The Geometries Of Innocence

Ernesto Spinelli

Cover design by David Higham

FOR GEORGES AND GREG

AND

FOR ALL THE SENIOR CITIZENS OF WOODSTOCK
NATION

— A NOTE FOR THE READER —

Most of this novel follows a UK English spelling and grammar style. The only exception is when direct quotes are employed. As all of the characters are living in North America, it seemed only fair to allow them their say in American English.

GREETINGS FROM YOUR TRIP GUIDE

Hello there, Time Trippers! Welcome!

Just a couple of bits and pieces before we travel back to The Sixties.

Like it or not, close to sixty years on from The Sixties, their ripple effect upon our present day continues to exert a heady influence. Everything good and bad, praiseworthy or deplorable, about life today can supposedly be traced back to what was said and done during that near-mythical era.

The thing is, The Sixties sound like pretty fun times when contrasted with the current 24/7 doom and gloom headlines and sound bytes blasting their way into our consciousness. Wasn't life a whole lot better when we weren't having to swallow our daily dose of proclamations regarding imminent environmental disasters, forecasts of food and energy costs going through the roof, inducements to stifle debate through dogmatism and cancel culture and warnings that existential threats of various kinds are about to attack and destroy every iota of our being?

But then again, what we tend to forget is that The Sixties were also chock-full of dangers and menace, not to mention wars and disasters, just as cataclysmically consequential as anything we face today.

So ... If it wasn't all that blissful Love and Peace stuff, what keeps us coming back for more?

Well ... Consider this: The Sixties became *The Sixties* because all those hippies and yippies and countercultural baby boomers positively *thrived* on uncertainty and ambiguity, wanted more and more of it, were bored to tears with all the soporific securities and sensible certainties the straight world had on offer. Whereas, uncertainty and ambiguity are today's big no-no's. Everybody's hankering after security, predictability and order. "Stand Out Only As Far As You'll Still Fit In" is the current Code of the Road. Like some horror movie we both don't want to keep watching and also can't stop peeking at through our fingers, this one big scary difference between The

Sixties and our present is hiding in the shadows ready to leap out at us.

Think about it: Our present-day leaders and influencers keep promising us more and more Order. Monsters like Trump and Putin and Xi Jinping and every other political, religious and social media bully hogging the online spotlight claim to be Agents of Order. But it's an Order that rejects and demonises its unruly and capricious counterpart. And because it does, we seem to be heading down a path taking us to the most destructive expressions of Chaos.

For an all too brief flicker of a moment there, The Sixties asked: What would emerge if Chaos was encouraged to infiltrate the current Order of things? What if Order provided the means to direct Chaos toward the creative and limit its most menacing possibilities? In short, what if Order and Chaos interacted with each other rather than went their separate ways? Great questions, right? If nothing else, our fascination with The Sixties might get us to start asking them again.

So ... With all that in mind, are you ready for your trip into The Sixties? Great!

One more thing: Back in the Psychedelic Sixties, it was a safe bet that when a group of people got together to fly high on their choice of reality-shifting drugs, one of them forsook the fun of going mush-brain and, instead, watched over proceedings just in case anybody freaked out and lost the plot. In which case, The Guide was there to cool things down and steer whoever was in trouble back to a more enjoyable state of mind.

Like those long-ago lifeguards, I'll be around so that your time-travel trip through the story will be as bummer free as possible. Flashbacks and flash-forwards are my specialty. This ain't no cosy nostalgia picnic we're on. It's a "tell it like it was, not as it should have been" trip. And, because of that, chances are you'll get confused or squeamish or possibly even horrified by some of the views and behaviours that the characters you'll meet expressed and maintained back then. When people weren't as enlightened as we are today. Even if they thought they were.

That voice you'll hear when the named characters aren't

talking? That'll be mine. And who am I? I used to be known as The Narrator. Or even The Author. But both those titles sound somewhat grandiose and all-knowing for our postmodern and post-postmodern sensibilities.

So, instead, in keeping with the spirit of The Sixties, allow me to introduce myself: I'm your Trip Guide.

Okay! Ready? Here we go!

PART ONE: McGILL

SEPTEMBER 1967 — APRIL 1968

'Hello ... Hello ... Hello!'

(to be sung in ascending scale and followed by the
melody from "Three Blind Mice")

— The Three Stooges Theme Song —

6 ERNESTO SPINELLI

1. INTRODUCTIONS ARE MADE

Hey, look! Here come Larry, Moe and Curly Joe.

What? You don't recognise them? Fair enough. Truth be told, they don't stand out that much one way or the other. They still visit barbershops when their hair's grown too rebelliously long and disorderly, watch their weight, keep ties and jackets on hand for special occasions, masturbate glumly and regularly. Like most other males in their late teens.

But, hey! As your Trip Guide, I'm here to help. So ...

Larry's the dreamily handsome one. Wide-shouldered, narrow-waisted, peek-a-boo fringe golden brown haired and blessed — or cursed — with a cherub-face look of quirky innocence that is straightaway appealing to the *Beatles* scarred women who enter his orbit. He remains, nevertheless, largely oblivious to his power and his shine. Larry's *Quebecois* born and bred but, for their own reasons, his parents have always made sure he's been enrolled in English language schools. Maybe because he's confused about this, Larry goes around telling everybody that he's a *Francophone.*

Moe, on the other hand, is the runt of the pack. Moe's the one who looks like Woody Allen doing an imitation of Michael Caine — or vice-versa — yet all the while, even if no one else can see it, believing himself to be the spitting image of Omar Sharif. Moe's from a blue collar background and likes it that way. He's a Fifties Fan-boy. Brando. Jimmy Dean. Montgomery Clift. When everything was more clear-cut. Like the music: straight ahead rhythm and blues, none of this Sixties fuzztone fuzziness.

As to Curly Joe? The only truly stand-out thing about Curly Joe is that he always writes and speaks in lower case. No Capital Letters for him. Other than that, he looks exactly like the person you'd imagine if you were asked to imagine someone named Curly Joe. Just tack onto your picture a black, hard-covered "thought-book" that he takes everywhere with him in case he should become poetically inspired, and you've got a foolproof description. And if that still isn't enough, search out the one with the anarchic mess of Mediterranean-origin, jet-black corkscrew hair. That'll be Curly Joe.

See them now? Sure you do!

And yes, those of you who have already made the link? Okay, smartypants, you got it right. They *do* share the very same names with a trio of slapstick comedians collectively known as *The Three Stooges*. The Stooges starred in a whole bunch of twenty minute movie shorts that came on as warm-ups to the Main Feature. Then TV repeats caught up with them and next thing they knew they'd become popular enough to star in their own hokey early 60s full-length films. When they got their start in the 1930s, the line-up was Larry, Moe and Curly. Then Curly got replaced by Shemp. After Shemp left, Joe joined in. Two years later, in 1958, Curly Joe came along and stuck it out until the end.

Not to worry. Definitely no troupe changes for *our* Three Stooges. It's been the same cast from the start. Which was four years ago now, in 1963, when they all met in high school. Moving things up to date, they've just begun their first year at *McGill University*. It's a good name to go to.

Moe's in McGill's Faculty of Science. He has no idea what he's doing there. Not that he especially minds being a science student. It's just that he hasn't learned much from it, is all. So far, what he *has* gotten wise to is that

a) A straight rope won't stay straight if you push on it.
And
b) Male elephants have pea-sized testicles.

That's it.

Even then, the only reason he's latched onto these two meagre facts is because, just prior to imparting them to him, both his physics and biology professors stated: 'Here's something you'll never forget.'

Moe never will, either. From now on, every time someone mentions the topics of physics or biology to him, these two shreds of dubious wisdom will pop up in his thoughts, all bright and bouncy and ready to entertain or enlighten. Consequently, Moe can't stop from musing how much more knowledge of all kinds of topics he'd possess by now if everyone began sentences with: 'Here's something you'll never forget.'

For reasons that remain a mystery to one and all — themselves included — Larry and Curly Joe have enrolled in McGill's Faculty of Engineering. They've only been there a couple of weeks, but already the rot's setting in. What Larry and Curly Joe really want to be doing, if the truth be known, is to write POETRY.

Some nights back, they're talking to each other on the phone and, just for the hell of it, Curly Joe starts reciting the liner notes to Bob Dylan's *Highway 61 Revisited* album. The words make no sense at all and fail to incite any intellectual response in either of them other than appreciative laughter. That Dylan has somehow soft-soaped The Straights over at *Columbia Records* to include this gobbledegook on the LP's back cover fills them both with unflinching admiration. Moreover, riding the whirlwind that the jingle-jangle jive onslaught of Curly Joe's oration induces, they are both awestruck by an instinctive, emotional secret chord which now won't stop reverberating.

'This is POETRY,' they proclaim. 'Pure and not at all simple.'

Consequently, on the day following this revelation, Larry scurries into *Classics Bookstore* and emerges, side-tracked and unashamed, page-flipping a paperback copy of Jack Kerouac's *Desolation Angels*. Soaking up the hip swagger and beat-ific, for-the-fun-of-it mayhem being recounted, the book's going-nowhere-fast influence casts a knockout spell over him. Now, wild-eyed and exuberant each time he reads aloud selected passages to himself or to anyone who'll listen, he feels a primal synergy with the other-worldly crazies, their intractable one-word chapters, and the sheer mind-fucking, razzle dazzle brilliance that cascades through the breathless writing. Like some vampire's hapless victim, Larry has become as bloodthirsty as his attacker.

Unfortunately, the Engineering Faculty doesn't approach

POETRY in quite the same way as Larry and Curly Joe do. To their fellow engineers, POETRY means something like this:

> *Yippidy-doo!*
> *Yippidy-doo!*
> *Wowee!*
> *I'll drink to that too*
> *Pat an ass!*
> *Squeeze a tit!*
> *We're McGill Engineers!*
> *Goddamn! Shit!*

The above is the Engineering Victory Yell. Engineers are required to shout it at hockey and football games, rallies, drinking expeditions and, best of all, while in the throes of orgasm.

Larry and Curly Joe had to memorise this particular ditty during Frosh Week when they, and some five hundred other identity-less blobs (four hundred and ninety-six of them being male), wearing plastic hard-hats so that they could be better herded together by their elders, made abject idiots of themselves Conga Line dancing up and down the stairs of the Students' Union, trying to capture one of the pigeons outside the McLennan Building and buying 44-D bras in *Eaton's* lingerie department. All of which were followed by the eagerly awaited climax to the merrymaking: glugging down as much beer as possible whilst in the convivial surroundings of *The Manse* (McGill Engineers' favourite watering hole), just to prove their right to be full-fledged members of the club.

As the Engineering Prospectus says: *McGill Engineers work harder and play harder than any other Faculty.* Whether barfing out your guts on beer is an example of one or the other continues to be a much-debated question. And, just to make matters worse for Curly Joe, one glass in and he's tumbled to the miserable fact that he doesn't even *like* beer.

All of which smoke-signals Larry and Curly Joe that there's no way on earth either of them will ever learn to love a sine curve graph, or handle a slide rule with eyes closed, or dream night and day of that Iron Ring they'll earn in five years time which, as the Graduate Goop in charge of festivities had piously proclaimed while holding up his right hand and showing off his own, 'is never, ever, going to be removed from chosen finger for the rest of your natural lives because you'll have worked your asses off for it.'

Larry and Curly Joe can't believe anyone could want *that*. Not that they have much of an idea what *they* want, but they're certain it isn't some cheap iron ring. That's just so *phony*. Trouble is, the only alternative they can come up with for themselves is to drop out and go find a job of some sort. Which, they both agree, is a course of action that isn't worth the bother of spending any precious time sweating over.

* * * * *

So here they are walking down St. Catherine Street, just to walk and talk, just to pass away the time.

St. Catherine Street, in case you don't know it, is Montréal's main shopping district. All the big department stores — *Eaton's, Simpsons, Morgan's, Ogilvie* — are there. So too, almost at its western tip and touching Atwater, is *The Forum*, home of the world famous *Montréal Canadiens* Hockey Team.

Why set our Sixties trip in Montréal? Well, why not? Canada's celebrating its One Hundredth Year in existence and it has chosen Montréal to lead the big parade. So up yours, Toronto The Good! And if that's not reason enough, how about the fact that Montréal's playing host to *Expo '67!*

Thanks to *Expo '67*, Montréal's *the* East Coast place to be right now. *Expo*'s a huge, huge worldwide hit. With its space-age Monorail taking you everywhere, and Bucky Fuller's giant Geodesic Dome as home to the USA pavilion, and the million-mirrored *Labyrinth* pointing out that we are all both Perseus and The Minotaur, and Henry Moore's *Locking Piece* sculpture and ... and ... and ... Wow! Even Emperor Haile Selassie has dropped by, with a couple of real live lions on a leash would you believe.

Oh yeah, if you aren't goin' to San Francisco wearing flowers in your hair, you might as well be waving around your passport to *Terre des Hommes*. And your ride over to it is bound to be via that brand-new, rubber-wheeled *Metro* which was opened less than a year ago by Montréal's feisty Mayor, Jean Drapeau.

Yessiree! *Bien sur!* Montréal rocks!

Moving on ... St. Catherine Street. Our Three Stooges, walking and talking. *Simpsons* at their back, *Eaton's* not far ahead. And, as they walk and talk, Moe gets an eyeful of the first male he's ever come across wearing a pair of ocean blue and burnt orange palazzo pants. Palazzo pants. They really did exist back then: high-waisted, ultra triple-x wide-leg, flare-out all the way to the ankles layers of gaudy-coloured nylon. Enough material in them to produce a decent-sized pup tent.

Moe's almost got used to seeing *female* backup singers and support dancers decked out in them. But a *man?* Grossed out, finding it impossible to stop gawking, Moe asks himself what depraved mind — even one belonging to the mammoth-sized schlub loping his way towards them — would *choose* to adorn his body with something so tastelessly hideous? Unable to come up with any worthwhile answer, he's aching to point his index finger and laugh his head off. Only thing stopping him from doing so though, is the queasy possibility that the approaching behemoth's inordinate bulk might well be matched by his equally supersized strength. Instead, playing it safe, Moe sighs dramatically allowing the frisky wind that's been following them to whisper into his ear. Inspired but still cautious, he waits until there's enough quick getaway distance between him and *The Incredible Hulk*. Then he turns, grins knowingly to his two pals, and pulls out his version of an old *Kinks* song:

> *They avoid him here, they run off there.*
> *He's got the clothes no one sane would wear.*
> *He has no idea that his taste has got to be the worst,*
> *'Cause he's a dedicated slaughterer of fashion.*

Catching on, Larry and Curly Joe burst into a combined chorus:

Oh yes he is!
Oh yes he is!

After that, all three of them need to stop right then and there, take deep breaths and hold back the collective belly-laughs until the source of their amusement has plodded his way out of their lives.

Moe's real good at cooking up bust-a-gut wisecracks. Especially when it comes to playing around with song lyrics. He has no idea how he does it. They just come to him fully formed and ready to be belted out. And as long as they keep doing that, Moe's not asking any questions. Besides, what really matters is that Moe's song re-writes and boffo one-liners are there to provide the proof all three of them require to see themselves as free spirits who think and feel and talk in ways which affirm that they are undeniably different. Because *being different* has become very, very important. Even if it's an ongoing worry as well.

As it happens, they're not the only ones obsessing over this. All sorts of people are playing around with any differences that might be found — or, if it has to be, created — to make US stand out from THEM.

The mindset has taken root.

It will flower.

It's the time for such things.

* * * * *

The September winds are blowing today. Their current is still comfortably warm but also cool enough to have shooed away most of the summer's swarms of mosquitoes and innumerable other fly-and-bite bugs. It's the best time of year to find yourself in Montréal. Larry, Moe and Curly Joe certainly think so.

Thing is though, this isn't any old September. It's that one-time-only, nearly the end of summer September *19fucking67, maaan!* And because it is, they can also feel the gust of other winds from every corner of the globe tickling their brows and necks.

Hey now, Tripsters! Shut your eyes and step inside. Maybe you can feel them, too.

Far out and outtasite! Here's that First Ever Rock Festival Wind blowing in from Monterey, California! Hear it whistling round everybody's ears!

Oh Boy! If you read the news today you'll know that the newly-released *Sergeant Pepper's* Wind is singing and dancing away like the Hendersons!

Watch it! The drug-busting Wind that got those Dartford Bad Boys, Messrs. Jagger and Richards into butterfly-on-a-wheel trouble back in chilly February London shows no sign of swinging out! No *Mars Bars* for you while you're in the nick, Mick!

Never on Sunday! That Greek Colonels Wind giving the Birthplace of Democracy a heavy beating has got every other constitutionally elected country wobbling from a bad case of Zorba-land giving them the creeps!

Trumpets and Drums! Here's that North Country Howling Wind comin' at ya from how many roads, caught on film cinéma vérité rough and rowdy daring one and all: *Don't Look Back!*

Say! Feel that Straight-from-Hollywood Wind whooshing washed-up Movie Stars now turned would-be politicians like Ronnie Reagan and Shirley Temple all the way to Washington, DC. Don't it bring on a full-flush shiver?

Shake Rattle and Roll! Did anybody notice that short burst of Six Day Conflict Desert Wind? Already come and gone!

Keep A-Knocking! How about all that Hot Air Wind De Gaulle's been puffing up with his *Vive Le Quebec Libre* rant?

Thunder and Lightning! Smell the napalm in that relentless Vietnam War Wind that's got so many thousands marching to the sound of "when will it ever end?"

Weather Warning! Threat of Snow Blizzard Wind blasts bringing added chill to ongoing Cold War thanks to Stalin's daughter defecting to the West!

Winds of Change Update: Cassius Clay Floating Butterfly Wind recently renamed and upgraded to Bee Stinging Mohammed Ali Squall is now dodging the draft and swirling up a storm!

And some Local News just in! Montréal area expected to bask in refreshing breeze brought on by Gently Billowing Wind until October's end, right about the time *Expo '67* shuts its gates for the very last time!

Blow winds blow!

Felt all at once, their combined effect makes it difficult to tell what's vision and what's reality.

Not to worry. It's 1967, right?

It's the time for such things as well.

* * * * *

Still walking and talking or not talking, they pass by movie theatres, record shops, hamburger joints, magazine stands. And as they walk, their eyes automatically note the physical appearance of each passing woman — nymphet or matriarch, it makes no difference — for their brains to evaluate, store away and create fantasies focused upon their aching desire to have sex with a friendly, free-thinking female who's eager to satisfy her own x-rated yearnings.

Like Moe never forgets to put it: 'Ya just don't make it, if ya don't make it.'

Or, when he wants his point to stand out even more unambiguously: 'I fuck. Therefore I am, Johnny-boy.'

Neither Moe nor Larry have ever fucked. If Moe's dictum is correct, this sad fact might be the source of their ongoing shared existential crisis. True, Larry *is* in love. But Angel lives hundreds of miles away and their relationship is one that would make Plato proud.

On the flip side, Curly Joe *has* gone all the way. Annoyingly, that was a fleeting experience dissolved months — though it feels more like years — ago, now. And since his current existential crisis shows no signs of being any less debilitating, it's all too apparent that Moe's pull-no-punches observation is, so to speak, premature. Perhaps frequency is the missing variable required to firm up his case.

Whatever the answer, all three find themselves in search of that elusive girlfriend who, in consenting to explore the mysteries of rubbing skin together, will prompt a shift in their circumstances such that, at last, the meaning and purpose to life will reveal itself to them. And, with that, they'll finally be able to stop degrading themselves with wads of Kleenex, milk bottles, folded pillows, vaseline palms, wet dreams.

They're sick and tired of speculating and wishing. Sick, most of all, of crinkled underwear that smell of cheap bleach. They desire someone their parents will welcome as a daughter and who, behind closed doors, will shyly, yet enthusiastically, lay bare the flesh beneath her clothes and lie down upon a bed, a couch, a beach, a carpet, a tiled bathroom floor, a lecture theatre lecterned stage, anywhere, in fact, where the desired target will be as explicit as her insistence that they begin to fuck, and then fuck some more and, after that, still be eager to fuck again.

Admittedly, there are numerous candidates cruising up and down Montréal's notorious Main ready and willing to play along with their every wish. But rentable by the hour, cash-up-front impersonal sex doesn't do the trick anymore. Like the rest of The Sixties Generation, they've caught hold of a new dread word: *relationship*. Which is why they are pining for a steady partner who'll hug them after they've done it, and say how wonderful they were, and how the earth moved for her and how she couldn't possibly dream of engaging in such a beautiful, stupendous act with anyone else. Ever. Ever. Ever. Sadly, they still haven't caught sight of any such creatures eager to be found.

Their way of dealing with this unrelenting *angst* governing their lives is to blame their early adolescence. The way they tell it, the Pavlovian conditioning each of them was subjected to during high school has succeeded in establishing a programmed response of rapid-fire, full-on fear and trembling the second they visualise going on a date with a female of their species. No, make that of *any* species.

The educational establishment in question calls itself *Heebie Jeebie High School for Boys*.

Well, not really. But it should.

Heebie Jeebie High was established some hundred years earlier by a little known sect of Roman Catholic priests whose 17th Century founder was Saint Nicholas Salvatore Magellan. Prior to setting up his Order, Saint Nicholas had been a Portuguese butcher. Legend has it that one day, while slicing slabs of beef, Nicholas allowed his eyes to inspect the well-developed cleavage of a smiling housewife customer. Just as the ignoble desire shoved its way to the forefront of his consciousness, he misdirected a chop with his cleaver and severed his left hand at the wrist. This caused him, as well as the Mrs. who'd stirred his passion, to faint in shock.

What happened to the lady in question upon awakening remains unknown to history. But Nicholas eventually came to imbued with the certainty that the occurrence had been God's way of informing him that he was to establish a new religious order whose major purpose would be that of creating educational environments for young men which, above all else, protected them from sins of the flesh by employing any means possible. Up to, and including, castration.

Three hundred years later, the castration clause has been removed due to the inadequacy of its effect. Instead, Heebie Jeebie High has rapidly established itself as a pioneering exponent of more modern aversive techniques. For example, some unforgettably colourful movies of syphilis-infested pricks continue to be projected on a regular basis as part of its Human Hygiene course.

What is truly mystifying however, is that entry to Heebie Jeebie High is so sought after that virtually every English Catholic Elementary School male living in Montréal seems willing to offer up *any* part of his anatomy to Saint N. S.

Magellan for the unbeatable privilege of being one of the hundred or so successful candidates chosen each year, who, after triumphantly passing a special Heebie Jeebie High School Qualification Test and whose parents are wealthy enough to pay the exorbitant Heebie Jeebie High School Fees, is made welcome as he makes his way through the Heavenly Heebie Jeebie High Gates.

In the four years they spend there, Larry, Moe and Curly Joe have their brains well washed, scrubbed, rinsed and hung out to dry until each emerges on a sunny Saturday June afternoon three months back, graduation diploma in hand, a Charter Member of the Heebie Jeebie High School properly-screwed-in-every-sense-of-the-word-bar-one *Class of 1967.*

The first test they're put through to measure the success of the Heebie Jeebie technique turns out to be The Graduation Dance. Moe and Curly Joe sail through splendidly by not even bothering to pretend that they might have a go at searching out willing dates for it.

Larry, contrariwise, begins badly by allowing his mother to talk him into phoning her best friend's daughter who, as pre-arranged, replies with a practiced 'Yes!' to his stammered invitation. He scrapes through in the end however, when, in the course of one of the slower dances, the unsuspecting girl momentarily presses her upper torso onto his. This entirely innocent act triggers an explosively erotic jolt that spreads forthwith throughout every cell in Larry's body. Getting horny right there in hallowed Heebie Jeebie High Hall is way too much for his mind to cope with. Pleading a spontaneous onset of fever, he escorts his bewildered date back to her home without delay. At long last in the privacy of his room, Larry undresses, masturbates twice and falls asleep feeling sinful and ashamed. And, somehow, relieved.

As luck would have it, it turns out to be Curly Joe who's the first of the three to experience a glimmer of de-programming salvation. A couple of days following his graduation, his parents reward him for his labours by packing him off on a three week YMCA-Approved Whirlwind Package Tour of Europe.

During one of the city break "do what you want" free days in his itinerary, Curly Joe's all on his own being a tourist in Athens, Greece. While buying a street-corner roasted corn-on-the-cob, he's overheard by an American student on her one-year Undergraduate Study Abroad Programme who's grown sick and tired of being unable to make herself verbally understood by people who don't speak any English. And especially, by the leering men who can't believe that any woman worth eyeballing would willingly walk around in crotch-outline cut-off jeans and a loose tank-top that displays, as effectively as possible within the limits of current Grecian Law, that she wears no bra. Overjoyed to bump into a fellow North American, even if he is Canadian and wet behind the ears to boot, she introduces Curly Joe to lamb souvlakis, gives him her copy of *Steppenwolf* to read, and effortlessly leads him back to her dirt cheap pension room off Omonia Square.

The subsequent events are as close to satori as Curly Joe has yet experienced. The consequences of his first non-imaginary sexual encounter with a woman aren't in the least like those predicted by Good Ol' Father Pious, the Heebie Jeebie High Personal Guidance Counsellor. First of all, on the following morning, much to his relief, Curly Joe doesn't find any purple pus emerging from his rapidly decaying cock. Which is what had happened to that young Catholic soldier Father Pious had sermonised about. *That* dumb jerk had allowed himself to be coerced into skipping Sunday mass by evil Protestant atheists in his platoon. Subsequently losing his virginity to a diseased streetwalker who'd infected him with medically untreatable syphilis, he up and died then and there, in agony, and worse, much worse, while still in the state of mortal sin which doomed him to suffer forever in the fiery tortures of Hell. Nope, Curly Joe's escapade, he's thrilled to report, has prompted nothing close to that.

Nor does his partner-in-sin break down in fits of sorrow and tormented contrition that can only be alleviated by a pure confession and Curly Joe's ensuing offer of marriage. Rather, she professes to have enjoyed the entire experience, especially as she'd never before had a virgin to initiate, and makes it clear that she requires more of the same — and preferably better — during the remainder of their alliance.

Most significant of all, there is no sign of *The Dark Powers* taking over Curly Joe's soul.

After a second day and night packed full of guiltless sexual indulgence, he reaches the conclusion that if what he's getting a taste of is the result of Dark Powers possessing him, he's more than happy to learn to live in their company. Matter of fact, he'll do what he can to make them feel so at home that they'll prolong their stay indefinitely.

Back once more on Canadian soil, Curly Joe wastes no time in relaying his pioneering adventure to his friends. Proudly, he even shows them the small bundle of near-black pubic hair that his ephemeral bedmate had snipped off herself, tied up with white thread and offered to him as a memento of their encounter.

Watching Curly Joe lovingly return the talisman to its home in his wallet, Larry and Moe determine right then and there that the Dark Powers are all right with them as well.

Alas ... All of that happened in late July and now they're in mid-September, and nothing's changed, and they're walking and talking or not talking, and grinning that rueful, expectant grin that asks the same forever question. In the end, as always, they cast their vote in favour of Heebie Jeebie High being bombed out of all existence.

And here's something you Tripsters might like to know: One night, several years into the future, long after walks and talks and innocent questions have lost their urgency and power, a group of anarcho-punks strung out on a weird cocktail of home-made meths and *poutine* take it upon themselves to heed their advice.

Whoever, and wherever, those persons may be now, should they be reading this, Larry, Moe and Curly Joe say: 'Thank you.'

2. A VALKYRIE, BOB DYLAN, A GUGGENHEIM, CHASTITY, AN ANGEL ... AND LENNY BRUCE

By the time the early-October wind eases its way under the sweaters and long-sleeved shirts they've begun to wear in subservience to its demands, our trio has resorted to taking up near-permanent daytime residence in the McGill Student Union Cafeteria. Class-day-after-class-day, they sit there for hours on end drinking machine-cups of cherry colas that, once emptied, are passed over to Curly Joe who manically shreds them into smaller and smaller strips of white, air-bubble styrofoam while they talk, or stare into the void or compose their poetic epiphanies.

The Union is a recent addition to McGill. It sticks out from all the other buildings like a mangled wart. Even at night. As unsightly and austere as the other teaching blocks are, the soot and grime they have collected over the years at least provide them with the dubious respectability of age. The Union, in contrast, just sits there, a grey monument to cold concrete and rectangle.

In any case, this is where we find Moe and Curly Joe today. They should be sitting in separate lecture theatres right now. But, hey! Blow it off! Their own table talk is infinitely superior to any lecture their professors might have on offer.

What's more, too much is happening that is begging for their undivided attention. So much for them to rap about! Some D.A. out in New Orleans has claimed that there was a conspiracy to assassinate JFK! *The Doors* have pulled a fast one on *The Ed Sullivan Show*'s censors by singing about getting high! Joan Baez just got arrested in Oakland, California, for blocking the passageway to that city's Military Induction Center! There's even reports of some sort of oddball automatic cash dispensing machines being introduced over in England. And weirder still, a bunch of physicists have claimed that something they're calling "black holes" can be found all over the universe. With stuff like that to throw around and chew over, going to classes has become *irrelevant* (another key mantra of The Sixties, in case you didn't know).

Today, like most days, Moe's taken centre-stage. Life, the perpetual bully, has been picking on him again. Like some possessed guitarist about to grind his axe through a rapturous progression of twelve-bar blues chords, he goes with the improvisational onrush, lets it take him where it will.

'Look, I dunno,' Moe says. 'Maybe I should do everybody a favor and show up at a Separatist meeting waving a British flag and leading a sing-a-long to *God Save The Queen*. Seriously, Jim. It's real balloon pants, ya know? Most of the time, I feel like I'm knee high to an ant. And a *midget* one at that!' He pauses for breath, then passes Curly Joe a squint that says 'are ya with me, man?' Assuming that he is, Moe sips from his styrofoam cup and then continues. 'Get the big picture? I'm a buff-A mess.'

Before there's an opening made for Curly Joe to jump in and counter this conclusion, Moe's off once more, pounding out another audience-pleasing groove. 'Sure, sure,' he riffs, 'I ask myself: Why? Why? The $64,000 question, gang. I mean, I talk to my Dad and all he can say is: "Ya turned eighteen and yer still a virg! What else can I tell ya?"' Moe smirks at the absurdity of that parental piece of wisdom. Then, grabbing hold of a passing thought, he gets caught in the head-grip of a loathsome memory he's wrestled to a repeated stand-still on numerous past bouts. He elicits a grin that might be a grimace. He's off and running.

'Hey! That reminds me of those stupid days in September when I had the hots for *The Valkyrie*. Yeah ... Who can forget *The Valkyrie,* right? Man, she had *some* tongue though, lemme tell ya. And me, never been French-kissed before, feeling like I'm choking on a live fish that's flopping around all over inside my mouth! *Jee-zus!* And then ... And then ... since she's coming on like raw sex unchained, I tell myself it'd be cool to inch my hand up her skirt and try to give her panties a feel. Christ, ya don't know what being scared shitless is 'til ya do something that *The Valkyrie* thinks is a no-no! She's foaming at the mouth and screaming into my ear: "What kind of girl d'ya think I am?" Like, I could see the muscles on her arms flexing, ready to give me one! Yeah, and believe it or not, while all this is going on, my wee-wee's got so excited it's squirting cum all over the place down my leg! It was a cinch for sure she was gonna pound me out. Man, I nearly wanted her to, so's I could groan in peace.'

Moe shakes his head to rid him himself of this godawful memory. 'I thought she'd notice that my pants were soaked. I prayed: God, please put me home and in bed right now. I'll believe. I'll go back to Mass. I'll even become a *Junior Jeebie*. No such luck, Chuck. So, I start into babbling about forgiveness and how her splendid body caused me to forget myself. I told her everything. Everything. That she was the first girl I'd ever danced with, much less necked. All that crap. Did she believe a word of it? Naw! No way! But, hey! It worked, right? She forgave me right away and we went back to trying to get our tongues into a double-knot.'

Having brought his extended solo to an end, Moe rapidly switches characters so that he's now a stand-up comic logging up various bits for possible future comedy routines. *'Kee-rist!* For two weeks after that, I was guzzling *Love Potion Number 9* non-stop. Worrying about whether you or Larry would be my Best Man. What we'd call the kids. Shit like that. Then, boom! Like some dumb jock, I go and tell her that I don't want her going out with anyone except me anymore. Oh yeah, she was pretty good about it. I mean, she laid it on the line that she was only seventeen and way too young to start going steady and that she liked me a lot but not enough to settle down, and love and adult things like that.

'Me? I put on a real Academy Performance. I very calmly told her that I saw her point. She was right. In spades. I was just being my usual brainless schlep. Sure, it hit me hard for a few days, there. Lots of singing the blues. And then, like wham-o, I wake up one morning and it's ... Hey! Wait a minute! I mean, who needs this, right? I mean, ya can't keep creaming over the same picture forever, Jim. What it comes down to, I guess, is that I need. Need what? Well, preferably a woman; but a dog'll do.'

He casts his eye over at Curly Joe, evaluating his single audience member's reaction to the just completed skit. Too bad, Curly Joe isn't on his toes enough to provide any feedback. Instead, he radiates an automatic "right on!" kind of smile that he hopes is what's being called for. Truth is, Curly Joe hasn't been listening to much of Moe's impassioned recital. He's heard variations on this particular sketch enough times already so that he's got a pretty good hunch as to what its punchline is going to be. Not only that, he's got his own stockpile of confusing topics to entertain him. No, he isn't mulling about romantic partners and the lack of them. Not so far, leastways. Suzie Q hasn't strolled into his life as yet.

Mainly, Curly Joe's been racking his brains over Bob Dylan: what he might be up to, and whether the rumours of a new record appearing pretty soon might be true. After a year's worth of motorcycle accident silence, it's about time, too! And wouldn't it be great if they could meet up some day, and maybe Dylan could help him put some of the poems he's been scribbling down to music that they'll record together. And ... And ... And ... Curly Joe doesn't believe in God; he believes in Dylan. Hard to tell if there's much difference.

Not that everybody holds the same view. Take Curly Joe's parents, for instance. Like most parents — okay, most *people* — they don't appreciate Dylan's rather nasal whine. Instead, to Curly Joe's constant irritation, they keep referring to Dylan as *The Squawker.*

'Turn *The Squawker* down, dear,' they say.

Or else: 'Haven't you got any records to play other than that damn *Squawker's?*'

Routinely, they even sink so low that they trot out the classic jibe: 'Yes, he can certainly write some very good songs. I'll give you that. But couldn't he find someone else to sing them? Someone who's got a voice, for instance?'

Blasphemy and sacrilege. Nobody sings Dylan like Dylan. Even *Columbia Records* admits to that. *Peter, Paul and Mary* might have made his songs sound more harmonious. And *The Byrds* might have turned them into folk-rock hits. But still ... What nobody's saying is that you can sing along to Dylan and not feel all that bad about your own voice.

Curly Joe went electric when Dylan went electric. At first, it wasn't an entirely positive goosebump experience. On Christmas Day 1965, going through the family ritual of unwrapping presents, he was staggered to find that his parents had somehow got hold of a ticket to Dylan's upcoming Montréal concert.

February 20th, 1966. Place des Arts. What a night! Curly Joe's been warned about the loud and raucous second half. He died and went to Heaven throughout the whole of that incandescent acoustic first half. No, he doesn't feel disappointed by what takes place after the intermission. He doesn't Hiss and Boo! He just doesn't *get it*. And he still doesn't get it when he rolls up to Father Bardo's class first thing Monday morning only to find one of his Heebie Jeebie schoolmates writing out the lyrics to *Like A Rolling Stone* on the blackboard, a new Holy Prayer to be recited at the start of every day. No, Curly Joe has to wait until his Summer '67 tour of Europe to finally and forever *get it*. A short seaside stop in Italy. Some nowheresville beach resort named *Silvi Marina*. Curly Joe all by himself, another stranger on the shore, mini transistor radio tuned to the Italian version of an underground FM station. The DJ blabs away about something or other and then *BANG!* That drumroll. That whispery organ. That undiluted uproar of sound. *Once upon a time ...*

Thought-zoning himself back to the cafeteria, Curly Joe's now lost in another fantasy. He's playing the increasingly regular game of seeing himself as one more misunderstood and unappreciated poet let loose upon a deaf and uncaring world. On the entire planet, he concludes, there are only two genius men who can truly understand him. One of them happens to be the aforementioned Mr. Dylan, and he's not easy to contact. The other is a little more accessible.

Curly Joe sits at the feet of this second guru on Mondays,

Wednesdays and Fridays, 11.00am to 12.00pm, in the Stephen Leacock Building. The man calls himself Guggenheim; he'd make a fine model for one of the painters whose works are exhibited in the Art Gallery that shares his name.

Guggenheim's uniform, which has undergone no noticeable change since the first day Curly Joe laid eyes on him, consists of a pair of dirty old jeans and a patched-up black turtleneck sweater. Invariably, his hair sprawls matted and unfurled, a dark semitic flag flying at half-mast over his ears, flawlessly setting off the brick-red jungle spreading abundantly over the lower part of his face. Guggenheim uses, rather than wears, his cheapo, square-frame glasses. They're forever being prodded down the lower part of his nose in some god-awful caricature of his colleagues or else slammed within his palms as he wipes their lenses with some vile looking, snot-soaked handkerchief that is otherwise stuffed, ball-like, in a back pocket of his *Levi's*. Naturally, he always wears sandals. Around a month from now, even with the threat or reality of snow taunting him, he'll be seen exchanging mud-smeared 10lb army boots and twin pairs of lawn green sweatsox for his Afghanis, placing the former among the innocuous and impersonal galoshes that lie on the rubber mat reserved for members of the Academic Staff. Nobody is *ever* going to pick up and slip into Guggenheim's boots by mistake.

Needless to say, Guggenheim is Curly Joe's English Studies Prof. Not that Curly Joe holds this against him. Unlike the disgusted opinions of the other nineteen Year One Engineering buddies who are required to attend Guggenheim's three-times-a-week course. English Studies is the artsy-fartsy subject that engineers have to sit through. Its avowed purpose is to keep young engineering minds open. Not that anybody can think of a single instance where a student was kicked out of the department because he was dead set on keeping his mind thoroughly shut.

Reality Check front and centre: to most engineering students, English Studies is seen as an hour's worth of snoozeville. They've tolerated Guggenheim during the first few classes just because he's so hilarious. His language, earthy and emotional and laced with innumerable "fucks" and "shits", has kept them all in stitches. Somehow, to be in the presence of a university lecturer — even one from the English Department — who swears like a drunken lumberjack is something that this roomful of engineers can approve of. And especially if the "fucks" and "shits" that spurt from his mouth are mainly directed at people holding positions of power. It's only when Guggenheim's rage and contempt begins to vent itself more and more precisely onto the Department of Engineering, its Deans and Professors, and, ultimately, its students, that the first intimations of rebellion arise.

World Politics puts an end to it all. Several times now, Guggenheim has declared himself to be a Classical Marxist. None of his students fathom what *that's* supposed to mean. But they're all pretty sure that Marx is somehow connected with the Soviet Union. And, as far as they're concerned, Russkies are the bad guys, even if they can play a mean game of chess, out-skate Canada to win the Hockey World Championship, and might just beat the Yanks to the Moon. But the way Guggenheim keeps on attacking the good guys for being in Vietnam, it's belatedly begun to dawn on some of them that maybe this panty-waist loudmouth doesn't think quite like they do. Which is why more and more engineers have opted to skip attending his class. Last time, there were six people in the room all told. And one of them was Guggenheim. *Plus*, two of them fell asleep minutes into his latest spiel.

The way Curly Joe's errant classmates explain it, they're fed up with listening to some dirty commie who wastes their time making them write essays on what they think about some lousy, centuries-dead creep's rotten poem that they don't think anything about anyhow. They have a point.

Curly Joe, in contrast, is awe-struck. From that very first session when Guggenheim pulls out the double-album cover of *Blonde On Blonde* and pins it to the wall so that everybody can goggle hypnotised at Dylan's out-of-focus face and hair, he's won over, his commitment sealed air-tight. Never, ever in Curly

Joe's life has he come across a crazy like this one in the flesh. Listening to Guggenheim rave on about things like the Biblical allusions contained in *Moby Dick*, William Blake's nudist-anarchic life style, why Hamlet was the first hippie, and how *The Somebodies* need to be denounced and stopped once and for all before it gets too late is flat-out technicolor heaven.

The Somebodies, by the way, are the members of a secret cabal that rules the university. Their weapons are oodles of ill-gained wealth, red tape and ostensibly inconsequential manoeuvres which, when shaken out of their guise, take the lid off the dark machinations of a system that has lost its very purpose of being, and, which, instead, has sold itself off to capitalistic greed as well as to an unwavering dedication to the cause of growing and multiplying future automatons.

Those are Guggenheim's words, straight no chaser. He has his point, too.

So how does Guggenheim explain away his presence in this hot-bed of intrigue? He claims to have infiltrated the system by having fooled it into thinking he's just one more of the faceless minions hired to daze and dull the minds of McGill's students. He is, he confides with no hint of humility, the enemy within. He'd signed on the contractual dotted line and now has the right to do whatever the fuck he wishes as long as he teaches the required number of hours. And what Guggenheim mainly wishes to do is to first expose, and then destroy, *The Somebodies*.

To Curly Joe, it all sounds like some story-line straight out of the pages of a *Marvel Comic*. It's not the plot that counts, it's the heroics. And Curly Joe's hooked.

That said and all polemics aside, Guggenheim's a shit-hot teacher. He knows exactly how much to explain about a passage and what to leave open for his students to figure out for themselves, or let their imaginations loose upon. He seeks out discussions, arguments, shouting matches. He'll even create such things, if necessary, by tuning in on some innocuous statement that a student has trotted out and turn it into a springboard for verbal jousts. The only views he disdains are those rehearsed as "right answers".

The one problem Guggenheim has, when it comes down to it, is in getting students to show up to his classes so he can save them from the dastardly futures being planned for them. So far, he can only count on one potential recruit to the cause. Which is what makes Curly Joe's hero-worshipping presence so necessary.

The fact that Guggenheim sees himself in this unreal role of guardian and protector blows the whistle on just how much he, too, is caught up in the prankster spirit of the times. Like so many others who could have something worthwhile to say, he's joined the long line of would-be wise men and leaders who refuse to look into the mirror and notice that the reflection staring back at them isn't all that distinguishable from that of their nemesis. Hey ho! Let the battle continue ...

Curly Joe isn't bothering to frown into any mirrors right now, either. This minute aware that he's been mind-travelling somewhere else for a while, he's not sure if Moe's waiting for him to say something. But what?

Having no idea, he asks: 'do you want another cherry cola?'

He sees Moe shrug 'why not?' and rises, off the hook.

By the time he's back, two more styrofoam cups in hand, Moe's moved on to another topic. Curly Joe resolves to pay attention this time.

'*East-West,*' Moe says. 'Ya heard it yet? 100% man, lemme tell ya. Guaranteed manic-depression any time.' Moe's talking music. The Blues, to be more precise. Moe loves The Blues. Especially the amplified city blues as recorded by *The Paul Butterfield Blues Band.* He's even thinking of buying himself a harmonica so he can play along to his favourite tunes.

However ... Having given mention to a much over-used diagnostic disorder, he sidetracks himself onto the topic of the new woman in his life. Chastity. He's only known her for a week, maybe a bit more. 'Chastity,' Moe winces, shaking his head in self-pity. 'Oh man ... I sure know how to pick 'em! Can ya imagine trying to get it on with someone with a name like that? Chastity. Ya gonna believe it? Still, I kinda like her, in spite of her name. Maybe she's the one. All I know is, I'm shit-scared. But I guess it's better to be shit-scared and wondering, than to be just shit-scared, right? Uh-oh. Philosophy time, gang. Okay ... So what'cha want me to do, go stuff birds or something?' As he raises the question, Moe guffaws. 'I am such a *dullard*, man! That's what I am! An honest-to-goodness, grade-A, first class *dullard*!'

That gets them both chortling and shaking like they've got a bad case of the DT's. They're so wholly caught up in it, they don't even see or hear Larry rolling in and plonking himself down beside them.

'What are yuh guys up to?' Larry says.

'moe's trying to figure out if he's in love with chastity. tell him, moe.'

Here we go again, Larry thinks. 'Are yuh?'

'Aw ... I ... Look ...' In a jiff, Moe tries out his adenoidal truck-driver voice. 'Ahh ... I dunno. Ah guess ah get these funny feelin's when ah'm on duh can, squeezin' out duh ol' joy-juice, Jim. Ah sez to meself: "meself, go find yerself a gal who's purer than the Blessed Virgin Mary an' therefore untouchable." Yeah. Good thinking there, Batguy! And while yer at it, pass me dat dere cantaloupe so's ah can stuff my schlong into it.'

Mention of unobtainable women precipitates a question that turns the spotlight on Larry.

'so?' Curly Joe asks.

'What?' says Larry.

'you know what.'

Larry shakes his head, then looks coy because he really does know what. Or rather, who.

Now Moe gets it, too. He puts the latest chapter in the ongoing Chastity saga on pause. 'Yeah,' he prods. 'Have ya heard from her yet?'

Larry frowns at being reminded of the miserable state of his own love life. As if he needs reminding. He grabs a quick sip of Curly Joe's cherry cola before answering. 'Nope. I keep mailing her letters pretty much every day. But Angel isn't sending any back.'

'what a drag,' Curly Joe commiserates.

'Yeah. Real Jean-Paul Sartre time,' Moe adds.

'Yuh bet. The thing is, I'm not even all that sure if Angel's receiving any of my letters. The address I'm sending them to is the one that she wrote down in the single post card I got from her so far. Supposedly, it's where some work pal who's actually renting an apartment lives. I dunno.'

'she still hasn't given you a phone number?'

Larry pouts. 'That's what makes things worse. I can't even phone her. Far as I know, she hasn't settled anywhere yet.'

'She's like her namesake,' Moe says. 'She seems to be flitting around everywhere and nowhere.'

Curly Joe gives him a disapproving eye. Bad joke.

'And, for some crazy reason, Angel outright rejects using a public pay phone so she can call me collect,' Larry whines, too caught up in his concerns to have heard Moe's dumb comment.

What Larry's keeping close to his chest is that when he's not worrying over something devastatingly deplorable having happened to Angel, her silence leads him to question if she cares for him anywhere near as much as he cares for her. What he and Angel have got going is something truly major league as far as he's concerned. Which is why practically every other day Larry dreams up some new way of letting Angel know that he misses her. Last time he did, he compared himself to a child who's lost his favourite toy. Which, let's face it, even if the initial ructions of Women's Lib are being barely noticed, this isn't the most inspired of analogies.

Enough ... Larry brings this particular discussion to an end by piping up that he's going to go get his own glass of cherry cola before he drinks down all the rest of Curly Joe's. Back minutes later, Larry's mooning over Angel is promptly distracted by something Moe's got off his chest about how matters are progressing romantically with Chastity. *Well,* thinks Larry, *this should be good.* He crosses his fingers hoping that what Moe comes up with might even inspire a couple of laugh-out-loud lines to be included in tonight's otherwise glum-ridden missive to Angel.

Pausing to squeeze out as much dramatic tension as he can, Moe eases into his spiel. 'Chastity let me kiss her goodnight last time. Would ya believe it? Nothing like *The Valkyrie*. Now *she* wouldn't lay off me. This one's the total opposite, ya know? Like, we neck for two minutes and it's as if I just used her to act out the whole of the *Kama Sutra*, or something. Crazy weirdo. How come I always get landed with the factory rejects, huh?' Settling down into his monologue, eyes darting back and forth to make sure he's got the full attention of both his pals, Moe shakes his head again in visible disbelief at what he's about to lay on them, and then begins to divulge.

'Ya know what she does for laughs? Ya gonna believe this? *She arm wrestles her father*! Yeah, she does. *And she beats the bastard, too!* Ya oughtta see this prick. Fat bowl of *Miracle Whip*, ya know? Like, ya touch him, and your finger buries itself outta sight. Slimy bastard. When Chastity introduced him to me he said: "How nice to meet you, young man'."' Moe pauses, then repeats the phrase in a highly effeminate voice: '"How nithe to meeth yew, yeung man." Yeung man! *Kee-rist!'*

'Thing is, they're *all* sick in that place, though. The mother paints her face up something *awful*. Like, purple cheeks! And she hates the old man, too. Just the way she looks at him, ya know she'd rather do it to a broom handle. Then there's the sister. God knows where she was when they were passing out the gray matter. Spends all her time in front of the box. In love with *Ilya Kuryakin* or some other TV jerk. She sits watching that junk with her legs apart and up in the air just to show off her underwear. At least she's wearing some! I haven't met the brother yet, but I can guess. Hell, no wonder Chastity's so screwed up. So many sick people, ya know?'

Moe falls back to the sidelines, pleased with his performance.

Time for Larry and Curly Joe to have their say. Taking their cue, they launch into long diatribes against inconsiderate parents, religion, Victorian morals, the price of cherry colas. Until, sooner or later, they segue onto the trio's *big* discovery of 1967: Lenny Bruce.

Already dead for over a year, nonetheless, thanks to Curly Joe's coming across a paperback containing transcripts of the stand-up comedian's most famous bits, he's never been more alive for them than now. Each has gone out and bought his own copy which, together or alone, they study and memorise as if it was a sacred text.

Moe sets them rolling. 'How's the old roll of tar-paper there, Johnny?'

'ah, you schtup! go fress your chicken!'

'Yeah, yeah. Let your chicken cook supper for ya.'

Larry finally finds a way to jump in on the recital. 'Oh right! That one's so *terrific!* The wife catches him fucking a chicken and —'

'Wait! Wait! I'll start over and put on a Brooklyn accent.'

'no! no! do it polish!'

'Or Indian, like Peter Sellers!'

'yeah! wow!'

The thought of it all sets Larry off again. He can't stop cracking up at his own list of Lenny-isms. 'It's his way with words, yuh know? I can't help it. What he comes up with and makes up, it's just —'

'yeah! like at the very beginning he says —'

Moe's too inspired to wait for Curly Joe to finish. 'And at the end he always says —'

'Emmis!' They all blurt out in chorus.

'Yeah, emmis,' Moe repeats, shaking his head in admiration. 'There's one for the books, right? I mean, where can ya get a better word than —'

Now it's Curly Joe's turn to butt in. 'schlep! that's another great one. like when he has the lone ranger —'

Hee-hawing Larry's up for it once more. 'Oh, that bit is just so fantastic! How's he come up with this nutty idea of The Lone Ranger wanting to get it on with Tonto —'

'no, it's with his horse, silver, ain't it?'

'Yuh, yuh. The horse, too. But that's before.'

'i thought it was after.'

'Are you guys sure? I don't —'

And so on ...

This keeps them busy through the rest of the afternoon.

By then, pooped out and hungry for supper, they all rise, tug at the seats of their trousers which have got damp because the plastic chairs they've been scrunched up on for hours and make their way to *Metro* Station or Bus Stop, wishing each other their 'so longs!' or 'see you in the mornings.'

One more illuminating, multi-eventful day put to rest.

3. DREAMS AND DRUGS

Talk about 1967 and you can't help but talk about dreams.

Sometimes, it seems like the whole world's caught up in one. Just the same, some parts of the dream don't feel right, as if some diabolical entity has possessed them. Looks like an exorcism is required.

Accordingly, on the Twenty-First day of October, a whole bunch of weirdos, freaks and whackos gather together in Washington DC, all of them shouting 'Out, Demons, Out!'

Not only that, but they're there to levitate the Pentagon.

Yes, you read that right: they're going to *levitate* The Pentagon.

To help them along, they invoke the cosmic powers of deities such as Zeus, Ra, Yahweh, and the Beak of Sok (whoever, or whatever, that is) to say nothing of The Tyrone Power Pound Cake Society in the Sky.

And, of course, the incantation works.

Up goes The Pentagon.

In their dreams.

All things being connected, some sprinkling of the Sandman's dust is bound to seep into everyone's dreams.

Even drab old McGill pays tribute to this with its yearly Revue. Some genius gives it the title *When Hippies Were In Flower.*

And, yes, it turns out to be as silly as it sounds.

* * * * *

As to our trio ... They've got dreams aplenty.

Maybe one of them will awaken heir to a mysterious super-inheritance that will permit the purchase of a "Stop the World, I Want to Get Off" secret island retreat.

Or, how about joining a commune? Living off the land. Growing your own food. Being self-sufficient.

And what if there's an invitation to direct the quintessential psychedelic movie?

Much less, the more conventional groovy standbys: Finding the cure for cancer. Bringing about everlasting international peace. Convincing everybody to vote for One World — No More Borders.

All the stuff that 1967 flower power dreams are made of.

* * * * *

Anything more specific?

A few weeks down the line and Larry and Curly Joe's poetic spree carries on undaunted. To amuse themselves, each keeps trying to top the other's efforts.

Consequence? Copious amounts of dubious doggerel that fill up page after page of their otherwise blank notebooks.

Worse yet, not only are they ready to recite this malarkey to whoever's dumb enough to ask to hear it, they have the audacity to slop numerous layers of made-up-on-at-the-drop-of-a-hat, chin stroking significance onto their efforts.

Well! Lookee here you lucky Tripsters!

Your Guide just happens to have a couple of their works on hand.

Want to see them?

Of course you do!

POETRY

A poem is a fun-house mirror
distorting ideas of ourselves,
bringing forth the truth.
And, as we all know:
we must never tell the truth.

GETTING OFF HENRY MILLER'S OVARIAN TROLLEY

> *a wise man walked up t' me one day 'n' asked:*
> *d'you b'lieve in*
> *monarchism*
> *capitalism*
> *socialism*
> *nationalism*
> *anarchism*
> *republicanism*
> *liberalism*
> *conservatism*
> *nazism*
> *fascism*
> *mccarthyism*
> *marxism*
> *catholicism*
> *hebrewism*
> *hinduism*
> *buddhism*
> *agnosticism*
> *atheism*
> *surrealism*
> *impressionism*
> *futurism*
> *popism*
> *existentialism*
> *?*
> *i said: i b'lieve in*
> *jism.*

And, just to wrap things up, here's one that Larry and Curly Joe composed together while their Applied Geometry Prof droned on and on about something no one wanted to hear about. Just for the fun of it, try to guess which one of them wrote each line.

TO A WORM

O joyous little worm
spelunkin' gaily up m' nose
Eat all you can find there;
ev'ry weed wuz once a rose.

o squintzy little yecch
Why does your head stick out?
or might that be yer ass
Which you're shaking all about?

what r'ligion are you, little-more-than-amoeba?
Dost thou believe in God? Might you be Jewish?
o little worm, i'm growin' weary.
O little worm ... SQUISH!

One glorious afternoon, they even persuade themselves that Latin is the root to all great POETRY. For days thereafter, every one of their inspirations is composed exclusively in a style they dub *Latinised English*. This Period in their creative endeavours reaches its peak with their endeavour to carry out all cafeteria gabfests in their newly created language.

Until ... Fed up with this esoteric bunkum, it is Moe who bushwhacks the proceedings. Threatening to contribute to all future discussions by relying exclusively on his personal take on Ancient Greek, he brings matters to a sudden and fitting end.

But not before the definitive put-down phrase in their private language is conceived.

Taurus caca.

It takes no time at all for it to become a nearly sacred profanity, reserved solely for the slimiest, vilest, most despicable SOBs who come along to upset their world.

For all that, they'll employ it a lot more often than they'd expected.

* * * * *

Moe's dreams are as reliable as the television programmes he's addicted to. Before and after supper, most nights he passes away his time staring into the black and white screen that rules his parents' home. What does he watch? Well ...

Recently, like seventy-eight million other viewers, he's sat glued to the tube eyeballing the very last episode of *The Fugitive*.

Then there's all those weekday re-runs of an old TV Western called *Have Gun — Will Travel*. Moe always makes sure he's got a ballpoint and paper on hand when it's on. That way, he can copy down all of the pseudo-philosophical statements uttered by the black-clad "knight without armour in a savage land".

And, of course, there's always the insomniac's last hope: *The Tonight Show*. Monday to Friday, Moe tunes in on the pale jokes and the near-desperate, egotistical rantings of Johnny Carson's invited guests imploring everyone out there in TV Land to run along and buy whatever it is they're hawking that week.

Moe's a reluctant witness to the cringe-making antics of over-the-hill Stars doing their best to remind some Hollywood mogul who might be watching that they're still alive and ready for their close-up.

He even masturbates to the black-and-white materialisations of legions of young starlets who appear, all capped-teeth smiles and low-cut gowns, willing to do and say anything within the limits of the broadcast censorship code just so they get themselves noticed. Mainly though, Moe laughs at all the phoniness and gloss and semi-restrained backstabbing that's on display before him.

It's a bitter laugh. A hoax, he knows, yet a good one. One that he'll play along to, regardless. Like believing in God, just in case.

And Oh My Lord, wasn't Moe's faith tested back in March with that nearly two-week US TV strike. It had him climbing the walls stuck with only Canadian TV crapola to get him through the passing hours.

Hardly unexpected then that Moe's special dream is that of

owning his very own colour television — an expensive, and therefore unlikely, event in 1967.

* * * * *

Trouble with dreams though, is that if they really and truly do contain messages of significance, their obscurity opens them to multiple interpretations, none of which is altogether satisfactory. Mostly, what's recalled is superficial flamboyance.

A bit like *Nehru jackets:* a fifteen minute 1967 flash in the pan that added up to a load of prodigiously toe-curling *taurus caca*.

* * * * *

And if it isn't dreams, what most people typically associate with The Sixties is the post-war generation's widespread fascination with mind-altering drugs. Drugs have catapulted *The Big Divide*: For every flipped-out space ranger claiming to have bashed the doors of perception wide open thanks to weed, buttons or tabs, there's twice as many nay-sayers prepared to tell you that drugs are the nightmare part of The Sixties dream.

It hasn't taken much for Larry and Curly Joe to lap up hippiedom as far as outward appearance is concerned. Larry's grown his hair longer so that it now covers the top half of his ears. And Curly Joe's allowed the wispy moustache he's sprouted to settle in on a continuing basis. He's even secretly encouraging it along by swiping his mother's mascara brush over it so that it shows up better and darker.

Moe, defiant as ever, sees this whole Dippy Hippie business as yet another Madison Avenue plot to conquer the world. Long hair and garish clothes? Don't hold your breath! Growing sideburns was a tough enough call to make. Swayed, in spite of his misgivings, by the revolutionary nature of the times, Moe's grudgingly crossed the Rubicon on that one. But he's drawn the line on mutton chops.

As to the underlying attitudes an ideals ... Well sure, all three agree that love and peace are the way to go. It is, however, the role of drugs in the countercultural scheme of things that has given rise to steadily more bad-tempered squabbles. As a result, their willingness "to agree to disagree" has been stretched to its limits.

Curly Joe, regularly first in such matters, has already tried pot. To be sure, it was a one-off event at a party he'd been invited to by a would-be-rebel rich kid son of friends of his parents. As he was already pretty blotto on the Singapore Sling that the host had mixed up as a way of greeting arriving guests, Curly Joe remembers very little of the experience. He *thinks* that he enjoyed it, and, sticking to that, has no qualms with the possibility of giving it another try. Likewise, joining the stoned ranks of the counterculture leaves him feeling really proud. Now that he's *in,* Curly Joe's even gone so far as to advance the view that LSD — or acid, as it's beginning to be called — sounds intriguing. Not to sound *too* extreme though, he waters down his verdict with the concession that the drug's uncertain lasting effects require appropriate caution.

Larry hasn't tried anything as yet, but is open to the possibility. Maybe drugs will help him find out what it's really like to *be here now.*

Moe's as terrified of drugs as he is about the laws surrounding them. His friends' disclosures of criminal curiosity bring on shudders and shakes. He's even begun wigging out to strangely alarming nightmares wherein Larry and Curly Joe — and, unaccountably, he as well — are put under the most heinously blood-curdling tortures by guilt-free, animal-like law enforcers who've caught them getting totally wasted on grass.

Okay Tripsters, your Guide has a pretty good idea what you're thinking right now. Brief history break coming right up. Viewed from the standpoint of the current worldwide scourge of opiates and opioids and all the wasted lives and unnecessary deaths linked to it, any proposal whose intent is to make a sympathetic case for recreational drug use seems irresponsible, if not downright offensive.

But what people today tend to either miss or forget is that, for an ever so brief window of time back then, those on the positive side of drugs saw them as being both revolutionary and transcendental. There was still some kind of status quo defying glory in forming little circles of criminals who passed around cannabis-filled roll-ups, or bubble-smoke water pipes, or Tibetan chillums stuffed full of ganja. Or, even more audaciously, stuck their tongues out and guzzled down blotter paper hallucinogenic dots. Dopers and trippers knew that what they were doing had a dangerous element to it, and not just because of its criminality. It felt like a true act of both rebellion and illumination that provided a direct link to the power lines of The Movement.

Best of all, the drugs really did work in those days. Timothy Leary instructing everybody to *Turn On, Tune In, Drop Out* was a call to explore, not to escape. Those words convinced a lot of people that they were on the same path toward spiritual enlightenment as an Indian ascetic who'd dedicated years of his life to the task. The only difference being that, via the drug route, the journey was just so much quicker and easier. Which was a scatterbrained error. But there you go.

And, when it came to it, in spite of all the media furore about drugs and how there wasn't a high school or college kid living in the Western World left who wasn't flipping out on LSD, there were probably more parents scarfing down tranquillisers worried sick over the possibility of their kids jumping out of windows at the height of some drug-induced delirium then there were high-flying sky pilots heading for zonker's paradise. For most people at the time, it was enough to be in the know about what *The Beatles* were *really* alluding to when they sang about *Lucy in the Sky with Diamonds* without personally wanting to join in on the actual experience. No question, a lot of the thrills were more about having a laugh sharing in a secret that the older generation didn't, and maybe couldn't, understand.

In 1967, the drug trade that mattered — grass and hash and acid — was run by independents, most of them baby boomers who took it to be their calling to turn on the world by expanding awareness and unifying The Tribe. There really was a distinction to be made between dealers and pushers. Pushers were part of international criminal organisations whose trade was primarily cocaine and heroin. Cocaine was what some people's grandparents had snorted back in the 20s and 30s or what Hollywood and 5th Avenue "suits" snarfed up their noses. Heroin? Heroin was for skid-row losers. People attracted to those kinds of drugs had nothing to do with The Movement. As to speed ... Well, speed was a sort of boundary line; both camps had it on sale.

Still ... Having promised to be honest with you all, this Trip Guide has got to admit that it wouldn't take too long for such dividing lines to fall apart. By the beginning of the 70s, rock stars and countercultural visionaries started to 'fess up that they'd been dabbling with coke and smack and crack. Some of them never stopped, either. And too many of the Janises and Jimis only stopped because they dropped dead. Just as bad, what were once holy herbal acts all too quickly became something as pointless and mundane as the pouring out of alcoholic drinks for the sake of relaxation and sociability. Besides which, once the worldwide cartels tuned in on what was happening they lost no time in taking control of the trade.

So ... Moe's fears are a peek into the future. And maybe, like him, those who got into radical revolutionary movements like the *Weathermen* and such like, and who were rabidly anti any sort of drug-taking saw what was round the corner more accurately than did the hippies and head-trippers getting off on a psychedelically awakened, peace-and-love fuelled planet.

But hey! We're back in 1967, when psychedelic only means something innocent and those in the know have good reason to snigger upon hearing *DuPont* and the like make claims for "Better Living Through Chemistry". Oh-hum. For a while there ... It's a here-and-gone flicker, Tripsters. Enjoy it while you can.

Meanwhile, over at Larry's house, a treaty is being hammered out. Because of his acute paranoia (and the fear that it might be contagious), it has been decreed that any discussion about drugs with Moe is now *verboten*. Besides, as Larry and

Curly Joe keep reassuring him, the whole issue's a non-starter, since neither of them has the vaguest clue as to how to go about getting a hold of any kind of drugs. Which, when they're left on their own to think about this, is kind of sad.

To make himself feel better, Larry returns to the same argument as the one he uses about his virginity: 'Not knowing is a beauty which yuh lose once yuh know.'

Curly Joe nods in agreement. All the same, he's keeping his eyes and ears and nose open. Just in case.

4. A REAL MEMORY

It has been proposed by those who claim to know about such matters that on the verge of death our thoughts are taken up with resurrected flashes of key events in our lives. That wise old con-man, George Ivanovich Gurdjieff, called these revelations "real memories" because, though they often depict allegedly trivial incidents, they are, without fail, what one's life truly adds up to. Assuming such speculations to be correct, here then is a real memory that the three of them will have in their final moments:

It's almost the end of November and Moe's just broken up with Chastity. This is nothing, of course, for a fortune teller to brag about. What provoked the crisis was Moe's confession that he didn't believe in Papal Infallibility. This pronouncement totally floored Chastity. How could Pope Paul VI *not* be infallible? Much less the saintly Pope John XXIII? No way was she going to keep on dating someone who couldn't accept something so evident! And that was that.

Conveniently, Moe had the good sense to choose a Friday for the tragedy to occur. Getting bored with watching him mope around all Saturday afternoon, Larry and Curly Joe decide that the best way to get his mind off the girl-he-lost is to arouse it with other candidates. Paying no attention to Moe's protests of love unrequited, they cart him off to one of Montréal's better known Discos.

As a way of getting Moe to stop complaining that the last thing he feels like doing is to go out dancing, Larry and Curly Joe nudge him towards worrying about Age IDs instead. They all need an Age ID because in 1967 Montréal in order to be served alcoholic drinks you need to be twenty-one or over or else in the company of someone who is. Appallingly, as far as they're concerned, you can't get into a Disco unless you're ready and able to buy a drink since drinks are what Discos survive on.

After a while, they agree that Curly Joe doesn't need an ID because his conveniently-sprouting Zapata moustache makes him look old enough in the dark to pass through without much bother.

Moe's going to use that fake ID someone gave him a few months back. So what if the face on the picture doesn't look anything remotely similar to his? If it comes to it and anybody asks, he was in a car accident that required extensive facial surgery.

As to Larry, he's sure to get in by speaking fluent *Joual* since the Outremont Disco they're headed for is a *Quebecois* student stomping ground, and what French-Canadian these days is going to say no to another?

Have no fear. As such things typically turn out, all the fretting and planning proves to be entirely unnecessary. The only proof they're required to yield is the correct amount of money for admittance and beers and tip.

It's at times like these that Curly Joe's intense dislike of beer is a godsend. As long as his glass stays close to full, he won't be hounded by one of the dozen odd waiters whose only job is to see to it that all customers pay more than adequately for their presence. Larry and Moe aren't quite that fortunate since they're more inclined to enjoying a glass of beer or three. They'll have to drink their *Molson's* slow.

The place they've ended up in calls itself *L'Onde Psychedelique*. It's a trendy place to hang out in. Though nothing mind-blowing, it showcases one of the city's largest dance floors, a passable light-show and the latest in Top 40 dance music. Mainly though, a lot of single women come to it.

While they're ordering their mugs of *Molson's,* the *Anglais* bartender connects with them and insists on clueing them in on the greatest scoop he's unearthed throughout the whole of his career. 'Buying a beer in a Disco gives away all your secrets,' he says. 'Beers are for lonely prowlers since they're the cheapest booze on the Menu and you won't feel so bad if the night's a write-off.'

They thank him for this exclusive news item, then head off to find a table. They don't need any Guru Bartender Wisdom to know that on the Disco floor women rule supreme. For once, the inegalitarian gender-roles that pervade all everyday interactions are reversed. They, as men, must bow to women for the honour of a dance, as well as suffer the humiliation of rejection or the pyrrhic victory of acceptance.

Which is probably why Larry and Curly Joe don't usually head off to Discos. Unlike his two friends however, Moe thrives on them. Giving up on any further attempts to badger his pals into letting him mooch his way back home, he magically transforms himself into "Moe Cool" and gets right into it. Age ID accepted, drink in hand, and "hell-if-I-have-to-be-here-I-might-as-well-enjoy-myself" attitude turned to MAX, Moe makes straight for the dance floor. In minutes, he's hit it off with a willing partner and finds himself frenetically undulating his hips in tune with hers to the kinetic beat of *Wooly Bully, Wild Thing* and *Chain of Fools.*

Mission accomplished, Larry and Curly Joe sit down in silence at their oval-shaped, formica-covered plastic table. Telepathy time! In unison, they set aside their beers and catch the attention of a passing waiter. Heeding the commands of their collective inner voice, they dare themselves to get blotto on scotch and soda.

Approximately two hours and three and a half scotch and sodas each later, they've managed to do just that. Problem is, now they can't stop giggling. Loudly. Strangers throw them dirty looks, and it gets them yucking it up all the harder. They home in on others' conversations, come-on's, or pleas from the heart and they're splitting their sides, ribs aching in response to it all. They're guffing so hard that they don't notice the guy who let them in at the Entrance is standing over them requesting that they leave. Immediately. Or else. They crease up in front of him, too. Still, they get the message.

However, trying to find Moe in the state they're in proves to be a teensy-weensy bit difficult. Try as they might, they can't pick him out on the Dance floor. Okay. Well then ... They shout his name, crawl under empty tables whispering 'Yoo-hoo, Moe!', check out the Men's, the Ladies', the Staff Room. Everywhere. A washout. Maybe they should take a second look at the Dance floor. Whoa! There he is! How'd he find a way to turn invisible before?

No matter what his pals might think, Moe hasn't mastered the art of disappearing. He is where he's been all night, he, too, by now thoroughly plastered on rum and coke but still in enough control to undulate in tune with his similarly pie-eyed partner. Right now, they're cheek to cheek in that unfading slow dance that is *A Whiter Shade Of Pale*. Just as the singer informs one and all that no reason exists, Moe takes a long-delayed plunge and works his hand into the best position so that it can casually slide down to his dance mate's nicely fleshed-out bum and stay there. Too bad. Right at that moment of meticulous timing which both boppers have been inching towards all night long, Larry and Curly Joe sidle up to Moe, grab hold of his shoulders, and lead him, too dumbfounded to protest, out into the dark.

Montréal. Dead November. Nearly 11.00pm, and the winds are blowing mean. Waiting for a bus to appear, wound up wild with free-flowing energy now, they shrug off the challenge. To prove they're not joking, Larry leaps into a fifteen minute flamenco number right in the middle of treacherous Cote-des-Neiges. There he is, dodging the speeding cars while impressively never missing a step. Moe and Curly Joe cheer him on, then they, too, caught up in the trance, bursting to take a leak, turn their backs and begin to pee onto the bus stand as if carrying out an act of bus divination.

When their coach ultimately does arrive, they leap on board and pretend to be unable to speak in any language other than their own bastardised form of Pig Latin.

Plainly unamused, the driver tells them to sit down and shut up.

Defiant, Moe launches into his *Elmer Gantry* preachifying zealot character and shouts 'Ya Sinners!' in a deep base Burt Lancaster voice while pointing an accusing finger at the dozen or so stunned and nervous passengers who, up to now, had thought it to be a pretty quiet night. Following his lead, Larry begs for forgiveness while crawling on his knees towards an attractive young woman who greets the events with a rigid grin that shows off her indented canines.

The driver repeats his command a bit more firmly.

Paying him no attention, Curly Joe invokes the ghost of the recently-assassinated Che Guevara and kick-starts an impassioned revolutionary rap that turns the bus into an allegory of the current social mess he claims they are all in. Caught up in his guerilla oratory, he urges the people to rise up and liberate themselves and the Montréal Transport System.

They are booted off the bus.

Big deal. They'll walk all the way downtown.

By the time they get there however, it's past midnight and they're ravenous. They need to eat something. Right now, if not sooner.

Curly Joe suggests Chinese Food.

Of course! Great! *Perfecto*!

But where? A deserted St. Catherine Street glares back at them in disinterested silence.

Larry to the rescue. 'There's an All-Nite Chinese place near my house!'

Cool! Let's go, go, go!

Somewhere in the great murky depths of their alcohol-addled minds, each of them is being reminded of a basic geography lesson that runs like this:

1. Montréal proper is an island.
2. Surrounding it is the St. Lawrence River.
3. Partially surrounding the opposite side of the mighty St. Lawrence is still more land known as suburbia.
4. Larry's home happens to be located in suburbia.
5. To reach suburbia, Montréalers must cross one of several bridges.
6. Usually, this is achieved by car and it takes some ten minutes to do so.

None of them has a car at his disposal at this moment, nor are there any buses that will transport them to their destination at this late hour. As to taxis, they maintain the reactionary view that they should be paid for fulfilling such vital social services. They look down at their already weary feet. Somehow, they'll have to cajole them into trudging over to the Jacques Cartier Bridge, illegally crossing it, and then going on further until they've reached Larry's particular suburb. Thanks to their sloshed-up skulls however, their determination carries on undimmed. Like Chairman Mao's Revolutionary Army, no obstacles placed before them will prevent the reaching of their destination. Let The Long March begin!

Just as they turn onto Clark Street, a snow flurry starts to descend. Rather than dampen their enthusiasm, the event unleashes untapped reserves of giddy energy. Eyes focused on the sky, they hear a Message From On High: as an act of good citizenship they should lap up all the snow before it hits the ground and thereby keep the street clean. Primed to obey, they scramble about in circles, heads tilted heavenwards, tongues flapping wildly like those of cats licking cream — or, better yet, tinned tuna fish — out of a bowl. A few minutes into this, the purpose behind their manic behaviour wiped from their minds, Larry shouts out that it'd be a great idea if they were to build a snowman.

Excelsior! *Cowabunga*!

Duly inspired, they set about their new task with a re-awakened tenacity. Too bad, the snow's too soft and unwilling to pack itself together. What now? Oh! How about changing strategies once more? Let's take up handfuls of falling flakes and start to pummel each other with them instead!

Aces!

Utterly soaked in minutes, they establish that they're cold. Or rather, they're freezing. Bodies shiver, teeth clack reverberating down the alleys they pass through. Jogging will warm them up! Consumed by an irresistible desire to break into a race, they stampede forward on all fours chanting Native Indian war whoops. Driven by some do-or-die *Light Brigade* stamina, they charge into the Bridge Street Tunnel and then right out the other end of of it. After that, inexplicably snapped back to cold turkey reality, they collapse onto the sidewalk heaving in painful gulps of air and questioning what exactly it is that they've been up to.

Still, what matters is that, somehow, they've made it to the Jacques Cartier Bridge. They scrutinise the overhead clock that ticks 12:45am. They calculate the distance still to be faced. They're close to tears. More out of despair than hope, Curly Joe sticks out his thumb appealing to each infrequent passing car to stop and show some mercy upon them. Too tired to walk any further for the moment, Larry and Moe just stand there, looking glum, lost sheep hoping for a Good Shepherd to guide them home.

Their faith is rewarded a few minutes later when a car pulls up. The man who's in the driver's seat reeks of alcohol and there's a definite slur in his invitation to 'get on in, boys'. But, hey! It's a free ride. Strengthened by this manifest thumbs-up from heaven, they take the drunk up on his offer. As it turns out, the guy's so plastered he's going in the opposite direction to that of his intended destination. They point this out to him once he's let them off a few feet away from the restaurant's door. He thanks them profusely for the information and drives off.

So here they are, on the wrong side of 1.00am Sunday morning, tucked into a red-leatherette dining booth of a plastic suburban Chinese All-Niter. They settle on the Chef's Dinner for Four. Asked if they want a drink, they demand *Sake*. Informed that *Sake* is a Japanese drink and that relations between the people of the Middle Kingdom and those of the Rising Sun are about as cordial as those between English and French Canada, they are invited to try a real drink — *Baijiu* — instead.

Sure, why not? But no cutlery. Chop sticks or nothing.

The food arrives. Egg rolls, beef chop suey, eight butterfly shrimps, pork chow mein, pineapple chicken, sweet and sour ribs, and anything else the chef was about to throw out. They each grab a bowl, cram one-third of every item onto it, mix things up until what's in front of them is some vile-coloured concoction and start to dig in. At the same time, the *Baijiu* helps to turn the red and yellow paper lanterns suspended above them into incredibly amusing ornaments worthy of prolonged attention.

Welcoming any new company, they cajole the sleepy-eyed waiter who's come to ask if everything's okay into sitting down with them. He half-squats on the outside ledge of their booth looking distinctly uncomfortable. When he lets slip that he's into Martial Arts, they plead with him to teach them some major moves right then and there. They're serious, they add. Just to make this point more forceful, Curly Joe tries to smash the table with the edge of his left hand and succeeds in providing a genuine experience of pain for himself while soaking Moe's shirt with plum sauce. Maybe it's best to focus on their meal. They eat up every scrap, stare at empty plates. Something missing? How about a Won Ton Soup to wash things down? And more *Baijiu*. The waiter, blatantly showing his relief at being able to beat a hasty retreat from these white devil loonies, sidesteps his way to the safety of the back-room kitchen.

Not far off from 2.00am, a wretched kind of drowsiness begins to creep over them. Concerned about his friends' long journey home, Larry volunteers to go on ahead to his house, borrow the keys to his father's car, and drive them back to their respective beds. They order another *Baijiu* to celebrate his gracious offer.

Shambling toward his street all by himself while the others wait behind passing away the time playing with their empty *Baijiu* glasses and inventing new aphorisms to be included in the next edition of Chairman Mao's *Little Red Book*, Larry can't stop shaking with laughter over the situation he finds himself in. Minutes later, still snickering audibly, he enters his parents' bedroom and begins to search for the necessary car keys. The noise he makes rouses his father out of a sound and peaceful sleep. Alarmingly awake, his body jack-knifed to a near-motionless position, he asks, with some temerity, what his son is looking for. When told, he points out where the keys are and then, not really hearing Larry's 'thanks and good night', slips back into a state of blessedly unaware sleep, hoping against hope that this will turn out to be one more half-forgotten dream.

Some twenty minutes and one last *Baijiu* later, they find

themselves driving back across the same bridge they were picked up from an eternity ago. Brazenly, halfway across, Curly Joe announces his burning desire for a vanilla milk shake. Hearing this, Moe chips in that he wouldn't mind a root beer and, come to think of it, a burger wouldn't be out of place either. Even though the snow fall's by now transmuted itself into a full-scale blizzard, they take a detour and head for a *Harvey's Take-Out.*

Another half hour flits by before they reach Curly Joe's home. A hasty "well, this is it, guys" smile is offered and then, he's set loose, lost to the storm, taking giant leaps for the front door.

Soon, it's Moe's turn to bail out as well.

'Good night.'

'Good morning.'

'Geronimo!'

Then, for the third time in less than four hours, Larry finds himself crossing the Jacques Cartier Bridge. Not quite believing it, he passes by the drunk who'd picked them up earlier and who, since then, has been driving up and down the bridge, totally confused by their directions.

Moments after Larry's turned up his street, the car's engine gives out on him. With the windscreen wipers at a stand-still, the pounding sleet has the car blanketed in seconds, his view of the outside world indistinguishable from that of a blurred TV screen. Prying open his door, Larry feels the gelid stab of bitter winds blowing from the North. Hunched up, he dives out to see just where he is and is in no time up to his knees in virgin snow. Taking it all in, Larry reckons *who's gonna be crazy enough to be out driving on a night like this?*

Answering his question in silence, he leaves the car where it whirred to a halt and sludges home to write to Angel and then at last, like the others, to sleep the peaceful sleep of those who've just notched up an award-winning real memory.

5. TELEPHONES

How's you trip through The Sixties so far? Enjoying yourselves? Maybe musing on where we're heading and how we'll get there?

Just so you know: no murder mystery or James Bond spy heroics around the corner. And definitely no three-headed radioactive spider biting our trio and turning them into superheroes.

My advice? Stay cool! Go with The Sixties flow. If it helps at all, keep in mind that what makes a time unique is measured not only by what existed but also by what didn't.

Like, for instance: social media and the internet — all that *Mac* and *Microsoft* sort of stuff we take for granted today — no sign of them in 1967 except in comic books and Science Fiction authors' imaginations.

Get this: you have to take several more backwards steps to truly take in how technologically primitive things are back in The Sixties. No social media of any kind. No *Netflix*. *No YouTube* or *Spotify*. No PlayStations, Nintendos or Game Boys. No blu-rays or DVDs. No satellite dishes. No laser discs. No PCs or laptops. No video players or VHS tapes. No Space Invaders or Donkey Kong. No Walkmans. Not much in the way of compact tape music cassettes, either. Even 8-Tracks are a rarity. It's reel-to-reel or nothing throughout most of these years. And no Men on the Moon either, until the end. As to credit cards? Who the hell has credit cards in 1967? Sure, there's *Diners Club* for Suits to flaunt, but really ...

Cameras? Yeah, you've got your *Kodak Brownies* and their variants, but it's thirty-six shots max and then you have to get the roll of film developed at some specialist shop and probably wait three days before seeing what's come out. Okay, so you can avoid all that if you have a *Polaroid* camera. But they're an expensive hassle to use and the prints fade to nothing if you don't smear on some gunk in the exact right way. Home movies are the same. A three minute roll of 8mm or Super-Eight is your lot. And they're *silent.*

Oh yeah! What's getting people all psyched up in 1967 are pocket calculators. *Ooh, look! It can do square roots too!* As if people need to do square roots of something all the time. Or even know what a square root is. And, in spite of the name, they're way too big and bulky to fit into most pockets.

What else is new in 1967? What matters?

Well, for one thing, something called underground radio is making its presence felt. Before you know it, the airwaves are worth listening to. Fiddling in the dark with transistor radios that probably only have a single, mono earpiece, you can tune in to the FM freak shows playing non-stop strange jarring music that goes way beyond the three-minute AM Radio Pop time-limit and keeps you up all night long curious as to what groovy sounds will turn up next. And, for the time being, there aren't any commercials in- between tunes, either.

As to the bands, they're mainly unknown yet extravagant in their stances and names. *Grateful Dead. Jefferson Airplane. Lothar And The Hand People.* They're ready and willing to call themselves anything. *Doors. Cream. Vanilla Fudge.* Even something really dumb like *Rhinoceros.* You name it, and *Hey Presto!* it's a rock group. And *psychedelic,* too!

It's through the laid-back lilt and doped-up cosmic chuckles of the station DJs that people learn that San Francisco is the Mecca and its entry visa is a flower. They're reminded that there's an LBJ and then a Nixon, a Chicago and a People's Park, campus clashes, Weathermen thrashes, hard-hat backlashes.

One more quick example: people only get to watch current release movies either in theatres or Drive-Ins. And they watch them really, really carefully, taking in as much as they can, because they know that, once they've been replaced with some new programme, they'll be gone for good, no longer available other than as memories. Want to revel in that film you totally loved one more time? Well, tough. Only chance you've got, if you're really lucky, is to wait some five years down the line when TV channels are allowed to air a square screen broadcast of your fave flick. And usually in some censored "TV Version" of it, no less.

Same thing with any TV show you're eager to sit through again. Maybe even binge watch the whole damn series. Forget it. There's no way you'll be able to stream, record or catch-up with your TV favourites. You get a single chance to give a show a go — and that's on the day and time that the networks ordain to put it on. The only exception is if the programme gets slotted in as a summer re-run. Trouble is, you'll probably be too busy having fun outdoors or else the rest of the family isn't about to let you take over the one TV in the house just so's you can make them all watch something they've already seen. Uh Huh. Not when there are *two* other channels offering some other repeat that nobody's tuned into before. *And* all this without a remote to flip and surf. More bad news: don't forget that most TVs in 1967 are still only black and white sets.

So many things that were and weren't which are now no longer or else are taken entirely for granted.

Which — finally! — gets us to telephones.

One of the most mind-bending things that Larry, Moe and Curly Joe keep going back to during their many visits to *Expo '67* is on display over at the *Bell Telephone Pavilion.* It's a video telephone — colour screen, too — that might become available some day in the future. And wouldn't *that* be super-duper? They can *see* themselves large as life while talking! No way! And ... And ... Here's an even more far-fetched possibility: what if, as well as having sound and vision, they could yak away to hearts' content with multiple people *simultaneously?*

Oh my God! A three-way hook-up! Outta this world! Talk about impossible dreams!

Whoa there, all you "how-could-I-survive-without-my-iphone" Tripsters! Let's get back down to Earth with the 1967 version of communication media reality.

* * * * *

Here's the thing: when Larry, Moe and Curly Joe have finished with their Student Union cafeteria chinwags and are back to their separate homes, it's not like they've run out of topics to talk about. For the most part, the walk or bus ride home is bound to remind them of how much more there is that they've barely touched on and can't possibly wait until tomorrow to be brought up.

Like what?

Well, for instance, has anybody figured out what's going on in this new TV show, *The Prisoner* and is it worth watching? Or is the *Jimi Hendrix Experience* more off-the-wall than *The Velvet Underground?* And what's CKGM's talk show host, Joe Pyne, going to be sneering about tonight? Failing that, there's always the old-faithful: did Adam and Eve have navels?

Thank goodness, then, for the existence of ordinary dial-up, landline phones. They're great. And they work just as well as these new-fangled push button ones that have started cropping up in Montréal's public phone booths, too!

The only serious obstacle to their phone gabs that they face on a regular basis comes from their parents. Of course. All of them never stop complaining about their sons' indulgent mistreatment of the telephone system. Which is a truly preposterous argument. Phones are there to be used, aren't they?

Just to make this point clear, one night Larry and Moe hold a marathon talk that lasts an eye-popping just under nine hours of uninterrupted telephone time. Amazingly, the call would have lasted even longer had not Moe's up-at-dawn Dad scuffled into the living room and come across his son still slouched on the couch and cradling the phone's speaker in exactly the same position as he'd left him around midnight.

Okay, even *they* have to admit that almost nine hours might have been a tad much. But they can't really see what all the fuss and bother is about. After all, it isn't as though their lengthy but local — and, therefore, *free* — phone calls are costing their parents any more than if their line had been left unused. (All you pay-by-the-minute phone company Tripsters shaking your heads and muttering 'that can't be right': Oh yes, it is! No charges for local phone calls, no matter how long they lasted was the norm in 1960s North America). As to the hypothetical someone who has to get through straight away at 3.30am in the morning? Come on! If it was that important, they could have easily gotten the Operator to interrupt them.

What Larry, Moe and Curly Joe fail to comprehend is that logic has got nothing to do with the issue. What hasn't occurred to them is that most people get totally weirded out at the thought of doing *anything* for nearly nine hours straight.

* * * * *

- Look Moe, I feel all right about it.
- Yeah, but how can ya? She just keeps you strung out hanging. Ya don't even know when you'll get to see her again.
- One of these days, I guess. When she's free enough from work. Soon, I hope.
- Oh. So what'cha gonna do till then?
- Wait.
- Yeah? How long until ya start to crinkle when ya walk?
- For fucks's sake, Moe!
- At least ya jumped the fence, Lar'.
- I'm *still* a virgin, Moe.
- Yeah ... But ya got a head start, though. This old spear-chucker ain't got no one ta chuck his spear at.
- ...
- Gotta do *something* in bed, Jim.
- Yuh.
- Hey, Larry. Ya do it often?
- Do what?
- Come on. Ya know. Blow the wad. Shoot the load. Play three-finger jiggy-jig.
- Oh ... Yuh, maybe.
- How often?
- Too often.
- What? Once a week? Ten times a day?
- Yuh! Ten times minimum! Twenty sometimes on weekends!

- Crazy frog. Touches it once and thinks it's a gear-shift. No, honestly, though.
- I dunno, Moe. Whenever it gets too bad, I guess.
- Yeah. Me, too. But it gets bad way too often. It's ... *Cold finger ... I'm the man ... The man with the Onan touch.*
- (mutual laughter)
- Yuh.
- What's really bad is, I don't even have anyone to fantasize about. I mean, at least you've got Angel. But who have I got? It's a real downer to fantasize over *The Valkyrie.* It *wilts* if I think of her. And if I start to imagine getting it on with Chastity, it'd drop off, for sure!
- So what do yuh do?
- I think of turn-ons in movies.
- Does it work?
- Yeah. Kinda.
- ...
- ...
- Uhm ... I don't always fantasize about Angel.
- Ya don't?
- No. Usually, I do. But sometimes I think of other people. Yuh know, like people at McGill.
- Yeah? Like who?
- I dunno. *People.*
- Ya ever think of the doll behind the caf' counter?
- Uhm ... Occasionally.
- Wow.
- What do yuh mean, "wow"?
- *Kee-rist!* If she ever knew. Both these total strangers creaming their sheets over her.
- ...
- ...
- Uhm ... Sometimes I do it with both her and Angel at once.
- Fuck, Larry! That's sick.
- They seem to enjoy it.

* * * * *

- hey, guess what? i was in *phantasmagoria* yesterday and the guy there told me that there's a new dylan lp coming out just after christmas.
- A *new* one? I thought he was at death's door.
- yeah. i did, too. but i guess he isn't.
- So what's it called, this new record of his?
- *john wesley harding.*
- Who the fuck's that?
- fuck knows, larry. some wild west outlaw, sounds like. but, anyway, the guy showed me a preview copy of the cover. man! it's black and white and there's dylan wearing this funny three-cornered hat and he's got these weird looking guys standing around him. no idea who they are. it's really anarchic, you know? it's just so stunning! he's really gone and done it again, man.
- Sounds great.
- yeah. and ... he isn't trying to copy *the beatles* and *the stones* with some far-out 3d psychedelic cover.
- Yuh. Real Fabba-Dabba-Do! I just hope the music's better than what's on that new Stones' LP. Crapola! *Their Satanic Majesties Please Give It A Rest,* far as I'm concerned.
- too right, man. how to go from kings of cool to total jerks in one jumpin' jack flash.
- *Ruby Tuesday's* okay. But that's about it. Uhm ... On another note: I'm reading Blake these days.
- blake? *william b*lake?
- Yuh. It's truly radical. The way he combines poetry and painting really gets to me. Yuh oughtta have a look and a read.
- i have.
- Yuh have? When?
- in guggenheim's class.
- Really?
- yeah, really. mind-bending stuff. i'd like to write like

that. put it to music.
- I just love his paintings. They're so simple in one way.
  Except they're not. I've tried copying them and found
  that out for myself. I ended up tracing some of them, just
  to get a feel for what he was doing.
- oh yeah? guggenheim hasn't said much about his
  paintings. he's more of a word man.
- Yuh know, there's another guy who's a bit like Blake.
  Word-wise, I mean.
- oh yeah? who?
- Somebody Angel wrote me about in one of her very
  occasional letters. Kahlil Gibran, he's called.
- gee-bran? fuck. sounds like a breakfast cereal or
   something.
- Yuh! That's the guy! He writes on the back of *Kellogg's
  Corn Flakes* packages.
- oh *him!* yeah, he's great ...

* * * * *

- hello?
- Hi, there.
- hiya, moe. how goes it?
- Same as ever. How're the curls growing today?
- straight and narrow, natch.
- Hey! Ya seen Larry around lately?
- uhm ... yeah. i seen him in class yesterday.
- In class? *You* went to class? *You?*
- well it's ... okay, i'll spill the beans. i showed up at
   chemistry class because there's this really attractive
   chick who i just figured out always goes to it. and she
   sits not far from where larry usually sits, so ...
- Ya talked to her yet?
- are you kidding? i told you, she sits a couple of rows
  down from larry. what should i do? scream hello?
- Nah! That'll get ya nowhere. There's one, sure-fire way,
   though.

- yeah, what?
- Well, next time, ya just walk up to her and say: 'Hey Doll, what's wrong? Ya on *the rag* or something?' Gets 'em every time.
- right. i'll try to keep that one in mind.
- Anytime, son. Now ... I've been re-reading that Father Flotsky bit. Pure Genius. Wanna go over it?

.

6. GIRLS! GIRLS! GIRLS!

As some of you will have already guessed, the girl in Chemistry class will prove to be more than some "really attractive chick".

She calls herself Suzie Q. The name suits her. No fakes. No frills. Real down-to-earth. Maybe she's a touch too tall for some. Perhaps a couple more inches wider around the hips than perfection. And, okay, a little more "oomph!" bust-wise might do the job. But, hey! From the moment he first lays eyes on Suzie Q, Curly Joe's convinced that his dream woman has materialised. There's that cinnamon brown hair of hers, flowing long and straight way past her shoulders, parted down the middle making her look like some Iroquois Indian Princess. Curly Joe dreams of losing his hands in it. And that crooked wisp of a smile she's got, aimed at no one in particular, more like the result of a question she keeps asking. Curly Joe wishes she'd notice him and admit to herself that he's the answer she's searching for.

But to really cap things off, there's her name. Wasn't that woman arm-in-arm with Dylan on the *Freewheelin'* album his long-time love and Muse? Sure she was. And her name was *Suze,* wasn't it? Suze. Suzie Q. Close enough, right? The signs are all there: this is meant to be.

And because it is, Curly Joe's been putting in a regular attendance at Chemistry class. Though, as far as he's aware of what's going on in it, he could be sitting in on lectures delving into the origins of Serbo-Croat Folk Tales. Which, come to think of it, might be more intelligible than the mumbo jumbo he intermittently tunes in to.

That quirky, all-knowing grin of hers bothers him, though. Especially as she's always already there in class, sitting in her usual seat, when he walks in. And as he passes by, trying not to look her way, there it is! ZAP! Which makes Curly Joe rack his brains: *does she know?* And even if she does, what can he do about it? The thought of going up and talking to her turns him into mushy, melting *Jell-O*. The one possible solution to the whole problem that Curly Joe can picture is so risibly remote from being fulfilled that even he concludes it's a waste of time giving it any heavyweight consideration.

Foregone conclusion? It's the very outcome that becomes a reality.

On the day that it does, Curly Joe has somehow found the courage to get to the lecture theatre early enough so that he can slide into his usual place before her arrival. There he is now, doing his best to look real cool and casual, spying behind an open book of chemistry equations so as not to be too conspicuous when she arrives. It would help if the textbook wasn't upside down, though.

Out of nowhere, he hears a voice asking if the seat next to him is free. When he looks up, irritated by this stranger's disruption of his holy thoughts, his awestruck eyes fix on those whose colour he's been trying to guess for the past three weeks. They're green; and all he can retain as he tries to curb the powerhouse_dizziness that has begun to rock him is that she's wearing this pale-blue, tasseled-hem dress which makes her look even more like some Iroquois Princess straight out of a Canadian History book. Somehow, he contrives to croak out a garbled reply to which she takes no notice whatsoever. Added to which, her question's rhetorical since she's already sat herself down while asking it.

The subsequent hour's nothing but sweat and shakes for Curly Joe. Worse, every time he steals a peek her way, she's already there silently challenging him to a staring match they both know he can't win. By the end of the class, Curly Joe's a broken man. A good sport about it, Suzie Q stands up and waves "bye-bye" hoping that even he will get the message that what she really means is "hello".

On the night of their first date, they go to see *Bonnie and Clyde* playing over at *The Seville Theater,* one of Montréal's premier-league cinemas. Curly Joe's already sat through it once and loved every second of the movie; there's no downside to watching it again. Except tonight, hunkered down next to Suzie Q, arm brushing arm, it feels like an endurance test is taking place within the movie house's darkened recesses. Which is nothing that comes close to Curly Joe's previous experiences of viewing dozens of 70mm epics — ranging from *El Cid* to *Lawrence of Arabia* — either in the company of pals and cronies or, far more commonly, all on his own right here, in this very same space.

But tonight ... Ah! Tonight! Two young hearts beat as one. Having guessed the movie's ending not long before it happens, Suzie Q begins to cry. Braver than he'd thought possible, Curly Joe slings his right arm around her in an attempt to console. His hand brushes hers. The heat of her skin is irresistible. So sensuous! She turns away from the screen, unwilling to witness the movie's final minutes. But she doesn't move her hand. Their fingers entwine. Then they kiss.

After that, both of them discover the ability to float on air.

* * * * *

Larry's walking the family pooch, a female cocker spaniel named Jolie, up and down the local streets bordering his own. He's been doing so for nearly an hour and Jolie keeps tugging on the leash doing her best to sway him into agreeing that they've been out long enough now and lying around back at home would be so much nicer. And warmer.

Not that Larry notices. He's too busy trying to grab hold of the inspiration required for the long, rambling, pathos-encrusted letter he'll mail tonight to Angel. Larry's suffering. And loving every moment of it. *Angel ....* Larry thinks. *Yuh couldn't have been given a more appropriate name. How could I have been so dumb to have avoided yuh for so many years?*

As children, Larry and Angel become friends in the wilds of British Columbia. Being nine and a half, Angel's one and one-quarter years older than Larry. When you're a kid, such matters hold great significance. Still, not so much that it stops them from spending as much time as possible together.

Typically, they play the types of secret games that lots of friends of opposite sexes engage in before their frolicking turns into all-out war. Practicing multiple versions on Doctor and Patient, they touch and pinch and squeeze and tickle each others' bums and genitals inside their hide-out in the forest.

When they feel especially daring, they even pee onto the ground in each other's presence. Off and on, while doing that, they take turns contorting their bodies into the most unnatural positions so that the other gains the least obstructed view of this mysterious event. Once even, Larry tries to pee while on his back, legs splayed upward, and does a great job in soaking his T-shirt and scarfing down liquid so acrid that all he can do the rest of the day is spit. It's a price worth paying; to watch Angel pee always fills Larry with awe. It also makes him laugh himself silly since it's so hilarious to see this jet of pale yellow fluid appear out of nowhere obvious between her legs. Young as they are, the awareness of their differences is already apparent: girls are nothing as simple and straightforward as boys.

Then one day, for reasons unexplained, Larry's parents announce that the family is going to move back to Montréal. And with that, they bring Larry's and Angel's games, and all the future variations of them that would have undoubtedly sprung up, to a crashing end. Muted goodbyes exchanged, the two chums swear eternal friendship, vowing to visit each other at the earliest opportunity.

For years, Angel sends Larry an annual Christmas card. Its arrival always leads him to speculate as to what kind of person she's become. Invariably, he promises himself that he'll find the time to write her a long letter bringing her up to date with all that's going on in his life. And then, feeling good about himself, he never fails to forget all about his plan until the next year's card appears. Tough as it is for Larry to fully accept, Angel has become just another lost pal from his past.

Surprise! Surprise! Angel turns up in late July to pay homage to *Expo '67*. As she's in Montréal, she gives way to her curiosity and looks up her long-ago friend. It takes Larry only three afternoons alone with Angel to convince himself that he's in love. She makes him feel so fabulously attractive and special. Which means that he has to be, right? Otherwise, why would anyone so devastatingly beautiful want to bother with him?

A week and a half later though, she's gone again. Irony time: just as her beauty has sealed a bond between them, it is now also the reason for their being kept apart. Angel's attempts to make her mark in a modelling career stand in the way. And, even worse, she's trying to achieve this in New York City, of all places. How many times has she sworn to come back to visit just as soon as she can? Larry believes her. But then, he reminds himself of how sure he was every year that he'd get around to replying to the card she'd sent.

At least she's mailing him postcards more regularly these days. Still no phone calls, though. And no permanent base either, as far as he knows. By her own account, she's in and out of various YWCAs when she's not off travelling somewhere for a photoshoot.

Juggling all these uncertainties has led to Larry being plagued by a recurring feeling of emptiness and unreality that had first come over him just as soon as Angel had got on that New York bound *Greyhound* bus last summer. They haven't lost their power either; if anything, walking aimlessly allows them to grow stronger over time.

So here he is, tramping the streets. Curly Joe's new-found relationship with Suzie Q intrudes on his thoughts. He's happy for Curly Joe. Delighted, even. He and Suzie Q make a great couple and they're having loads of fun going to movies and coffee houses and concerts together. It's so splendid ... and it's driving Larry nuts. Why does Curly Joe get to have a steady girlfriend who lives in the same city and he can meet up with any time he wants? As opposed to ... Curly Joe. Curly Joe. Why's *he* always getting to be the one who's first? The first to tour Europe. The first to get laid. The first to get high on grass. Larry sucks in the crisp December air. When's it going to be *his* turn to be first? Which, for some improbable reason, takes him back to earlier in the day, some twenty minutes into calculus class.

There he is, trying to make head or tail of what the Prof is busy scribbling onto the overhead projector. At the same time,

Larry's doing his best to transcribe the mathematical symbol for 'set' — $\in$ — which precedes each incomprehensible equation he's been copying down. Poring over his spiral bound notebook, its margins filled to bursting with doodles, unfinished poems, and attempts at caricatures of lecturers and students, Larry becomes aware that it's main entries are made up of what appear to be a swarm of giant E's followed by arcane combinations of lower-case letters and arithmetical calculations.

And then he hears the Prof announce: 'Better to integrate than disintegrate.'

Well, okay, he can live with that one.

It's what comes next that causes Larry's ticket to explode.

'There's an integer lurking somewhere here in the tall grass.'

Whether the rest of the class guffaws out of authentic amusement, or as if to say 'Christ, willya listen to this jerk?' isn't of the remotest interest to Larry. It's all too plain: he's been thrown into some sick-o, paranoid William S. Burroughs world surrounded by the mind-manipulating Nova Mob. Seizing the moment, he chucks pens and notebook and useless slide-rule straight up into the air, leaving everybody around him nonplussed while he makes his dash for freedom.

At last outdoors, alone in the quad, stomping across the lawn near the Three Bares, blowing deep breaths to regain his sanity, Larry can't stop asking himself what's happening. Why is he acting like this? And why has everything and everyone turned grey on him? Even his thoughts.

Which, come to think of it, is the very same feeling that came over him again a moment ago, walking with Jolie, when Angel came to mind. *Hey! Wait a minute!* An astounding, out-of-nowhere answer nearly knocks Larry sideways. Of course! Having fallen in love with Angel is what's making him so crazy! Like that Hit Parade song he used to sing along to with his parents, *That's Amore!* No doubt about it. The proof's right there, out in the open, not "lurking somewhere in the tall grass".

Too much! So *this* is what it's like when you're in love! All this grey misery turns out to be a total blast squared to the nth degree! All the pandemonium that the ferocity of his ongoing romance with Angel has rustled up in him? *That's gotta be a first! Sure. Why not? Beat him at last!* Larry thinks. *Curly Joe might be feeling something similar, but I got there first on this one!*

Freed from the hollowness that's been hounding him, embodied once more, Larry experiences a red-hot desire to thank Angel again for what she's brought to his life. It's Angel, after all, who's opened up his eyes to the Arts. Angel who writes him — when the mood takes her — of plays and films and paintings she's seen, of Happenings she's participated in, of poems she's memorised because they're simply so beautiful. Just as it's Angel who informs him, weeks ahead of anyone else — even Curly Joe who keeps up with such things — what new records to buy, movies to go and see. And where would he be now if not for Angel and her angelic advice? Still playing the same old *Ventures* and *Kingston Trio* albums from his now-contemptuously juvenile record collection, that's where.

In paltry return, Larry wants to tell her about his confusion and loneliness, as well as the welcome peace that descends on him at the most unlikely moments. Like now. But over and above that, he wants to remind her — and himself — that he loves her more than ever, even if she's several hundred miles away and hasn't been seen since August. Turning to the snow, following it fall and mix in with the grime that cakes the streets, he wishes he had a pen on hand so he could capture it all. Instead, he'll have to memorise what now fills his head.

'Let's go home, Jolie.'

Somehow decoding the message, Jolie throws him a look that says 'And about time, too!'

Regrettably, when Larry's back in his room and able to write, all he can scrape up is unworthy crap. So trite. So facile. Not even worth reproducing. Some day ... Some day, that masterpiece which will make him, and Angel, and Curly Joe, and maybe even Moe, feel so proud will come rushing out of him.

In the interim though, poor Jolie's going to have to resign herself an awful lot of tiring, near-endless walkies.

* * * * *

Moe sits in his bedroom facing a window that looks out onto a cold and snowy Montréal morning. He's thinking of Curly Joe and Suzie Q. He's thinking of Larry and Angel. He's thinking ...

Basically, Moe's jealous. But he can't admit that.

So, instead ... *Time for some down-and-dirty city blues. Record player on, let the sounds lead you to places that act as reminders of what a pitifully dumb putz you can be. Like the Joy Incident for example*, Moe tells himself in his best Perry Mason voice. *Joy. Now there's a tale worth kicking yourself in the teeth with.*

It begins with Moe and Larry finding themselves at a party. God knows where Curly Joe is. Out with Suzie Q, all too likely. Be that as it may ... Somebody from Engineering that Larry hardly knows at all has invited him and, having nothing better to do, he's moseyed on over with Moe tagging along for the hell of it.

Aside from the food and the booze, both of which are plentiful, it's still the case that the party's pretty boring. Especially the music. Every other tune seems to be some *1,000 Strings* piece of crap being belted out by Andy Williams or Vic Damone or ... or ... Taking a shot at drowning things out, Moe's gotten into the juice with the result that his tongue's loosened itself up way more than usual. Which has turned him into the centre of attention. He's unleashed his night-club comedian character and he's burning hot tonight. So much so, to give him credit, that all sorts of people are scribbling his name down as reminder of who to put on the *Must Invite* list to their own parties.

Riding high, full steam ahead, Moe's now surrounded by a devoted audience mostly comprised of attractive single women who keep passing him love-sick stares. *Wow!* For once *he* gets to pick who to dance with. And maybe Ol' Andy W and his pals and their schmoozy violins ain't so bad, after all.

The dance partner Moe chooses is a rather sultry-looking student nurse named Joy. She has flamboyantly wavy flame-red hair that falls just below her ears and a pair of breathtakingly beautiful bouncy breasts straining to escape the confines of her tight, low-necked dress.

Moe lacks no courage tonight. After much internal debate, he's pressed himself ever closer and tighter against Joy's delicious bosom and, much to his amazement, hasn't been told off for it. Risking further experimentation, he flexes himself, his full erection prominent. This too, brings on no sign of scorn or indignation. Instead, Joy flutters her eyelashes and then finds some judicious means to ensure that their embrace becomes ambitiously even more body-hugging.

As night turns into early morning, there's virtually no guests left — not even Larry — hanging about and the host is producing loud yawns intended to attract the pair's attention. Vaguely hearing them, Joy comes round to noticing the time as well and signals that she has to get back to her apartment in case she's called in for emergency duties.

Oh well, it was great while it lasted. It's only when Joy asks him if he's brought a coat, that it even occurs to Moe that she might want an escort home. Thrilled by this unforeseen windfall of good fortune, he enquires as to where she lives and, establishing that it's reasonably close by, suggests that they saunter their merry way over to it. Joy's renewed fluttering of eyelashes assures him that he's said the exact right thing.

As they shuffle out into the chilly early morning, Moe becomes aware that he's gliding some distance above Cloud Nine. Holding hands, they stop halfway through the park they've cut through and sit on a wooden bench to gape at the Moon which, being in its new quarter, is invisible. They see it anyhow. In-between long, gooey, tongue-tangling kisses.

All too soon, they've reached the stairway leading up to Joy's apartment. Giving it his utmost gung ho derring-do, Moe seizes Joy by the waist then and there, and kisses her harshly, just like some Hollywood Bad Boy Star would do. Then releasing her, congratulating himself, ready to turn away and stride off manfully into the closing shot night, he hears something that stops him cold.

'Would you like to come in for a cup of coffee?' purrs Joy, following this with an extra-animated fluttering of eyelashes.

Moe's entire body goes numb. The last thing on earth he wants right now is to force down even more liquid. Still, he can't insult her. Forcing himself to mime affirmatively, he follows her up to her 1 1/2 room studio.

Inside her modestly furnished apartment, Joy directs Moe to sit down on the couch which, she tells him — flutter, flutter — also happens to be her hide-away bed. While she slides into her walk-in closet of a kitchen, Moe does as he's told and eagle eyes the two oversized, black and white framed photograph posters taking up most of the wall facing him. One of them is of Paul Newman in T-shirt, the other of Brando in leather — modern Christs to watch over and protect their sleeping faithful.

Before Moe can think of anything amusing to say, Joy pokes her head back out and owns up, in a convincing state of regret, that she has no more coffee left but that she could make them a pot of tea instead. *Or* — and here, the fluttering of eyelashes reaches its climactic peak — she could shake up a killer Martini in no time at all.

As easy as the test she's given him is to pass, Moe crash lands with the loudest bang possible. 'No, it's all right. I don't really feel like anything right now, to be honest. You must be tired. I'd better get going.'

And with that, Moe rises, bestows a quick peck onto his hostess's left cheek and waves goodbye, leaving behind a stupefied Joy and her impressive breasts and dejected lips and no-longer-fluttering eyelashes.

Making his way home, Moe can't stop reliving the best bits of this most wondrous encounter. Next afternoon, it's left to Curly Joe to open Moe's eyes as to what Joy had been not-so-subtly hinting at. Another chance to be rid of his bothersome virginity bites the dust! So long, Joy.

Moe snivels mournfully, taking another sip from his glass of chocolate milk. Somewhere in the act, he hears himself wish that there weren't any such creatures as women to get bent out of shape over. Elaborating on this theme, he rustles up a Lenny

Bruce inspired romance of a peaceful world where he and Larry and Curly Joe ride off into the sunset on horseback every night and never for one moment stop to consider that there might be anything at all unacceptable about bestiality.

7. NEW YEAR'S EVE, 1967

For a lot of people — Larry, Moe and Curly Joe included — the only thing that gets them through Christmas without going on a killing spree or putting an end to their sorry lives is the thought of New Year's Eve and the socialising possibilities it dangles before their eyes. Sadly, New Year's Eve l967 doesn't seem to want to play by the rules. It's a case of being all keyed-up with nowhere to go.

Angel has some modelling job in Nassau she couldn't get out of. Suzie Q's off visiting relatives up in the Laurentians. And Moe's on his lonesome, as usual.

So that's that. Even the half-hoped-for invitations to bohemian in-tune-with-the times parties have failed to materialise. Evidently, they've been emphatically forgotten by all their old acquaintances. Looks like their solitary option is to get together and have a go at some sort of celebration, regardless.

So here they are right now, straggling back from their tootle through The Main. Moe's put on his Hick-From-The-Sticks face, and adds to the caricature by picking his nose with his thumb while fumbling around like a drunken Charlie Chaplin tramp complete with itchy arsehole. That gets them in a good mood. But it's a brief respite and, moments later, they're back to speculating what to do with themselves.

They pass by people rushing off to prepare for tonight's extravaganza. *They* have no need to rush. It's not only the Montréal winter wind that makes them tremble through their McGill jackets. Moe pulls on his aviator's hat. Curly Joe tugs his old *Boston Bruins* hockey cap farther down so that what's left exposed is an eye-slit between it and his black-and-white imitation Bob Dylan checkered scarf. Larry wears an ear band; he likes it because it allows his growing hair to tussle with the wind.

They trundle past the *System Theater* which is said to be infested with rats and winos. Larry and Moe have never set foot inside it. Curly Joe says he has. Of course. Hang on though ... What's the most absurd thing they can think of doing on New Year's Eve? It's staring them right in the face: go to a flick. Even if only to find out who else is insane enough to do the same on such a night.

The only downside is picking what to go see. That's guaranteed to start up an argument between Moe and Curly Joe.

Curly Joe's tastes veer him towards foreign "art" films directed by people with unpronounceable names. The only American stuff he rates is made up of so-called "underground movies" that the *McGill Film Society* shows every now and then. He's even sat through the whole of Andy Warhol's snoozefest, *Empire*. Twice. What Curly Joe loves most, though, is European films. *Zazie Dans Le Métro. Closely Watched Trains. Blow-Up. Persona. Juliet Of The Spirits.* Sheer bliss! The ones that really, really impress him most are what's being called French *New Wave*. Truffaut. Godard. Rohmer. Movies where not much happens plot-wise and dialogue reigns supreme. He could watch those non-stop, over and over again. Hell, he can even picture himself directing his own one day.

For Curly Joe, *Expo '67* will forever be that cinematic godsend, full of first time sight and sound experiences that open up his consciousness as to what movie magic can be like. He watches films where block parts of the physical screen plunge out toward the audience creating the weirdest of 3-D effects. He eagerly heads back a dozen times to marvel at a Czech film that pauses at various key points in its story and invites the audience to choose the narrative direction that it should take. He thrills to the physical illusion of movement while standing still surrounded by an imposing 360° projection that takes him canoeing, flying a plane and racing through a forest. And most of all, he's blown away by a movie where the on-screen story splits into any number of smaller segments so that different events and characters can be followed simultaneously. Which isn't just about speeding up the narrative; more radically, a whole new form of storytelling unique to cinema is being showcased right before his eyes.

Moe, *au contraire*, is very Star-oriented. For him, there's nothing better than Hollywood movies from the 40s and 50s deliver on that demand. Granted that it would take the most hair-raising tortures for him to admit it, but if Moe wasn't so paranoid of being laughed at, he'd be happily buying up all those Hollywood Tell-All type magazines that are sold in drug stores.

Second best, he settles for something almost as good. This is Moe's *Big Hollywood Production Number:* One day, Moe's walking down Cavendish Boulevard in the rain. Bang on cue, out of the corner of his eye, he notices something strange happening on one of the side streets across the road. Curious, he heads over and finds a young dirty-blonde-haired mystery woman wearing a trench coat with its collar turned up being rough-housed by a Warner Baxter B-List type drunken lout. Without giving it a second thought, he rushes to her defence. Using some innately-available new-found skills in Karate combat, he somehow pounds the shit out of the bully, hails a conveniently passing cab, and is pleased to find that, beneath the trench coat, lies a woman with the body of Rita Hayworth, the face of Greta Garbo, and the elegance of Katharine Hepburn. And, miracle of miracles, she finds herself immediately as madly in love with him as he is with her. All before the camera fades on that sloppy Hollywood sunrise kiss they've just enfolded themselves into. *Xanadu! A classic!*

Pushed to expressing their contrasting takes, Moe and Curly Joe's debate runs something like this:

'*Jee-zus!* What *is* this crap?'

'c'mon moe, it's art!'

'Bullshit. How the hell can this be Art, huh? C'mon, you tell me what's artistic about this piece of shit, willya?'

'uhm ... it's symbolic.'

'Oh, yeah? What's it symbolizing then, huh?'

'uhm ... a lotta things ... his angst.'

'His *what*?'

'his angst! angst! his *pain*, you illiterate schmuck!'

'His pain?'

'yeah, his pain!'

'Well, why's he have to go and symbolize *that*, huh? Why doesn't he just make it plain and simple, if what he wants is for everybody to go cold sweat?'

'because.'

'Because ... Because, bullshit Jim! Because he doesn't know what to do with his joy-juice, son. That's why.'

Larry tries not to take sides. Mainly, he partly agrees with both of them. Besides which, he's already come up with a solution that he's got no doubt will appeal to everybody. Hand raised, bouncing up and down, he's back in Second Grade trying to grab his teacher's — Miss Whitby – attention. 'Me Miss! Me Miss!' *Success!* Taking advantage of their curiosity, Larry points out that there's this one movie playing that he and Moe have been wanting to catch, and which will also appeal to Curly Joe because it's got an "experimental" feel to it. Definitely not your typical Hollywood gloss. Trying to get seats has been a waste of time because the counterculture crew's been raving about it since its opening. Hey! What better time to give it a look-in?

Not quite an hour later, now inside the *Place Ville Marie* shopping mall, they're no longer feeling the chill. *Place Ville Marie* is the first of several interconnected malls that form Montréal's underground city. The big vision is that of Montréalers traipsing from one end of the city to the other without once having to catch sight of blue sky or rain clouds, much less breathe open air. Sounds great, doesn't it? The promised pay-off is that, in this underworld, it's warm enough in winter to unbutton coats, unzip parkas, remove mittens and gloves. While, at the other end of the scale, it's always air-conditioned cool during the worst of the summer dog days. Best of all if you're a bag-lady, begging bum or homeless street person, it's an optimal temperature all year round free hotel.

The Little Cinema, tucked away in one of the mall's quieter corners, is dark. It looks closed and there isn't anyone inside the ticket booth. When the matronly cashier deigns to appear, they each feel as if they'd just tried to buy a porno rag off her. Tickets purchased and now being presented, they receive a mournful look from the ticket-taker as well, just to make them feel even worse. He grouches that he'd have had a night off if it weren't for malcontents like them. They hand over their paper tickets for desultory inspection and obligatory ripping in half.

Ritual completed, shame-faced and stripped of any remaining self-worth, they seek out the soothing darkness. In keeping with their usual brand of luck, the lights come on full blast just as they're making their way down the main aisle. Regrettably, the theatre isn't entirely empty. About a dozen faces turn around in collective curiosity, recoil out of some kind of unpleasant recognition and look away post-haste. Then the bodies to which the faces belong sink lower down into their seats. All men. All tired, sad-looking, grizzled old men who seem to have saved up their pennies all year long just so they can get through this grim *soirée*.

Unambiguous message: something murky and malevolent has resolved that the three of them be a part of this Hell. The realisation hits them hard. Though they say nothing, they know they're all thinking the same sad thought: *what the fuck am I doing here? What's so odd or terrible about me that I find myself in this wretched place, sharing stale air with this even more woebegone company tonight of all nights?* Receiving no reply, they wait for the lights to dim. When, at long last, they do, their breathing becomes a little easier.

Fade to black. Then the opening chords to a song they immediately recognise as *The Sound of Silence*. The singer greeting his old friend, darkness, one more time and on their behalf. The screen lights up and projects a shot of a young, hung-up, as yet unknown Dustin Hoffman standing in an airport, looking lost. Split-second empathy. They slouch down into more comfortable positions. This might just turn out to be a pretty good choice.

A second screening of *The Graduate* later, they force themselves to leave. They've each felt it. Somehow, the movie has captured something that soothes their fears of being so all alone in their difference and still nebulous specialness. Sometimes, movies truly can be like mothers providing a cuddle and a reminder.

* * * * *

Back outdoors, it's a lot colder now. The sun set nearly three hours ago. Night enfolds them and they're faced with the odious anticipation that, any time now, the entire city of Montréal — except them — will begin the carousing and singing that marks every New Year's Eve. Hell-bent on enjoying themselves regardless, they agree to buy food and wine and then congregate at Curly Joe's house — since it's empty of parents as well as being the nearest at hand — to drink and laugh away the old year on their own.

So the hunt for an appropriate meal begins. In due course, they come across an exotic-looking delicatessen that attracts Larry and Curly Joe with its display of seafood. Moe would have preferred burgers and 'fries but is by now too hungry and freezing cold to care much about what's bought. In the end, fighting off suggestions of lobster and Canadian caviar, he gets the others pumped up about knockwurst and sauerkraut instead. The added enticement of fresh corn on the cob ends all disagreements.

Definitely on a winning streak, a few blocks further down Sherbrooke Street, they feast their eyes on a *Liquor Board Store* that's still stocked with wines and whose cashiers ask no questions. Larry buys a cheapish French claret, Curly Joe two Italian vinos, and Moe a *Faisca Rosé*, since it's his favourite and it's the closest thing to champagne he can afford.

Thus armed, they stride off to begin *The Feast*.

* * * * *

Now in Curly Joe's kitchen, they follow instructions: place corn and knockwurst into water-filled pots. Turn on stove top. Wait.

However, waiting's pretty boring. So Larry suggests they begin to sample their wines while the food cooks. Sounds mighty fine to one and all. Tragically, the corn's taking much longer than they'd expected. By the time it's edible, they've drunk their way through the claret, and are half-past a *Chianti*. The room swirls. Fascinated, they note that their plates of knockwurst and corn have turned into artistic masterpieces. They admire and appraise them as though they're on exhibit in a museum.

Eating such works of art, however, is another matter. Curly Joe's in there and attacks the corn with gusto but it is only hard to swallow bravado that allows him to finish it up. Sozzled and famished, Moe leaps upon the knockwurst, pigs out on his portion in a matter of minutes, and turns upon Larry's which lies there untouched except for a couple of thin slices that Larry's somehow forced down his gullet. Part-way through his third sausage, even Moe gives in to the perceptively strange rumblings in his belly. While nobody's looking, he cuts up the remains into bite-size chunks and sneaks them to the floor where they are rapidly gobbled up by Diana, Curly Joe's family's wire-haired fox terrier.

Sad to say, the carefully planned dinner comes to its rather hurried end. Still, they're now feeling in a party-time mood and, just to prove it, they bravely continue to drink on, though perhaps more slowly than before. Minutes later however, the wine, too, loses its allure. Staying seated for a few minutes longer will get them totally focused on the upcoming fun and games.

Three green-gilled faces beam idiotically at each other for what seems like the longest time. Scanning the kitchen clock, Larry has to blink twice before he's convinced it really does claim that it's only 10.30pm. One and a half more hours of agony to live through just so they can say they've been up for the New Year. What's worse, the leftovers on their plates have become gag-worthy to look at. They agree to move on over to Curly Joe's bedroom.

Cruelly, even this change of scene doesn't help much. In order to stay awake, they turn on the bedside transistor radio. *Uh-oh.* The underground station run by drug-crazed hippies has come up with this really *fantabuloso* idea: how about it plays the complete recorded works of *Guy Lombardo and his Band of Royal Canadians* all through the night? Aw, what a shame: Guy Lombardo bombs.

* * * * *

When Curly Joe's parents return home from their own merrymaking, they find the three of them plus Diana dead asleep in different parts of Curly Joe's bedroom while the radio continues to blare away old-fashioned dance band music at full volume. They switch it off, cover the trio with spare blankets and, carrying Diana, go off to their own bed bewildered as to what youthful debaucheries their son and his cronies have been up to. Hopefully, nothing that they will ever hear about.

* * * * *

On the morning of the first day of 1968, Larry meets Curly Joe coming out of the bathroom. Both their heads ache and it's painful for either one of them to speak.

'i just pissed out the old year,' is all that Curly Joe feels able to say.

Larry can't even be bothered to crack a fake smile at this. He shuts the bathroom door behind him and feels an impulsive urge to masturbate.

Meanwhile, deep in his heedless sleep, Moe waits for the occurrence of the midnight that has passed him by some nine hours ago. Once awake, he won't be too upset to have missed it. He'd always been ready to bet that 1967 was going to be a lousy year. Great to be finally rid of it.

8. ANIMA SOLA

Having settled itself in, February resolves to curl up against the city like a sleepy cat that, for the moment, has permitted your lap to become its bed. The marriage of darkness and frost makes it so unbearable that to emerge from one's home for reasons other than extreme necessity is unquestionable folly.

Undeterred, relishing the challenge, alone and unannounced, Angel arrives in Montréal on an late afternoon *Greyhound* driving in direct from New York, New York.

Despite the early sunset and inhospitable weather, she roams about the city aiming her way towards Old Montréal, where she prays a bit and snoozes a bit in the little church at *Bonsecours* dedicated to the sailors who had cast off from the harbour on their journeys back to Motherlands or onwards to even wilder wilderness.

More than out of a desire to see Larry — though that's definitely there as well — Angel has come for this. It is a pilgrimage, of sorts, in honour of her newfound Master — a Montréal poet turned singer-songwriter named Leonard Cohen — who released his first album of songs less than two months ago. Angel has been a disciple of Cohen's ever since reading his novel, *Beautiful Losers.* It's a book that outraged many upon its publication. Result? Censorship problems, low sales and a major disappointment as far as newspaper and magazine reviewers are concerned. But Angel loves it. It speaks to her in ways that no other piece of writing — not even Larry's — has ever come close to.

And so, here she is. Another *Anima Sola,* so like the Mexican religious painting of a lost soul suffering in Purgatory that is on the LP's back cover. Huddled up on an empty bench, shivering in the lamp-lit stillness of almost deserted street and falling snow, she identifies with that spirit, shares the fullness of her suffering.

A twenty-something Montréaler breezes by and comes to a standstill, immediately taken with Angel's striking beauty.

Rustling up the evidence required to establish she's on her own, he secures the necessary arrogance to approach her. Noticed now, he smiles coyly then waits to receive that okay smile signalling her agreement for him to come sit next to her. Neither speaks the other's language terribly well. Still, Angel's remembered Elementary School French is enough to get across that she's from New York, while he — Daniel — in turn mimes that he's a hairdresser. After that, he somehow finds a way of communicating his happiness that Gene McCarthy has opted to run against LBJ as the Democratic Party's anti-war presidential candidate. Which, all things considered, is far from being the most romantic of get-to-know-you patter. Luckily, Angel shares his political leanings. She makes it easy for him to invite her to a local bar, then to a restaurant meal and, eventually, to guide her back to his one-room apartment.

At first rebuffing Daniel's ardent advances, she makes him switch his TV from its French channel to the American one broadcasting *The Tonight Show.* She tries to explain that this is a special night. And it is. Johnny Carson is on a week's break and has invited Harry Belafonte to take over as guest host. Race relations being what they are, Belafonte has agreed — but only if he can bring in Black guests. This is something way out radical for broadcast television and because it is, Angel sees it as her Civil Rights duty to watch and support the event. Three commercial breaks later, conceding that Daniel's been appreciably patient, she gives way. Nicely warmed up, and about to feel warmer still, she snuggles closer and gives up her perfect body to him while her mind continues to invoke her Master's voice.

* * * * *

Next morning, feeling relaxed and bored with Daniel's stilted small-talk, Angel waves a stranger's so long and heads for the nearest phone booth.

'Hi. It's Angel. I'm in town. Do you mind coming to pick me up?'

For Larry, this event is the highlight of a thus far pretty blah year. Since January, life seems to have shrugged itself into a standstill. The threat of exams is looming and he hasn't yet begun to study for them. Not that he's overly concerned. All that matters most mornings is to get out of bed and keep vigil for the human being he detests most on Earth to pass by and deposit the day's mail. Usually, there's nothing postmarked from New York. But now, with Angel next to him sipping her café bought *chocolat chaud*, the world takes on a glow that not even bleak mid-winter snow storms, nor curious parents wanting to know whether he and his impromptu guest will be back in time for supper, nor the McGill Engineering Department can extinguish.

A couple of hours spent in catching up and asking questions as to why she's appeared now, without warning, pass speedily by. Instead of answers, Angel demands that Larry, in spite of his protests, takes her to McGill so that he can attend all his classes. Pretending not to notice the jaw-dropping and eyeing-up she's being given by all the other engineering students in the room — including the four female ones — she sits with him shoulder-to-shoulder throughout and makes certain he jots down notes for each of the four courses of the day. While Larry submits to her edict, Angel finds herself charmed by the cartoonish portraits of who she guesses must be Profs and other students that fill up the pages' margins.

'Hey!' she whispers. 'I didn't know you could draw. These are cute!'

'Aw, they're just dumb doodles,' Larry blushes.

'No, they're better than that.'

'Really?'

'Yes, really. Now get back to your class!'

Tasks accomplished, it's time for a quick hello and cherry cola with an equally open-mouthed Moe and Curly Joe. Angel's only met them once before but she enjoyed their company then and still does today. What she especially likes is how positively happy they both are that she's come over to visit Larry. She's aware that their happiness is mainly for him, but they've spread it out enough to include her into it as well. She wishes she had friends like them back in New York.

Later that afternoon, once again on their own, Angel whispers that she's brought something special for Larry but that they have to go somewhere that's private. In one of the tutorial offices of the McConnell Engineering Building, crouching over a desk scribbled-over and compass-point scarred with initials, boasts, and predictable four-letter oaths, Larry is presented with his very first little ball of tin-foil wrapped hashish.

Angel informs Larry that it's called Red Leb, which means nothing at all to him. Then, she takes out a miniature pipe, stuffs a bit of the resin into its mini-bowl, and tells him to inhale just as soon as she lights it. He tries but is right away coughing non-stop, blowing the smoke out of his mouth and hating the sensation of itchy, dried-up throat. So she shows him how to do it, revealing, in her expert enactment of the ritual, personal secrets Larry hadn't dared consider. Pride duly injured, he attempts the act again and again until he begins to hear the beating of his heart pronounce itself louder and clearer than he's ever heard it before. This is all so curious to him, though not so curious as the thought of where they are and what they're doing there. And then ... *What the fuck! Yowzah! Ugga Bugga!* In no time, Larry knows for certain that he's high and all he wants is to be more so.

* * * * *

On their way back home, still stoned but coasting now, Larry treats Angel to a smoked meat sandwich at *Bens* and, avoiding her eyes, tells her that he loves her. Leaning closer, Angel kisses Larry's cheek then whispers into his ear that what she'd really like to do now is go to bed with him. Paying no attention to Larry's efforts to hide his incredulous reaction to what Angel's proposed, she lays out a plan: they'll wait until his parents have gone to sleep, then he can tuck her into the fold-away down in the playroom, and, in the process, tuck himself in next to her as well. He'll have to leave, later, to keep up the facade for his family's sake, of course. But, for an hour or so, they'll be in heaven.

Larry's all-consuming need to know stops everything in its tracks. 'Angel, are yuh a virgin?'

She pauses long enough to make him aware of the good vibes he's just done a great job in destroying. 'Yes ... Of course I am. But why should that matter?'

'It doesn't,' he lies. 'I just wanted to know, I guess.' He can't think of what else to add. Besides, his question

had nothing to do with *her* lack of sexual experience.

Then, as though she's just understood exactly what all this has been leading to, she begins to clarify matters. And to punish him. 'I gotta tell you, though ... I'm not on The Pill.'

'Well,' Larry blushes. 'I don't have any ... any ...' His mind won't summon up the word "condoms", and he feels too tongue-tied to bring himself to say "safes" or "Rubber Johnnies", so he lets things drop, certain that she's filled in the gap. 'I guess I could try and find a drugstore somewhere —'

Angel grimaces. 'No, don't. I can't stand the thought of those things.' Then, taking in how sad and hurt he looks, feeling sorry and once more in love with him, she smiles. 'I guess that fucking isn't on the cards as yet. That's okay. It'll be enough to re-introduce our bodies to each other. It's been a long time, and I've got a feeling they've changed a little.'

Larry's never heard a woman say "fuck" before. And so unselfconsciously, as well.

* * * * *

Past midnight, the rest of the family hopefully asleep, at last it's just the two of them alone, in the darkness. They've been groping their bodies all over, absorbed like the little kids they used to be. From the way his fingers push and rub between her legs, Angel no longer has any doubt that Larry's new at this. It's frustrating, especially following Daniel's adroitness, but also pleasing to know that she's teaching Larry something new.

Still, there's a limit to her patience. Angel takes hold of

Larry's penis, cradles it in-between her palms, feels its heat. She draws back the foreskin until the smooth secret inner flesh is at her disposal. Seconds later, the trembling becomes pronounced and there's no turning back for him.

And later, lying next to Larry, listening to his soft breathing, feeling the stillness of his body, knowing that he will have to leave her soon, she becomes that *Anima Sola* once again.

* * * * *

The following day, much to Larry's disappointment, it's already time for Angel to go back to New York City. Larry accompanies her to the Provincial Bus Depot feeling sick and tired of such acts, though he knows full well they'll continue to be a part of his life for some time to come.

Just as she's about to climb aboard the *Greyhound*, Angel turns, eyes sparkling and carefree, and ordains that it's high time that Larry paid *her* a visit. And more than that, she scolds, it's high time that Moe and Curly Joe did as well.

Before he knows what he's saying, Larry agrees that all three of them will be coming down in May so they can celebrate his birthday in style.

Then, the bus, with Angel seated near the front and blowing kisses from an unopenable window, drives off.

And Larry's left there, waving at nothing.

9. PARENTS - A BRIEF INTERRUPTION

But wait! By now many — if not all — of you Time Tripsters are probably asking: what about The Stooges' parents? Don't they have a role in this tale? So far, the few times they've been mentioned, they just seem to be reacting in befuddlement to all the things their sons get up to. But they're *their parents,* for heaven's sake! They can't just have a walk-on part

Okay, here's the deal: Something happened to parenthood between 1967 and today. Today's parents want to be much more present (some might argue intrusive) in their children's lives. Parents and kids dress more alike, eat more alike, play more alike and dream more alike these days. From early on in their kids' lives, parents talk to them in a very adult-to-adult way. They explain their financial situation, express their worries and concerns about jobs, illnesses, emotional states, family tensions. Parents today want to be as much *friends* with their kids as they might want to ... well ... parent them.

This current view of parenthood would have been pretty alien back in The Sixties. Not that 1960s parents didn't love their kids as much, or worry over them as much, or weren't attentive to what they got up to as much as today's parents do. They just lived out their relations with their children in a different way. A sort of *Parent Knows Best* way. Which, of course, didn't always make for easygoing relations between them.

During The Sixties, the Generation Gap felt more like an abyss, and any surviving bridges were pretty rickety, requiring tons of open-minded concentration on both sides if the intent was to reach a meeting point. 1960s parents and their kids mostly interacted with each other at the breakfast and supper table and in front of the family TV. Which, contrarily, turn out to be the very same places where today's parents and children are *least likely* to connect. The rest of the time, the lives they all led and what they did in them mainly stayed separate. And, preferably, private.

Which takes us back to Larry, Moe and Curly Joe.

Hopefully, all of the above helps to clarify why their parents don't get much of a look-in. It's not that they are irrelevant. They're present all right, but they're hovering in the background, loving their kids in their "1960s parents" way.

Still, since we've got them here ...

Curly Joe's parents are European immigrants who left behind a war-torn and Iron Curtain divided continent to seek out a better life in the New World for themselves and their son. They have sacrificed a lot but their hard work and commitment has paid off financially such that they now all live in Montréal's bastion of upper middle class Englishness, Westmount.

Larry's mother and father see themselves as French-Canadian rather than *Quebecois*. They're proud of their Gallic roots, but it is to Canada that they pledge their allegiance. Larry's mother is related to one of the stars of Canada's home-grown soap opera, *The Plouffe Family,* which everybody watched back in the 50s when Canadian TV only had one English language channel and one French language channel and the show's cast had to run through the same show twice to appease its language-divided audiences. As to Larry's father, he's a bit of a dreamer who likes nothing more than to travel, eat fresh Atlantic oysters and buy his wife fur coats of every animal species available.

And Moe's Mom and Dad? They're the oddballs. And, because of that, they're the most attuned to all the changes going on around them and the least antagonistic to their implications. Moe's Mom grew up in a Canadian Socialist cult that modelled itself on the Israeli kibbutz movement. In due course, she ran away from it but still espouses radical left-wing views and regularly goes on marches against nuclear weapons and any form of censorship. Moe's Dad is, to put it kindly, a retired con-man who has flimflammed everyone he came across into buying whatever he had on offer, including his selling snow to the Eskimos. Yes, really. Putting up roots in one of the less salubrious corners of Montréal West, he's now Manager of a local Corner Store and claims to be a poet. Although all that anyone has ever seen of his efforts is a single couplet:

I'm a hard-working man
Yes I am. Yes I am.

Okay. Back to the background, folks!

10. ANGEL AND SUZIE Q

Now here's something to get your heads around: Angel and Suzie Q have more in common with each other than either suspects. For one thing, each, in her own way, has led a fairly happy existence until the arrival of Larry and Curly Joe.

Angel's only real burden over most of her twenty years has been her physical beauty. Though she'd undoubtedly miss it were it to be abruptly taken away from her, she's never gotten used to the lewd once-overs and brazen snuffles of approval that her body arouses in men. When she hit her mid-teens, Angel was certain that her calling was to be an actor. She took up a two-year diploma at a community college and would have gone on to a more professional acting studio, except ... Sensing that she was already being straightjacketed into "glamorous bimbo" roles, she got it into her head that she might as well take up modelling for a few years since it was easier and probably paid around the same, if not better. Also, modelling gave her the chance to turn males' drooling attentions to her advantage. Her motto goes: if you can't change the status quo, at least get what you can out of it. Most of the time, it sounds convincing enough.

Decision taken, Angel's casual flirtation with modelling sputtered into life back in 1966. Mainly formal and casual wear for provincial seasonal catalogs, that sort of thing. She wasn't pinning all her hopes on it going that much further. What she hadn't bargained for was a photographer doing outdoor shots in B.C. hell-bent on sweet-talking her into becoming his "discovery". He wrote out his address over in the *Big Apple* and begged her to come on over and allow him the pleasure of opening as many doors to fashion modelling superstardom as she could dream of.

Six months later, Angel's just about surviving in New York City. The promised contract she'd expected to sign fell through all too quickly due to an unwritten clause she wasn't — and still isn't — prepared to agree to. Luckily, since then, she's shamed a few modelling assignments out of the bastard while she reputedly thinks things over. With the money she's made out of these, she's been able to join an Agency. That keeps her work status legal on top of providing her with enough cash to pay up-front for her apartment until this coming June. So far, there have been no life-altering breaks but the job offers teeter on the right side of regular. For now, her waitressing provides what's needed to cover the few extras in her life.

Angel hasn't mentioned any of this to Larry. She knows what he'd say if she did, and she doesn't want to hear it. Instead, her irregular letters to him enthuse about the career that is advancing as quickly as she'd hoped. In reality, she hates New York City. It's too spread-out for one thing, and, more than that, it's frightening. And lonely. When she's not modelling or on her usual four-day stint as waitress, she makes sure she's inside her multiple-lock apartment, reading or watching crap on the second-hand portable TV she's bought.

Nearly every night she cries herself to sleep. Many of her tears are focused on Larry. Angel feels she loves him, but somehow it isn't enough. She knows she can get up and run to Larry anytime she wants and wallow in all the attention and security and love that she could ever hope for. And yet, though she passionately desires these things, Angel weighs up their cost and concludes that the price demanded isn't one that she's ready to pay either.

When all's said and done, Angel feels that throughout all her life she's been forced to follow other people's rules. Mainly, men's. *Well, fuck that.* Little by little, she's started to make up her own rules. And what she's found is that as much as she reviles and despairs about her current circumstances, she can also turn around and luxuriate in them. Just because they are her's and no one else's.

* * * * *

In a pretty similar way, Suzie Q hasn't gotten any further in making sense of her divided attitude toward Curly Joe. As weeks pass by, her thoughts keep going back to those Chemistry class days. She questions if she did the right thing. Well, she had to do *something*, didn't she? If she hadn't, Curly Joe would still be sitting there, bombarding her with lovesick stares. Could somebody male be *that* innocent? On the other hand ... Isn't that what's so attracted her to him in the first place? Okay, maybe that and that it feels devilishly arousing to be the focus of such barefaced desire.

So now, Suzie Q has a steady. She's happy. She's miserable. All through high school, having a steady had been her greatest wish. Now she's at university and she has one. Somehow, it hasn't turned out to be as towering an achievement as she'd once envisaged.

Not that she doesn't really, really like Curly Joe. She maybe even loves him.

And her parents approve of the fact that he's studying something sensible like engineering. She hasn't told them yet that he's failing miserably and has confided to her that all he'd really like to be doing is writing poetry. Poetry! Of all things! Well, she has to admit that she gets a really nice tingly feeling when he hands her a poem he's just written about his feelings for her. It's as good a sensation as when she's skiing. Or when she touches herself. Better even.

And it's great to be busy every weekend now. Going to movies or to the *Yellow Door* or *New Penelope* to listen to live music. Which is another thing. Suzie Q can't *stand* Dylan. That voice! And, after all, music's for dancing to. *Tom Jones. Dave Clark Five. Herman's Hermits,* even.

Still, Curly Joe's attentive and respectful. He kisses real nice, too. Which is as far as they've gone up to now. But that feels right for where they are in their relationship. Kind of.

As always, it boils down to sex. Suzie Q worries a lot about sex. Mainly, she worries about how much she enjoys it. Probably *too* much. She's been fingering herself since she chanced upon the effects of doing so at the age of twelve. She knows it's a sin, although she's not sure if it's a venial sin or a mortal one. Whichever it is, she also knows that she should be admitting to it every Thursday when she goes to Confession. Except ... She can't. Not really. It's too mortifying. *Bless me Father for I have sinned. It has been one week since my last Confession. I touched myself twice ... No! Not on your afterlife!* Instead, as a compromise, she admits *I have had two impure thoughts.* Well, she's not fibbing, is she?

And on top of that, why what she does should be deemed to be a sin is so confusing. According to the sex education book she keeps going back to, there's that part of her — her clitoris, it's called — whose only biological purpose and function is to provide pleasure. Now why would God create clitorises for women if He didn't want them to explore their possibilities? Suzie Q guesses that her Catholic Catechism would say that it was God's way of testing women's resolve against temptation. *But God wouldn't be so mean, would He?* Not the female-knowing side of Him, anyway. No, that side would be saying *'Hey, I made female bodies that way. And I'm God, which means I can't be wrong, can I? So you go right ahead and do what you will. It's your body, after all. Don't go letting anybody tell you different.'*

Suzie Q wishes that she could accept that view through and through. But she can't. There's still that ever-niggling guilt that won't go away and keeps insisting that it's all so sinful.

Which takes her full circle back to her divided feelings for Curly Joe. Or, to be more precise, back to her divided feelings about sex with Curly Joe. Or, rather, the *lack* of sex with Curly Joe. Now *that* totally mystifies Suzie Q.

Not that she's repelled any of his advances. It's more like he hasn't really tried anything beyond kissing.

Which reminds her ... On their third date, they'd gone back to his home because he was desperate to have her listen to — yes, you guessed it — this seemingly endless Bob Dylan song, *Sad Eyed Lady of the Lowlands.* They were alone in the basement playroom, his parents were out somewhere and ... well, for some crazy reason, she kept worrying that he was going to try go all the way with her. She wasn't ready yet for that so when the morbid tune finally came to an end and he asked her to pick a record she liked, she was so nervous she'd ended up putting on one of Curly Joe's parent's soundtrack albums, *The Pink Panther*. Suzie Q blanches now, rewinding the scene in her mind all over again. Him asking 'are you sure?' and she insisting 'Yes! I love it!'. He must have guessed that something was wrong because minutes later they were out of the house and kissing goodnight at the bus stop.

Going over things again, Suzie Q could kick herself. There was never anything to get all antsy about and she's sure now that Curly Joe wouldn't go further than she'd allow him to. Maybe it's her fault that he hasn't really tried anything since then. Or, to go back to where she started, maybe things are moving along at their own speed and she should be more grateful and less impatient for that. Being fair on him, Curly Joe's fine in public. Always wanting to hold hands when they walk around, even putting his arm around her, not caring who sees. So it's not that he doesn't find her attractive. She knows for sure that he does. And it's also not as if he doesn't pay attention to her body, either. On some occasions, excruciatingly so.

Like when, a couple of Friday nights ago, he'd come by to collect her and she'd put on this girdle that she'd been told by her mother smart-looking women always wear. Curly Joe had spotted it right away when they'd greeted each other. He'd even felt it. Squeezed it, actually. Which Suzie Q sort of enjoyed. When she'd told him what it was, he'd made a face and just about insisted that she go and take it off right away because girdles were dishonest. He'd made it sound like doing that was the same thing as setting herself free from some sort of slavery. Which maybe it was, when she thought about it. Anyhow, she loved Curly Joe so much in that moment that she'd have willingly gone all the way with him right then and there. But nothing happened later except for some deep soul kisses. Which were great, for sure. But ...

According to the scheme of things as Suzie Q deciphers it, they should be quite a ways into a necking stage by now. Maybe even at the below the belt level. Which is both exciting and guilt provoking to fantasise about. But would be even better if it was happening for real.

And she knows Curly Joe's done it already because he's told her he had. Just after asking her if she was still a virgin. Which was ghastly, to say the least. And the way he emphasised *still* made it sound like she was way behind everybody else. Which isn't true at all. Assuming that her girlfriends aren't lying to her.

Above and beyond all that, being a virgin still means a lot to Suzie Q. It isn't something dumb like tearing her hymen. Nothing like that. Let alone the fact that horse riding, and Tampax, and fingers have made the continuing presence of a hymen highly uncertain. No, being a virgin is more about that innocent state of not knowing, and the delirium and the fear that come with it.

It shocks Suzie Q to accept that she's all set to give up her precious virginity to Curly Joe. But *he* has to make the first move. Surely, he can't be waiting for *her* to take the initiative! Not like at Chemistry class. No! Not in a million years! In not fending off any advances that he might make, Suzie Q tells herself that she's gone as far as she can. As is appropriate.

It's up to Curly Joe now. He has to start acting like a man.

On the plus side though, Suzie Q's girlfriends all envy her. And, no question, she knows how lucky she is. She can even picture Curly Joe way, way down the line, being a wonderful husband, a loving dad.

Which, funnily enough, is the real problem. Suzie Q takes a long, hard look at her future — their future — and sees that it's already been all mapped out.

Friendship.
Courtship.
Engagement.
Wedding.
Married Life.
Kids.

Nothing wrong with that, she supposes. So why is it a pattern so well set that it's succeeded in upsetting her? Why should what she's always dreamed of coming true turn into something so ... so ... *icky*?

Being with Curly Joe, beginning to fall in love with him, makes Suzie Q feel like life has opened up its door to give her a peek at something that words like freedom and independence get close to, but don't quite capture. *And then,* having done so, it's gone and slammed that same door shut before she can even begin to walk through it.

All of which makes Suzie Q relate to Curly Joe as if, strangely, he was both her saviour and her destroyer. And equally, unsettlingly, neither.

* * * * *

Odd stirrings in the underbelly of the dream.

The times have struck an unfamiliar note that reverberates in the minds of women as disparate as Angel and Suzie Q.

So far, though disturbed, the dreamers will continue sleeping.

Soon enough, the awakening will begin.

11. GOODBYE, GUGGENHEIM

Time, having its way, passes. And, impossibly, it's already Guggenheim's last class.

As has been the case for some weeks now, Curly Joe's the only student in attendance. Guggenheim's political views had been bad enough, but now his lectures are also being boycotted because of McGill's *Obscene Libel Scandal*.

What was *that?* you ask. Okay Tripsters, here's the lowdown:

One fine morning, near the end of November last year, the *McGill Daily* appears on campus like normal. This particular issue, though, includes an extract of an article written by "hip satirist", Paul Krassner. Far out, right? Well, no. Not by a long shot. See, Krassner's piece claims to contain some censored passages from William Manchester's *Death of a President,* a seven hundred plus pages tome that's gone into over-the-top detail covering the events on the day JFK was assassinated. According to Krassner, an avowedly excised section of the book contains a rather attention-grabbing interlude during which Lyndon Johnson is caught fucking the Kennedy corpse in the throat while on the flight back to Washington just prior to his being sworn in as the new President. What can I tell you? The Sixties had a warped sense of humour.

Including Krassner's filthy joke in the *Daily* is bad enough, but what really galls *The Somebodies* is that this profane imitation of Manchester's prose style is right on the money. So when most people — possibly, even some of *The Somebodies* as well — get around to reading it, it doesn't take much to persuade them that the article must be genuine. Which says a lot about what people back in 1968 think of LBJ.

Next thing you know, the Montréal newspapers get wind of what's been published and immediately hack out numerous exposés deploring the sleazoid state of today's decadent youth. Predictably, deducing that a sacrificial scapegoat is deemed necessary to be presented to the mob, *The Somebodies* point the finger at the poor schmuck who'd given the go-ahead to insert the article. And — guess what? — a McGill-wide Free Speech Movement arises overnight.

Having the loudest voice and take-no-prisoners presence, Guggenheim is right in there, immediately identified as the outlandish leader of the anti-establishment pack. He thinks the whole incident is hilarious in a blood-chilling sort of way. *The Somebodies* agree with him that events have turned ghastly. But they fail to find anything to laugh about in them. Not to speak of the negative publicity for the university that comes with the unrest. Having gained *The Somebodies'* attention, Guggenheim has become a marked man. Which he's been loving no end and happily regaling his solitary student with all the latest side-splitting developments.

But all this was some months down the line. You'd think that everybody would have gotten over it. Uh huh. Today is bite back time.

By now, Guggenheim and Curly Joe are on a first name basis. This was a difficult breakthrough for Curly Joe to have made. He's never before called anyone who claimed to be a teacher anything but Mr. or Father. It's a major challenge to address one of these people as *Zeke* (short for Ezekiel).

In line with this shift toward familiarity, the seminars — if they can be called that — have become a lot looser as well. Usually, they take the form of discussions whose focus and topic only take shape once the two of them have started talking, and, as uncertainly, might either continue on well past the official hour or last only a few minutes. As to grades, Guggenheim sees these as forms of supremacist subjugation and power. As a substitute option, he's challenged Curly Joe to assess himself and any ranking he proposes is what Guggenheim will hand in to Registry.

These changes in their relationship notwithstanding, what remains as strong as ever is how much both participants *need* each other. For Curly Joe, Guggenheim provides the proof he demands in order to continue seeing himself as different and special. And, maybe, a little weird as well. But in a good way.

As to Guggenheim, behind his radical cool facade, he is really pretty insecure about ... about ... take your pick. What it mainly boils down to is his agonising desire to be valued.

There are possibly a great many reasons as to why Guggenheim should want this, but there's only one real reason: Guggenheim's petrified of growing old. He even started to write a book dedicated to all the people who peer out from their windows on starry nights in hope of catching a glimpse of *The Ship of Lost Boys* heading for *Never-Never Land*. He didn't get very far with it but neither has he completely given up on the dream. Most nights — be they starry or not — Guggenheim's right there, in front of his window. And then he peeks into the nearby mirror. And the stars change very slowly. Much, much more slowly than the likeness being reflected back at him. Becoming an academic is Guggenheim's way of trying to make the lines on his face slow down a bit. The tactic isn't turning out to be much of a success.

A few years past, catching himself yet again asking what the point of it all was, it struck Guggenheim that of all the dumb questions he could have picked, this was the dumbest of all. Death has enough of a monopoly on answers to that particular line of enquiry. Why bother making any effort to set up a rival trade?

Still, Guggenheim is smart enough to know that telling this to Curly Joe is only going to confuse and disappoint him. He's still too young to really hear it. Just like Guggenheim once was. That in mind, he does his best to remind Curly Joe that each one of us is unique first and foremost so that any and all attempts to generalise about anything regarding who we are is an insult to our very being. He attests that all knowledge is of value — even engineering — and that this value can't be measured by narrow concepts like "good" and "bad", but by the humanity and honesty through which that knowledge is put to use for one and all. And most, Guggenheim tells him about how *bona fide* acts of creation — be they in the Arts or Sciences — construct a bridge between the uniquely personal and the universal. Like Blake's grain of sand and the whole of the world each unveiling and being unveiled through their interconnectedness.

Not that Guggenheim himself has fully accepted any of these insights. Not so far, anyhow. Which is why he still needs Curly Joe. And today he needs him more than on any other because today, sorrowfully, is Guggenheim's last class. And not just his last class of the semester, either. It's his last class *ever*, as far as McGill is concerned. It turns out that *The Somebodies* always had a well-tucked away clause, among the many hundreds of clauses that Guggenheim had failed to take into account when he'd signed his name on that dotted line, which allows them to be rid of him.

Here is the last thing that Guggenheim tells Curly Joe: 'There are always going to be such clauses. Sometimes they come typed on paper and, other times, they come out of the barrel of a gun. There's no avoiding them, either. All you can do,' he says, patting Curly Joe's shoulder, 'is see them for what they are and laugh even if all you feel like doing is crying your heart out. And if you can, accept that the bastards who are busily trying to convince themselves they're so powerful for having got one over on you are well and truly shit-scared, no two ways about it. Why? Because they can see that no matter what they throw at you, unlike them you ain't about to fall to your knees and beg for their mercy. Let 'em realize that. And then ... when their mouths are open in disbelief, aim your spit so that it slides down their fuckin' throats.'

12. FULL MOON MAGIC

Exams have come and gone.

Moe's gotten by with clear, if unexceptional, passes in the B- to C+ range. They'll do.

Larry's not that far behind; although he's been landed with the irritating tribulation of having to take a supplementary exam in chemistry near the very end of July. Which is light years away.

Curly Joe ... Well, he's just worked out how stupid he's been in not even making any attempt to pass. Now he's having to face the reality of starting his university career all over again by going back to another first year in a new Faculty.

'Engineering's gonna miss yuh. But, what'cha gonna do? Switch to Science next year?'

'yeah. guess so. i wouldn't mind going into arts, but what the hell are you gonna do with a ba?'

'Suck cocks in the Hawaiian Lounge, Jim.'

They are, at this moment, celebrating over at Larry's house. No one's bothered to define what exactly there is to celebrate. "So what" to that. It's enough that Montréal's into late April and the squelch of boots onto dirty melting snow is a fading memory. Flowers are springing up everywhere and the nights are getting shorter and warmer. Outdoors, you can even get away with just a sweater on some evenings.

From the backyard of Larry's home they gaze up at the stars. The suburban sky's clear enough tonight for that. They don't know it yet, but Magic is afoot.

Larry's raided his father's bar and emerged with a 3/4 full bottle of Vermouth and a whole one of gin, three glasses, ice, swizzle sticks and canned strawberries. The strawberries are there because he couldn't find either olives or cherries and since he's got his heart set on making official Dry Martinis, he's assured himself that the canned fruit provides a decent enough substitute. Nobody's complaining. More importantly, the drinks are working.

Even Curly Joe's laughing about his grades. Five F's and one A — the latter in English, of course. One of those F's has made history, being the grade given to the first-ever free hand technical drawing submitted to the Engineering Department for assessment. There's even talk of having it framed and hung in the McConnell Building.

Just as Moe's about to launch into some new tirade, Larry bolts up from his deckchair as though the ultimate secret of life has just landed right there on his lap. 'Holy shit!' he says. 'It's a Full Moon! It's a fucking Full Moon!' True enough, it is. It shines down upon them silently, somehow still majestic, even if it's already being cluttered up with metal bric-a-brac from Earth.

'what's got into you, man?' Curly Joe says. He's been quietly replaying memories of him and Suzie Q over at *La Ronde* last weekend going on every thrill ride available. Suzie Q screaming her head off and glueing herself onto him. So animated she didn't even notice that her skirt had ridden way up until she felt his hand on the inside of her naked upper thigh. Seeing as she'd taken her time in politely lifting it away, there's no way she didn't get a kick out of his taking such liberties. *Sigh!* And now Larry's inexplicable outburst has brought things to a *pop!*

'Dont'cha see?' Moe says. 'Larry's secretly a werewolf. Look at him: he's getting hairier by the second.'

At last, Larry makes up his mind that it's time to testify. 'It's a Full Moon,' he repeats once again to the others' visible irritation. 'I've figured out that every time something really loony happens to us, it's *always* a Full Moon. There's just something funny to it, is all. Here we are, all saying how strange and peaceful we feel tonight, and I look up and there's a Full Moon glowing down on us. Isn't that weird?'

Curly Joe says nothing. He isn't all that sure about Larry's theory, but he has no real argument against it, either. He's in the mood for adventure. If the Moon's to be used as an excuse, so be it.

Moe, naturally, isn't about to take any of Larry's hocus pocus claptrap. He wants to schmooze about his problematic virginity again. 'Come off it, Larry. What kinda bullshit are ya throwing around tonight? Maybe ... Maybe *once* when something wild happened, ya noticed that the Moon was full. Okay, I'll give ya that. But you're loading the dice when ya start insisting that something crazy's *gotta* happen tonight because there's a Full Moon that says so. Furthermore, I'm gonna prove ya wrong. I'm gonna drink up this here fire-water and then I'm gonna say goodnight. After that, I'm gonna catch a bus which'll take me to the nearest *Metro* which, in turn, will take me to the end of the line where I'll hop onto another bus which'll take me right home and I'll go to sleep, wake up with a hangover that's too painful to think about right now, and then phone ya just to show ya how hollow your Moon theory is. Emmis.'

However, the one drink quite casually stretches out to another and, by the end of them, Moe's forgotten all about the Moon and his virginity and his resolve to go home. Dependably, they've all forgotten. The peculiar beauty and stillness of the night has beguiled them.

'you know,' whispers Curly Joe, "this has gotta be one of the most fantastically beautiful nights i can recall. i mean, look at it.'

They do. For once, there's no disagreement.

'but still ...' Curly Joe continues, regaining their attention, 'look at us. here we are standing on carefully-mowed lawn, surrounded by a white picket fence, with our backs to a brick wall. what we need to make this night ultra-magnificent is to be someplace out in the countryside. somewhere that's completely wide open, you know? a dirt road, maybe. or no road at all, come to that. where we can lie out on the ground, stretch our legs. watch the stars shine ...'

Overcome by Curly Joe's evaluation of things, it becomes vital now for them to turn this vision into reality. In principle, this shouldn't be too difficult to achieve. There's still a few nearby scattered bits of wilderness, as yet untouched by brick and concrete suburbia, waiting to welcome them. Their only difficulty is how to get there. Hitchhiking's no solution. First of all, it's already past 11.00pm, so the number of cars driving by is going to be severely limited. *And*, even if there are passing cars, what bobo is going to stop to pick up three quasi-drunken teenagers wishing to be let out in the middle of nowhere so's they can see the stars in their natural habitat? Self-transport's out to lunch as well. Ever since that Night of the Chinese Restaurant, Larry's father's car has been off-limits. When push comes to shove, walking seems to be the only solution. Not that any of them mentions this because then they really will pack it in and go home to sleep things off.

It's Larry who gets to the buzzer first. 'Bikes!' he shouts. 'What we want are bikes!' And, remarkably, he even knows where to find some. Invading Larry's garage, they immediately find their means of transport. There are exactly three bicycles lying around waiting for them.

Larry grabs hold of his rusty and years-unused *Raleigh*, treating it as if it was some old race horse long since put out to pasture and now being called upon to perform one final errand of mercy.

Curly Joe takes the bike belonging to Larry's younger brother. This one's newer and in better shape and amazingly has three gears for him to fiddle around with.

Moe's landed with Larry's little sister's two-wheeler. It's much smaller than the other two and has a saddle that swivels in all directions every time he lifts his ass in the air to work the pedals. Worse, the handlebars are so low that his knees scrape against them if he speeds things up. Inconveniently for Moe, there's no choice in the matter. Larry's and Curly Joe's legs are too long so that they wouldn't even be able to steer the thing. They appease Moe with the promise of cycling slowly and not laughing at him. Not when he can notice, anyway.

Then they set off. After some twenty minutes, Curly Joe's country vision is rewarded with something even more breathtaking. And all because Moe had to stop to pee. As he empties his bladder, Moe fixes on an apparition that confounds him. 'Hey!' he says, 'Do you two see what I'm seeing or am I just going nuts here?'

He's not. Off in the distance, initially semi-obscured by trees, beautiful waves of bright green light are dancing in the sky.

'what the fuck is that?' says Curly Joe.

'I know! I know!' Larry says. He's seen this before as a kid back in B.C. 'It's the Northern Lights! *Aurora Borealis*! Wow!'

And he's right, too. Totally bedazzled, all three marvel at the spectacular light show being put on just for them. Before long though, they begin to feel the early morning cold come seeping through their clothes. In order to keep warm, they start to jog along the roadside and, as they get going, more enchantment happens. They chance upon a decrepit-looking, rarely used dirt road just about twenty yards from where they'd stopped. In truth, it's more a footpath than a road, but it's still exactly right.

The pedalling they'd been complaining about earlier takes on a new energy as they turn their bikes toward the bumpy and difficult to manoeuvre dirt track. More natural than man-made, it soon opens out into an expansive pasture overabundant with wild new-born grass. They let their cycles slide to the ground and crouch down onto a field that is still too damp to lie upon. Squatting instead, all they can hear are sporadic cricket chirps. Mainly, though, they allow the silence to dazzle them.

Unusually, the first of them to be firmly drawn into the mystic is Moe. Spontaneously, unwilling to stop himself, he stands up, approaches each of his friends and hugs them one at a time as if each were both lover and brother combined. Then, for once sticking to the original, he quotes a couple of lines he's still got memorised from Heebie Jeebie High's Third Year English Lit class. John Keats. *Ode To A Grecian Urn*:

> *Beauty is truth, truth beauty,—that is all*
> *Ye know on earth, and all ye need to know.*

Later, he won't be able to get a handle on his gesture. Nor will any of them. The only thing that matters is that its purity leaves them all electric.

After an exquisitely long, silent while, their ears become attuned to a novel, faintly insistent sound. Since it's still indistinct, they nail down that it must be originating from the outlying regions of their field. Still, if they had to put a tag on it, they'd say that it has the unmistakable ring of a howl. Maybe even a baying, to more more precise.

'Just like in the wilderness,' gushes Larry. 'Almost as though it was a coyote crying out to the Moon.'

Curly Joe smiles, thinking of a line from a Dylan song about the sounds in the night. Then smiles again, keeping the thought to himself.

Moe isn't saying anything either. He's too busy picking out the not-quite-that-faraway whine. Coyote or whatever, it's certainly attracting his attention. Seconds later, the yowling takes over every other sound that reaches his ears. God knows what it is, but it's approaching them at charging-level speed.

It doesn't take much longer before their disquiet is cast aside in favour of unadulterated terror. Snatches of sounds much too similar to ugly snarling are clearly being given voice to by an as yet unknown creature that is doing its best to assure them of its malevolence. Just then, an especially villainous bark emerges from the darkness. There can be no other conclusion: *It* has nearly reached them. It's Curly Joe who yells 'let's get outta here!' By then, they're all three already on their bikes, their minds exploding with visions of some devil-spawned demon incarnate descending upon them furious to chew out their hearts.

Larry and Curly Joe, adrenalin pumping madly away, are burning rubber as fast as they can, with Curly Joe taking and maintaining an early lead. Possessed with the stamina of a superhero, he's far out ahead of Larry, pushing himself to go at a roaring speed which flies him over rocks and bumps and puddles that rip and muddy up his jeans.

Moe's not as lucky. Having raced to his bike along with the others, he gets only fifty feet with it before its saddle falls off. Panic-stricken, trembling and cursing any and every god there may be to hear him, he finds a way to fit the seat back on and is about to start stepping on it when, like magic, a fearsome dark shape in the form of a ravenous Husky dog appears to his left and, with startling ferocity, takes a bloodthirsty snap at his ankle. At this, Moe's hightailing it like a man caught up in a veritable race for his life. His knees bump and scrape against handlebars while his feet rotate furiously. Yet, somehow, every time he turns to sneak a look behind him, it seems that the Hell-Hound's forever no more than an inch or two away.

Improbably achieving an astonishing speed, Moe hurtles onward until, to their shared incredulity, he overtakes Larry who, in turn, savvies that the mastiff is now eager to treat him as its prime victim and scares up the required amount of additional energy to catch up to Moe. Now side-by-side, they curse and shout in hope of warding off the brute until they catch sight of the highway lights once again.

Only when their tires have been in contact with cement for over a minute does either of them permit himself to relax just a little and dredge up the courage to look behind his shoulders. In relief, they confirm that they're once more alone. The apparition has disappeared back to the Hadean depths from which it had emerged. About a quarter mile or so down the road, they come upon Curly Joe's doubled-up body lying in a heap beneath his bike. Though his chest heaves and his heart pounds, he grins the unmistakeable grin of a man who knows that he's just cheated Death.

By the time they get back to Larry's house, they've reasoned out that, somehow, they must have blundered upon a farmer's plot of land and one of his guard dogs had sniffed them out. In the security of suburbia, it sounds like a rational argument.

'well, looks like we're crashing out on larry's floor again,' Curly Joe says, stifling a yawn.

Moe eyeballs the sky. The sun's not got too many hours to wait before rising. 'Guess so.' Then it dawns on him. 'Hey, ya know what, Larry —'

'Never mind, Moe. Let's just get some sleep.'

And the Full Moon, counting three more in the ranks of her worshippers, allows herself to give way to the daylight.

PART TWO: FREEDOM

MAY 1968 — AUGUST 1968

'Under the pavement: the beach.'

— 1968 slogan —

13. ANGELS IN NEW YORK

Guess what, Tripsters? It's May 1968, and everywhere our trio turns they hear people talking 'bout a revolution. A lot of them are even done with talking and are busy starting one up.

Thing is, revolutions come in all sizes and shapes. Sure, there's always revolutions in some socio-political kind of way. And there's plenty of those going on in 1968. There are workers and students in Paris doing the equivalent of storming *The Bastille*. And over in Britain, their counterparts are taking possession of factories and universities. Look around and blood's being spilled in the streets of Rome and Berlin and Prague and Shanghai and ... just about everywhere. Add to that all the heroes and martyrs to shed tears over. Martin Luther King's already lying dead and buried. Red Rudy Dutschke hovers on the borderline between life and death. Bobby Kennedy has just a few short weeks left to live. Even Andy Warhol's being targeted for assassination. And, if that wasn't enough, *The War* — that stupid, pointless war over in Vietnam — rages on.

One way to look at all this is to conclude that by the middle of 1968, the Days of Love and Peace have given way to the Hour of the Gun. That said, it's also a 1968 where, in spite of the headline news reality of death and pillage, a pungent optimism has also flowered bringing with it another sort of revolution. For as many who take to arms and ready for battle, an equal number turn inward, plunge into a drug-induced, me-focused cosmos. The East has been voted in as the pathway to any and every spiritual quest that captures the imagination. That mantra, "the personal is the political", captures this revolution's stance in a nutshell. Consciousness Raising. Encounter Groups. Bioenergetics ... Anything promoting the idea that revolution must begin from within each individual before it can express itself in some wider, external way has attracted many to enlist as inner change guerillas.

Two competing revolutions happening simultaneously

makes for crazy times ahead. Real *Yin/Yang*. Or *Kali*-like *Creator* and *Destroyer*, if you prefer. Times containing Alan Watts and Watts in flames. Times nurturing both Tao and Mao. Times enraptured by Astrology and Astronauts. The *Summer Of Love* meets the *Long Hot Summer*. Crazy times indeed! And with opposing sides convinced that their way to revolution is the *only* way, a split in The Movement is becoming more and more apparent. There's the hippie revolution and the radical politics revolution. And while there's still some dialogue going on between the two, both keep asking: which side are you on? It won't take long before each starts seeing the other as its worst enemy. Which is one sure way to guarantee that a revolution — no matter its focus and shape — is going to fizzle out and fail. Now and again, it can even fail so bad that people start to wish it had never happened.

But hey! Get with it, Tripsters ... It's 1968. Revolutions are in the air. It's in their nature to shake things up one way or the other. And by they way: which side are *you* on?

* * * * *

As to Larry, Moe and Curly Joe, their own experience of revolution begins with a letter that Angel's just written. When exactly, she wants to know, are the three of them going to come down to New York City and visit her? She's even got a one-bedroom apartment with her own phone in it now so Larry can ring with their chosen dates of arrival.

For a couple of days after that their imaginations are buzzing non-stop, inventing wild New York adventures to be savoured for years to come. And then, Moe goes and spoils it all by getting a fit of the Doubting Thomases. Nearly a week goes by with him doing his best to prevail upon the other two to accept that Angel doesn't really want him and Curly Joe to make it over. Sure, she's being kind and all that. But, come on, she only wants Larry to be there with her. It's an open-and-shut case when you think about it. Larry's reaction is to blow his stack and get all sarcastic, wondering aloud if Moe's expecting a printed invitation to appear in his mailbox. Which only clinches Moe's suspicions that he's been right on target all along.

Cue Curly Joe to the rescue. He's been passing the time reading Freud and Jung and some living Scottish weirdo genius named R. D. Laing. So it's left up to Curly Joe to analyse the situation and point out to Moe that he's busily making up reasonable-sounding excuses so that he can evade the unpalatable truth that he's basically just plain scared of going on a trip all by himself, without any parental presence and protection. To everyone's astonishment, this pseudo-analysis strikes home with barely any resistance on Moe's part. Matter of fact, it convinces him that this is his chance to stop stalling and take charge of his life.

It's May 1968, and Moe's breathing in the spirit of the times. Just to prove to himself that his own private revolution is finally off and running, Moe lets it be known that right now is the perfect moment for him to go and buy that car he's been yakking on about for months on end. This way, they can drive into NYC in full-fledged, independent glory. To hell with *Greyhound* buses.

Four days, twenty three used-car dealers and forty-seven FOR SALE ads later, a suitable vehicle is found to meet Moe's stringent demands. Naturally, they've come upon his dream machine by accident. The garage they'd just stopped at to buy some cherry colas has been trying to get rid of it for weeks. It (or more correctly, *she*) is a 1962 *Ford Falcon* with an allegedly brand new engine and an equally doubtful recent paint job. She runs, as they say in the trade, like Pierre Elliott Trudeau (Canada's P.E.T. and new Prime Minister), on political heat.

It's love at first sight.

Dowry set at $475.00, Moe dubs her, now and forevermore, *The Flacon.*

* * * * *

Crisis averted, Larry's back to feeling pretty good about things until Curly Joe, who's caught the pseudo-analyst bug in spades, comes right out and asks him how come he's so pleased? Given the choice, wouldn't he rather be passing away a few days alone with Angel?

It's a question that Larry hasn't got any sort of answer to. All he knows is that the thought of going to New York and spending a week with Angel all on his own brings on cold sweats and uncontrollable shakes. And it's got nothing to do with being a lonesome traveller. Not that he tells this to Curly Joe. Instead, he laughs and tells him to fuck off. Which works. But only to the extent that now Larry's infected with the analytical bug as well. Why *does* bringing his friends along seem so necessary? What's his unconscious know that he doesn't?

* * * * *

When he's not so up to his neck in playing disconcerting mind games, Curly Joe is flying high at the thought of it all. What an adventure they're about to have! Moseying around in The Village and bumping into Ginsberg and Corso. Maybe, even Dylan himself. Hanging out in esoteric record shops and alternative book stores. Easing back to watch the latest underground movies in tiny, twenty-seater cinemas. *Oh Holy Joy*!

* * * * *

And when the three of them are together, riding in The Flacon just to test her out, they keep cracking-up like little kids telling each other their first dirty jokes.

Naturally, it's Moe who takes centre stage, reeling off his collection of phobias and foibles. All those indispensable bottles of pills he's going to have to cart along as necessary aids against multiple allergies. The duck-down pillow he just *has to* bring with him in case the place they'll stay at only offers capoc-filled ones. And also, don't forget, there's his rubber sheet! No, it's not because Moe's incontinent. Its function is to provide further protection against the numerous possible inflammatory skin reactions that strange beds might elicit. Add to all this Moe's quaint habit of staying up late to get his nightly dose of Johnny Carson, which, naturally, he follows up with a 1.00am shower, and you've got NON-STOP LAUGH-ORAMA each and every time.

No kidding, it's May 1968, and who knows what will happen next?

* * * * *

hiya suzie q,

guess what? we made it! we're in new york city! the ride down was a trip even if we didn't drop no acid. this guard who stopped us at the amerikan border was an absolute pig who was positive he'd hit it big time with three hippie-politico-anarchists just because he glommed on a copy of "logos" lying on the back seat. so naturally, he gets into rifling through all of our belongings, practically ripping the flacon apart and trying to use subtle interrogation techniques such as suddenly going over all friendly and keeping a straight face when he asks if we have any of them there roach-clips on us that he could borrow. a real clown. naturally, he didn't find anything, since there wasn't anything to find in the first place, so he had to give up and let us cross the border. just as we were leaving, larry shouted 'so long, porky!' and moe gunned the motor down hard.

at any rate, we made it over alive. just about. new york. wow. whaddaya say to that? where to begin? the first thing that hits you is the déjà vu effect of its skyline. i mean, how many hundreds of films have we all watched that begin with an aerial shot of this place? you know: 'there are seventeen billion stories in the naked city. this has been one of them. ta-ta-ta-ta. the end'. and all that sort of stuff.

one thing, it's real easy to find your way around in new york. every street's a number, so you just follow numbers until you get to where you want to go. you wouldn't believe where we got to! first thing we did was to go straight to "green witch village" to find a place to crash. we couldn't find nothing even after asking a couple of sidewalk freaks. all they gave us was these weird

*looks that moe was convinced unmasked their sexual
predilections. sensible game plan failed, we picked up an issue
of "the village voice" instead. larry bought it while trying to act
as nonchalant as possible, just striding up to the newsstand and
asking the guy there for "duh voice", as though he's been living
in new york all his life. the guy stiffed him with a two-week old
issue! which pretty much sums up this town.*

*we deemed it likely that any places advertised two weeks
ago would probably still exist, so we studied the classifieds.
first one we saw read something like: "friendly, clean
establishment. reasonable prices. single-double-triple rooms.
$20 per person per week." That sounded altogether okay to us.
so we walked to where this place was supposed to be. not too
far from the chelsea hotel, it turned out. when we saw it, we
were flabbergasted. here was this run-down heap of rubble just
where our hotel should have been. on closer inspection, we
realized it <u>was</u> our hotel.*

*there were what seemed to be 20 bums lying on the steps
leading up to it, hanging about in various states of
degeneration. one guy practically lurched his way over to us,
pulled out some beat up old transistor radio and asked: 'wanna
buy an am/fm, real cheap?' when all he got was polite refusals
from us, he turned to moe and whispered 'wanna try a bit a'
skag, man?' moe was really shaken up. first of all, he had no
idea what skag meant (come to that, neither did larry or i - we
later found out it's slang for heroin). and second, the guy gave
him the creeps. so he (moe) just started to get the shakes like
nobody's business and tried to splutter out: 'no thanks'.
whereupon the bum presented moe with this almost toothless
grin and cackled: 'hey man, looks to me like yer on it awready!'
then he shimmied himself away, laughing non-stop at his joke.*

*for some totally pointless reason, we continued our way into
the hotel. indescribable, suzie q. there were twice as many bums
inside as there were outside on the steps. plus, there was this
godawful stink of puke and crap everywhere. out of some
warped sense of curiosity, we asked to see a triple room. one of
the bums stood up to show us. unbelievably, it turned out he*

was the bellhop. you could tell that by his ratty-looking stained jacket which he'd been wearing for so long that it was now an inherent part of his body. it had this insignia on it: "hotel baron". somehow, it didn't seem to matter to anyone that the hotel we were all in wasn't called anything even vaguely like "hotel baron".

he led us down this decrepit corridor. you know: cracked plaster ceilings, musty torn wallpaper utterly caked with dust and riddled with innumerable (and unimaginative) obscenities. having reached our destination, he stops in front of what once might have been a door. it looked as though someone had kicked it down and later vented out all of his frustrations on it with a 20lb sledge hammer. the bellhop muttered something about needing to repair the lock. we just stared and pretended to agree. though it was hardly necessary, he pushed the wooden remains 'til they swiveled inwards on their one shaky hinge. we were greeted with a spectacle just so unbelievably appalling that we got shocked into a state of utter facial apathy. what hit us right away though, was the foul stench that made the rest of the hotel smell like roses. it was as if a platoon of infantrymen had lived in the room for a month and that every night of that month each one of them had drunk himself into a stupor during which he'd barfed and peed onto the walls and floor. add to this the aroma of years-old rat shit and you maybe get a hint of what swooped up into our nostrils. and the floor! oh my god, the floor! it looked like it was into its twentieth layer of dust. on closer look-see, the dust was moving! it turned out to be a carpet of cockroaches! as for the furniture, what we could see was a sagging double bed and a mattress leaning up against a wall (to prop it up perhaps). this was, as you may recall, a triple room. oh yeah, there was a sort of chest of drawers with a jagged corner of a mirror taped to the wall above it. and that was it. except for the aforementioned cockroaches which were everywhere on the walls as well.

our silence was broken only by the smiling bellhop who took it as his chance to inform us that the toilet was down the hall (no, we didn't have the guts to go look at it), and that sheeting *cost an extra $2.00 per week. we told him where he could stuff his sheeting and practically ran for the sanctity of the outside world.*

no need to tell you, suzie q, we were getting scared. i mean, here we were in new york city, it was moving into late afternoon, angel wasn't anywhere to be found (more on that, below) and we had visions of having to sleep in the flacon rather than try out any other hotels. boy, were we depressed. larry worst of all, as you can imagine. not knowing what else to do, i went and bought a new issue of the village voice. lo and behold! there was an ad there for an international students residence. we sort of got worried by its address — on the fringes of the bowery — great, more drunks to fight off. but we figured: what the hell. if it only took in students, it might be some ways better.

we found the place: way down on 4th street and avenue d. really close to the wharf and a pretty rough and tumble bit of the jungle. 'positively 4th street,' as dylan says. there were mainly puerto ricans around, a lot of them sitting on sidewalks or doorsteps, kids kicking basketballs around, a few guys drinking, more playing craps out in the open, mongrel dogs everywhere. an incredible picture. yet an appealing one to me, in some odd sort of way. it struck me that i was seeing a side of new york that tourists never bothered to go near and that guide books pretended didn't exist. it was seamy and noisy and maybe more than anything else, ugly. but it was real. it was exciting just to think i'd be living in it, if even for only a week. thank goodness.

anyway, to get on with my story: the sun was about to set so we took up courage and knocked on the residence's door. it opened right away as though somebody'd been standing behind it all along, waiting for a knock. the somebody turned out to be "ron levitt, head of hostel". really! that's what he told us his name was. but, that aside, he likes to be called <u>the warden.</u>

<u>the warden</u> looks and speaks like he's either a retired wrestler or a bouncer from the hawaiian lounge back home, even if at the same time, he sports a pronounced beer-belly

which probably helps to make him look even puffier and flabbier than he undoubtedly is. naturally, he has a crew-cut (marine-style) and a pair of glasses with an elastic band that wraps itself round his head. he wears this t-shirt that's shrunk two sizes too small and has its front emblazoned with the fading legend "miami beach" which is tucked into the crevice between his boy-breasts. his pants, on the other hand, are about two sizes too large (he must have bought them from a circus show fat-man because the warden *is mighty big himself), and just hang there almost like flags draped on his lower body and supported by — of course, what else? — a single piece of rope which he's twirled about half-a-dozen times in the region just above his navel area. when we first set eyes on him, he made a picture so brilliantly dopey that we'd have burst out laughing in his face if he didn't look so wired and mean.*

'whaddaya want?' he scowled.

larry was first to speak up. 'we're looking for a room, and —'

'who sent'cha?' he scowled again.

'we read your ad in the village voice,' i said.

'that commie rag ... students are ya?' yet another scowl.

'yes, we're from mcgill university in—' larry tried to finish.

'prove it.' a tough scowl this time.

'we've got id's,' moe spoke up.

no reply from the warden. *just another scowl that was answer enough. this was followed by a loud huff when the cards were turned over to him.*

'yer all boys, right? can't tell with the long hairs these days. no girlies allowed in here.'

'all three of us are male,' i piped up.

'no girlie boys wanted neither.' the warden *gave us a long, paralyzing evil eye. I guess that we passed the test because he handed back the id's. 'okay. i got an empty room. might not be so empty tonight, though ...' at this point he produced a scowly-looking grin. then he added: '$3.00 the first day, $2.00 every following day. each. free bathroom, shower, cooking facilities and any out-of-date grocery food i can scrounge up. color TV's in the living room. DON'T TOUCH OR ADJUST IT. ONLY I*

ADJUST IT, RIGHT?'

we nodded. who'd be dumb enough to disagree? besides, moe was already in seventh heaven at the fact that this place really does have a color tv. the big-sized room (six beds in it) has proved to be decent. only the bathroom shows any noticeable signs of cockroaches.

and ... here we are. we've got a room-mate tonight as well. he's some sailor on leave. it seems sailors are bona-fide students, too, as far as the warden's concerned. when sailor-boy found out we were from montréal, the first (and only) thing he wanted to know was how much montréal prostitutes cost. great guy. we told him what we guessed might be the going rate and he just flipped out. wanted to leave for montréal right away. we weren't about to discourage him.

we couldn't get in touch with angel till really late at night. larry, by that point, was pretty frantic. he was certain she'd been mugged, raped and killed while skipping her merry way home.

what had really happened turned out to be even worse than that: she'd forgotten that the date we were arriving was today. yup, you read it right. angel insisted she was sure larry'd written that we were arriving tomorrow.

larry, naturally, got pretty upset. but they seemed to get things straightened out over the phone. angel said it was too late for her to come over and see us tonight, but that she'd call by first thing in the morning.

pretty strange, huh? larry couldn't make things out at all and nearly got into a fight with moe when he (moe) suggested that he'd been right all along about angel wanting to have larry come visit on his own. thanks to my quick thinking, i stopped things by reminding moe of the color TV and taking larry out for a walk.

wow! new york, lower east side, 10.30p.m. what an in-your-face feeling, suzie q. fear and disgust and, still, that feeling of belonging. of being part of it all. it did the trick. larry got cooled out and calmed down, so we walked back home only to be greeted by the warden who handed over this musty-looking apple pie and said it was ours to eat. we were too scared to turn it down.

as i write this, larry's asleep, moe's next door in the common room still sitting spellbound in front of the TV watching some old humphrey bogart flick on the late late show, and i cringe at this piece of pie in front of me wondering how in hell i'm gonna get rid of it, while at the same time, doing my best to finish up this letter to you.

it's been a looong day. a promise of what's to come, maybe. at any rate, i'm dead on my feet. i'll write again soon.

miss you already.

love

— curly joe —

ps. see? i told you i knew how to write words like everybody else and make it easy reading for you. that's how much i love you! i'm sticking to my guns about capital letters though. got to preserve some dignity.

* * * * *

Newsflash! Angel hasn't gotten the date of their arrival mixed-up.

Three days ago, her Modelling Agency twisted her arm into trying-out as a Go-Go Dancer for a live band's two-night residency at one of those new discotheques opening up all over Manhattan. Angel didn't much like the idea of being ogled while gyrating half-naked, but it was good exercise and, more to the point, it paid well. Plus, tips were no problem so long as they didn't involve any illegal hanky-panky. Bottom line: she could use the cash. To get the time off though, Angel had to agree to taking on extra night shift at the restaurant she works at.

It's only after she's been scribbling down pre-theatre customers' orders for an hour or so that she allows herself to feel sorry about today. That upsets her for a few minutes and then someone wanting to pay his bill motions in her direction. And that's that. Customer satisfied, she gets back to thinking about her reaction. Why is she feeling so little guilt knowing how upset Larry will be? Trudging her way back home, she's still puzzling over that one.

Inside her apartment, crashed out across her couch, an exhausted Angel judges that the inevitable is happening. Too much is going on, too many thoughts getting in the way. Most of them having to do with men. Angel's learned a new word: *chauvinism*. It's a word that's not yet in most people's consciousness. You decades-later Tripsters might not believe this, but it's something that men growing up in The Sixties can usually get away with without being called out on. Even male fantasies of the 4F variety — Find them, Feel them, Fuck them, Forget them — are still considered cool enough for men to own up to and for women to put up with.

Angel's moment of illumination came about slightly over a week ago:

There she is taking orders from four Columbia University pre-med students. Long-haired, bell-bottom jeaned and sporting black arm-bands because of *The War,* they don't notice her standing there waiting because they have such burning issues to discuss first. Okay, hearing them going 'right on!' that the US Supreme Court has ruled all State laws prohibiting interracial marriage to be unconstitutional is something she can feel good about too. Same with their calling to mind that the world's very first successful heart transplant patient is still going strong. One of them even happens to mention not quite under his breath that British Courts have just decriminalised homosexuality and — who knows? — it could happen here, too, some day. Fine. She'll just stay where she is, pencil hovering.

What changes everything happens but a breath or three later. Having taken his time to acknowledge her existence, one of these guys gives Angel the eye, licks his lips and says 'Let's go PUAB tonight.' Angel knows what PUAB means. Pick Up A Broad. To be fair, a few of her waitress pals might have said the same thing. 'I wanna PUAB tonight!' Meaning: Pick Up A Boy. Or, if they happen to be lesbian, implying the same as this prehistoric prick sizing her up.

Angel's all for the sexual revolution. Never before in history have men and women been able to engage in worry-free, open-aired, anywhere, anytime, anyhow sex. And, yeah, maybe that might still only be a dream for a lot of people. But just the same ... Schmucks like the ones she has to go on smiling at just to keep her job are making sure the dream gets forgotten the minute you wake up.

Thinking back on them, Angel knows for sure that Larry's not anything like those clowns. And that matters. Or, at least, it should. Except, truthfully, it doesn't matter enough. And because of that, all she can hope for now is that she'll be able to delay things until after Larry's left and the renewed physical distance between them will lessen the pain that's bound to follow.

The insistent ringing of her phone brings an end to any further soul-searching. Larry. Of course. Anxious to hear that she's okay, unable to bring himself to ask where she's been. Although it does its best to, his voice fails to hide his confusion, suppressed anger and disappointment. Little by little, Angel finds herself wishing that he'd shout at her, order her to come over to him right now! She knows that, were he to, she'd obey him without a second's thought. But ... He doesn't. Which only makes things worse because it proves how weak Angel is for wanting him to be so ... so ... male. And how she hates him now for making it crystal clear how much she hates herself for being so weak, so unliberated. Swallowing hard, she lies to him and to herself. The days got mixed-up in her mind because of tiredness. But, there you go. She'll be free tomorrow and they're all going to have a ball, right?

They both pretend to be appeased.

* * * * *

Happily, for the next few days, Angel genuinely enjoys being in The Stooges' company. Her laughter is both carefree and warmhearted. And more, Angel is touched by how effortlessly she's been welcomed into their tourist world and how eager they are for her to explore it alongside them.

Like the others, she, at first, allows Moe to draw up the timetable that will take them up and down the Empire State Building, all around the UN, criss-crossing through Central Park, swanning down 5th Avenue, parading along Broadway, tip-toeing along the edge of Harlem and being ferried over to the Statue of Liberty. All in two days.

Then: rebellion. Curly Joe wants to find Andy Warhol's Factory and hang out with the Superstars. Larry demands that they're to spend an afternoon in the *Museum of Modern Art*. And Angel urges them to visit *The Electric Circus*. Unwilling to admit defeat, Moe tries to mollify them by suggesting they spend the day in a line-up to get to be part of *The Tonight Show's* live audience. The bastards pretend not to hear him.

Luckily, at the height of their argument, they find themselves on Broadway and 51st, right smack in front of the *Lowe's Capitol Movie Theatre*. What's playing is *2001: A Space Odyssey* which recently had its world premiere. And it's in *Cinerama*, to boot.

Afterwards, they huddle together inside a coffee house booth till the early morning hours, eating blueberry pancakes and sipping lemon tea while discussing the impact that the film has had on each of them. Eyes shimmering and heads in the clouds, they defend personal interpretations, embark upon philosophical speculations, muse over key points that demand deeper analysis. As a matter of fact, none of them has the faintest idea what that ending is all about. But, hey! What's it matter? They're electric, transporting themselves thirty-three years into a future that seems so unimaginably far away.

Still buzzing, they begin to make their way back to the underground car park where they've left The Flacon. It's 2.00am on Broadway, though you wouldn't know it. Lights pulsate and sparkle, neon signs blare out the latest necessities, cops patrolling two by two troop by while people of every size and shape, shade and colour shamble about tangibly indifferent to the time of day.

The city's energy, as unnatural and hyperactive as it is, courses through them. They wait for a traffic light to change, and then keep going. Their footsteps sound loud and dimly foreboding. They've fallen into a spontaneous regimental march: Curly Joe skirting the sidewalk curb, Larry and Angel arm in arm, between him and Moe who's on the inside, erratically brushing against brick walls and shuttered shop doors.

'okay, tell me,' says Curly Joe, 'where's the *real* new york?'

'I think it's the Lower East Side,' says Larry. 'Now *that* is real. Not like all the touristy places.'

'naw,' says Curly Joe. 'i would've agreed with you a day or so back but now that we've been here a while i think it's *exactly* the tourist places that make new york what it is. it's why people come here. it's the uniqueness. slums ain't unique. you can find those anywhere.'

'Will the real New York please stand up and reveal itself?' says Moe. His stab at a joke dies an instant death.

Which is enough for all the pressure that's been building up inside Angel to pass its breaking point. In her mind, she's back in the restaurant waiting on those four — now reduced to three — jocks from Hell. Which is unfair, she knows, but there's no stopping her. 'For pity's sake! Can't you guys just be satisfied with f*eeling* things instead of having to analyze everything so that it fits into your preferred slot? That's exactly what our parents do. And what our would-be political leaders carry on doing. And, guess what? All they end up with is no feelings at all! That's what you're doing to yourselves going on like this!

'Each of you's being caught up in some full-on beautiful emotion. Okay, I get that. But can't you just give into it instead of trying to put some useless stamp on it? If it feels good, do it, right? *That's* what The Revolution's going on about, you know!

'People are getting beaten up, arrested, even killed just for giving their feelings a right to breathe! I mean, twenty-six people were assassinated right next door in Newark last summer! Or didn't you guys hear about that yet? And the cops have got orders to shoot to kill everybody in the Black Panther Party. Even teenagers like Bobby Hutton. But maybe that's news to you, too! So I guess that you haven't picked up on what's happening in Rhodesia either, right? Well, for your information: last year, they made Apartheid legal. Can you believe that? And now, they've gone ahead and executed three Black guys just for being Black to prove that they mean it.

'Get with it, you guys! It's not just clothes and hair, you know. Total war's been declared. There's people protesting for freedom everywhere without having to come up with "sensible reasons". They don't need "sensible reasons" to know what really matters. So who could care less about trying to define anything? It's 1968! The word is Freedom, right? No need to define *that*. So stop hogging the sidelines, will you? Join the party!'

They've stopped in their tracks while Angel has her say. Her words are too emotional to walk to. It's either dance or complete stillness.

To feel the feelings. To welcome them whether they bring on pain or happiness. Naive or inspired, they have just been let in on the soundtrack to The Sixties. And, struggling, led by Angel, they've begun to absorb it into their hearts and bones.

* * * * *

Larry's over the moon. Angel's words got the three of them listening to her as an individual, as an equal, and not just because she's his girlfriend. This woman. He loves her. He's sure of it. He loves her.

* * * * *

Five days gone already and it's Larry's birthday. Moe and Curly Joe treat him to a mega-lunch at *Mamma Leone's* and then, fulfilling his wish, they all head off to *MOMA* to catch this madcap exhibit on Surrealism complete with Mae West Lips sofa and water-sprouting limousine in the museum terrace pond. *Like, zany!*

After that, it's a parting of the ways. Moe and Curly Joe, swept up by Angel's *cri de coeur,* are off to experience the dangerous delights of 42nd Street. Larry? He's going to spend the rest of the day and — fingers crossed! — all night over at Angel's.

* * * * *

Angel's apartment is tiny and smells of air-freshener. She and Larry are inside it right now, trapped in reciprocal silence, pretending not to have an inkling about what's going on. An hour earlier, she'd brought out a tray with half-a-dozen cupcakes bunched together, each of them with a lit birthday candle stuck in their middle.

'This is the best I could do for a birthday cake,' Angel confesses.

'It's beautiful. Thank yuh. And thanks for the present.' Larry points with his chin to the dozen tubes of acrylic paint and collection of brushes on the spare chair. 'I'll try them out back home.'

'Make sure you do.' Angel almost adds 'I'll want to see your efforts next time I'm over' but stops herself just in time.

It's Larry who breaks first. 'What's the matter?' he says, trying to find an answer in her eyes.

'Nothing.'

'Yuh look like you're about to start crying!'

'It's nothing.'

'C'mon, Angel. Tell me.'

It takes every ounce of will power, but she finds the courage to face him. As soon as she does, her confidence nearly melts away. How can it not when he looks every bit like a doomed Romantic Poet seeking salvation that only she can provide? 'I wanted you to be so totally happy.'

'But I am! I'm with yuh. It's just yuh and me in yuhr apartment, sitting on yuhr couch next to each other. It's my birthday. I'm happy.' Waving his left hand as though shooing away all the demons who might be floating around in Angel's thoughts, Larry nearly knocks over half a glass of red wine that, earlier on in the tortuous evening, had been placed on the floor, next to where his feet have just gone. He starts to offer an apology and then rebels. 'I haven't been able to keep up with yuh all week. Yuh're happy. Yuh're sad. Yuh're ... Aw, I don't know. What is it? Will yuh please just tell me?'

Angel wants to apologise as well. She really does. But the desire to hit back takes over. 'Oh ... Look, I'm really, really, sorry. But don't you get what's happening here?'

'No,' Larry says, grinning stupidly. He's counting on the effect that his *enfant naif* pucker will have in forcing the miserable play they're in to bring down its curtains so that, hopefully, something new will start and take things in the direction he's wanted them to go all night.

His ill-disguised manoeuvre incenses Angel once again. 'All right then. Have it your way. Make matters as difficult as possible.' She pauses, then gives up. 'Listen, what you need to know is that on that first night you arrived I went through a really crummy time because of you. I was determined to pretend to be who you want me to be. I've tried, Larry. But when you came over tonight, I knew I couldn't any longer. You deserve a lot better. I've got to show you the truth. Who I really am.'

Larry shakes his head in disbelief. Now he's caught up in some dumb TV soap opera. 'Yuh're just making things so complicated, Angel. Yuh —'

'No! *You* listen! How many times have we seen each other since we met up again last summer?'

'I don't know.'

'Don't lie!'

'What's the point to —'

'Two times, Larry. Twice. A couple of days in February, and this past week. It doesn't add up to much, does it? Small chunks in the gaps that make up our separate lives. And then what? You go back to your world and I go back to mine. And that's it. We're strangers again.'

'Yuh're the one who seems to find it necessary to work in New York.'

'And *you're* the one who seems to find it necessary to stay in Montréal! Even though you're not doing shit there! So don't go all "I'm more important because I'm male" on me, okay?'

'And what are *yuh* doing that's so important? Modelling. A plastic world full of cardboard people. That's *really* relevant, Angel.'

She nearly smiles, predicting his reaction to her next revelation. 'I've decided to give up modelling. You're 100% right. It's crap. I don't want to subject myself to it any longer. I'll probably just keep on working as a waitress for a while.'

It takes some seconds for her words to sink in. '*What?* Holy shit, Angel! But that's great! Yuh could come back to Montréal!' Larry blubbers on, totally carried away, now confident of the golden future that lies ahead for them. 'Listen,' he says, doing his best to talk her into agreeing with him. 'Don't worry. I'll help yuh out any way I can. Yuh should have told me sooner. Why didn't yuh?'

'Why didn't I?' says Angel. 'Well first of all, you didn't let me finish what I wanted to say. I'm really desperate to get back into acting. And New York's the place to be for that. There's so many Drama Schools to get me into focus again. I'll see what happens ... But the more important truth that stopped me from saying anything earlier is that I was scared you'd react in exactly the way you just have.'

Gut-punched into breathlessness, head spinning at full tilt, Larry's lost it now. 'How the hell *am* I supposed to react? What am I expected to do? Shake my head and just say "good", or something?'

'Yes, exactly that,' Angel says defiantly, knowing full well he won't get it. 'If you knew *me*, Larry, you *would* react that way!'

Okay. Calm down. Larry tells himself. *Try to make some sense of this.* 'But why? Can yuh tell me why? It's something we've dreamed of, being able to live close to each other. We've fantasized so much, so many times about it.'

Angel grabs at her glass, swigs down the wine to give herself the added resolve to continue answering him honestly. 'It was *your* dream, Larry. I wish it was mine, too. I really do. But it's not.'

Larry reels from another unanticipated uppercut. He's still

determined to stand, though. 'And what's yuhr dream, Angel? Hey?'

'Nothing more than what I've just tried to explain to you. No one, if that's what you're really asking.'

'And that's what yuh want?'

'I don't know. Really ... Sometimes, I'm convinced I do. Other times, I hate the thought of it. I tried to want your dream, too. I really did. But I couldn't. All I can say is that what I'm doing is necessary for me. For now. For today.'

Okay, come back fighting, Larry. 'But I love yuh. We love each other. Doesn't that matter at all to yuh? Doesn't it?'

'Of course it does! But the other thing's just as important. More important, even. Maybe.'

That's it. Larry's on the ropes now. 'I really can't figure out what yuh're saying. I really can't.'

'I *know* you can't. We're on different wavelengths. You don't understand because *I* don't really understand, either.' Before she can think about it, Angel finds herself cradling him. Propped up inside her arms, Larry responds, hoping that the connection between their bodies will end all argument. But it's only seconds before Angel breaks away.

'I thought that being a model was going to be something fine and good. I tried to tell myself that I wasn't setting myself up to be just another lump of meat for men to slobber over and try to fuck!'

She sees him flinch at her use of the word. It makes her feel very hard. 'Every man I've ever known has wanted to fuck me, but I pretended that that wasn't it at all. Even when some of them *did* fuck me —' Angel blushes, conscious of her slip. She knows she's just torturing him now. She almost giggles. 'Oops! The truth will out ...' She shrugs. 'Just one of the several lies I've told you, Larry ... Except, it wasn't totally a lie. A part of me honestly *did* believe I was still a virgin when I was hanging out with you. Can *you* believe that too, Larry?'

Larry shakes his head trying to take in her words within all the whooshing going on inside his head. 'Believe what?'

'That I'm still a virgin for you, even if I've been fucked by different men already.'

Angel takes Larry's silence to mean that he doesn't believe her. Or that he can't. Or won't. Not wishing to, she begins to cry. Without thinking about it, Larry moves to calm her, but she won't have it. 'We're still those kids,' Angel wails. 'I had a little girl crush on you. Then you left. Years went by. We became what's laughingly called adults, separated by thousands of miles and a lifetime of different experiences. And then we met up again. But we met up as if we were still those little kids. Except we've got grown-up bodies now. Bodies that want what they want and if they get it are gonna destroy those little kids forever and ever. I can't let that happen. I won't let those little kids disappear.'

'So yuh'd rather tear those two kids apart from each other? How's that gonna keep them from disappearing, hey? Isn't it gonna do the opposite and make sure that they do?'

Angel's hand finds his and clings to it. 'Oh ... Who knows? Maybe what you say is true for you. But ... But for me ... I can't ... I've got to find out who this grown-up me is. And I can't do it if you're here beside me. As much as I'd love you to. Don't you see? Being together, those two little kids stop us both from growing up because they're too tempting. I can't back out of doing what's right, Larry. You know I can't. And you can't, either. It's too precious. For both of us.'

Larry's hand goes slack and loosens itself from her grip. 'Good luck, then,' he hisses, unable to listen to anything else she might have left to say.

She starts to tell him something, but Larry doesn't hear her. He's already at the door, already too far out of reach for her to stop him from running away.

* * * * *

Larry runs because it's the the only thing he can think of doing. Luckily, New York's a good place for running. Strangers swerve out of his way and look daggers or swear as he rushes past them. Images and sounds beset him, too quick to analyse, too slow to flit by as a blur. Tearful, bitter and positively lost now, however hard he tries, Larry keeps returning to the memory of the elevator operator from Angel's apartment block vacantly droning on and on about the baseball season. Somewhere in his confusion, the man's voice becomes Angel's. 'I don't love you, Larry,' it jeers. And although she's never spoken them, those have become her final words to him.

* * * * *

Something's changed. Larry shouldn't have heard it, but he has. The curiosity it creates forces him to stop.

Music.

It's only a street violinist camped out at the entrance to an alley directly across from the main doors to a Broadway theatre. The show's over, the customers are escaping, and he's trying to slow them down with his desolate tune, make them feel guilty for receiving something for nothing until the guilt guides hands to pockets and coin atonements are thrown into the open case at his feet. The melody slithers so that it reaches Larry, entices his body and mind to open up and take notice, to enter into it. *Surely, this man, too, must have known love, suffered rejection and despair,* Larry tells himself. *And here he is now, reshaping those experiences into music he offers to passing strangers.*

Not long later, two cops march over and order the violinist to move on. He stops playing in mid-note, as though the police had interrupted nothing. As though the moment he'd stopped at had been his chosen moment. More exactly, the best possible moment. The musician's eyes flicker and blink, awakening. He replaces his instrument into its case, and begins to fade away into the night.

Like some pilgrim approaching a holy shrine, Larry heads over to where the violinist had been standing. He's overcome by sensations that, unprompted, bring on a contemplative serenity. From deep within himself, Larry sees the light: Once Love has been offered, its unalloyed beauty inhabits the world ready to be accepted, though who accepts it is something left for the fates to determine.

His feet kick at some unknown object on the ground. Curious, bending down, he feels the edge of a coin. There are more like it all around. Offerings made that have been left behind thanks to the violinist's readiness to appease the cops. Or, maybe, he just wasn't all that bothered. He sure looked like he could use the money, though. Larry picks up as many quarters and dimes as he can find and then runs over to the side alley he recollects seeing the man make his way towards. He searches frantically, his breath in spasms. On the point of despair, he locates him, taking his time, case tucked under his arm, whistling to himself.

'Hey, Mister!' Larry shouts.

The violinist pauses and stops his whistling. Then he begins to walk faster.

'Mister! Hey, wait! Yuh left some of yuhr money behind when yuh finished playing!'

That brings the man to a halt. He's still cautious, but he's now ready to bet that it isn't a mugger getting ready to pounce on him. He waits for Larry to reach him.

'Here it is. Here's yuhr money!'

'Thanks, kid.'

'Thank *yuh.*'

The violinist gives him an odd look. 'What for?'

'For the music. For the way yuh played.'

The violinist shakes his head, amused. 'It plays itself, kid,' he says. 'It plays itself.' Then, wasting no more time, he stuffs the coins into a pocket and limps away.

Following his example, Larry turns to face the neon-lit street and drags himself back to the hostel.

* * * * *

They leave in silence. So long, New York.

Larry is stretched out across the back seat of The Flacon, worn-out after a night's worth of soul-searching, yet still far too aware of the calamitous change in his life to allow himself any sleep. The peace he'd felt from what the violinist had pointed to has lingered, but it has changed subtly from some solid block that he can focus on to a thin veil of ether which is everywhere in his thoughts yet too intangible to grab hold of. It's Angel who's the centre of his attention now. He recreates again and again how she'd looked, what she'd said, the way she'd moved during their last time together in some hope of exorcising her from his thoughts and life. Instead, the incantations succeed in making her more and more present. And, with each new appearance, his sense of loss grows in proportion. He's certain they'll never see each other again. Their roads have split irrevocably; he can't envisage any possible junctures ahead. Even if she ran back to him, he tells himself, even if she begged him to give her another chance, he won't give way. His pride's dictated that he can't. She pretended to love him. He refuses to forgive her for that. He shrugs. *You loved and lost. You'll love again.* Brave words to repeat to yourself each time you wake up knowing you're alone. Not that he believes them entirely. But they'll help. They'll keep him sane tomorrow. As for today, at least they're succeeding in restraining the more harrowing fantasies he's invoked to a stalemate.

Moe's driving. It's still early morning and they've contrived to get out of mid-town Manhattan with as few hassles as possible. No one's argued or agreed with any of the route options he's taken. What mistakes he's made have been met only with loud curses from him and silence from his two passengers. Somehow, he realises, curses or silence in response to his turning up or down the wrong street don't seem to matter much right now. Moe has things on his mind as well. Angel's shocked him. He's hated her since last night, because she's hurt his friend so deeply. He isn't interested in finding out the causes or reasons. He doesn't want to accept what's happened. Plus, he's really, really angry. He'd planned to pass the ride back reminiscing over the week's events, laughing and blowing them up into legendary proportions. Angel's destroyed all that. Now the trip to New York will forever be looked back on as the time Larry and Angel broke up. And that's not fair. Because it's been a lot more than that. It's been a great time for the three of them. Except for last night. A chuckle, then. A silent, uproarious, uncontrollable, hysterical cackle for all the memories.

Curly Joe's mind is playing around with memories as well. Somewhere in them is his sadness for Larry. And for Angel, too, when it comes to it. But dominating his musings are sights seen and sounds heard in cafés and down in Washington Square, and everywhere he'd been where others his age had congregated. Mostly, he recalls their afternoon in the *Cheetah Club* when a couple of unknown bands played for free and a strange Indian guru talked of inner peace and enlightenment. There hadn't been many people around, so the guru didn't hesitate to pass away a half-hour or so with Curly Joe.

'*All Power to the Imagination,*' he'd said. 'That is what we have opened our doors to, is it not? A gift, no mistake. But, as with most gifts, it manifests a dual nature. What emerges from the imagination is always unpredictable. It can call forth all manner of new questions. But it can also fill up our thoughts with an endless number of false answers. The generation before yours, given what they have lived through and endured, fears Imagination. A pity, yet it would be wrong to blame them. But this, The Sixties Generation, of which you are a part, flocks toward the Imagination. Ah! But are you braced for it? Have you the necessary strength — and the humor — to meet it? Grow from it? The Imagination can turn anything down to earth into something all to mystical. And it can make any mystical-sounding, pretty words sound sensible, down to earth. The Truth? Choose to run with Imagination, you might be granted great visions. But also be prepared to make a complete idiot of yourself every once in a while.' They'd both laughed at that. And Curly Joe had felt at ease enough to ask for an example of the guru's idiocy. The guru swept his hands over his impeccably ironed, loose-fitting white robe. "Are these clothes I feel duty bound to wear, even though I was born in Brooklyn, not gaudily comical examples? There will be many more, no doubt. For who among us who seeks to embody the Spirit of the Age will not, one day, awaken and wince in red-faced remembrance of deeds committed, words spoken, clothes worn or objects purchased because of the allegiance given to this era?'

Curly Joe's more awake than he's ever been. Without thinking about it, he's agreed to join the ever-swelling ranks of those in tune with the times. If humiliation at some point in the future is the required price, then bring it on!

Moe grunts. Real loud. He's vainly hoping that with his outburst he can crush the silence. 'Well, so long, New York,' he says, stoking the fire. 'It's been *some* week. Won't forget it for a long ol' time.'

From the back of the car comes a noise vaguely similar in sound to a 'yuh'. It's taken Larry close to insurmountable pain to voice it.

'yup,' echoes Curly Joe sweeping his eyes over the patches of country that pass by his window.

The city skyline fades into the background and they are on the super-highway that will take them almost directly back to Montréal and ordinary life.

Defeated, Moe buckles down and gets back into the driving.

14. WORKING THINGS OUT IN MONTRÉAL

Lamentably, being set free from McGill also means finding some sort of summertime paid work. Not that Larry, Moe and Curly Joe are trying that hard. It had been so much easier during the previous, near-miraculous *Expo '67* summer when there were so many different jobs to choose from that it was "pick whatever you like" all the way. Not any more. Now, it's like 'Hey! Here's what's left over that nobody else wants. Take it or leave it.' Which adds up to being the rawest of raw deals.

Moe's university life is being supported by government loans. He considers these to be grants. Come the revolution, they will be.

Larry and Curly Joe, however, got dealt a rotten hand. The Quebec government has ruled that *if*

a) you're under 25,

b) you're living in your parents' home,

c) you've been living on your own for less than three years,

d) you aren't disabled,

and e) your parents' income supersedes the government's cut-off line,

then it's tough break, pal. Pay up Annual Fees in full and in advance, thank you very much.

Summertime jobs help to offset the tuition costs that are going to come out of their parents' pockets. In the event, Larry and Curly Joe's parents put a lot of value on their sons' attaining a university degree and are more than willing to splash the cash on their behalf. The problem isn't with them. It's that accepting parental help compromises that independence Larry and Curly Joe have been so busily attesting they've achieved. Which is downright humiliating. Finding work partially appeases their wounded pride. Luckily, resolutely *intending* to get a summer job achieves the same. Which is a welcome relief.

So far though, every attempt at holding down any sort of paid work hasn't lasted beyond a few days at most.

During the back end of May, Curly Joe tries his hand at a heavy labour job in which he's hired to carry crates of *Orange Crush* bottles onto waiting trucks for eight hours at a go. His arms give out on him just before lunch on the second morning, causing him to drop a crate and thereby shatter all the glass bottles stacked inside. Even worse, the liquid orange fizz that oozes everywhere along the pathway rapidly congeals into this glue-like sludge that sticks to the soles of everybody's shoes and results in slowing down the factory scheme of things. Not only is Curly Joe given the shove, full damage costs are taken out of his one-and-only pay cheque leaving him with a grand total of 89¢.

At about the same time, Larry contrives to infiltrate a road construction gang somewhere in the north end of Montréal. He cracks on for four days drilling holes into sidewalks and streets before having to recuperate for a week from the backache and tinnitus his efforts precipitate. At least he comes out of the experience with more remuneration than Curly Joe.

It's up to Moe to come up with the topper.

* * * * *

One morning, Moe comes across an ad in the *Montréal Gazette* that offers a minimum pay of $250.00 per week in an "educational sales" job. In summertime 1968, $250.00 a week is simply outtasite, man! Even that, however, pales into insignificance when Moe reads a little further. Unless his eyes are going whacko on him, the ad clearly states that hard-working, dedicated and intelligent *students* are encouraged to apply.

Encouragement duly noted, Moe rings up the number in no time flat, certain that all the positions must have already been taken. Instead, a friendly female voice informs him that he is one lucky boy. Would he like her to slot him in for a private interview later today? Would he? Boy! Yes, Moe most definitely would!

Arriving at the right place at the right time, Moe is handed a brief — *very* brief — Application Form to fill in as a warm-up. Desultory questionnaire completed, he is invited to step through the closed door up ahead and to his right. When he does, Moe is wrong-footed to find that there are nearly twenty other candidates in that very same room. And ... All of them are going to be interviewed simultaneously by the same interviewer.

Grabbing everyone's attention before they pick up the smell of rats, the buoyant host is pleased as punch to inform them that, by a once in a lifetime turn of events, the analysis of results obtained from their completed forms has indicated that all of the present applicants turn out to be ideal candidates and should consider themselves hired as of now. And not only that! Their new boss is on his way to meet and greet them!

The main man in question turns out to be some pipsqueak hustler with thick, L-shaped bad-ass sideburns who swaggers into the room, picks out one of the applicants and hands him $250.00 in bills. 'Working for us means that you'll be earning that kind of moolah *this* easily,' he asserts, giving everyone the glad eye. Then he snatches back the cash. Scam completed, Big Boss Man scores big time in implanting dreams of wealth into all the bobbing heads that stare back at him in awed silence. Out-mastering Svengali, he soon has the vast majority of those present salivating to affix their names to the list of people who have agreed to work for him on a "full-commission basis" rather than on a measly, insignificant $250.00 a week "straight salary" that is a blatant insult to their abilities and intelligence.

But what about those three dumb-nuts who've stubbornly opted to stick to a straight salary in spite of his persuasive arguments? Well ... it's all too evident that their unscrupulous attempts to hide their woefully impaired rational wherewithal have failed miserably. Now that they've been exposed, they've been invited to attend a further, more detailed, interview. Expected outcome? The Top Brass is saddened to report that, with sincere regret, those deadbeats are about to be given the old heave-ho.

As to those who've signed on, it's only once their expectations are raised to fever pitch and they are practically drooling at the thought of the vast wealth they'll accumulate in no time flat, that the "educational aids" they are about to spring on an as yet unsuspecting public are brought to light. 'Are you guys ready for this? How about ... Ten volume sets of *Grassroots Encyclopaedia,* created especially to suit the interests and IQ of every ordinary working man and woman in the country! They're sure to sell like hot cakes!' However ... Before this year's millionaires can start shovelling in the shekels, they'll each have to undergo a specially-designed, rigorous training programme provided exclusively for them by a hand-picked sales-training crew. And all for the specially-reduced and laughable sum of $25.00 total (sales tax included).

Wholly taken in like all the others, marvelling at how little it's going to cost for these hot-shot experts to take the wraps off their arcane success guaranteed secrets, Moe doesn't hesitate to write out his cheque. Tomorrow, he'll begin his three-day course on the art of double-dealing, back-stabbing and ruthless advantage taking of any possible suckers who might let one of these soon-to-be-outright-bastards into their homes and allow themselves to be bamboozled into buying a ten volume set of overpriced, fifth-rate information.

'And never, ever forget! Always knock on doors *certain* that you'll make a sale. *Maybes* or *perhapses* are for losers! High sales salesmen always think positively, have a couple of working ball-points in their top pocket, and carry a stack of sales contracts wherever they might be!'

The two-hours-per-day of training completed, Moe is primed and ready to go. If ever an embodiment of the dictum "never give a sucker an even break" walked the earth, he is it. Even Larry and Curly Joe, who've been practiced upon past the point of no return, are forced to concur that Moe has morphed into a salesman to be reckoned with. Too bad he's also turned into a grade-A shithead along the way.

Before he knows it, the first money-making evening descends. Moe's Section Leader picks him up to take him to Moe's very own private turf. On the way over, they try out the rehearsed patter one last time. Greasing the wheels of greed,

The Leader blows up Moe's head even higher with tales of the big bucks Moe will earn tonight and all the phenomenal things that'll follow. Women. Sports cars. Expensive suits. Women. $100 tips. More women. Moe, naturally, laps it all up, loving every second of the pipe dreams on offer. Then, at last, he's dropped off at what Moe considers to be a rather ill-lit — seamy, even — neighbourhood somewhere in a Montréal he's never before set foot in. So be it. It will be a worthy challenge.

Moe waves to his Leader who is already driving off. He takes a deep breath and sprints over to the nearest front door, arranges his information pack, crooks it under his left armpit in exactly the way he's been practising, runs over the first few lines of his speech, brushes back his hair, takes another deep breath, waits, indulges in one more deep breath to brace himself, waits again, allows a final, this-is-definitely-it deep breath, and knocks in a firm and confident way.

Seconds later, the door opens and a gruff-looking face belonging to an even gruffer-looking man clad in undershirt and baggy trousers being held up below his abundant stomach by frayed braces appears. He's showing no signs of wanting to hide his irritation at the disturbance Moe has inflicted upon his life.

'*Oui? Qu'est-ce-que tu veux, Chalice?*'

Uh-oh. *French!* Panic, terror, and the aroma of his customer's recently ingested supper and beer being released into his face stop Moe dead in his tracks. How is he going to appease this guy with a bunch of glossy brochures for an *English Language* encyclopaedia? The ace team hadn't prepared him for this.

'Uhm ... Good evening, sir. I'm representing a new company dedicated to improving the education of all citizens of this great, growing country of ours —'

'*Quoi? Je'n comprends pas. Pas d'Anglais ici. J'suis separatiste, moi.*'

In double quick time, a medium-sized, utterly vicious-looking mongrel appears between the man's legs. It gnarls a guttural kind of gnarl that gives notice of its FLQ sympathies.

And *that* is more than enough for Moe's week-long flight of fancy to evaporate on him posthaste. Gabbling '*Pardon. Au revoir*', he hotfoots it to the nearest bus stop and somehow navigates his way home.

Looking back on the days of his life and the twenty-five smackeroos he's wasted, Moe can't be bothered to return the Sales Folder the shyster company had loaned him. Let them come and try to get it off him. He bares his teeth in imitation of that mongrel. As far as Moe's concerned, several new bastards have just joined his list of people to be placed up against the wall come the revolution.

* * * * *

More days pass by and their job situation fails to improve. Curly Joe is the first to give in to the inevitable and hires himself out as a dishwasher to the first restaurant that will take him on.

Larry grudgingly follows suit.

Moe holds out for a while longer; but then, arguing that at least they'll all be working together, he, too, throws in the towel and picks up the dish-rag.

* * * * *

The couple of dawdling weeks before spring officially comes to an end make their presence felt with dull, humid blasts of heat that enfold Montréal island. Point impossible to miss, Montréalers are left with no doubt: the approaching summer is sure to be as a harsh a dictator as winter ever was.

On the campus lawns of McGill, the growing numbers of street people bask in the sun, soak dirty city feet in the pond that surrounds the statue of The Three Bares, or prance about showing off their tie-dyed, crazy-colour jeans and T-shirts which, in 1968, are still an antagonising novelty for the ever-Silent Majority. Guitars are strumming, voices chant, children laugh. Anarchic as the space may be, its abiding ethos embraces harmony and tolerance. Small wonder then that the three of them escape here as often as they can during their non-working hours. Alone or together, they seek it out to lie upon its cooling grass, close their eyes, and allow their thoughts to carry themselves away wherever they will.

Curly Joe has been at the dishwashing game for nearly two weeks now and it's become something way too awful to even think about. Except, a lot of the time he can't stop doing just that. Even when he turns his attention to what he and Suzie Q are going to do on their next date, the possibilities keep returning him to the behind-the-scenes kitchen world he inhabits and whose unappetising secrets he now knows much too well.

Mainly, what he focuses on are the people he has to share kitchen space with when Larry and Moe are on different shifts. There are two dullards in particular who drive him up the wall. They're both somewhere in their forties, and look upon life as something you have to put up with. To see things through, they've allowed themselves a couple of highly specific kicks.

The first, not unusually, is alcohol. Every half hour it seems, one of them pulls out a hip-flask, knocks back a shot of rotgut whiskey and then passes it over to his pal so that he can do the same. After that, they'll both throw Curly Joe a nod and a wink before turning their attention once more to whatever needs cleaning.

Their second, far more original, source of lacklustre gratification is derived from what they proudly brag is their complete collection of *Playboy Playmates of the Month* — going all the way back to the Marilyn Monroe "all I had on was the radio" nude right up to the current issue's wind-up toy — that they keep bundled together in some ratty-looking briefcase they take everywhere with them. What the story is as to how they came to co-own this most prized of possessions is something that Curly Joe hasn't dared ask. All he knows is that the pin-ups make the duo inseparable and seem to be the sole topic of the opinionated verbal exchanges between them. Adversely for whoever else might be around, the daily, ritualised slanging matches that follow are far from private.

'April 64!' one of them is likely to come out with for no apparent reason other than to wind up his pal. 'Now there's a beautiful pair a' knockers for ya!'

'Yeah,' the other answers, falling into the groove every single time. 'She's real fine, but if ya want one of the best, take a gander at September 66.'

'Aw, she's awright,' the first retorts, 'but the *finest's* gotta be August 65. No bull.'

'Yer crazy!' the other screams, 'It's September 66 with them big brown nips of hers! Nobody comes close to them!'

'Ya turd! Whadda *you* know? Any idiot would see August 65's are tops!'

That sets them off and running. A shouting match comprised solely of the words "September 66" and "August 65" begins its incessant repetition. And, all the while, their bodies, like super-automatons, continue to wash industriously while the infinite supply of dirtied dishes keeps coming through from the hole in the wall in front of them.

In due course, as a steadily more regular last resort, one of them flicks his neck in Curly Joe's direction, turns to his partner and says: 'Hey! Let's ask *this* guy what he thinks.' So they scamper over to their bundle, select the fold-outs in question, and present them to Curly Joe, breathlessly awaiting judgement.

It has taken Curly Joe a while to catch on. The first few times, he'd been stupid enough to vote in favour of one of their choices. Such an act only ended up escalating their argument as well as sucking him even further into their inane rants.

Lately, however, Curly Joe's come up with a far better response. 'you're both way off,' he tells them now. 'it's gotta be january 59, for sure.'

The designated date, or any other he thinks of on the spur of the moment, has the effect of sending them scuttling back to their briefcase and feverishly flipping through the treasure trove in search of the desired centerfold, their thoughts now uncertain as to whether to consider Curly Joe a fool or an indubitable Master in the field of Playmate Picking. It's mind-numbing, but the main thing is that this ploy secures their silence for a few blessed minutes.

All of which has led Curly Joe to begin to ponder how much longer he can keep going before he succumbs to some equally pitiful ritual that will take over his life. Lying on the cool lawns of McGill, he concludes that today's the day: it's high time he put an end to his dishwashing career.

Bowled over by Curly Joe's resolve, Larry and Moe agree to strike out as well.

To hell with stupid jobs! To hell with all the revolting people they have to square off against! To hell with left-over food, and greasy plates and lipstick-stained cups and glasses! There's gotta be something else out there that's more suited to their capabilities.

Yeah ... But what?

* * * * *

A couple of afternoons later, in a blinding flurry of brilliance, Larry and Curly Joe cook up a real blast of a fall-back plan: they're going to do a Lenny Bruce. Inspired by the infamous Father Flotsky, they will set up a worthy cause — The Charitable Fund for Needy Young People — solicit the wealthier areas of Montréal for donations, and reap the profits.

As to the ethics of it all? Here's their defence: Nothing to worry about! See, legitimate charities, as everyone knows, by the time they've paid out for administrative costs, salaries, and advertising wind up with only about 20% of what they took in to spend on their chosen project. Whereas, *their* charity will be magnanimous and give away 40% of the money they'll rake in to needy families in the East End by passing out food, clothes and amusement vouchers to whoever's around who looks like they could use them. Admirably generous or what? Theirs will be a revolutionary charity, just like *The Diggers* and *The Black Panthers*! Feeling supremely pleased with themselves, they pass away a whole afternoon kicking around the various ramifications and ploys of such things, until they're one hundred per cent convinced they've knocked up an out-and-out foolproof plan.

Disastrously however, Curly Joe then goes and does something really dumb by mentioning their easy-money plot to Suzie Q who promptly turns all hysterical, babbling out less-than-rapturous visions of the two of them being carted off to prison, their names in headlines.

Just like what happened to Lenny, they both rush to remember.

Now plagued with doubt, but still wanting to believe that they haven't wasted their time, they seek out Moe's advice. Fatally, Moe's the one who hammers the final nail into their scheme's coffin. He informs them that they'll need to put forward a formal proposal in order to be granted a certified Provincial Permit. Which will take time and cost them a wad of cash they don't have on hand. Added to which, it's never going to be approved. He should know, Moe sniffs in conclusion, he'd looked into the matter already. Ages ago.

Emmis, as Lenny would say.

* * * * *

Still ... The enterprising audacity of the idea fills them with a newfound readiness to revolutionise their thinking.

That being so, a few days later Curly Joe finds himself earning $3.00 an hour tutoring high school students on subjects he's actually failed in. And all because he's used the magic words "McGill Engineering Student" on each ad he'd tacked up on the Notice Boards of half a dozen nearby *Steinberg's* supermarkets. For once, he tells himself, he's getting something worthwhile out of McGill.

At about the same time, thanks to his having slept in late one morning, Larry totters outdoors to breathe in the air and ingratiates himself with the family gardener by offering him a cup of coffee. Next thing he knows, he's mowing lawns and pruning hedges as the man's assistant, much to his physical and financial satisfaction.

As for Moe, he thinks of all the bureaucracy stifling people's desire to be educated and vows that the most radical thing he can do to bring this state of affairs down as fast as possible is to go on strike for the holidays.

* * * * *

Job concerns set aside, the three of them are free to reclaim the beautiful absurdity of living for the hell of it.

The soundtrack's pretty good, too. *Wheels of Fire. The Notorious Byrd Brothers. The Resurrection of Pigboy Crabshaw. We're Only In It For The Money. Music From Big Pink* (Curly Joe always chokes up when *Lonesome Suzie* comes on). Every one a winner.

The picture that most clearly evokes this point in their lives captures them, ping pong rackets in hand, showering more and more scurrilous, expertly honed, totally harmless abuse upon each other from opposite ends of Larry's beat-up table while the record player — turned to automatic — repeats the B side of *Bookends* over and over and over again. *Mrs. Robinson* is their theme song for the summer. Multiple nights are passed riding in The Flacon down Montréal streets shouting along to its words and tune. Once, they even cross the U.S. Border on the northwest tip of Vermont and back just to try out a new *Howard Johnson*'s Ice Cream flavour.

Most times, though, like rebel angels, they simply cruise a few miles, park in a country lane and take a close look at nothing in particular while the radio blasts out just released anthems or keeps them up-to-date with the latest news.

And sometimes (nearly *all* the time it seems to Larry and Curly Joe), Moe guns the motor, wild and reckless, possessed by the ghost of James Dean who's somehow acquired the truculent Bronx voice of a character Moe's invented this Summer. Catching sight of an unsuspecting stranger, Moe hits the brake bringing The Flacon to a standstill, leans out the open window as if to ask directions, then yells out: 'Let's see that ol' roll a' tarpaper there, *Jawnny*!' And with that, foot down flat onto the accelerator, he drives off again, delirious and diabolical, in search of new victims.

That always gets them laughing the laughter of the demented.

Starry, standout days.

With no hint of what's just around the corner.

15. THE VIRGIN AND THE GYPSY

The Gypsy's real name is Anne. But for them to ever think of her as anything but The Gypsy would be absurd. A true child of her age, The Gypsy, as her sobriquet suggests, is a wanderer. The territory she travels through however is purely ethereal, the more otherworldly the better. Philosophy's her game; the more Eastern the better. George, of course, is her favourite *Beatle.* She doesn't mind Bill Wyman either; it's the way he stays so still throughout that *Rolling Stones* whirlwind.

Her body, which she's quick to admit can provide appreciable pleasures, is nonetheless something of a nuisance, plaguing her with its demands and weaknesses. She'll have no truck with any all-consuming fanfare for the flesh. For one thing, The Gypsy is diabetic. Every day, three times a day, she has to lock herself away somewhere or other, pull out the little red plastic case that holds her syringes, and fill up her body with the ration of insulin that will maintain a steady blood sugar level. And even if The Gypsy is committed to ensuring that she keeps her body healthy, regulates its weight, enhances its appearance and, on occasion, succumbs to its delights (within the limits traditionally expected of a single woman), it still seems to her as if once, long ago, this still alien entity had somehow attached itself to her, and now, in spite of their incompatibility, repulses any command to let go. If anything, her body reminds The Gypsy of her mother's neurotic poodle.

* * * * *

The first time that Larry and Moe meet The Gypsy, they're inside a movie theatre.

She floats in all on her own, wild, androgynous hipster clothes turning heads and raising eyebrows. And then, honing in on the visually ideal place to land, she plunks herself down on the seat right next to Moe. Less than a minute later, she remembers. She taps the little red plastic case hidden in the invisible pocket lining of her homemade boho pantaloons to make sure it's still there. A quick wrist-flick and her watch confirms that there's enough time before the lights go down. Up on her feet, The Gypsy turns to Moe, catches his wary eye and asks — more like *tells* — him to watch her coat and purse for her.

Before he has a chance to say anything, she's already on her way to the Ladies. Moe can't believe what this *complete stranger* has just done. He passes Larry a *what the fuck?* Larry shrugs back at him. These days, thanks to their New York City adventure, Larry's convinced himself that he's an existentialist. So everything is meaningless as far as he's concerned.

When The Gypsy eventually returns, she camps herself back down in her seat and throws Moe a smile. 'Thanks,' she says.

'No problem. But ... Weren't ya the least bit worried that I might steal some cash out of your purse?'

'No, of course not.' The look she gives him makes it plain that she thinks Moe's question is pure fiddle-faddle to be dispensed with as quickly as the syringe she's just used.

'But I could've easily just got up and walked out of the theater —'

'No you wouldn't.'

'What'cha mean, "no ya wouldn't?"'

'I trust you,' The Gypsy says in her very best matter-of-fact voice.

Larry's zoning in on every word of this exchange. Still silent, still cool, but becoming openly intrigued, he surmises that her argument could have something of a Heideggerian turn to it.

Back to Moe, who blusters on. 'But ya never even met me before! Ya don't even know who I am —'

The Gypsy stops him, already bored with the topic. 'Look, let's cut to the chase. Did you take anything?'

'No! Of course not!'

'Well then, you see? I was right. You could be trusted.'

That shuts Moe up. Larry offers The Gypsy a smile that he hopes she'll read as a thumbs up from one *savant* to another. Seconds later, the room starts to go dark and the fitful audience wheezing and coughing dies down, causing any further interrogation to cease for the time being.

The movie's a total blur to Moe. His mind keeps going over all that's just been said and done. Why's he so zoned out over a complete stranger? Yeah, but a complete stranger who *trusted* him. Just to give Moe something else to play mind games with, The Gypsy manages to do the unbelievable yet again. From what little Moe can recall, reviewers have praised the film as a five star exercise in terror. (In case any of you Tripsters are curious, it's Polanski's *Repulsion*). That it is exactly that can be judged by the hear-a-pin-drop silence in the hall.

Except for The Gypsy's whispered voice. 'Can I hold on to you? I'm super-duper frightened!'

As before, she doesn't bother to wait for Moe's reply. Turning to grab hold of his arm, one of her breasts inadvertently snuggles itself against his shoulder. The impact has its unsurprising effect. Much to his chagrin, Moe's grown an erection that will not deflate on him. And the only thing to do is to sit stock still with it because if he starts to shuffle in his seat, she's bound to notice what's — literally — up with him and then recoil at this weirdo pervert right up close to her. Nothing to do but hope for the best. One good thing: she's so engrossed by what's happening on screen that she's taking no notice of anything else. *Relax. Stay cool. And, come clean now, how long's it been since you've been this close to a woman, Jim?*

During one of the more brightly-lit moments of the movie, Moe offers Larry another of his *can ya believe this?* looks. But Larry's too busy dropping his jaw in reaction to the unnerving scenes he's taking in. Leaving him to it, Moe goes back to asking himself if he's just died and gone to the weirdest of heavens. Not that he's complaining.

Sadly, the film has reached its end. While the credits roll, people breathe loudly in relief, chatter, get up from their seats to leave. The Gypsy takes her hand away. Back to reality. Still, at least she's staying put. *And* just in time, Moe's stiffie has unstiffed.

'Good flick, wasn't it?' Moe says. Not that he's got the first hint as to what it was all about. But he's still onto a good bet that his question is a safe conversation starter.

'It was all right. But her madness was too rational. The Director thought things out too logically. He should have let himself go a bit more insane.'

Yeah, whatever that means, Moe thinks. Still ... Seeing as she's open to chatting, he presses on. 'Listen, getting back to what ya were saying earlier: do ya *always* trust strangers with your things like that? I mean, just on account of some belief on your part telling ya they can be trusted?'

'Yes,' The Gypsy shakes her head. What does she have to do to make it clear that she's really, really bored with the topic by now?

'All of the time. And you're never wrong.'

'I didn't say that.'

'Oh?' Moe perks up. 'Ya mean sometimes people steal your things?'

'Yes. Usually, just money though.'

Just money? Kee-rist! Is she a millionairess to boot? 'And ya stick to it, anyway?'

'Stick to what?'

'I dunno. What ya said. Trust people. Strangers.'

'Sure. Of course. Don't you?'

'But don'tcha gotta know someone before —'

'Why?'

'Well, if ya don't *know* them, how can ya trust them?'

The Gypsy shakes her head in consternation. 'No. You've got it the wrong way around: if you don't trust them, how can you know them? I trusted you. Now I know who you are.'

'But ... Ya don't know me from Adam!'

'Yes I do. You're the guy who watched over my things.'

'Yeah, okay. But I could have stolen your money. We both know I didn't, but I *could have*. Some people will.'

'Of course! It's your choice. I have the choice to trust you or not to trust you. You have a choice to accept or reject that trust. It's all about choice.'

Moe turns to Larry for some backup, but Larry's just sitting there nodding like he agrees with everything this madwoman's saying.

'But then sometimes ya come out of it with no money.'

'Well? So what? I chose. I trusted. I learned. When you get right down to it, the money's inconsequential.'

'But ... But what *about* your money?'

'What about it?'

'Ya said that some people *steal* it! Doesn't that bother you?'

'Yes, sure it does. But only because I feel so sad for them. They plainly think that paper's worth more than trust. If it means that much to them, they're welcome to it. Paper's always replaceable. Trust isn't. You only get one chance at it.' The Gypsy looks into Moe's eyes. She should have gotten up and walked away by now. Ended this ridiculous debate. Although ... There's something about him. Something she's feeling but remains unable to identify. Fine then ... 'Don't you see?' she offers, absorbed by her unfamiliar reaction. 'It's not the *result* of the act that matters. It's the act itself. I choose. I choose rightly or wrongly. It makes no difference. Either way, I become more aware of myself. Of others. The person I trust has a choice as well. He can guard or steal. He chooses. Whatever his choice, he learns more about himself. And about me. The money's secondary. It just makes the choice more materialistically real.' The Gypsy smiles to prove she's human. 'Apart from that, it's not like there's ever wads of it in my purse.'

Ah. Maybe Moe's caught her drift at last. 'So money doesn't mean anything to ya, huh?'

The Gypsy hoots. Wrong again. 'Don't be silly! Of course it means something. I just want to put it at its proper level of importance. It allows me to buy things. Food. Clothes. Movie tickets. Okay, that's fine. I enjoy all those things it can offer. But it's second in line to what really matters to me. Which isn't to say it's unnecessary. It's just not as important as it's made out to be, as far as I'm concerned.'

' ... '

'What's wrong? Don't you get it?'

'I ... I'm not sure ... It sounds nice, but ...'

'But *what*?' Before Moe can come up with an answer, The Gypsy notices the time and reports that she's sorry but she's going to have to leave them now. A moment of hesitation. A choice. 'Still ... Maybe we can catch up with each other another day?' Once again not bothering to wait for Moe's reply, she writes her phone number down on the back of an old prescription sheet she's found in her purse and passes it to him. 'It's your choice whether to call or stand me up,' she says. 'Whichever's fine by me. But, I'm hoping that you'll get back in touch. Bye for now!'

A couple of minutes later, when he and Larry are about to leave as well, Moe's a changed man. 'This is it,' he repeats to himself and to Larry all night long. 'This is it. At last. This is it.'

* * * * *

For Moe, The Gypsy will always be his first conscious experience of Magic. And, caught up in its throes big time, Moe feels just like Billy Batson. He's yelled 'SHAZAM!' and, in so doing, has turned himself into *Captain Marvel*. Infused with the novelty of this super-power, Moe's able to act in ways that once seemed impossibly absurd, but are now totally easy-peasy.

Like, for instance, before he's even bothered to think twice about it, he's gone and asked if there's any work available at his favourite music emporium. Minutes later, he's offered the sales and stacking job of his dreams. Implausible as it may seem, he's actually being *paid* to listen to all the records he's always wanted to hear. *Cosmic!*

The Gypsy has something to say about that during their third date, taking a break from some serious, but still pretty innocent, smooching. 'See? Everything that teaches you something, it's like a finger pointing at the Moon. The finger shows you where to look but it, itself, isn't what you should be passing away your life staring at. The problem is that that's *exactly* what most of us do. We get caught up in studying our own and other people's fingers — we compare their shapes, the lengths of their nails, their prints, their lines — and what we forget is their real purpose. Which is to point us to the Moon.

'The thing is, there's so many sorts of pointing fingers. Like religion, academics, philosophy, psychology, spirituality, sex, love, drugs and every buzz and blast imaginable. Even Good Ol' Rock 'n' Roll! All of them can be great fingers. Nothing wrong with that. But that's all they are. Just fingers. Except ... Any one of them can give us such a high that we start believing that this or that particular finger *is* the Moon ... Until it starts to bore us, like all fingers will after a while. And so we move on to another finger. And then another. And another.

'And, all the while, right in line with whatever finger we've trapped ourselves in, is that same Ol' Moon waiting for us to follow our pointing finger and, at last, get around to noticing what it's pointing to.'

Moe, naturally, doesn't get his mind around any of this. He can't see either finger or Moon. All he sees, and wants to see, is The Gypsy. At last! At last! Unaware that he's totally missed The Gypsy's point, Moe's busy worshipping yet another finger.

* * * * *

The Gypsy's particular brand of Magic will have its effect upon all their lives.

One afternoon, Larry meets up with her and Moe. They walk a while, shoot the breeze, then stop for a cool drink at an outdoor café on Crescent. All done, Moe insists on it being his treat and heads inside to pay.

'Moe's real happy these days,' Larry says, just to say something.

'And you're so very, very sad,' The Gypsy says.

'Me?' Larry shakes his head. 'No. No, yuh're off beam on that one. I was sad for a while after New York and what happened there. But that's in the past. I'm happy now. Well ... I'm trying to be.'

'And why are you doing that?'

'Doing what?'

'*Trying* to be.'

Larry shakes his head again. 'I don't get what yuh're saying.'

The Gypsy's certain that he does, but plays along regardless. 'Why are you trying to be what you aren't? Why are you so dead set on fighting yourself? You're sad. Okay, *be* sad. Experience the sadness you're feeling. Let yourself go with it, Larry, because it's a feeling. An honest feeling. Neither good nor bad. It just is, right? If you're sad, let it take you. Take the trip to your place of sadness and find out what's there. You might be blown away by what pops up.'

Larry's tempted enough to follow The Gypsy's advice. But not until later that night, when he's home and alone. And all the pain, and anger, and confusion and self-loathing that he's held back since splitting up with Angel comes flooding out of him in one raw burst of rancid power which pushes him down onto the linoleum tiled floor, crunched up in primitive foetal position howling over his broken heart. Until, drained, there's no tears left and he can begin to laugh again. More than that, for the first time since Angel gave him the acrylics and brushes, Larry finds the desire to make use of them. Right then and there, he attempts a portrait of Angel from memory. What he creates is nowhere close to what he'd seen in his mind. But you know what? Even if he's failed, the undeniable thrill that came with making the effort has found a way of putting up with the frustration following it. He'll fail better next time.

Curly Joe's close encounter with The Gypsy also has its persuasive impact.

He and Suzie Q bump into her and Moe at *The Palace Theater.* Some movie called *Petulia.* Afterwards, they're sitting around in *Bens.* Curly Joe and Suzie Q and Moe are sharing milk shakes and a smoked meat platter. The Gypsy's mainly just sitting and listening. Every so often, she takes a dainty sip from her glass of water. When asked why she's not joining in so much, she gives them that classic Sixties line: you are what you eat. As far as The Gypsy's concerned, eating what the others are eating isn't in line with her goal to become pure spirit. Fair enough. When all's said and done, it's too pleasant an evening, and the food's too tasty, to be much bothered by The Gypsy's take on things. Honestly, when the mood takes her she's joking around and giggling no differently to the rest of them.

Part way through their meal, The Gypsy zones in on Curly Joe. 'What's on your mind?' she says.

Curly Joe knows what's on his mind but he isn't about to make it public. Earlier in the evening, Suzie Q casually let it be known that she'll be in Vancouver from the middle of July through the whole of August, visiting her grandmother. Just like that. The whole of fucking summer gone belly-up. Not that that's stopping him from playing it cool.

'nothing much. just thinking this and that,' Curly Joe says to The Gypsy. 'no big deal.'

The Gypsy's reaction is as far as he can get from what he would have expected. Much to Curly Joe's shock — and Suzie Q's and Moe's as well — she reaches out to grab both his arms and starts shaking him.

'Thinking's *always* a big deal,' she says, meaning it. 'And when its cut off from any feeling, it's horribly dangerous is what it is. Every evil thing that's ever happened came out of thoughts that denied any feeling.'

over the top or what? 'come on! it's not that heavy-duty. i'm not gonna go and start murdering people just because i'm letting passing thoughts go through my head.'

'Maybe not. Not right now, anyhow. And probably not ever. But you looked so hard, and cold and scary that it made me feel that you could have been that murderer. You get what I mean? I just had to wake you up.'

The Gypsy won't say any more. And Moe and Suzie Q aren't hiding their relief that this strange interlude is being put to bed. Just to make sure, they jump in and start gabbing away about how beautiful Julie Christie looks and isn't it great that such offbeat movies are being made these days?

For all that, The Gypsy's words still find the means to worm their way into Curly Joe's mind and find a lasting nesting place. What did she mean? What was she implying? Maybe there was something there that made a senseless sort of sense. Come to think of it, it's possible that he's become too buttoned-up emotion-wise. Maybe he needs to *feel* more.

Like with Suzie Q. She just up and announces that she's going to take herself over to the other end of Canada for the summer so she can spend some time with her grandma. And what's he do? He takes a deep breath and says 'have yourself a great time.' Meanwhile, he's cracking up inside. Same with his friends, too. There's been a growing distance on his part toward them all. Okay, so maybe he owes her one. The Gypsy's woken him up to noticing his detachment.

Which is kind of strange, when Curly Joe thinks about it. Because in lots of ways, The Gypsy is one of the most detached people he's ever met. Except ... She's not, really. When she's caught up in what's happening, she's also the most "into something" person he knows. It's like everything really, really matters to her but not so that she won't let it be. *Wow! Is that what freedom is?*

* * * * *

As far as Moe's concerned, the flush of freedom — or whatever — he's been feeling is pinpointing one simple truth: he can only plough on like this so long as The Gypsy's there to make it happen. He needs her, is what it boils down to. And because he does, Moe knows that it's time. He has to tell The Gypsy that he loves her. The thought of doing that makes him want to puke. It also makes him replay the reactions he got on the other couple of occasions he'd made such a pronouncement. And his memories of those make him want to puke some more.

But still, there's nothing he can do about it. It's his heart that's speaking, and he knows he's incapable of shutting it up. Okay then, how to go about it? Should he spring it on her out of the blue? Or should he work his way to it slow and easy? Should he hold himself back for some other, better, time if it doesn't seem like she's in a receptive mood? Or should he go ahead, no matter what? Maybe he should just forget all about this lunacy? Will he have the strength to keep to any resolution that he makes? And what if he'll need to puke while dealing with it all?

By the end of all this self-questioning, Moe feels ready to drop. Lying on his bed scheming, it dawns on him how to get through all this uncertainty in a secure, impersonal way. Paper and ink. That'll do the trick. A letter? Possible. Or ... How about ... a poem. Yeah! Something simple. Something profound. Something that will leave him totally defenceless and yet which is unconnected enough so that if all goes up shit creek it can simply be treated as some sort of failed venture at literary creativity on his part. *Start writing, man!*

Two hours pass by. Two hours full of frustration and crumpled scraps of paper. Fear keeps hitting him right between the eyes. A poem's become a necessity now. But nothing's emerging. He's got creative constipation. And then: *Bingo! Curly Joe's poem. Now we're talking!* In his best handwriting, removing Curly Joe's irritating Dylanesque style, Moe copies a draft of a poem Curly Joe mistakenly scribbled down on the back of one of Moe's spiral-bound notebooks while whiling away his time in the Student Union.

> *You know*
> *that love's a word*
> *spoken in silence*
> *crushed between*
> *the brushing of two lips.*
>
> *You know*
> *that love's a gesture*
> *unnoticed in the turmoil*
> *waged inside*
> *the mystery of two lovers' loins.*
>
> *You know*
> *that love's a person*
> *shouting in the distance*
> *caught only when reflecting*
> *the shadow of someone being born.*

Moe doesn't have the teensiest damn idea what it all means. He suspects that Curly Joe doesn't either. But ... The words satisfy him. On top of that, they'll make his declaration safe.

* * * * *

Four hours later, the date's been going tip-top smooth. The Gypsy's in one of her rare states of jubilant good humour. She's even snuggling up him at the slightest whim and offers no arguments or resistances to anything he proposes. She doesn't even demand to pay her own way as she usually does. To make matters that much better, they've both been blown away by Sonny Terry and Brownie McGee's two sets over at *The Back Door Coffee House*. All of which helps to make Moe feel even more certain.

At last, they're sitting in The Flacon holding hands and smiling at nothing and everything. *Now*, Moe tells himself. *Showtime!* He inches one sweaty hand into the side pocket of his casually rumpled sports jacket.

Empty.

A moment of panic. Letting go of The Gypsy's hand, he reaches into its other pocket.

Empty.

Moe's *really* beginning to sweat it now. Maybe he put the poem in one of the two outside pockets.

Empty. Both of them.

It isn't in any of his jeans pockets. Or in his wallet, either. In despair, Moe frisks himself again. Nothing. He wants to bang his head against the steering wheel.

'Moe! What's wrong with you? You're acting like you've got a case of the fits!'

'Aw, I was searching for something to give ya.'

'What was it? What were you looking for?'

'A sheet of paper.'

'Was it something you wrote?'

'Uhm ... Yeah.' Strictly speaking, that's no lie.

'Well, just tell me then. What did it say?'

' ... '

'Uhm?'

'What?'

'What did it say?'

'Aw ... Nothing much.'

'C'mon, tell me.'

'I love ya.' Moe speaks the words softly and then begins to squirm.

For once in her life, The Gypsy finds it difficult to accept what's happening. She's not totally dazed; maybe she'd even expected it. All the same, she's stunned into silence.

She looks into Moe's anxious eyes knowing that he wants her to say something. But she can't. So she shuts down. Eyes riveted on the windscreen, she says: 'I think it might be a good idea if you drove me home now.'

Twenty eternal minutes later, no awareness as to how they got to it, they're parked right in front of the drive to The Gypsy's house.

Nobody moves. Neither of them dares turn to face the other. Time passes, but The Gypsy just keeps sitting there, either unable or unwilling to get out.

Moe sure doesn't want her to, even if her silence is driving him nuts. 'You're home,' he manages to say.

The Gypsy fidgets, pushes open the car door, wiggles out. 'Thanks for the concert. I loved it. Goodnight.' Too late to backtrack on her klutzy use of words, she hurries up the pathway, unlocks the front door, disappears.

* * * * *

Back in his room, Moe sits in the silent darkness for hours. He thinks and feels blurs.

The poem, of course, is lying neatly folded on his desk. Right where he'd left it.

* * * * *

As to The Gypsy, she's beginning to worry how long it will be before she can no longer live up to the title they've bestowed on her. The title she loves and feel so proud of. Because of Moe, she's not so sure she deserves it any more. Any day now, she'll have to go back to being plain old Anne again.

Moe continues to awaken confounding desires inside her. Nothing uncomplicated, like sex. If it was only that, she'd have allowed it to take its course. No, it's something else. It seems like years ago now since their first meeting when she'd known straight away that here was a person she *had* to get to know. Intuitively, she was certain that in being with him she'd gain a deeper understanding of herself that she'd avoided. And so far, she admits, she's been right about that. Only, she's not necessarily liking what she's homing in on. Being with Moe, especially tonight, makes her think ludicrous thoughts of settling down, saying goodbye to wanderings of any kind.

It should be so easy to let him go, forget all about him. Except, it's not. Incomprehensible as it seems, her heart leaps in disorderly pleasure knowing that Moe's there in her life. She's even caught herself pining away, waiting to hear his voice or looking out of her office window dreaming that he'll be there calling for her to come join him.

She knows what she wants. What she's always wanted. To love freely.

But with Moe ... It's different somehow.

And because it is, she feels anything but free.

* * * * *

Four evenings later The Gypsy phones Moe. Why hasn't he called her, she wants to know. And, oh yes, would he like to come over to supper at her house one night during the weekend?

* * * * *

When he arrives, Moe expects a sermonette on the stupidity of his remarks, followed by the inevitable "there's no point in our seeing each other again" conclusion.

Needless to say, he's wrong. There's no lecture, no ultimatum. Just an enjoyable evening with The Gypsy and her family. She even kisses him when he arrives. In front of her parents, too! And she repeats the act — tongue-to-tongue, as well — when they're alone outside, whispering goodnight. The way she allows their caresses to go on feels more like the act of a lover than a friend.

Confusion reigns. Is The Gypsy hinting that she feels the same way? Or is she just trying to smooth things over, making sure he'll never give a repeat performance? Who cares? They're back together. And enjoying it every time.

As often as possible, on after-work afternoons, they drive out of the city and have picnic dinners. Frequently, they even bring poetry books and read out loud to each other. Mostly, they just stretch out side by side, or with one's head on the other's lap, and gaze up that sky. And isn't that enough?

Besides, don't forget: a straight rope won't stay straight if you push on it, right?

16. CUPID'S MISDIRECTED ARROW

One morning, three days into July, Suzie Q finds herself at the CN Train Station in *Place Ville Marie*, waiting for her old Elementary School friend, Edna, to arrive from London, Ontario. Now separated by some five hundred miles, she and Edna used to be the bestest friends as kids. Not that the physical distance seems to matter, they've retained some sort of friendship that still feels strong and true.

When, at long last, they set eyes on each other, Suzie Q is confronted with the appearance of a not-quite-six-foot tall, gangly urchin in too-short mini-skirt and page-boy hair-do giggling non-stop at the reality of once again being able to hug her old sidekick. Pleased as she is, Suzie Q is consumed with envy. Edna's gained the sort of presence that fits all the ideal feminine requirements laid down by icons of the age such as Twiggy and Jean Shrimpton. *And* she's got the naivete not to be aware of it. In short, she's dynamite. When placed next to her, it makes Suzie Q feel like a simple background shadow to Edna's blazing sensuality. On the positive side though, at least Curly Joe isn't around so she doesn't have to worry about him falling under Edna's spell.

As it happens, Curly Joe's a good distance away, gone with his family for their annual week in the resort town of Old Orchard Beach, somewhere in Maine. Which leaves Suzie Q in a bit of a dilemma. She needs to find two male companions to accompany her and Edna on some of their adventures. Who could *possibly* fit the bill?

Uhm ... Suzie Q tells herself. *Edna's sure to go wild over Larry. And, if it turns out to be two-sided, then it'll have the added bonus of getting Larry to stop moping on and on about his lost Angel. It might even encourage Edna to come over more often. Which would be a treat.* As to a companion for herself who isn't going to try to hit on her ... Well, who better than Moe? With Moe involved, loads of fun and laughter come guaranteed! Conveniently, that strange woman he's been dating is off on some yoga retreat up in the Laurentians. So joining in and helping out will remind Moe what it's like to be around more normal company for a change. Suzie Q's offer of a free restaurant meal seals both Larry's and Moe's fate. Spot-on, right? What could possibly go wrong?

* * * * *

It's as though they were setting eyes on each other for the very first time. Real *Strangers In The Night* dreaminess.

On the first evening's get-together, they all head for a disco and some dancing. After a while, Suzie Q announces it'd be fun if they keep switching partners to dance with.

The next day, they go horseback riding in the countryside and Larry's and Suzie Q's horses somehow contrive to take off on their own and in the same general direction.

By the third day, the clandestine couple are busy making sure that whatever it is that's happening isn't noticed by anybody else. Every chance they get to be left alone to themselves, Larry and Suzie Q rapidly embark on another round of delirious kissing. So far, they've found the self-control necessary so that no hands have strayed into far too dangerous territory. But their matching desire to devour each other is definitely picking up steam. All that's putting a brake on things is their equally shared guilt at the thought of betraying Curly Joe. It's that very same guilt, as well as the fear of their being caught out by Moe or Edna, that brings their current canoodle to an unwelcome end.

'This is absurd,' Suzie Q says.

'I know,' Larry says.

'It's so, so wrong.'

'I know.'

'I mean, it has got to stop.'

'I know.'

'I don't understand what's going on, do you?'

'Nope.'

'For Heaven's sake, it's not as if we haven't known each other before this. How long is it since we first met? Eight months?'

'Maybe more.'

'Okay. Maybe more. But during all that time I never once wanted to ... You know ... To do something like this with you.'

'Me, neither.'

'Really?'

'Uhm ... Yeah, really.'

'Oh ... Okay. And, let's not forget, I'm Curly Joe's steady girlfriend, right?'

'Sure. Of course yuh are.'

'And I still want to be. I don't want to —'

'I know yuh do. I want yuh to keep being —'

'Oh, shut up and soul kiss me again!'

* * * * *

Moments of excruciating temptation aside, Larry and Suzie Q force themselves to pass away the rest of the week making sure that they behave in public as though nothing has happened. Okay, so maybe their kidding around with each other has become more loose and playful, but it's nothing that raises any suspicions. They hope.

Edna's been too busy taking in all that Montréal has to offer to be doing any hinky head-scratching. As to Moe, he's not showing the remotest signs of being suspicious that something weird might be going on. From what they can tell, the only thing he's picked up on is that Suzie Q's got into the habit of mixing in some French every time she has something to say to Larry. Even more hilarious, she's gone and renamed him Laurent. *Laurent! Laurent!'*

Moe thinks it's a gas. It gets him gasping for air every time. 'Wait'll Curly Joe gets to hear it, too! He'll split his sides laughing!'

All of which is a relief, as far as Suzie Q's concerned. In her room at night — blissed-out, bone-tired, sleeping Edna lying next to her in shared bed — Suzie Q can't stop swooning over the thought of Laurent and the carnal feelings his memory inspires. Worse, she's longing to let her fingers do the walking, but can't. Not with Edna maybe waking up and catching her at it. In the end, unable to resist her wheedling lust any longer, Suzie Q heads off to the family bathroom, makes sure its door is locked and does her best to keep the unbridled self-pleasuring on mute.

Suzie Q can't believe that she's behaving like this. The sex-mad bombshell grinning stupidly back at herself in the mirror is *definitely* not her. Or, at least, not who she thought she was. *Especially* when she's being so unfairly unfaithful to Curly Joe and not caring enough to do anything about it. She's sneakily read about cold-hearted creatures like that. *Lady Chatterley's Lover. Peyton Place. The Carpetbaggers. Fanny Hill.* That Henry Miller book which her parents keep hidden in their bedroom. Sure, she's enjoyed the dirty-minded craving they provoked in her. But it was all make-believe! She never once considered the possibility that it might become her reality. Adulterous housewives. Cheating partners. Two-timing floozies. She's not anything like them!

Honestly, she's still so innocent. No, really! Even with Curly Joe, she's only ever felt "it" up against her; she's never taken steps to actually touch it. The furthest she's ever gone that way was to slide one hand along the target area of this guy's pants at her High School Graduation Dance. Once. Now, all she can think of is doing the same sinful thing with Laurent. Only, the hand sliding would be a lot, lot slower. And it wouldn't happen just once, either.

That thought in mind, Suzie Q decides she'd better stay locked away in the family bathroom for a little while longer.

* * * * *

Back again at CN Station, Edna nuzzles them both goodbye and heads off to board her train back to London Ontario repeating for the thousandth time what a magnificent week she's had. Then she's gone and they're left all on their own not sure as to what will happen next. Luckily, they haven't got Moe to deal with as well since he's driven off to go and pick up The Gypsy.

It's Larry who makes the first move. Hand on Suzie Q's shoulder, he draws her closer toward him.

For a moment, she allows herself to respond and then resists. 'No, we can't. *I* can't.'

Larry lets go of her, then gestures his sad agreement.

'It's not fair on Curly Joe,' Suzie Q reminds him.

'No, it's not.'

'Or on me and you, either. We can't go on with this.'

'No, we can't.'

'So let's agree that everything that took place this week was just some momentary madness and nothing like it is ever going to happen again.'

Larry bows his head one more time. 'Yuh're right. For all our sakes.'

Their eyes burn into one another.

Suzie Q forces herself to think of Curly Joe. She loves him. She's sure of that. And he's so nice to her. And ... And ... *Thank God I'm off to Vancouver soon!*

'Oh, Laurent!' she bleats, turning to allow him one last kiss.

17. A MOMENTARY RESPITE

It's nearly the middle of July now and Montréal's being walloped by week after week of unrelenting heat-waves. Mosquitoes rule the land. And, not all that far in the distance, the reality of McGill threatens to encroach itself upon The Stooges' lives once again. But no. Not yet. Surely, there's still time left for some more freedom. Of course there is. We're in The Sixties after all.

On an impulse, Larry's parents declare that it's too hot and sweaty in suburbia. So they and Larry's brother and sister all pack their bags and head off for a beach holiday in Virginia. They're even taking Jolie with them! As to Larry, on the paltry excuse that he needs to study for his make-up exam, they've felicitously agreed that he should stay at home and keep hitting the books.

Which means ... The house belongs to Larry while they're away! How fantastic is that? Curly Joe and Moe are sure to hang out as often as they can, and then ... Then they'll be irrevocably, undisputedly, *free*.

For a whole two weeks.

* * * * *

And what a time it is, too! At one point, they invite a homeless draft-dodger all the way from Tennessee to stay over, catch his breath, weigh up his options. Turns out, he can play a mean guitar as well. Too bad he's got something against washing himself. They learn pretty quick to avoid being too up close to him. After he heads on, they make sure to strip Larry's brother's bed of its sheets and pillow cases as well as leave the room's window wide open for the next couple of days.

As is its habit when you're having fun, time speeds by. Not that they're paying much attention to calendar dates. Or much else, for that matter. The three of them — plus The Gypsy when she can make it over — have gotten into such a free and easy groove of being the only residents, they haven't stopped to notice that the house is in a visibly advancing state of degeneration. Anyone else dropping by and taking in the condition of this once pristinely-maintained home would be bound to add up that its current inhabitants are savages. And exceptionally filthy ones at that.

It's a possibility that doesn't bother them in the least. True enough, the kitchen by now has been pronounced an official disaster area. Reeking dishes piled into a plugged-up sink. Mouldy cheese that they've been too lazy to store in the nearby fridge. Left-over take-out food containers taking up table and counter space. Scattered bottles of wine and beer and empty glasses leaning up against walls or lying on their sides in various parts of the room. The odours that drift from this no-man's land have seeped their way all-too-conspicuously into every nook and cranny of the house imbuing it with an unmistakable stench of decay.

No, their sense of smell remains intact. It's just that they've gotten attached to their home's raunchy aroma.

As to the record sleeves, library books, newspapers, stationary and pens, sketch pad and new tin of watercolours, music sheets, astrology charts and unfinished life-maps that lie scattered all over the living room parquet floor? Well, they, too, look just right exactly where they've landed.

* * * * *

Another idyllic evening begins. At first, it seems no different to any other. But it is. Tonight's the night they come up with *The Plan*.

It's way past their usual bedtimes. The meal cooked by The Gypsy turned out to be vegetarian. How novel and weird! But they've licked their plates clean for that matter (saves on washing), and now they're all lounging in the living room, busy chatting, full of ideas and feelings too powerful for any of them to consider going to sleep.

A couple of hours ago, Moe and Curly Joe rang up their

parents to say they'd be staying over at Larry's yet again. The Gypsy insisted that she didn't need to, which wowed the trio and left her smiling because she chose not to add that she'd already told her mom and dad she wouldn't be back that night.

Then, magnanimously, Larry invites Curly Joe to phone Suzie Q even though it means a long distance call to Vancouver. Fuck the cost! I'll just be another item on the home phone bill, and who's going to notice, right? For good measure, the act helps soothe Larry's conscience about what happened between him and Suzie Q that can't, and won't, ever happen again.

Duties done, clock ticking and about to chime midnight, suburbia gone into its silent weekend sleep, they're ready for anything to happen.

Outside, it begins to rain. No hassle. The streets could do with a clean and it'll cool things down a bit.

Dylan's on the record player. Two songs to warm them up and then just as *Visions of Johanna* gets through its first stanza, the sky explodes. In one cosmic, madly soul-rattling moment, lightning turns on the heavens with a display of power so awesome and majestic that they're forced to open the bay window's curtains all the way and gaze out at the fearful beauty which begins its dance in front of their eyes. It's a luminous moment. The song's lyrics merge with the crackling storm so that when lightning strikes once again, their faces shimmer, quivering ghosts caught in the glow of this electric night.

They're somewhere else now. Somewhere outside their bodies. Beyond time and space. Beyond anywhere or nowhere that words can explain or capture. They're in that unbroken here and now. No past, no future. No there. An awareness so total that even when they veer away from it, they can't do so completely. A door has opened that none of them will be able to shut. Not tonight. Nor on any night and day to come.

When Bob's sung himself out, they play Beethoven loud and emotional. And, inexplicably, it all fits in. The music and the thunder and the light-show heavens and the four of them, still and silent, swaddled up close to its heart. A moment of total, inseparable unity. Dancing so free up there in the skies. They don't bother to try to unravel any of it. They know that they're stuck in plastic-land suburbia and they know, as well, that probably in every other house on the street people will be rushing around to shut and bolt all windows, or will be busy calming down tearful kids, or will just simply be cursing and tossing about in bed unable to get back to sleep. Missing the point of it all, one more time.

Never mind. *They* see the point.

Indeed, they *are* the point.

* * * * *

The visionary experience ends a little past 1.00am. They've sat through it all, rarely moving, saying nothing. All they're able to do, in the end, is to turn to each other and smile a once-and-forever-in-a-lifetime smile.

What better moment for the *The Plan* to be hatched?

'Let's go,' Larry says, unable to contain himself.

'where?' A jittery question, followed by a semi-worried look, from Curly Joe who's already aware Larry isn't talking about anything less than grandiose.

'Yeah, man, where?' says Moe, also curious and, like Curly Joe, also more than a bit queasy.

'West,' says Larry, spreading out a wide grin that's making it all too clear he isn't joking.

'west! you mean, all the way? to vancouver?' Curly Joe nearly shouts. He's going through the motions. *obviously* Larry means Vancouver. *oh my gawd! imagine the look on suzie q's face when we all turn up!*

'Oh wow. You are so warped, Jim,' says Moe. He looks over at The Gypsy who's signalling go for it!

'No, I'm not kidding. We've got a bit of money saved up. We'll hitch. Right across Canada. Bring sleeping bags. Camp out in The Rockies. We can do it real cheap.'

'But ... But you've got a supp to write! We don't have time, man! School's in September. We'll never make it!' Moe keeps his eyes on The Gypsy. Okay, so she's still egging him on and he's already most ways copacetic with the idea.

'Look, I've got my supp on Tuesday, right? Okay. So, I write it in the morning and we leave in the afternoon. What's to stop us? We've still got nearly the whole of August to go. That's ages 'til registration. There's *plenty* of time. Hell, we could even make it to Kitimat. *Yuh!* We'll make it to Kitimat!'

'christ, larry! that's what? way, way north of vancouver! just some backwards aluminium town hundreds of miles from nowhere... this is just crazy!'

'Yeah, but I lived there for awhile. So I know it's also some of the most spectacular country yuh'll ever see. As wild as yuh can get. Forests. I mean, out of this world redwood forests. It's worth it. Come on, yuh guys! Don't yuh wanna see my roots?'

'I've seen your root, Jim, and it ain't much to brag about.'

That makes The Gypsy blush. Which gets everybody sniggling away.

'three thousand miles west and five hundred miles north just to see your roots. we *gotta* be off our rockers.'

Arguments against?

None raised.

Motion passed unanimously.

The Gypsy is bouncing up and down on the sofa, barking her approval even if she's telling herself that she'll miss Moe like crazy. There's no denying that it isn't altruism which allows her to be so willing to send him away on adventures she won't be joining in on. Crucially, the time apart will give her a breathing space to meditate on her life and where it's heading. Mostly though, she'll be on her own and facing her own version of freedom once again.

A celebration is called for. More music plays, another bottle of wine from Larry's father's stock in the cellar is uncorked and drunk. For old-times sake, they go ahead and order a take-out for four from the all-nite Chinese.

Then they all collapse.

* * * * *

Mid-morning, while they're still in dreamland, Larry's family turns up back home from its holiday. Their return date is right there on the kitchen Message Board. But who notices such mundane things?

The first ones inside, his parents are stupefied to discover how quickly and easily a house can be turned into something resembling The Black Hole of Calcutta. To add to their horror, they find their son sprawled out on their best sofa, egg-roll splattered shoes caressing one of its recently reupholstered arms. Worse than that, lying next to a heap of filthy dishes and unwashed glasses, they take in Curly Joe knees to chin on an armchair, seemingly dead, embracing a guitar. And, worst of all, there's Moe and a strange girl lying side by side on the carpet with one of the girl's hands resting casually on Moe's jean-covered genitalia. Had they previously met The Gypsy, they'd discern that this is an innocent gesture on her part, performed in the midst of sleep. But since they haven't, all they can do is speculate. And, with that, they conjure up unleashed demons of rampant Eros prancing about in their home from the moment they'd abandoned it.

Unable to contain herself, Larry's mother lets out a blood-curdling screech. Which, naturally, wakes up the four of them with heart-in-the-throat shock horror.

And then, seeing that the worst possible thing that he could imagine happening has, no question, happened, Larry does his best to disavow any mindfulness of the unfolding disaster. Shaking himself awake while his friends hover like cornered animals sniffing out the territory to take advantage of any avenues of escape, Larry rises, and, after owning up to his family's presence, informs them casually and in the sincerest of tones: 'Moe and Curly Joe and I are heading off to Kitimat in a couple of days.'

He'll never live down that line.

18. CROSS COUNTRY

They've stopped at Wawa.

Wawa, Ontario. High up there in the north country, near Lake Superior. Famous for the *Wawa Duck*, a monolithic wooden statue that stands somewhere on the outskirts of town. This is all they'll get to see of Wawa. The *Greyhound* bus, after all, has only parked here for half an hour. It's a rest stop, is Wawa.

There's still a couple more hours or so to go before the other passengers will begin experiencing hunger pangs that will get them shuffling about in their seats until lunch stop looms into view. The Stooges will have no lunch. Worse, they'll have no supper tonight, either. It's their first test: two days of fasting.

The early August sun shines on them through the *Greyhound's* special sky-light top. Having been the last ones to climb on board, they're scattered about in various parts of the bus, stuck in the crap seats that everyone else has steered clear of.

Larry's right behind the driver: no window, no possible way to unbend his legs.

Moe's in the back seat between a mother with the inevitable crying brat and a sleeping man whose breath carries the stench of cheap liquor. With each bump, the man's head leans on Moe's shoulder so that he has to keep shoving it off him.

Curly Joe's close by. He's in the seat in front of the toilet. This is probably the crummiest seat of all since not only is it not possible to recline in it, but also something's happened to the mechanism belonging to the seat in front such that it leans quite a ways back beyond its proper boundary. As a result, Curly Joe's trapped at the knees, incapable of movement below the waist. Even more of a horror show, the woman sitting next to Curly Joe appears to be the female twin of the palazzo pants guy who inspired them way back when. Because of her inordinate size, her over-abundant flesh has slunk its way into a good half of his seat, thereby pinioning him into a position he can't wriggle out of. To top off Curly Joe's misery, on those rare moments when he's found the means to let his mind drift into a painful sort of unconsciousness that might encourage him to sleep the trip away, one of the passengers inevitably uses the toilet, and, unmercifully, his ears are treated to an undreamed of array of the gross noises people allow themselves to make in the avowedly sound-proof privacy of a *Greyhound* washroom.

Wawa, then, is a godsend, an opportunity to slouch out of their despised seats and learn how to walk again. Breathing in the North Ontario air, they feel as though half their lives have been spent inside that bus. Already, Montréal has become a blur, the events leading to their departure encased in a history all their own.

* * * * *

As per *The Plan,* on the morning of the day they leave, Larry's back at McGill taking his supplemental chemistry exam.

He'd spent most of the day before reputedly psyching himself up for it. Mainly, he just worried. He tried again and again to read the required texts but his brain scorned all attempts to interpret any meaning from the garbage it was being fed. So he stopped and instead passed away a couple of hours drawing various self-portraits while staring into the downstairs bathroom mirror. This relaxed him for a while until he started panicking about wasting time. Which got him hitting the books again until the blinding pointlessness of the exercise made it impossible to keep going. Back to the drawing pad. And so on ... A steady START-STOP cycle that repeated itself right through into the evening. Happily, having taken a extended supper break, Larry hit on a way out: since he's going to be sitting through an IBM pick-one-of-five-answers sort of exam, he'll rely upon his latent skills at precognition to see him through. And, with that, he headed for bed and a well-deserved night of undisturbed sleep.

The exam has lasted a harrowing three hours. Answer paper handed in, Larry breathes in his new-found freedom. No doubt about it: chemistry is some primordial spawn of the devil designed to weaken any sensible being's will to live. When he meets up with Moe and Curly Joe who ask him how it had gone, he blows it off convincing himself as much as his friends that notching up a Pass is a dead cert.

* * * * *

In their initial discussions, one and all affirm that hitching is the only way to go. The Flacon's been brought up once as an alternative, but everyone agrees that she probably wouldn't survive the experience.

Discouragingly, on the afternoon of their departure, the weather turns unseasonably cold and very, very wet. Rain storms over the next thirty-six hours are being forecast. The prospect of hitching through that, and at night on top of everything, suddenly doesn't sound much like an adventure to look forward to. How about if, instead, they opt to hop a ride on a *Greyhound* bus that will take them as as far as Winnipeg?

'Half and half,' they assert.

Pleased with how coolheaded they're being, they phone the bus depot and are informed that it'll cost them $30.00 to get to Winnipeg or $37.00 to make it all the way to Banff.

'Well,' they tell themselves, 'those extra seven bucks will take us a long way down the road, and save us time we could be wasting by hitching our way through the boring prairies.'

So Banff it is. Dowry set, a two day fast sounds like a tolerable way to make up for the added costs.

* * * * *

Their bus is due to depart at 11.00pm.

Larry appears lugging his father's WWII duffle bag.

Curly Joe makes it over with his mother's cream coloured suitcase, an 8mm movie camera, and a brand new pair of white sneakers.

And Moe drags along an airplane case complete with

allergy-free pillow.

So what if those already on board are narrowing their eyes in disdain? They're about to take off!

Uh-ho. The bus breaks down in Ottawa and they have to get out and wait two hours for a replacement. It's pouring down here as well. Their shoes and socks are soaked and Moe wants to head back to Montréal.

Their stomachs growl, so they share a *Coffee Crisp* Curly Joe has brought with him from home. They pretend to feel full.

And then ... Hallelujah! Their new bus is ready to roll.

* * * * *

Sometime during the early dawn morning they pass through Sudbury. Curly Joe twitches at its ugliness and films it just to preserve the memory.

'desolation row or what?' he whispers to Moe who's gotten out of his seat to take a better look. 'what the world's gonna look like after atomic devastation.'

Moe agrees. Anyone would.

The near-lifeless trees emerging from the dark-brown land speed by.

* * * * *

Here they are then, landed in Wawa. Green Ontario woodland.

'Wait'll yuh guys see Kitimat,' says Larry, sniffing his nose at it all.

Stopping at a tourist shop just to have a look around, Moe comes across a postcard of the *Wawa Goose* that he just *has to* send to The Gypsy, even if it'll cost him part of his first breakfast. He writes: *Wawa. Where we stopped to drink a glass of wa-wa. Miss you. Love. Moe.*

'I can't believe it,' Moe says to no one in particular. 'Here I am on my way West with no food, little money, and an airplane case stuffed with a rubber sheet and a pillow. I've given up warmth, security, a bed to whack off in, three or more free meals a day, the gal of my dreams and The Flacon ... And all for what? To go and see a bunch of places I don't really care if I ever see or not. Like Wonderful Wawa here, for instance. I feel like writing a song about Wawa. First line goes something like this: *You and me and Wawa makes three.* I'll think up the rest later, when I'm stuck on a buff-A mess of a bus with a drunken wino and a brat I'd love to punch out. Somebody must have got my brain and balls mixed-up. Again.' He smiles in spite of himself.

Then the bus honks its horn, and they hurry on back to their lousy seats.

* * * * *

By the time they reach Winnipeg, general depression has set in. Even the fact that the bus has settled down to a half-emptiness which allows them to stretch out over two seats and make the best of the situation, doesn't cheer them up all that much. Long distance buses might be quicker to get you to where you're going, but they can also be dull, dull, dull. For one thing, their windows are tinted green — ostensibly, to keep out the sun's rays. And maybe they do. But, they also create a strangely monotonous tinge to the outside world which, at times, goes beyond mere distraction and veers towards revulsion. One good thing, they seem to keep out the clouds of insects living it up in the August sun. Mainly, though, the effect just turns everybody chronically drowsy.

They've been on their bus for the past twenty-four hours, stopping only for passenger meals, washroom breaks and changes of drivers. Temptation too great, they've opted to stay where they are inside just in case the smell of food might drive them to the point of breakdown. It doesn't help things at all when they remind themselves that they've gone ahead and *chosen* this squalid life.

Still, arriving in Winnipeg means that they've caught up enough on their funds so that each is now allowed 65¢ per day to do with as he wishes. As would be expected, their fortune gets spent on food. Lunch today consists of a chocolate bar or ice-cream cone. For supper, they'll feast on a packet of chips (or popcorn, if they're wanting something healthier), another chocolate bar, and a quart of milk. Two of the finest meals in their lives.

As well as provide them with such gastronomic delights, Winnipeg also means a four-hour stop in their bus journey. Which is an unprecedented period of time for them to regain a vertical view of the world. Emerging, they make a circuit of the city's streets, in and out of the *Hudson's Bay Building*, past the movie house advertising *Rosemary's Baby*, up and down Main Street scanning newspaper headlines ballyhooing Nixon's winning the Republican Party nomination to run for President, the rioting in Watts, the Russian Politburo's increasingly bellicose grousing about Alexander Dubcek's *Prague Spring* over in Czechoslovakia.

What sticks in their minds the most, however, is that the drug store near the Bus Depot sells postcards of itself. It is, the message states, one of Winnipeg's major attractions. Looking around at what appears to be a typical, unadventurously arranged Drug Store, they conclude that, somehow, the card is telling the truth.

The outing does them good. By its end, they even find themselves laughing about all the drongos, bozos and goof balls who've inhabited their bus world. The characters who get them howling the loudest are the drivers themselves. They've never seen such an collection of weirdos quite like the ganefs they've entrusted their lives to. Every five hours, give or take, a new one takes over to come clean about his unique set of identifying features, gestures or apparel that serve to provide him with the requirements for a quick stab at his very own fifteen minutes of fame.

Some merely get on the bus, adjust their seat and wing mirror, then switch on the microphone to quickly introduce themselves: 'Hiya folks, I'm ... Dave. Long John. Wally or just plain Wal, whichever's fine with me. Wild Bill from Pecos here an' rarin' to go, podnuh.'

Others gleefully inform their passengers of the estimated time to their next rest stop and then settle down to a long bout of wordless driving.

A few, as if given their entertainment chance of a lifetime, keep returning to that microphone as and when they're so inclined and supply their captive audience with action-packed documentary monologues, intuitive weather forecasts or even dramatic readings:

'This here bend we're comin' to on your right, folks, is where me an' a bus load a' passengers just like you nearly ended up in that Great Big Bus Depot in the Sky 'bout six years back. I always take it slow an' turn real quiet while I go by here. It'd help a heck of a lot if you all hushed up, as well.'

'Whew! Round here we call days like this Devil Days 'cause they'se so hot some folks estimate that Hell can't be much hotter and go doin' all sortsa rotten things. I'll turn up the AC real cool just so none of you's go gettin' no such notions, okay?'

'Goddamn! Did any of you folks catch the number plate of that sunnabitch that just cut me off? Aw hell, when I make sure to get up close to that li'l so-and-so, he ain't gonna know the difference 'tween his mouth and his *derriere*. If you pardon my French, ladies.'

As if following a ritual straight out of *The Bus Driver's Manual*, nearly all of them place rosary beads over their rear-view mirrors, chew on toothpicks or tobacco and spew quarter-sized gobs of phlegm out the only windows that will open before going back to casually rubbing the back of their necks while mumbling inane oaths to themselves. Usually, they're beefy, overweight duffers resigned to the boredom their job induces. Their smiles are hollow. Their eyes, too long accustomed to highway lines, don't react to people except to note possible misfits, troublemakers and slow returners from rest stops.

The driver who gets on in Winnipeg blows all other contenders out of the water. He believes himself to be a Marine Sergeant and throws a menacing look at each passenger as they climb on board just to make his delusion a shared one. As soon as everybody's sitting down and accounted for, he flicks on his mike and snarls: 'Settle down folks, this ain't no picnic. My name's Duane. Do something stupid, and your name's Mud. We'll be in Regina just 'bout in time for when you'll wanna eat again. Till then, settle back and relax and leave the drivin' to me ... Oh, and by the way: I ain't no piker, but I sure hate hikers. So if'n I speed up a little at any time, peek out your windahs and have yourselves a laugh or two. One final thing: I will not tolerate alcohol being drunk on this here bus. You just try, and the next town is gonna be yours. Over and out.'

* * * * *

Once again then, they return to the green-tinted views and to the tatty newspapers other passengers have left behind. Most of these predict a major confrontation, perhaps even violence, at the upcoming Democratic Party Convention in Chicago. Just about all of them slant their commentaries that little bit to the right so as to make Mayor Daley and his hoods sound like true Defenders of the American Republic. Moe, having nothing better to do, studies the reports and questions, with more than a touch of cynicism, if all those people who've gotten *Clean for Gene* have any idea they're about to be royally shafted. He sympathises with them; he, too, feels more than a little grubby in a manner that has nothing to do with either his skin or his clothes.

What Moe's mainly thinking though is that he's made a terrible mistake coming along on this trip. He's missing The Gypsy to the point where he's started daydreaming that she'll climb aboard at the next stop. Agonisingly, thanks to the power of his imagination, he's now turned on non-stop, sweating it that someone is bound to notice the tent pole inside his pants. All of which keeps him griping more and more loudly about how bored and stupid he feels being on this trip.

This has made Larry and Curly Joe aware, like never before really, that while neither of them is leaving anything much behind, Moe's given up quite a lot in getting out of Montréal. They look at their friend and they, too, guiltily wish he'd stayed behind. Moe's disgruntlement brings out the differences between him and them once again. They've accepted their current situation more easily, even welcomed it. Food, comfort, warmth — all take second place to their insatiable urge to be on the road. Visions of Kerouac and Cassady fill their heads so that they see themselves as a new generation of desolation angels ready and willing to travel anywhere just for the sake of saying they've been there. But Moe's not like that. Moe isn't made for the road. He's the one you come back to, the one you write your letters to, the one you sit with quietly when it's all over and it's time for words to re-live the tale. Somehow, Moe's out of place being right there when the adventures beckon. Alarmingly, his presence might even stop those adventures from ever happening. Unwilling to face such awful possibilities, they try to set their minds at rest by insisting that all will change once they reach the mountains and never again have to get on a bus.

* * * * *

Sitting behind a man with an enormous bald head, Curly Joe gets his first view of The Rockies.

Having just travelled through a whole day and a night of prairie wheat lands, looking out onto a monotonous world which is so flat, so continuous into the distance, he now appreciates why so many have compared it to an ocean. *wheat risin' high into th' sky,* he writes in his Thought Book. *risin' tall n' free in deep summer, when it's too soon yet f'r cuttin'.* He shakes his head. What in hell does he know how tall wheat grows or when it's time to cut it? Never mind, what matters is that his memory of the days going by remains picture-perfect. Each little scene, apparently significant or not, is as vivid now as when he first experienced it.

He remembers waking up somewhere along the prairie ocean in the early morning just in time to catch the Midwest sun come up and cast crazy wheat-field shadows everywhere. He sees an old abandoned shack, dark and misshapen, slowly growing lighter as the sun rises higher. The black over the land disappearing as soon as the red sun touches down. Then ... Indescribable. *Bauer* camera aimed and running, shooting seconds-long impressions that will be enough to capture the scene without taking up too much of the film he's got available. And the silence. On the whole bus, only he and the driver awake; the latter too engrossed in his engine to notice such miracles taking place.

Curly Joe records it all through eyes and camera and gasps of unalloyed, punch-drunk joy. He laughs to himself recalling the early evening hours they spent in the Regina Bus Depot. A realisation that a mistake's been made in counting out their cash. They've overspent. Result? Their fairy-tale meal: a pack of stale *Melba Toast* and a 10¢ box of chocolate-covered peanuts to share between the three of them. Gloom turning to hilarity as they engage in the absurd by placing the sweets between two crumbly slices and eating them as if they're sandwiches. And, of course, the chocolate-covered peanuts keep rolling off and onto the depot floor where they're picked up again for them to nibble away at as if they're prohibitively expensive delicacies. Which, in a way, they are. Filled with such memories, he writes: *saskatch'wan nights 'n' days. august 68. 'n' somethin' clicks ...*

So now the Rockies. Though they're still distant and vague, they'll be reached within the next few hours. They mark the end of buses, the end of lumpy seats and contorted sleep.

The future becomes a bigger blank. Where will they go? Where will they sleep tonight?

The bald head turns sideways, cutting off Curly Joe's view.

Cutting off his thoughts.

* * * * *

If proof were necessary, Curly Joe's movie will later verify that they make an odd trio sweating and cursing their way up the tourist trail leading to Lake Louise.

It's early afternoon, and they're starved, tired and restless to reach the site before they die. Bellyaching over the unwieldy luggage whose weight threatens to tear off their arms as the climb gets steeper, the sun hotter, their strength weaker, they push on regardless, possessed by unrelentingly demanding demons.

Curly Joe's white sneakers stand out, an irresolvable aggravation. He's tried scuffing them up, mixing them into the dirt and dust of the various trails they've followed. He's even attempted jumping into dried folds of mud, hoping for soggy miracles. But it's all useless. Protected by their own unique form of White Magic, those shoes continue to shine on brightly.

Wow! The Lake! Double-Wow! The view! Out of relief (and, perhaps, temporary insanity) they praise it as though it were a Goddess. Sweating from every pore in their body, they collapse, knees to the ground, and laugh in spasms. Sweet success! They made it!

* * * * *

(From Larry's Log)

Jasper, late at night.

We lie in a tent owned by a giant Moe has named Tiny Tim. No tiptoeing through the tulips for this guy, though. He's American, wears aviator glasses and crimplene shirt and trousers, weighs 300 lbs, drinks beer, refers to female fire rangers as "hon", owns a majorly intricate super-8 camera along with several thousand feet of film which lie, cartridge-scattered, in the front of his '66 Ford, and addresses toilets as "little boys' rooms". Mostly though, he stinks of the bucketloads of vinegar he keeps splattering onto his body. 'Keeps the skeeters at bay,' he says while sticking more vinegar-soaked cotton balls around the opening to his tent. In sum, a real bozo. A chooch. A bimbo. A classic case of incurable dullard-itis.

Still, to be fair ... He picked us up somewhere outside Banff where we'd been hitching for about three hours. I guess, by the *looks of us, he judged that we were crazy in a safe kind of way. As it turns out, we're all sleeping in his tent tonite which is a lot better than the laundromat we'd tried sleeping in last nite.*

He's a nice enough guy, though Moe's convinced that Tiny's after his bod'. That's only because Tiny nearly busted a gut when Moe pulled open his suitcase and took out the pillow. He just turned red and broke out with this over-the-top roar pretty well scaring the shit out of all of us, and then bulldozed his way towards Moe, patting him (all the while, still laughing) and clasping him closer. It was too much for Moe who turned white and took it all in silence while Curly Joe and me stood by laughing in a wary sort of way.

After that, he made us cut logs for the fire. Curly Joe's first attempts with a hatchet practically sent him to the nearest hospital. I took over.

This tent's gigantic. It could hold at least twelve. Tiny usually sleeps in it all by himself. He's gone now. He tried to interest us in some bar beer but his keenness sank to less than zero when he found out he'd have to pay for it all by himself.

So we're alone now. The three of us by a log fire, feeling sleepy and a little crazy. Moe seems happier than in the bus days. Maybe he's getting used to the uncertainty. Curly Joe's in a world of his own. The green and the mountains and the whole feel of the place have gotten him into some sort of Thoreauesque rhapsody. He walks around grinning and shooting from the hip with his camera.

Me, I grin a lot, too. I feel good. I feel it's working.

Jasper, pre-dawn morning.

We'll be on the road again in a few hours. Curly Joe woke me up sometime back shaking like a leaf because he'd gone outside for a slash and found a bear scrounging around for food. A ginormous Grizzly, he called it, then zipped up his sleeping bag and went back to sleep.

Over on my right side, Moe snores on. And not far from him a living, breathing mountain heaves up and down. Tiny, he sure ain't.

I can't sleep. Dreams of Suzie Q by flashlite infest my head. I can't stop them, even though I keep telling myself to. I try to work out what it's gonna be like meeting up again when we're all in Vancouver. Seeing her with Curly Joe. Holding hands and kissing. Wanting it to be me, instead.

Never mind. Nothing's ever gonna happen between us. And, if nothing else, it's stopped me having nitemares starring Angel.

* * * * *

They leave Tiny Tim asleep. A "Thank You" note pinned to the tent flap, they promptly proceed to get lost somewhere inside a wood that Larry's just finished convincing them is a short cut to town. It doesn't matter much except for the fresh tracks they come upon which look like those of some colossal fantasy creature that's sure to be lying low waiting to pounce on them. Still, getting lost will be one more yarn to recount. It's not like they're in any sort of hurry to get anywhere. Anywhere is where they already are.

Soon after they find a way out, they're greeted by a friendly black-and-white dog who follows them along their path, tail wagging as though he's just re-found his masters. They resolve to adopt it, hitch with this mongrel all the way to hallowed Kitimat, have it become a part of their own mongrel lives. Then, as they near the town, the pooch goes one way while they head for the other and scampers out of their lives.

Destination reached, they lie down on the grass in the town square and smile up at the sun. On an impulse, Larry buys a half-pound bar of milk chocolate. Then, sheepishly, he attempts to persuade himself as much as the others that chocolate's a great source of nourishment for the travelling man. And who would want to contradict this point?

When they finish eating, they push on once again. They're aiming for an unknown somewhere they believe to be rural Western Canada. Maybe they'll head North. Possibly West. Depends on the rides they'll get.

Even from a distance, you can see them walking slowly down the road, Curly Joe's shoes still glistening white while, somewhat half-heartedly, not entirely resigned to his fate, he stamps the ground so as to create little clouds of dust that fail to scuff them.

Having come across what looks like a good hitching place, they read the salutatory messages for their brothers and sisters that previous hikers have left.

> *This place sucks! I been here 6 hrs!*
> *— Sunshine Phil —*

> *I beat ya! Been here 7 1/2 hours now! Love 'n' Peace*
> *— Lady Day from S.F. way —*

> *Shit. I beat 'em all. Nine hours, man!*
> *ps: Don't forget to hide the roaches.*
> *— L.S. Dee —*

They laugh in a subdued sort of way.
Two hours later, they strike gold.

* * * * *

(From Larry's Log)

Valemont.

Where the fuck is Valemont? A good question. Valemont is nowhere. It's not even on the map. Not our map, for sure.

Mount Robson in the distance. Highest peak in the Rockies, we're told. Don't think we'll be climbing it. So I'll do a sketch of it instead.

Before that though, back to Valemont ... It's the place where the highway to Prince George is supposed to begin. Only it doesn't. There isn't even a paved road in Valemont. Just dirt. And people who look at us as though we're Martians.

Valemont is where we got driven to by this guy who went around picking up everyone he could find. Including us and a stinky old man with a long spittle-strewn gray beard that Curly Joe stuck his face into every time he couldn't stop himself from falling asleep.

It's the place we wait at for somebody to take us to some other god-forsaken place, the name of which I can't recall now (McBryde, I think) where we might be able to hop a freight train which'll take us to Prince George tonight.

If all goes according to plan.

Curly Joe's swooning. He's just found a cache of licorice pipes complete with red sprinkles on top for sale. He's now re-living his childhood.

Moe sits glumly on the Post Office steps. He looks very lost while tearing up page after page of foolscap trying to capture this place for The Gypsy's mind.

I write in-between munches on this super-juicy apple I got cheaply in Valemont's one-and-only General Store.

We're all nervous. And happy. A hopped freight train ride. Can ya dig it? It thrills and frightens me all at the same time.

Kerouac in my head again. Sal Paradise and Dean Moriarty madly racing east and west and back again in a matter of days. Smoking. Loving. Crying. Dying. Living. Every day. All the nutty races — and for what?

Does there have to be a "for what"?

If there is, I guess it's the "for what" that's making us break our backs to get to some implausibly out-of-the-way town in the B.C. forestland.

Three of us. Two never having been there, having no connection with the place. No past there, no memories. Yet still going.

And me. Me with roots and past and memories. Yet certain that those aren't the reasons. That there's more to it than that — whatever it may be.

Kitimat, we come.

Or, at least, we fucking well are gonna try our damnedest to.

* * * * *

(From Moe's letter to The Gypsy)

Help! Two fugitives from the local padded cell have just shoved me into a wagon car from a freight train and it's starting to move! They <u>think</u> it might be the right one! God knows where we'll land up. They ain't sayin'.

The floor's dirty with grain. Larry's trying to tell me it's okay to eat it as he stuffs a mouthful into himself. It's time for the net-boys to take us all away.

I must have stepped beyond The Outer Limits.

* * * * *

(From Curly Joe's Thought Book)

— m' first freight train —

fantastic. it's th' first 'n' only word what comes t' mind. i mean, christ, here we are, three punk kids tryin' t' act like bums, 'n' against th' odds, succeedin'.

we're onna fuckin' freight train, man!

who th' fuck hops freights anymore?

its like all our highway dreams amazingly comin' true.

moe's got his harp out an' blowin'. me an' larry, we bin hummin' 'n' singin'. but mainly, we all three jus' stare.

a while back, we pushed th' freight car door open, 'n', after a few minutes, when we wasn't so scared of bein' caught, we started t' peek out into the light, takin' quick, surreptitious glimpses at first, catchin' furtive vistas of th' world outside, till, at some point, we got brave enough t' lean t' th' side of th' doors 'n' look. or even just sit down with our legs hangin' outside th' car 'n' danglin' with th' wind that th' train's speed created.

it's just indescribable. i never seen woods like these. rain forest, we say t' ourselves. it's really all we can say. even moe's dazzled by it all. by th' dizzyin' wildness 'n' peace of this railroad ride, of them trees 'n' leaves 'n' creeks. it's like we're right where nobody's bin before. we've just never been exposed t' wilderness this joltin'. we just wasn't prepared.

i can see grins shinin' on each of moe's 'n' larry's dirty, unshaven faces. mine's probably th' same.

as far as i'm concerned, th' trip's been made right here 'n' now.

everything what's happened, or'll happen from now on, th' trip's a total success because of this here train ride.

i started t' feel chilly, so i put on my ugly grey jacket. it reeks a' sweat, 'n' dirt, 'n' dandruff, 'n' even grain now, i guess. as i put it on, i leaned outta th' car at th' same time that larry was filmin' somethin' or other, 'n', just as i leaned, the sun hit me square on, totally bathin' me in this eerie orange light. i had my hands in the pockets of my green jeans, 'n' i tried t' look real cool, like as if all this had happened t' me countless times before. 'n' larry's filmed it all. i can see it already: my face comin' outta th' darkness, lit orange, snarlin', hair flyin' everywhere, mustache long thin 'n' nasty, a look of utter contempt that i'm hopin' will show up on film.

'n' inside, my heart's beatin' faster than it ever has.

'cause all this is real.

th' train's real.

th' scenery's real.

all of it.

not a film i'm watchin' or a book i'm readin', man. no, it's all happenin'. t' me.

th' kid who's gonna get off this train for sure ain't gonna be th' same as th' one who got on.

somethin's took him over.

or somethin's got out of him.

kerouac's right.

i'll never be able t' look at a freight train unemotionally again.

* * * * *

Prince George is pitch black dark by the time they arrive. Playing it safe, they scramble out of their freight car, darting into corners every few seconds, just to put the non-existent, watchful railroad guards off their trail.

Prince George is pretty far up there. Close enough to the Alaska border to give you chills even in August. They shiver. Though not only at thoughts of Alaska. Prince George late night silence is creeping in and, wherever they look, they see nowhere that seems friendly enough to want to welcome them into its bosom. More trains are out of the question for now. Far too expensive to ride the normal way and, from what they've overheard, the next freight to Terrace — the closest town to Kitimat — won't be leaving until 2.40am. The winds that are building up tell them there's no chance they'll survive till then, and even if they were to somehow manage that they'd freeze so much in the freight car that they'd need to be thawed out by the time they arrived.

So what's there left to do? Hitch? Yes. They try to. The few people who bother to stop laugh in their faces when they hear them say 'Terrace?' *No one*, it seems, is crazy enough to want to leave for Terrace at this time of night. Thoughts like those, you keep away from till the morning.

Given all this, it's little wonder that Moe's started griping again. He's cold and tired and still too hopped up from the train ride to deal with the dismal reality they're facing. He just wants to sleep. The grumbling's infectious. Curly Joe picks it up from there. He starts cursing the weather, the city, his light clothes, people who don't pick up hitch-hikers, the hair blowing in his face, exorbitant train fares and expensive hotels. In short, a whole litany of places, events, and circumstances that have demonstrably conspired to keep him icicle cold and awake.

Then Larry puts on his thinking cap: *Salvation Army*. Surely, even in this godforsaken town there's some kind of Mission House for them to crash at?

Twenty odd minutes later, dog-tired thanks to the burdens of their luggage and minds, they come upon *Brother Anthony's Refuge for the Needy*. They knock. A very Christian-looking guy somewhere in his early thirties answers and informs them that the place is full up. *But* ... If they hang on, he'll ring another House he knows and see if it'll take them in. On the phone, he refers to them as transients. Being labelled that brings home exactly what's happening: here they are, three middle-class university students used to luxuries and pampering being treated like they belonged to some flop-house world full of derelicts, alcoholics, junkies and god knows who else. Unintentionally, they've joined the ranks of all the wretches and deviants who inhabit the underbelly of civilized society. They take that as a compliment.

And they're on a roll. This other place has room for them. They walk to it contentedly, no longer noticing the winds blowing through their clothes and hair. With shelter in the offing, Prince George takes on a much more benevolent guise. They're way up in B.C., further north than they've ever been. Three thousand miles away from home. And they're official bums. What more is there to life?

The distracted man who greets them gives them a quick, tired scrutiny. Leading them into his office for the signing in, his face conveys a look of dismissive pity. On the wall behind him hangs an imposing portrait of Christ looking down in divine sorrow over his lost sheep. Puckering his lips, the man casually asks if they know how to write their names. Not that he seems to care one way or the other. Their reply is bursting with mock sincerity. Taking their word for it, the man opens up the Nightly Admissions book and shows them where to sign. He makes it explicit that they keep the ink between the lines he's pointing to. They do so. For the first time since entering the hostel they begin to feel ill-at-ease. It comes as a shock to be made aware of what it's really like to be seen as being near-worthless, almost less than human. Their hands shake and sadness creeps over them. What if they had to do this every single night?

'Have you got any money to pay for your beds?' Before they can say anything, the man answers for them. 'Naw, I guess you wouldn't.' He looks them up and down, gives a mocking snort, and shuts the book.

They follow as he leads them over to the dormitory. Some sixty cots, lined up in rows of ten. Three-quarters of them already filled with tired or drunken old men sleeping off yet another forgettable night. They find three empty beds next to each other, stick Moe in the middle one, and try to go to sleep, pretending that the sheets are clean, that it's just their imagination that makes their skin tingle as though bugs were crawling over it, that the coughs and jeers and barfing and constant flushing of the toilet are sounds unheard.

Sometime during the night, one of men begins to cry. Bitter, forlorn, swearing at the world for his situation, spitting and gurgling he drones away at the woes and miscarriages of his life uncaring or unaware of all the ears that hear him. Awake and alert, they lie there in the dark listening to the sobs and rants and naked anguish, feeling the old man's pain, and, somewhat guiltily, trying to suppress the grins that his drunken ravings bring on. Long minutes later, a light's switched on. Eviction is threatened. All goes quiet.

They close their eyes again. Their minds are, by now, very much attuned to the salival silence, to the shifting of bodies and the squeaking of beds. And they realize that, if only for one night, they're where they belong: sleeping with the hapless wretched and forgotten scum of the earth.

* * * * *

(From Larry's Log)

Prince George Outskirts.

Hitching. Early Prince George awakening. The bums got restless when the breakfast bell rang. Forty starving down-and-outs giving it all they've got for their bowl of mush. We couldn't hang around any longer. The thought of passing away breakfast — even a free one — with a bunch of snot-nosed, barf-stained old men turned us off. You see things differently in the morning, I guess. So we gave up our meal tickets to some wino who was cold and starved and looked like he really could eat four bowls of mush.

Long story short, we left. Walked to the highway. It seemed like miles, but the sun was shining so it wasn't all bad. Still and all though, a tiring walk. It felt like we were heading away from everything. No cars. No houses. No woods. Nothing except highway stretching out to nowhere and everywhere.

I notice a stick out in the distance moving closer. The stick gets bigger, mutating slowly into a human being. Long and thin. Jeans and Logger Jacket three sizes too big. A Native Indian. Or maybe half-breed. Not red-skinned really, more a tanny brown. Unshaven. Gaping holes where some of his teeth should be. Swagger. Whisky breath. Looking so much older than he should.

I wish I had the guts to pull out pad and pencil and try to draw him. He'd make a great contrast to Tiny Tim if I drew them together. Something for later, I guess. He's stopped. Stooping down from his tired six-foot-six frame. Squinting at us heading out.

- Where ya for?
- Kitimat.
- Long ways.
- Yeah.
- Oughtta stay in 'George.
- Oh yeah?
- Lotsa good bars. Whiskey. Wimmen.
- We been there. Gotta get to Kitimat.
- Job?
- Nope.
- How cum, then?
- Dunno. It's there, I guess.
- Yeah ... Wanna smoke?
- No thanks.

He wouldn't go away. Cars started to pass us by but wouldn't stop when they saw "the injun". He wasn't gonna move on, though.

More cars drove past, kept on driving. We turned silent, hoping he'd get up and go.

He didn't. He took up position by the side road smiling and smoking his Players. It seemed like he'd made plans to set up roots there, pass away the rest of his life right where he was standing. He yawned and lit up another cigarette. More cars. More frustration.

In the end, Curly Joe suggested we pick up and walk down the road a bit more. We did so immediately.

He stood firm on his ground, still smoking, mouth open wide into some toothless perversion of a smile. He half-nodded us away in silence.

We walked until the shadow faded, and the highway borders altered and the sun blasts turned hot and very, very British Columbian.

Now, we're in some nowhere clearing where a couple of people fish and three starving loonies wait for salvation.

* * * * *

(from Moe's letter to The Gypsy)

Good evening. Welcome to my nightmare.

I find myself writing to you from a bed. Not an ordinary bed, mind you. What kind of bed, she asks? Would you ever guess? Okay, I'll take you out of your misery. Would you believe: one of the three extra beds owned by a used-car dealer who also owns this gargantuan 4-bedroom trailer that he keeps for himself and umpteen women (so far fictitious) and who goes by the handle of Donny DeSoto (or, as I've taken to referring to him, Donny D)? I know all this is getting hard for you to accept — I find it hard too, believe me — but here's more: all this is taking place in dynamic, up-and-coming Kitimat B.C., home of the world famous Kitimat Spanish Soccer Team.

*Yup! We got here! God knows why or how, but we got here!
We've reached rock bottom.*

*It took seven rides to reach Terrace (world capital, Terrace,
has three movie houses). Then, the unbeatable pick-up: Greasy
Pierre and Tonto. Two dozers. Real buff-A types.*

*Greasy Pierre stood 5'4" and looked like he'd cast a 1\2 inch
wide shadow — if he spread his legs full stretch. He wore
brand-new vintage 1958 needle-point black shoes, a
phosphorescent orange shirt with blue spangles over the
nipples, and matching green Official Arnold Palmer golf pants.
He was sporting a Presley-greaser hair-do which reeked of the
four jars of Brylcreem he'd slopped into it.*

*Tonto, in total contrast, seemed like the "ugh-me-like-white-
men-fire-water" type, and had a belly to prove it. He was
average height and picked his teeth on what looked to be a
Bowie knife. When we told him where we were from and where
we wanted to go, he went silent right away. Maybe because his
jaw fell to the floor board.*

*Greasy Pierre though couldn't stop talking. Rambled on and
on about all the things Kitimat has to offer — cars and a good
biker shop. He admitted "duh gals" weren't so easy to pick up.
They read more books than Terrace wimmen. He was nice,
though. Even stopped to point out the site where the rockslide
had happened back in '66. Biggest thing to hit Kitimat in years.*

*The sun began to set and I got to admit that even with those
two bozos in front of us, it was real pretty. Okay, I'll come
clean: it was beautiful. Larry and Curly Joe thought it was
tremendous. I'm close to agreeing with them.*

*Okay, better get back to the story. The Bobsey Twins left us
right in front of the Kitimat Hotel — a clever ploy to get us to
invite them in for a drink. We fooled 'em by laying out our stuff
on the sidewalk and sitting on it. They skulked in and left us in
peace.*

*To tell the truth, it wasn't all that peaceful. Our minds were
racing pretty fast. now that we'd got here, where were we gonna
stay? It was too cold outside, too expensive at the hotel, and
Larry didn't think anyone would still remember him. None of us*

could face another night inside a hobo hostel. *Assuming that Kitimat even has one. So we sat there. Silent. Starved. I'm down to the last notch on my belt. Just thought I'd mention that.*

Suddenly — words fail me for once, but literally suddenly — this car comes roaring by at full speed, stamps on the brakes as it passes us, and stops at a dead-standstill fifty feet away. By now, the inmates from the bar have all come out to take a gander at what's making all the racket. Something to tell the grandchildren about, I guess.

Tension builds. We're rubbernecking this Volkswagen that's stopped in the middle of the road, its engine purring. Everybody else is taking an extra good look at what's going on.

Then, a voice bawls out: 'Hey, you three! Ya wanna go to a party?'

Now, I ask you. Put yourself in our situation: lost somewhere in Kitimat, starved out of our gourd, tired to the point of exhaustion, freezing, and some lunatic voice invites us to a party.

What party? Whose? Where? When?

Do these questions really matter?

Nahh!

We ran like we were being chased by the devil to that car carrying all our 400 pounds of junk as if it were feathers. We smiled into the driver's window ... and we drooled and dribbled out inanities like: 'Party? Party! Par-tie? Ugh! Me like party. Party, Party. Where-um-at, Kemosabe? You like-um me go to party? Goody. Goody. Party!'

We kept raving on like that even after the driver had opened the passenger doors to let us hop inside.

It was Donny D.

He went insane when we told him we were from Montréal. 'Montréal? No kiddin'? Montréal! Whadda you know? Holy shyte! Montréal!' On and on.

Then we really rocked his boat when, for some screwy reason, we got into our "let's pretend we're..." game and lied and told him that Curly Joe was really a draft-dodger from California who went by the name of Rick The Digger. That was really too much.

'I bet you play music too, huh?' Donny D asked Curly Joe, waterfalls of saliva dribbling down his chin. He was like a little kid now, so we didn't have the heart to disappoint him.

'Well ... uhm ... sort of ...' offered up Curly Joe.

Then Larry got into it: 'Don't listen to him! He's always under-selling himself. Why Rick here, he's an artist. Best goddamn folksinger in the world. Only Dylan. Nobody else. You got a voice as good as Rick's, you only sing Dylan.'

I couldn't stop myself and started singing

Hey Mr. Tangerine Man,
Peel yourself for me ...

(I don't know where that one came from, either. My mind works in mysterious ways).

The way he looked vacantly at me made me pretty sure that Donny D had never even heard of Dylan till then. Maybe he thought I was a Byrds fan, or something. In any case, he was too stunned to waste much time thinking about that. Hell, he had stars in his eyes. He'd picked up a California draft-dodger from Montréal who was a goddam folk singer and artist. He went into a whole new series of "Holy shytes". Then he started to let us in on his great plan. He was gonna save up some money and build a coffee house in Kitimat. Shake up the town. Get real bona fide musicians like Rick here to appear. Start a whole Head Colony right in good Ol' Antiseptic Kitimat. Yikes!

When he found out we had no place to stay, he practically begged us to crash in his trailer. We didn't say no. He was over the moon. A draft-dodging folksinger and his two friends from Montréal sleeping in his trailer. Holy shyte!

So he took us to his trailer, raved about all the girls he'd had in this place — how it turns girls on to make it in a trailer. (Would it turn you on to make it in a trailer?) Sneaky li'l devil. Right off the bat, he wanted to know if we had any of that there "merry wanna" on us. He said he knew where he could get some but it was too late now. We told him that was cool, no sweat.

The party came up again. There really <u>was</u> a party. Somehow, I found a way to beg off. I'm too wasted to make it to a party when there's this too good to be true bed waiting for me. Curly Joe was the one Ol' Donny D was hopped-up about, anyway. Larry figured he'd better tag along to give Curly Joe support. And they left.

That was about an hour ago. I stole some bread and ham and tomato and lettuce from the kitchen. Dee-licious! As soon as I finish this letter, it's gonna be off with the strides, hit the sack, and catch up on a few well-earned zzzzz's.

I really can't believe it. It's like some warped dream. All that's missing is a certain Gypsy I know. And, somehow, that's a lot.

See you in a while if I ever make it back alive. Love.

- Moe -

* * * * *

Talk about warped dreams ... Buckle up, Tripsters! Some Sixties Sordidness up ahead! The more faint-hearted among you? See if you can ride the wave through its turbulence, okay? You'll get through it.

It seems to Larry and Curly Joe that they've been thrown right into the middle of a Fellini movie being shot on location at Shearwater Avenue, Kitimat, Number ... Number something or other.

On one side of the crowded living room sit an all-male group of short-haired, lost Fifties Generation hangers-on. They're decked out in what seem to be red-coloured long-johns and matching long-sleeved undershirts. They're the *Kitimat Baseball League.* And feeling tickled pink about it, too. A few feet away, a smaller gathering of similarly time-warped jocks wearing black windbreakers huddle together backslapping and swapping the latest scuttlebutt. Coaches? Good guess. But, no. They're part of the *Kitimat Sky Divers Association.*

On the opposite side of the room, turning in unison to pass an eye over whoever drops in, is a gaggle of gals, Kitimat's most eligible bachelorettes. They're dressed to kill in loose-fitting, pastel-coloured, v-neck short-sleeved blouses and skirts daringly cut at two or three inches above the knee. As trendy as they believe themselves to be, most of them are well on their way to replacing the matronly school teachers from their school days who they used to make fun of and never once dreamed of becoming. As if already rehearsing for this role, they do their best to sip daintily on their Okanagan Valley wine. The night's just beginning, after all. Wait for the record player to be turned on before getting into the harder stuff. That way, chances are they'll still be sober enough to pick out a decent partner to neck with.

Observing them all, making sure that everything's running smoothly is the Mistress of Ceremonies, Nora. She's the one wearing a wide sleeve, plum-coloured billowing evening dress. She's plastered and sprayed all sorts of gunk onto herself in order to attain a look of maturity suggestive of someone who's spent years and years mastering the skills required to be a successful party hostess. Beneath it all, though, Nora can't hide the fact that she's still quite young, really. Twenty-three at most. And, like everyone else, she's thrilled to bits about her two special guests. Paying them the most careful of attention, she keeps on topping up their glasses as soon as their liquid content goes below the "glass half full" level.

The cheapo wine that Larry and Curly Joe have slurped down on empty stomachs because they didn't want to seem rude has already taken effect. Hoping to counter-balance this, the guests of honour slouch on an old-fashioned sofa madly munching away from a large bowl of potato chips that someone's passed over to them and which they now guard over with all the protective zeal of a wild animal devouring its kill.

Donny D has squeezed himself in there as well, patting shoulders with Curly Joe. He's busy recounting over and over to every new arrival who stops by to say hello how he came upon his new lifelong pals. Donny D is really popular tonight.

Grateful for this, he's competing with Nora to make sure that the stars' glasses are never less than filled to the brim.

As if all that isn't enough to contend with, strange faces insist on moving in upon Larry and Curly Joe to ask the dumbest of questions.

'Why did you come *here*?'

'Where are you heading for *next*?'

Or, unbelievably, and yet in complete seriousness, 'What do you think about Engelbert Humperdinck?'

At first, "the extra-special guests" do their level best to provide superficially sensible answers. However, by the fourth glass of wine, the boredom of the non-stop inquisition turns them into snobby, pretentious, sarcastic above-it-alls, talking down to these wretched buggers. Bad move. Much to their horror, the faces begin to appear more frequently and old ones keep coming back for more.

Worst of all, while putting up with this , someone new arrives. Pattie, going by the shouts of welcome and recognition she receives. The assembled part so that she can make her way unencumbered towards them. What's that she's got pressing against her? Oh, it's a fucking nylon-string guitar, is what it is!

Sarcasm, chips, and way-too-much-wine rise up in one tremendous heave-ho from somewhere deep down in Curly Joe's stomach. Pattie's guitar is handed to Donny D who, in turn, reverently passes it to Curly Joe. Immediately, the entire room adopts a hushed silence.

'what's this?' asks Curly Joe. His unsuccessful shot at humour is rewarded with scattered nervous snickers. He attempts a couple of open-fret twangs, then pretends that this act has musical significance. 'uhm ... a bit outta tune.' A few in the audience bob their heads in appreciation of his acoustic know-how.

Curly Joe's doing his damnedest to look cool while inside he's going bughouse crazy. *what the fuck do i know if it's outta tune or not after four glasses of wine? oh god, let me have control over my fingers. give me a voice to sing with.* He strums a few more strums, then works out what to play. *all right. here goes nothing. please, god. please!*

With the first stanza of *It Ain't Me, Babe* accurately remembered and sung, it starts to sink in that he's pretty damn hot tonight. Everything sounds fine; immaculate even. He notices Larry's head swaying in silent harmony. Next to him, Donny D is in Pig Heaven. When he's greeted with long and eager clapping at the end of his opening number, Curly Joe revs up the courage and blasts off, his muse right there spurring him on. Two stanzas into *Only A Pawn In Their Game,* a protest tune to shake everybody up a tiny little bit, one of the baseball players turns his crew-cutted head towards Curly Joe and begs him to tell it like it is. With the mad wine working up his insides, the utterance strikes Curly Joe as being hilariously funny. Like a pro though, he keeps up his straight-face solemnity. Not that Larry's making it easy for him to stop from busting a gut. Thoroughly drunk, he's going around slapping people on the back and bawling nutso absurdities like 'Yeah? Yeah!' or 'Goddamn!'

Somehow, Curly Joe leads them through every Dylan song he knows how to play and some he hasn't yet got round to figuring out their chord sequence. No worries. His audience loves it. A boy genius has landed in Kitimat. He brings the show to a close with a particularly fine version of *The Times They Are A-Changin'*. Everybody's screaming and shouting, begging for more but he declines to play another note. To make this clear, Curly Joe passes the guitar to some faceless character who does what he can to get people into a sing-along about Courting Froggies and the Merry Merry Dew. Shot down in flames, poor bastard. Time to put the guitar away and get up and dance.

An hour later, Curly Joe's wildly shouting out to the chorus to Tom Jones's *Delilah* along with everybody else. He wonders on and off what he's doing losing his voice to this crap while contorting his body to its irritatingly catchy tune. Guessing by the number of times this same single's being played, it would seem that Tom Jones is the only guy who sells records in Kitimat.

Facing him, Hostess Nora is swivelling her body in line with his. Oh yes, now it's come back. They'd each gone a few rounds with other dance partners and then agreed to stick together. She'd also fed him a cheese sandwich at some point, as well. She'd sat down next to him and watched adoringly while he ate it. And, when he'd finished, she'd leaned over and kissed him. Their tongues coiled like a worm hacked in half.

'happy new year,' he'd told her. *did i really say something that corny? not that nora seemed to mind.* Muddled fleeting fragments of thoughts do what they can to distract him from further humiliation. *god ... what in hell's going on here? wait'll moe hears what he's missing. and, speaking of moe, where's larry? oh yeah, larry's dancing somewhere or other with pattie, the girl with the guitar. can't see them, though. where have they headed off to?*

The next song to come on is a slow number. A great excuse for nuzzling up and grinding away at each other without anybody else giving it much notice because they're all doing the exact same thing. Curly Joe's hands have moulded themselves onto Nora's abundant posterior. After a few feeble attempts at trying to slide them off, she's given in and is now busily working one of her hands lower and lower, slinking dangerously close to his straining penis. Oh well ... Giving in to Nora's insistent exploration, Curly Joe hears himself repeat 'nice and soft. nice and soft,' for reasons that elude him.

'Nope, you've got that wrong,' Nora whispers back. 'It's nice and *hard.'* Then, sniggering, she finds the mark and begins to knead her palm over the crutch of his jeans. She's breathing fast, a look of power in her eyes. In response, Curly Joe sneaks an arm inside the back of Nora's evening dress and slips one hand into her panties so that it wriggles its way down her bouncy bum cheeks until its tickling the back end of her rather juicy quim. The act makes Nora jiggle lecherously, and, the more she jiggles the faster her hand moves over his hardened cock. Recklessly kissing, sucking, biting, and clawing each other, they both give way to glorious lust.

Aroused beyond the point of no return, Curly Joe comes. His body releases a long, tremulous spasm that feels as if a bucket of water's been thrown onto his lap and which, seconds later, nearly brings him to his knees. Urging Nora to wait right there for him and not move an inch, Curly Joe slithers his way to the bathroom. Jeans and underwear now around his ankles, he looks down at his much-pummelled manhood. Already shrunken, still tender and numbed, it droops defeated. Still, open to the possibility of another work-out, he pulls up his pants, stuffs a wad of toilet paper into his trunks and clomps back out.

Darkness. Too many couples getting in his way, wanting to thank him for his performance once they recognise who it is. *thanks. great. glad you enjoyed it.* Everybody off somewhere, he's left in peace to look around. *where's nora gone? oh! there she is! who's she yakkin' with? some local chooch, trying to make out with her. and she ain't resisting. no way, man!*

Face-to-face now, the two rivals give each other a grilling. Even as they smile out their fake 'hello's', one monumental silent argument begins to take place:

'what the fuck do you think you're doing? she's mine!'

'Whaddaya mean? She was all on her own waiting for me to take her on.'

'fuck off!'

'No, you fuck off, kid. I'm the one she wants. Go on, beat it!'

'i ain't going nowhere, pal. i'm staying put.'

'Then it's a race, kid. Winner takes all.'

'you're on!'

Their unspoken wrangling is so self-evident that even Nora catches its drift. She chortles at the thought of all the fantastic possibilities waiting to happen.

As if reading her mind, the other guy jumps in and makes the first move. Pulling Nora towards him, he presses close against her, waits for her positive response, and then begins to slide his tongue over lips, and ears, and cheeks, and neck. Amply encouraged by her coos and impassioned whispers to keep going, he semi-lifts her while still in a bear hug and slurs something about finding the direction to her bedroom.

Wriggling free, Nora takes his hand and leads the way. But before he can claim total victory, she also grabs hold of Curly

Joe and drags him along as well.

Inside the room, door shut, all three fall in a heap onto the bed. Not being slow to continue taking the lead, Curly Joe's unnamed rival unbuttons the top of Nora's dress, pulls down her bra, and puts his tongue back to work. Mewling in approval, Nora lets herself be carried away, her nipples hardening in excitement, legs akimbo in dizzy expectation.

Curly Joe has no doubt that it's time to get in there now or he's lost forever. Trouble is, he can't tell if he's a spare wheel or a co-starring player. Maybe Nora picks up on his hesitation and that's why she yelps 'More! More!' Was that her way of inviting Curly Joe to join in? It doesn't take much to win him over that it was. Lying flat beside her, he shoves the other guy sideways to give himself some space. *Okay, here goes nothing!* He pushes up her dress as far as it will go. Then, before he can think twice, he slowly slides down Nora's expensive-looking, hot pink, frilly lace underwear until they're fully removed. Not hearing any infuriated protests nor noting any move to restrict further activity, he begins to stroke and spread her nicely moist labia. The result is heart stopping. Nora's bouncing up and down thoroughly caught up in moment.

Not being slow to wise up to what's happening, Curly Joe's adversary goes for broke. Kneeling across her chest, he unzips his jeans, and wedges his prick between Nora's pleasantly plump breasts. She, in turn, now eye to eye with the tip to his wiggling cock, stretches her tongue as far as she can in a bid to create a further point of erotic contact.

The sounds being aired don't take much to distract Curly Joe's five finger exercise. He sits up to absorb what's going on. For a second there, he catches Nora's attention. She allows herself a passing what-are-you-gonna-do-to-top-that-big-boy? smile before returning her attention to more urgent pursuits. Accepting this to be good enough encouragement, Curly Joe unzips his jeans, throws away the toilet paper still lodged inside his underwear, and quickly, oh so easily, penetrates her.

Contest ruled to be a tie, the three of them turn into a perpetual motion beast with three backs. In and out. Up and down. In. Out. In. Out. Faster. Pump. Faster. Pump. Pump. In. Out. Faster. Faster. Aahh! *Yes!*

They nearly all come together. First Nameless. Then Curly Joe. And, half a second later, Nora.

Three satiated sighs.

Three emphatic heaves.

Three gasps for air.

Three grittings of teeth.

Three shit-eating grins.

All that Curly Joe is aware of after that is finding himself in a car being driven by the ex-rival who by now is treating him as his best buddy. Half-scaring the guy, Curly Joe shouts: 'where the hell's larry?'

The next moment, he's in a bed inside Donny D's trailer. All is silence about him. He only has time to raise his question once more. Then, thankfully, sleep.

* * * * *

To answer Curly Joe:

Larry finds himself somewhere he's never been before. He's lying right between two cushions of female flesh while seven inches of him shakes and empties itself in a once-in-a-lifetime tremor of gratification. It's all quite insane. Back to Kitimat. Back here for his first ever full-on, non-fantasy fuck. His drunken mind reels. The place that had given him his innocence is now taking it away.

She'll become known in their private mythology as Pattie Pubes. Though it's doubtful that she's ever heard the word tantra, much less actively studied its philosophy, she is a true Tantrikim seeking higher fulfilment through the expert use of her body. From the moment she first fixes her eyes on Larry and reckons he's the cutest-looking male she's seen not on a movie screen in a very long time, she knows that she wants him. Nothing lasting. Nothing to try to grab a forever hold on. Just a desire that will last as long as he stays. Or as long as she doesn't tire of him. She makes no attempt to seduce him, nor has any need to; she simply lets him know she's approachable.

So when, in his drunkenness, Larry's reduced inhibitions allow him to press himself up close against her, she bends to his advances, though her bending has little to do with surrender. They dance an hour or so longer, prolonging their separate pleasures. Then she suggests that she show him her apartment. She's pleased to note how grateful he is to be invited. They steal a bottle of rosé wine and sneak into the night, arm in arm.

On the way over, for her own unstated reasons, Pattie starts talking about her past affairs. She speaks at length of some Canadian Army guy who'd promised, and of others who hadn't. She tells him of her first. And then of her last, two months earlier. All of which gets Larry going all ga-ga nervous. What will she say about *him* at some point in the future?

With that unnerving thought in mind, as soon as they're inside Pattie's apartment Larry uncorks the bottle of rosé for succour. Having been shaken all the way home, it spurts and spills all over the place, turning Pattie's grey skirt into a red bubble swamp of evaporating alcohol. She swears loudly, and then laughs lustily. He wants to slink back to Donny D's trailer. She mothers him. They drink up what's left over. Wine trickles down the sides of her mouth, dribbling along her neck, onto her white shirt. She doesn't mind. Instead, she encourages him to remove her wet clothes and prances around like some pin-up, wearing only white bra and black cotton undies.

Enough. No more time to waste. She leads him to her queen-size bed. At first, Larry's totally lost. Hard and up, yet uncertain of where to aim or even how to aim. All he has to guide him are the blind stiffness of his prick and the expression on Pattie's face. Worst of all, he begins to worry that he'll come in seconds. Does she know she's about to have her way a full-fledged nineteen-year-old virgin? Not that he'd ever tell her.

So here they are now, their bodies going at it. She's enjoying the sensations, but she can tune in to Larry's tension by the machine-like way he pumps away inside her. 'Relax,' she whispers into his ear before giving it a quick bite. 'There's plenty of time.'

Her words turn him on even more. *What am I expected to do? Think of baseball, like in the jokes Moe tells?*

Increasingly aware that Larry's lack of confidence threatens to restrict her pleasure, Pattie clamps one hand to his neck then shoves his body downward, pinioning him so that it's now she who looks down from above, he who looks up wide-eyed, expectantly, from below. Relishing her control over him, she pushes her legs forward and wriggles until her labia are wet and slippery enough to allow uncomplicated access. She lowers herself onto him slowly, expertly, wishing to prolong the sensation being induced. She feels the elemental thrill of total attachment, as if some new umbilical link between her body and this boy's has just come into being. And she knows that her body and his body are no longer theirs, that they've become entities of their own. Taking command. Transporting. She tenses her muscles so that they close in upon his cock and bring on escalating havoc to her stiffened clitoris. *If there's any good in the world*, Pattie reminds herself, *then this is it. This is Life's explanation for itself. Just this conjunction. Union and transcendent intoxication. All at once.*

She notices a change in his exertions, has no doubt as to what they signal. Wanting to share it, she bobs up and down even more rapidly transforming herself into the All-Cunt fucking and being fucked by a thousand million males all at once. Well on the road to excess, she pleads for more. This primal urge she feels now is reflected in her eyes that bulge open yet see nothing, in her mouth which lies agape, a thin spread of spittle trickling down its lips.

He comes. She feels the volcanic thrust followed by that moment when motion ceases, when breathing stops, when eyes snap tightly shut. And now, she knows it's her time. Legs and thighs caught in a rush of ardour. Hands clawing and pummelling air and skin. Panting mounting in pitch and volume. Puffs of air escaping from mouth and nostrils. Tongue licking already dampened lips, running back and forth across teeth, extending itself out as far as it can stretch. And ... Oh yes! There! Back arched upwards now, pelvis grinding quicker. Then quicker still. And ... Oh! One never-ending growl while the inner walls of her womb explode.

The after-silence is finally broken by Larry. He whispers a tentative, fatuous: 'Was that good for yuh?'

She laughs at full volume, then puckers her lips in melodramatic severity. 'Judging by the advanced state of mental decay your head must be in at this stage in the game, I'd say you handled that poker of yours with clear-cut expertise and manliness. Yes, it was good. In fact, it was great, all right?'

Not picking up on the mockery, Larry's so grateful, he farts. One loud, long, nose-turning trumpet of air that shocks them both at first into mute embarrassment and then sets them off, hooting and howling and rolling on the bed, stopping only when the sheets shift and he sees the crack between her spread-out legs and then throws himself upon it.

An hour later, not quite knowing why, Larry is blundering down silent, deserted Kitimat streets. The sun hasn't risen yet but its threat is evident. Stillness. And cold. Only his footsteps to remind him that all this is real.

'The night has a thousand eyes,' he says out loud. That sounds appropriate even of he's not quite sure what he means. Chalk it up to simply being alone, trying to find a trailer park in Kitimat.

Inside their temporary home at last, he looks in on both his friends. Moe's curled up in a loudly innocent state of stillness; unshaven, hungry probably, yet peacefully asleep. Larry wants to cuddle him, he's so much the replica of a child.

Opening the door to Curly Joe's room, Larry trips and wakes him.

'oh god. what the fuck have *you* been up to?'

Larry's face gives away the answer.

'you're kidding!' Curly Joe's bright awake now.

The sun begins to rise while they laugh and congratulate, compare notes.

Light filters through. A good day coming.

* * * * *

'Kitimat to me, when I was a child, was the one and only Lost Horizon. I was happy the first moment I set foot into Kitimat Valley at the age of seven. I'll never forget the days-long train ride from Quebec, followed by the boat trip from Vancouver along the B.C. coastline and then up the Douglas Channel that leads to Kitimat.

'I remember how frightened I was the first night we sailed because I'd never been on a big passenger ship before (incidentally, it was named *The Prince George*), and because the portholes looked unfamiliar and cold. When yuh're a kid used to square windows, round ones make everything seem weird.

'I was in the bunk of our cabin. My parents had gone out to some other part of the ship for the evening. I guess it was a Saturday night. I must have fallen asleep because I had a dream. I dreamt I was passing under some giant-sized bridge that was darkly silhouetted against the sky. I suddenly woke up, and it wasn't a dream at all! The ship was streaming under The Lion's Gate. For a few minutes, I lay there in my bed petrified. Scared because I couldn't make out reality, didn't know whether I was still sleeping or totally aware of maybe experiencing a new kind of consciousness. After a while, I got up the courage to stick my head out the porthole to get a better view. There's just nothing lonelier or more forbidding than a night-time sea. We were well into the straight between Vancouver Island and the mainland by the time I was ready to get myself into bed once again.

'Daylight came and my whole family went up on deck. B.C. coastline. Got to be one of the most scenic and beautiful anywhere. Green-covered mountains sloping steeply down into the water, land indented by rivers and creeks and man-created patches of sea that never heard of waves. Yuh could catch the reflections of the mountains off that ship. Wild country. Just as wild as the country we passed through on that freight train we hopped. No sign of human life. No settlements. No roads visible anywhere. The only sound coming was the wind bouncing off the ship's port and starboard. Maybe the occasional scream of gulls every time the galley hands threw out potato peelings.

Other than that, a flat-out beautiful, deeply natural silence. Impossible to relate the feelings then. But they must have been powerful because a seven year old kid could cast his mind back to them, and keep them inside.

'I think that boat ride to this place was the first time I began to think, in a very dim and uncertain way, that my life was maybe gonna be something different. What was I doing on this boat traveling away from people I'd known and into a wild virgin coast? No man belonged here. No white man, anyhow. Yet, here I was, a little French-Canadian kid wrenched away from a normal life in Montréal. What was going to happen to all my friends back there? What was going to happen to Lucien who I'd go catching grasshoppers with and keep in glass jars? What was going to happen to my First Grade teacher and the other teachers the older kids would scare me about and who would now never teach me? Why the fuck had my father accepted this job which would take us all some 4000 miles into Haisla Indian Legend forests? Was it only for some financial benefit? It couldn't be just that. He could have stayed where we were, found a way of moving up the Montréal corporate ladder if that was what he was after. Was it more then? Was he looking for something when he took his family to this godforsaken place? Maybe he never found it. Maybe he did. Or maybe he got this far, and then passed the search onto me.

'That day remains a very clear picture. Going ashore from Kitimat wharf — that's what they called this bunch of logs rammed into the earth and covered over with makeshift planks — and seeing mountains sloping down upon the river, rain forest trees standing tall, smell of seaweed, fresh wind, Native Indian faces with quizzical brown eyes, pure blue sky, and high white clouds trespassing here and there. And, most of all, this gut-down feeling of peace. The mountains and the emerging town were peace. The river was peace. The isolation and solitude of the valley we stood on, they were peace.

'Kitimat 1956, and a kid could look anywhere and he'd be sure to be happy. A kid's Paradise. Water falls. Trees to climb. Green grass and mountains. All free. All open to him. I'd found complete freedom to be — though I guess I didn't conceptualize it then. Noble Savage land. Yet it wasn't just that. Adults saw the same things I did. They just reacted differently. They couldn't quite feel all the Indian Spirits and Legends that filtered down into me.

'Maybe that's why I wanted to come back here. Maybe I'm searching for that peace and freedom I lost long before I ever even left Kitimat. Maybe I thought yuh might be able to feel it with me. Or even in spite of me.

'Okay. Kitimat. K-I-T-I-M-A-A-T. That's the original Native Indian spelling of it and it means, in the Haisla language, as I may have told yuh a couple of times or more in the past, *People of the Snow*. It's necessary as an introduction to my favorite of the many beautiful Indian legends which now infest my mind ...'

* * * * *

When the night starts moving in and the legends have been recounted, when they've trekked up and down and around the valley, gloried in the mellow August weather, felt the heat on their skin, and watched their shadows lengthen until they've become indiscernible from all the other shadows cast by the setting sun, they straggle back to their trailer home.

Donny D is already there. Eager, anxious to please, offering up yet another party full of more people to entertain and act superior to.

Moe wants it now. More than anything. After what he's been told had happened at last night's party, he's fired up with the faint hope of losing his accursed virginity as well. The idea of making it with some beautiful stranger he'll never see again, and who won't be around to remind him of how sexually inadequate he's certain he'll be on his first time, is pre-eminently appealing.

A visitor appears just as they're about to leave. Ex-Hostess Nora. In slacks and tied-back hair, looking younger than Curly Joe recalls. She's nervous; the greetings she offers aren't trying to be sociable. For some reason unknown to him, Curly Joe trembles. He tells the others to go on ahead, he'll catch up later. He watches them leave, smug we-know-what-you're-up-to grins plastered all over their faces.

They're alone now. Silence hovers like a patient vulture. A few stabs at politeness: coffee in their respective cups, radio on at the right volume playing some silly North Country love-lost ballad.

'well, here we are,' Curly Joe stammers, still feeling the tension.

Nora peeps back. She sits alone in an armchair opposite him. She considers, for a moment, if she's made an error of judgement, then shrugs the thought aside. 'I've come to ask a favor, if that's okay,' she says at last, then blushes.

'i'm all ears.'

She looks him eye-to-eye. 'When you go, will you take me with you, Rick?'

For a moment the question almost passes him by. Then confusion sets in. 'what ... what do you mean?'

She hesitates, gives in. 'I ... I like you, Rick. Maybe even a lot. I'd just want to spend more time with you. For a while, I mean. A few weeks, maybe. A month. See how things go. I've got a life here, I know that. I keep telling myself that I'll want to return to it. But then, maybe not. I'm just not sure any more. You're my chance to find out.'

Curly Joe's stunned. How on earth could what happened last night lead to *this*? How could she turn a drunken threesome into such a big deal with life-changing potential to boot? This is nothing like how he and Suzie Q gave birth to their love. And ... Oh God! Suzie Q! How's he ever going to bring her existence into this? What does he say to some stranger who's fool enough to tell him how she really feels, even if what she feels makes no sense at all to him?

Before he can think of anything, Nora finds her courage again and continues. 'You see, you're such a change, Rick. I don't know if I can find the words. You come along, sing for us, get physically close to me, and then you leave. And we're all left waiting here for someone else to come by. I can't stay here just waiting anymore. There's so much out there in the world ... I mean, I like this place, you know? I like the country, the air, the feel of belonging to nature, being so close to it. It's great running out late at night to watch the stars. Or in the mornings, seeing the sun rise over the hills. It's incredible, no doubt about it. It's *so* relaxed. So ... So ... You know? But then people like you bring tales of big far-off cities you only read about up here. You're eager, tired, full of beans about about where you'll go next, playing your songs and being open to whatever happens. And we listen. And something says: This is alluring, you know? It's like some steady hum that you can't get rid of. Then you leave and the strange thoughts evaporate and we go back to our security.'

Nora pauses, gives him a despairing look. This isn't what she wanted to say. Another pause. She begins again. 'I found myself looking around this town today. I know it so well, know everyone, everyone's secrets. They get around so easily. There's nothing *else* to get around, anyway. I found myself feeling very smug and settled, quite sure of everything. Of my lot in life. And then, I thought of you and what you had to offer: Fun. Confusion. Living for the moment, not knowing what happens next. Uncertainty. Scary, yes. But, somehow, in that moment it all seemed so excitingly attractive. I don't know why. I'd just like to go with you now for a while. I guess I want to share your life and ways for a little bit. Maybe even find my own. If you'll let me.'

Listening to her, to the defenceless honesty in her voice, Curly Joe still can't put two and two together. How can this person in front of him be the same one who'd simply used and had been used the night before? Why can't people stay as simple as they first appear to be?

Nora sits fidgeting, tears threatening to erupt. She's in some self-imposed limbo, waiting for his words. She sees him stare back, expects the worst. Is she to get some fatherly advice to grow up, accept her fate?

Curly Joe's cowardice wins. As far as he's concerned, on this occasion the truth isn't going to set anybody free. Him least of all. 'okay,' he says. 'you're welcome to come along if you want. i can't promise you very much, but —'

'It's what I really, really want,' Nora interrupts, full of hope. She could be eight-years-old and it's Christmas morning.

'yeah. fine, then. we'll go tomorrow, okay? or is that too soon for you?'

'No ... No. That's no problem. The earlier, the better. I'll take only a few things. Leave the rest at home. A friend can look after things.'

damn. 'yeah ... that sounds good.'

'When?'

'what?'

'I mean, what time tomorrow?'

'oh... well, we *should* go early but i'm still pretty bushed from last night so i doubt i'll be up before ten. and by the time i get around to packing and saying good-bye, it'll probably be close to eleven. let's say you come round a bit after eleven. we'll leave then.'

'Maybe I'll pack a lunch.'

'yeah. good idea. we'll eat on the road.'

'A picnic.' Nora pauses. 'Thank you.'

'for what?'

'You know. You've made it terribly easy somehow.'

'yeah. well, we'll see tomorrow. uhm ... look, if we're gonna go, we'd better both get to sleep soon.' Curly Joe tries to make himself look tired.

'Wish I could stay,' she hints, wanting to please him.

'me, too.' Another in a growing number of lies. 'but there's no place, really, and i'm not sure how donny would take it.'

'We could make love now, if you like.'

He freezes. That's the last thing he feels capable of at this moment. As far as he recalls it, what they did last night was fuck, not make love. 'yeah. we could. but i'd hate for you to have to leave right after. let's save that for the trip.'

'Tomorrow night, then,' she agrees, almost letting slip her own relief.

'yeah, tomorrow night.'

He walks her to the trailer door. Before he can react, she's whirled round, clung to him. She breaks into a series of loud sobs while furiously kissing him.

'Thank you again.'

'for nothing.'

Curly Joe stands by the door until he can't see her anymore. He studies the stars and chokes up out of fear and self-loathing. He's pulled it off. She'll hate him tomorrow and that hatred will haunt him for many tomorrows to come. Never mind, he can put up with that. *kitimat. goodbye kitimat. who'd have thought it'd come to this?* Back inside, he searches for a pen and some paper.

moe 'n' larry,

sorry, but i gotta move on from this place without you. you'll be asleep when i go. here's suzie q's phone number in vancouver: 737-9430. call her when you get there. i'll probably be there. or else, she'll know how to contact me. sorry. it's too complicated to explain right now.

- curly joe -

He'll leave that out for them in the morning when he goes.

To bed, then. 6.00am's an ungodly hour to leave anywhere.

But better to play it safe and scram while everybody else is bound to be sleeping things off.

* * * * *

'Yeah, well he could have stayed around till the morning! He could have woken us up!' Moe's angry, chomping on his breakfast toast while staring up at Larry who averts his eyes and pretends to read Curly Joe's note once again.

'Maybe he couldn't, Moe. We don't know. We —'

Moe's in no mood for excuses. '*Kee-rist*! That's it exactly. We don't know. We don't know nothing! He just picks up and goes. He leaves us a note that says fuck all. Where's that at, Jim? What's he trying to pull off anyway? He's almost treating us like we're goddamn strangers or something.'

'Well, what can I say Moe? We'll find out when we get to Vancouver.' Larry's full of questions too. But for some reason he's feeling the need to defend Curly Joe just the same.

It's Moe's chance at last. Larry's just given him the way out to this whole sorry mess. 'Naw. I guess *you'll* find out, Larry. Because I've had it. Christ, it's not really Curly Joe that's got me so steamed up. I guess ... I guess he's just made it all too plain and simple. He's heading for Suzie Q. And you're mad keen on seeing Vancouver. And here I am fressing away what's left of the summer traveling further and further away from The Gypsy. Shit, it's been good. I'm not really made for this, but it's been great with you guys. Even the busses. I mean, I'll never forget it. But maybe Curly Joe's right. We've come this far. We got to where we wanted to get. And now, we gotta split up. I can't go on kidding myself, Larry. I miss her. I just gotta head back.' Having revealed all, Moe looks to Larry for a full acquittal. But Larry's saying nothing, still unable to keep up with what's going on. At last, worried he may have been too ruthless, Moe prods once again.

'Larry?'

'Uhm?'

'You're not mad at me, are ya?'

Larry looks into Moe's face, takes on board what he's been saying. 'No. No, I think yuh're right. We oughtta split up. I think I'd better be heading for Vancouver, find Curly Joe.'

Tensions cleared, Moe allows himself a cautious smile to share with his friend. 'Ya know, I wonder what wouldda happened if we hadn't come here. Maybe —'

'It wouldn't have been us if we hadn't.'

'Yeah. Trust us.'

* * * * *

There's a bus leaving Terrace late afternoon. Moe gets a ride to catch it with one of the people he'd met the night before at the otherwise totally unsuccessful party. Larry tags along to see him off. It feels strange to say goodbye from a place neither one of them lives in.

'I'll see ya soon,' Moe shouts as the bus pulls out, looking happier than he has since they'd set off from Montréal.

* * * * *

The car ride back to Kitimat goes by in silence. The last thing Larry feels like doing is to talk to anyone, much less this near-stranger who plays incessant steel-string guitar cowboy ballads on his car radio.

For the third time in less than a week, Larry finds himself travelling on the only paved road between Kitimat and Terrace. He sees the same trees, breathes the same fresh Kitimat air, has the same thoughts.

Still, something's different today. He's being tormented by the past. *By going back, yuh find out that there is no going back,* he hears his mind tell him. He's all too aware that this isn't a new nor unfamiliar conclusion. It is, however, the first time he's believed it. He feels a confused sort of anger directed toward Kitimat. After all the trouble he's taken to return to the place, it's treating him wrongly. As though he doesn't belong. That thought shocks him into an even deeper silence. Contemplating ghosts, Larry soon finds himself walking the old paths again, back to the house he'd once known as his home.

Who lives here now? Would they know anything of me? Would they have come across that corner of the basement wall where I once scratched SHIT on a dare by now? Would they have looked out from the window of my old room and seen the Kitimat sun rising in the summer as I did, when I was a kid on school vacations that lasted so long they were almost forever? Would these people have noted the strategic position of this house as free ground for Cowboys and Indians, tag, and innumerable other games? Would they have calculated that the height and thickness of the back yard bushes are terrific for hiding from enemies or for the peaceful bilateral exploration of the secret parts of each other's bodies?

Larry shakes until tears, neither forced nor controlled, begin to trickle down his eyes and cheeks. He weeps out all the fears and bitterness he feels. He mourns the loss of this house. For the clay pits he used to play in as a kid that aren't there anymore. For all the chipmunks he'd killed and skinned in nearby woods with the child's dream of making a chipmunk fur coat for his *maman*. For all the people living unawares in this unawares little town. He cries for himself, mainly. And for his coming back which maybe, after all, shouldn't have been. Finding a fallen tree to sit on, he uses his Log Book and a black-ink ballpoint pen to sketch the house and its surroundings.

Dissatisfied with what appears on paper, Larry stops. Something new comes to mind. That woman. Pattie Pubes. His first fuck. He'd been sure that Angel would have been his first. Wrong again. Pattie Pubes takes over his thoughts, brings him slowly back to the present, fills him with lust. He'll go to her now. Yeah, that's what he'll do. Spend tonight and maybe tomorrow fucking and then leave. Back on the road. Head for Vancouver and whatever's there for him.

But that's in the future. His prick is throbbing. Right now, it's all that seems worth paying attention to.

* * * * *

Somewhere outside of Burns Lake, B.C., Curly Joe freezes.

The sun set two and a half hours ago. The workmen up the road have all gone home to wife, kids and supper. The farmer across the way closed his gate one last time. Everybody's somewhere else in fact, except for all the planet's kamikaze mosquitoes.

The neon sign on the the opposite side of the highway he's on is flickering its red and blue message: SLEEPY-TIME MOTEL. He wants to destroy that motel brick by brick, neon light by neon light, until only rubble points out its former whereabouts. Unable to achieve that, he instead keeps giving it the evil eye. He could conceivably move on down the road till the place slips beyond his vision. He doesn't, though. It's something conspicuous to vent his rage upon. Something to keep him going.

It's cold. More than cold. The breezes blow through his bones. Strangely, focusing on the motel provides him with a solace that he isn't feeling cold and hungry on the edge of nowhere. Nowheres don't have motels.

* * * * *

The cross country bus has at last left the Rocky Mountain town Moe spent the better part of the first day of his return journey in.

He'd scrutinised all the tired looking Native Indians who slouched around, waiting for bars to open. A cowboy had spent an hour talking crap to him, wanting to know what Montréal was really like. The corner store had supplied him with sandwiches and *Pepsi*.

What's keeping these people outwardly sane? He takes in a couple of Mounties shoving a very drunken Native Indian into the back seat of their patrol car, and guesses that he's been asking the wrong question.

* * * * *

Squeaking bed. Murmurs of encouragement. Heavy breathing. Bed damp with sweat and sex-juice.

The swooning joy of fucking. That sublime torture of holding it back as long as possible while everything else, even the woman beneath, blurs into a formless jumble of sensations.

Minutes when a whole life seems fixed on the tip of your prick that burns and thrums with all its new-found energy.

The moment when you know. Even before it happens. You know.

* * * * *

Howling! Can it be wolves?

Curly Joe gets up out of his sleeping bag. The cold blasts away at him once again. *if it's wolves, let 'em have me. i'm as good as gone in any case.*

He curses some more at the motel. Then he curses the manufacturers of his useless sleeping bag. Momentarily spent, he burrows into it once more, head covered in deep and tries to sleep.

* * * * *

A young woman's now sitting on the bus next to Moe.

Pretty. She'd smiled as he'd moved aside to give her the window seat.

He casually — probably accidentally— nudges her thigh.

She doesn't seem to have noticed.

Should I speak to her?

* * * * *

Oh God. Oh God. Oh God.
She's coming.
She's moving around so fast I might slip out.
Oh God.
Look at her go.
Too much for words.

* * * * *

He tries to jerk off just to make himself feel a little warmer.

Somehow, it reminds him of Nora. The cosy bed they were all bouncing on.

Reduced to this. No! Get her out of your head! Think of Suzie Q. Be faithful!

* * * * *

'Pretty packed bus, huh?'
'Yes.'
'Nice night, though.'
'Yes.'
Well, at least she hasn't told him where to shove it yet.

* * * * *

God, won't she ever stop coming?
It's like her ass is on fire.
Look at her go!

* * * * *

'suzie q .... suzie q .... suzie q .... suzie q ....'

* * * * *

'Going far?'
'No. I get off at the next town.'
'Oh ...'

* * * * *

WOW!
WOW!
WOW!

* * * * *

'There's Vancouver!' the truck driver shouts over the din of his engine, waking up Curly Joe.

It's mid-afternoon, two and a half days since he's left Kitimat. It feels like forever. Still he survived.

A man from England and his Korean wife driving by in the early morning hours had noticed him lying half-out of his sleeping bag and looking very close to frozen death. They'd bundled their spare woollen tartan blanket over his mosquito-bitten body, turned on their car's heater to the max, and fed him sandwiches. All of which restored a smile back onto his face. Happily, Curly Joe got along so well with them, he ended up spending the next night recuperating at their house.

Then it was back on the road, hitching, experiencing floating thoughts of himself and Suzie Q in Vancouver. Summerful, sunny Vancouver. Close enough to 'Frisco and The Haight to have received much more of the vibrations than Montréal ever could. Vancouver ... A truck had stopped and a voice was calling out 'Vancouver?' It belonged to a skeletal figure behind the wheel of one of those get-out-of-my-way juggernauts that nearly knock you off your feet when you're standing next to the highway, waiting. The skeleton spoke next to nothing and Curly Joe almost immediately fell asleep.

'There it is,' wheezes the skeleton, 'That's Vancouver. Nice place for a city.'

Left off at the outskirts, Curly Joe quickly gets a new ride that takes him straight through Stanley Park.

'It's, like, real psychological,' explains his fashionably-cut long-haired driver. 'All the nine-to-fivers have to make their way in and out of it when heading back home, and it's so goddamn beautiful that it's enough for them to forget what a fucking awful job they've got, so that they'll go do it again the next day.'

Curly Joe's dropped off at the end of Cornwall Avenue, close to where the beaches are. He has no idea where he is, but he loves the place already. It's exactly as he's imagined it. He begins to walk around, not knowing or caring where he heads. When he stops, it's simply because he likes the name of the street he's just passed by. Arbutus Street. It's the right place to make a phone call to Suzie Q.

He looks forward to staying at her grandmother's. Him and Suzie Q. And then, later, Larry and Moe as well. Oh! The heavenly treat of a shower. Maybe even a shared one. His hands shake for some reason when he dials.

- Hello?
- can i speak to suzie q please?
- Just a second. Hold on.

(*a nice grandmotherly voice. she'll probably cook up a fantastic welcoming meal*).

- Hello?
- hi ...
- Oh! You made it!
- yup.
- That's great. Hang on, I'm eating an apple. Tell me all about it.
- oh, it's hard to say. hard to talk about, you know? there's so much. it's been great though, can't really begin going through it on the phone.
- Uhm ... Oh, thanks for the card.
- what?
- From Winnipeg. The Drug Store that took a picture of itself.
- oh ... it's nothing.
- So funny. I loved it.
- i bet you did.
- What do you mean by that?
- nothing.
- C'mon, I'm such a fool. What do you mean by it?
- nothing! i swear.
- All right ... Well, tell me something.
- what?
- About your trip. Did you get to that place where you all wanted to go?
- where? oh, kitimat? yeah. yeah. we made it there.
- How was it?
- interesting.
- Are Larry and Moe with you?
- no. i left early. on my own.
- On your own? Why?
- oh, a couple of things came up.
- *Things*? What do you mean?

- i'll tell you, soon. not over the phone.
- Where are you now?
- somewhere called arbutus street.
- That's near one of the bridges to one of the rivers, isn't it?
- uhm ... yeah, i think so.
- Oh, the beaches are *so* great! The water's beautiful!
- yeah, i'm sure it is.
- We'll just *have* to go there one day.
- yeah. we'll —
- Where are you staying?
- wha? uhm ... i dunno ... say, can i —
- Oh, well, I hope you find a place soon.
- ...
- Hello? Are you still there?
- yeah. i'm here.
- Let me know where you're staying, okay?
- yeah. i guess. hey —
- Hang on. Nan's calling me. I'll be right back.
- okay. *god! what's happening here? no invite. maybe she's gone to speak to her grandmother about it.*
- Hello?
- hi again.
- Nan says I've got to get off the phone because dinner's ready.
- oh.
- Call me up as soon as you can, hey? And we'll go to the beach together, okay?
- yeah, sure. uhm ...
- How long are you planning to stay?
- uhm ... i dunno. a while.
- Well, I've got to go. See you. It's great to hear your voice. 'Bye.
- 'bye. *oh my god! what the fuck? was she giving me the brush-off? how? why? but what else could it be but that?*

In his arrogant innocence, it never occurs to Curly Joe what the social ramifications of his staying over at Suzie Q's grandmother's would mean to an elderly woman who'd grown up in late Victorian England. For sure, somewhere in the back of his mind, he's figured this out. But he'll have no truck with it. He feels totally betrayed by Suzie Q. He's come all this way, nearly frozen himself to death, just to reach Vancouver to see her ... Feeling like a balloon that's soared higher and higher and is now on the point of bursting, he slips out of the phone booth in a daze, positive that it must be over between them.

Curly Joe flounders around the city streets taking in very little. He has no idea where he's heading nor does he care. He's so far and away lost in his thoughts, he even fails to notice the three people who've laconically shuffled up alongside his path looking as though they have the most heavy-duty questions ever, ever, ever to ask him.

Two males and a female, all around the same age as Curly Joe. Vancouver hippies.

One of the males has long curly hair spiralling down to his shoulders. A headband (which is, looking more closely, a green and black striped strip of left-over fabric fastened tightly around his skull) keeps it in place. From a squinty-eyed point of view, he kind of looks like a white boy version of Jimi Hendrix. Maybe.

The other guy lowers his fly-eye glasses to give Curly Joe a spot check. He's a bit shorter, but about as lean and hungry as his buddy. He's covered his body and clothes with a sizeable variety of beads and trinkets as well as a yellow-dotted red bandana, the necessary accoutrements of those who seek inner, personal revolution. There's plenty more like him living that dream in Vancouver. This *is* Canada, and not Amerika, after all.

The young woman has straight blonde hair and wears bell-bottomed blue jeans onto which she's stitched brightly-coloured outlines of the peace symbol, a cannabis leaf, a daisy, and the astrological glyph for her Sun sign, Cancer (though she refers to it as Moonchild due to the bad vibes associated with its original name). In order to avoid being hauled away on a morals charge, she's also donned a wildly tie-dyed pink and purple T-shirt, torn at all the right places.

Attractive as she is, the young woman fails to jump-start

Curly Joe out of his stupor. Neither she nor her compatriots have filtered through into his conscious thoughts. Instead, his mind dwells on matters that seem at once trivial and yet which sum up his whole relationship with Suzie Q.

Flashback! A meal with Suzie Q and her parents. His hand, reaching for a glass of wine accidentally stroking hers. That second just before her impish smile forms itself. Its moment frozen forever.

Flashback! Suzie Q's screw. There they are, enjoying the vibes of Old Montréal, sitting on a bench somewhere, smiling. Then ... *Abracadabra!* She's holding this loosened screw that she'd spied sticking up from one of the seat planks and is making out that it's the biggest thing in the world to her. Something for them both to joke about for a couple of minutes before moving on. Except, weeks later, she finds that screw again in her purse, pulls it out and asks if he remembers. When he doesn't, her teardrops fall non-stop. Broken-hearted, the only thing that gets her smiling again is hearing him say that he loves her.

And after all that, what does she do now? Writes him off with a phone call from Hell! How could everything change so instantly and conclusively? The question forms a connection with Curly Joe's memory of his last exchange with Nora. He'd been as non-plussed by events then as he's feeling now. Is this his cosmic comeuppance for how he'd treated her?

The questions disappear as quickly as it takes the hippie woman — Nature Girl, she calls herself — to lay her hand on his shoulder. 'hey,' Curly Joe begins to say. *who are these people? pan-handlers hitting on easy bait, i guess. well, they're on a losing streak today.*

Nature Girl interrupts him. 'Hey, yourself. Don't be so down, man.' Her concern is sincere. His hair, wild curls and all, identifies him as being on the right side of the culture wars. That's enough of a reason for her to want to help. 'Look,' she continues, 'The sky's blue. The sun's out. The ocean's waiting. And there's always the flowers. No reason at all to be so down in the dumps, man. You know that.'

Her dopey grin makes it unthinkable for Curly Joe not to reciprocate with a sliver of a smile.

Which is good enough for Nature Girl. 'That's better. See? Life's pretty okay after all, right?'

'naw. it's a hassle. but thanks, all the same,' Curly Joe says. Then he asks himself what he's doing pretending to be happy for these strangers. Still, maybe they can be of some use to him. 'uhm ... do you guys know a place i can crash at? i just blew in and —'

Nature Girl eyes up his clothes, then is all smiles again. 'Look, if you're all messed up about a crash pad, you can hang out with us. No hassle, man. We got plenty of floor. Can ya dig it?' She waits for Curly Joe's silent response to shift from suspicion to grateful relief. 'See? Troubles just fly away if you let 'em.'

'well, it's not every day i get a free place to stay in —'

'Nothing's free on *this* bus, man,' the maybe Hendrix look-alike hippie pipes up .

bus? what's he going on about? do they live on a bus? Curly Joe hasn't picked up on the allusion to Ken Kesey and the Merry Band of Pranksters travelling around in their psychedelic bus, *Furthur.* Not that it stops him from playing it cool anyway. 'oh, right ... uhm ... so how much is the rent then?'

'No paper. Can't pay with paper, man. We ain't fuckin' capitalist pigs, man,' the other guy says, causing his acid-head Tibetan brass chime earring to tinkle. 'What Vic means is that if you come in with us, then you're part of us, dig? You lose what you gain by being alone.'

'i guess i can afford that.'

The guy called Vic sniffs contemptuously. 'Not that many cats seem to think so.'

'yeah. guess so.' Curly Joe agrees, not really clear as to what exactly he's agreeing to.

'Well, if you're coming, let's go then,' Nature Girl says. 'Time's passing!'

'where? to your place?' Curly Joe hopes so because he could do with a wash and somewhere to slip inside his sleeping bag so that he can tie himself up in knots over the cruel knocks his life has had to take on board.

'Are you for real? On a day like this?' Nature Girl clucks her tongue. 'This boy's a head case,' she tells her hippie brothers, who nod back in sad agreement. 'We were making for the beach before you stopped us,' she explains.

'the beach?'

'Yeah. You know: swim-swim, splash-splash. *The beach.*'

'oh.'

'Well? Are ya into it?'

He's not. But what's he going to say? 'sure. why not?'

'No. Not why *not*!' they all shout.

'That's a negative action, man. You should be asking "why"?' Vic says.

Curly Joe gives in to their crazy logic. After all, everything about this encounter has been bizarre so far, so why stop now? 'why?' he says. 'uhm ... well ... because it's sunny?'

'And ...'

"the beach is there?'

'And ...'

'my hair could do with a soak?'

'And ...'

'it's cool and refreshing on a day like this?'

'And ...'

Curly Joe turns to face the Nature Girl. 'i'd like to see what you look like in a bathing suit?'

Nature Girl laughs. 'And ...'

'uhm ... i dunno. i just really feel like it now.'

'That's it!' the three cheer in sync. 'You got it. Let's get going then.'

And with that, they all take turns patting Curly Joe on the back, welcoming him into their world.

* * * * *

The first thing Moe does when he's arrived at the Provincial Bus Station on Dorchester is to phone his mother and tell her he's fine and that he'll be home later on so can she please leave him some home-cooked food because he's sick to death of eating sandwiches? Then he heads over to the Men's washroom and slams himself inside one of the stalls. He pulls off the clothes he's been living in for the past four days and changes into cleaner, though just as wrinkled, replacements. Task achieved, he studies the Station's clock, making sure that he's locked into the right time zone. Yep. Nearly 6.00pm. She'll be home from work by now. With the bit of money stashed into his jeans pockets that he's kept hidden away for emergencies he hops onto one of the three buses he'll need to take, and then heads for The Gypsy's house over in Mount Royal.

Answering the door, she's shocked by his unannounced reappearance. Not hesitating, she embraces him proudly, refers to the event as *The Prodigal's Return*, and welcomes him indoors. Watching Moe devour the scrambled eggs she's cooked for him, The Gypsy can't avoid asking herself what impact this is going to have on the freedom she's been wheedling back into her life. *It will be what it will be,* she reminds herself, pushing the concern aside so that it won't override the happiness she's feeling.

Life, however, has other plans. In response to The Gypsy's encouragement, Moe starts to recount their adventures. He tells her proudly of Prince George and their night in a doss-house. Her upset and anger at how they'd used people, lied to them, raises his eyebrows. All right then, how about if he lists some of the terrible ordeals he'd been put through during the first few days of the journey when they'd had no money? She pronounces such times as being patently beautiful and definitive moments that he should savour. And so it goes. Like some never-ending tennis match, every volley is returned with equal, if opposite, fervour. Until, a shared comprehension sets in. Somehow, in the time that's passed since they've last seen each other, their whole world's gone madly out of orbit. Not knowing what else to do, they revert to desultory, safely polite small talk.

The result of this for Moe is the experience of an emptiness so total that it won't even permit him to feel despair. He wants to be with the woman he's come back for, to hold and caress her. The things he's been through just to make it back alive for her. The blur of the last four days, sweating it with assorted hicks and farmers, killing his back, starving himself so's he could afford to take her to a nice restaurant some night once he made it home. It's all failing dismally.

The Gypsy, too, is shaken by the pace of what's happening to them. While Moe's been away, she's allowed herself to build up an illusion. She wants to love Moe just because he's another human being. Yet she knows he's different; she wants to be in love with him. And the subtlety and extremity of the tension provoked in that difference continue to pull her apart. How quickly and easily she's allowed possessive love to fill up her mind. So long as its heart and focus kept itself to a safe distance, it was an enjoyable diversion. But now that the distance has been conquered, she experiences the first shockwaves of that relaxation. And it feels like one prodigious hiccup that resists leaping out.

Regrettably, their divide exposes a shared awareness of defeat; their affair of the heart, hardly born, is already preparing to die.

* * * * *

'I don't know! What's wrong with him? I've waited and waited for him to phone back since he arrived. But, nothing. Not a word. Why's he being so cruel, hey?'

Larry shrugs. He can't work out what Curly Joe's up to, either. But now that he's here, in Vancouver, sitting across from Suzie Q in her grandma's living room, it doesn't really bother him all that much. It just feels great being where he is, giving in to the feelings taking him over. He can see that Suzie Q's really upset, that she still really cares for Curly Joe. Loves him, probably. No, definitely. As he does, too. But he's not worried. Even if he has no idea what's going on for him, Curly Joe is bound to be taking good care of himself. He's sure about that.

Hearing the whimpers Suzie Q's unable to subdue, Larry

fixes on how humiliated she must be feeling. Without thinking about it, he stands up, moves toward her. To hell with Curly Joe and where he might be. What matters is that this beautifully seductive woman sitting across from him is crying and feeling unloved. He's here to prove her wrong.

Sensing that something has changed, Suzie Q stands as well. She doesn't flinch when Larry crooks his left arm around her waist while, with the other, he gently cradles her face, looks into it, and, not hesitating, kisses her fully on the lips. In spite of everything, Suzie Q responds. And *voila!* She, too, forgets all about Curly Joe.

'Come on,' Larry says. 'Let's go.'

'Where?'

'I'll show yuh the dump of a room I'm staying in.'

She'd like to believe that she hesitates ...

The hotel Larry's staying at is on Granville and Davie. It's the cheapest he could find. They pretend not to notice that he's hit the jackpot on that one. A bed, a chair, a foldaway plastic table and a closet. Not much space left after that.

Still, who cares? Door locked, chair up against it just in case, Larry wastes no time. A week ago, he wouldn't be feeling so certain and assured. A week ago, he wouldn't even have made the suggestion to Suzie Q that she should follow him here. This change that's come over him? That's thanks to Pattie Pubes. She's taught him that, when it comes to sex, taking is a form of giving and the worst mistake to make is that of hesitation. Confident that he can be the lover she deserves and hopefully desires, Larry starts to unbutton Suzie Q's shirt and unclasp her bra, then remove it. Stopping her hands from covering herself, he bends to take each of her already erect, pale-pink nipples into his mouth, allowing his tongue to slide over and curl itself about them until they stand out even more taut than before.

Suzie Q moans.

Outside, unusually for the time of year, it begins to rain.

Larry fumbles with the zipper at the back of her skirt. He yanks, but nothing happens.

'I'll do it,' Suzie Q whispers, scatty in her impatience. Her only words to him.

The skirt slips down onto the dust-covered wooden floor. She sucks in her breath (and stomach) as his impetuous hands begin to caress the elastic band of her panties. Swept away by desire, she doesn't resist as he stretches their elasticised band, bringing the blue cotton briefs down to her knees where they pause for a moment and then sag to her ankles, covering her toes, waiting to be kicked away. She shuts her eyes, finding it too wanton to meet him face to face. Her legs begin to tremble of their own accord and Suzie Q feels a rush that cancels out all sounds other than the rain, which pours down even more fiercely now, and of running feet clickety-clacking hurriedly past the window, retreating for shelter.

Free to explore, Larry's hands encircle her loins, travel up and down her thighs, fingers circling ever closer towards the already dampened slit, wet from secretions that aid his campaign to bisect the outer lips and gain partial entry.

Suzie Q moans again. Her entire body convulses in involuntary spasms.

Rain splatters onto the hotel room window providing a staccato beat and a vague reflection which, once noticed, makes them aware of what an odd picture they create. Feeling somewhat silly, Larry begins to undress himself. Be it courage or curiosity, Suzie Q opens her eyes enough to peek, eager and ashamed.

He strips hurriedly, leaving on only his underwear. There's a ruthless reason for this act that has nothing at all to do with modesty or precautionary sensibility. Rather, Larry is dead sure that if his shorts come off, their loss of control will be complete. Which would bring on a demand to confess his guilt that he won't have the will or the skill to keep hidden from Curly Joe once they meet up again. Same goes for Suzie Q, he supposes. Under no circumstances is he going to allow that to happen. So it has to be that they go as far as possible without going all the way. Fair's fair. After all, Curly Joe's been unfaithful, hasn't he? He'll have to deal with that one. Until then, why can't Suzie Q have some fun, too? And better with him than someone else because at least he knows where to draw the line.

Guilt tolerably appeased, Larry eases Suzie Q down onto the bed so that her body is fully open to him and then begins to probe it with his tongue. It's the closest, and furthest, thing to fucking that he can think of while still qualifying as an act of love. He forces his mouth to slide little by little down her neck, to her throat, and then, once again onto her breasts. Pausing only momentarily, he runs his tongue lower to her navel, and onto her hips, and up again to her belly where his caresses tickle, causing her to laugh nervously. When it reaches her mound, he sees that she's placed one of her hands over it. He chooses to avoid the obstacle and continues his downward route, stopping only once his tongue's just an inch or so below her knees. There, he begins once again to kiss and lick at the inside of her legs, enticing such pleasant irritation that she feels no fear in spreading them apart.

He's so close to her vulva now that the odour of her secretions distracts, compelling him to turn his attention back to the secure smoothness of her thigh. Yet her scent's irresistible and alluring, so exquisite in its aroma that he licks his lips, then lowers them gently until they hover over the bristly hairs. Giving his tongue free reign, he allows it to play in the pubic forest, bathe it, until, too curious, it unfolds the pliant flesh, urging itself deeper into the cavity, exposing a cavern-like network of ultra-sensitive skin to slide between and lubricate into arousal.

Inflamed by his slippery advances, Suzie Q's body initiates a series of ever-more determined thrusts intent on goading his tongue to increase its feverish lapping at the inner walls. Giving in to an insistent rhythm, Suzie Q is taken over by an involuntary pandemonium that travels lower and lower down her body until, at last reaching it's terminus, it swells into an extended gasp of elated gratification. Then everything comes to a standstill. The caresses. The whispers. The world. Everything. Except for the rain that continues to drown the world.

Aware now of what has happened, Suzie Q tries to get used to the reality that it is Larry, not Curly Joe, who is the first man since her childhood to see her nude, much less to possess her in the way he has. While that admission shocks her, at the same time it fails to give rise to the slightest feeling of remorse. She'd enjoyed looking at Larry's eyes as they took in every bit of her body. She'd blushed with pride at the admiration reflected in them. She wants him to know all this. But not through words. Spurred on by the lascivious need to fulfil her demand, she grabs hold of the top of his boxers and, before he can do anything about it, pulls them all the way down.

She's never seen *that* part of a man before. Not erect, anyway. It fascinates her in a repulsive sort of way. It looks so silly and bordering on the ugly, and yet it is also, somehow, perfect. She knows enough from books what she should do now. What Larry must surely want her to do now. Nope, sorry! She isn't able to bring herself to take his cock into her mouth. But she is brave enough to touch it, then fasten a tighter hold and begin to tug in a way she hopes will be a good enough imitation of what she'd learned from her furtive, nimble-fingered readings.

Oh please! Please! Let me do it right for Laurent! Let me make my handsome, masterful lover come in intoxicating urgency just like the novels say!

And when he does, when his sperm spurts everywhere onto her hand and stomach, bed sheet and floor, she's taken aback by the messy reality of it all. No book could have ever opened her eyes to this. She feels an urgent longing to wipe the goo off immediately but manages to stop herself from doing so. This jelly-white gunk which is already hardening into a wafer-like solid is one of the ingredients to the creation of life. And here it is, lying wasted on her body. Overcome by a mixture of profound sadness and pride, Suzie Q reminds herself that, after all, it is *her* body he's chosen to waste it on.

Snuggled up now, still light-headed, beneath the sheets, Larry kisses her once more. 'I'd better get yuh home soon. Yuhr grandma will start getting worried.'

Suzie Q reluctantly agrees. Then, a barely audible whisper. 'Laurent ... *Je t'aime.*'

He pauses. 'I love yuh, too.'

'But —'

'What?'

'I thought I heard a "but" about to follow.'

'No, there's no but.'

'Only Curly Joe,' Suzie Q says, at last finding herself able to remind them both of his existence.

'Yeah. I guess.'

Suzie Q sits up. 'Can we forget about Curly Joe for as long as we're both here in Vancouver? We'll deal with things when Montréal reality sets back in. Let this be our dream-world.'

Larry smiles. 'I like that. A lot. Okay. Let's carry on dreaming in Vancouver.'

'One thing, though ...'

'Yeah? What?'

'I just noticed that I've been lying on my shirt and now its all wet with ... Well, you know. Not just yours, mine as well. So can I borrow a fresh one from you?'

'Sure. I don't know how fresh what I've got to offer is, but yuh're welcome to pick what yuh like.'

And, with that, Suzie Q is certain. She gazes at her Laurent and sees everything that matters. Not only is his hair falling long and straight, he's also begun to grow a moustache. He's an erotic dream come true.

But then, she has to admit, in an altogether different way, so is Curly Joe.

* * * * *

Nearly forty minutes have passed by since Curly Joe dropped.

He sweats freely, a permanent foolish grin etched across his face. He keeps glancing over at the others, Nature Girl most of all. She's dropped as well. It strikes him that he can't backtrack on what he's done. Once you've knocked back the little yellow pill, you're committed to whatever it's going to do with you.

Never mind. He feels so much love for his commune friends

that he forbids himself from worrying. Five days now, he's been with them. Years, really, for all the unflagging carefreeness and peace they've brought him. He's thought little and worried over no one from Montréal while in their presence. Now and again, it has passed through his mind that Larry and Moe may be somewhere in the city searching him out. He can't do anything about that. If they find him, well and good. And if they don't, well, that's okay, too.

Suzie Q also settles into his thoughts now and then. But the pain he associates with her is small and the thought of Nature Girl sleeping next to him at night makes that pain quite bearable. Nature Girl's given him so much; she's made him her pet worry. And responsibility. Her eyes dart every which way and her forehead curls upward whenever he confounds her with his doleful words. But her mouth, behind it all, always comes up with an easygoing grin for him.

Once upon a time not all that long ago, Nature Girl went by the name of Lily and worked as a front-desk receptionist at one of San Francisco's bigger advertising agencies. She used to have ambitions to be an air stewardess but meeting her ex-boyfriend, Rex, had squashed that one. One day, she'd woken up, Rex snoring away. Just to drown him out, she turned on the bedside radio. It was tuned in to her favourite station, KYA, and it was playing Aretha's *(You Make Me Feel Like) A Natural Woman.* In double quick time, Lily saw her most likely future. Not liking it one bit, she dumped Rex, quit her job, threw out her work appropriate clothes — especially the various sets of tights that had a habit of rolling down on her or generating unwanted static — and bussed her way to Haight-Ashbury and a new life.

Not long after that, she met and got entangled with Vic in a free and mellow sort of way. Telling him the story of her musical moment of illumination, Vic gave it some thought and proposed that from now on she should call herself Nature Girl. Somehow, changing her name made a goofy sort of logic to Lily. Besides, it gave her the excuse to stop shaving her underarms and legs. And so it was that Nature Girl came to be.

Then, a couple of months later, Vic got this job moving

people's furniture and such to new locations. One time, he was going to drive all the way to up to Vancouver so he asked Nature Girl to tag along for the ride. Once they'd arrived, they both got zapped by the really great vibes of the place. Plus, being holed up in Canada, meant that Vic had a foolproof way to avoid any possible future draft calls. And that was that.

Now Nature Girl is a solid point in the Vancouver Scene. And more, she's dedicating a whole lot of her time attending to Curly Joe. Still, he knows that even if she's his for now, he can never possess her. Her love for him is free and simple and totally open. Just as it would be to anyone else who wanted it. She'd not thought twice at putting him up in her room, giving him her bed and her body, allowing one more lonesome stranger to experience makeshift peace through her.

Now and then, Curly Joe wonders if Nature Girl is the person that The Gypsy is trying to become. And, with that thought, it comes to him that more than love Nature Girl, he idolises her. Here's a creature he could never feel any of that protective jealousy he'd always assumed came naturally with someone you loved. Long-held assumptions thrown to the wind, Curly Joe has to admit that, for once, he's face-to-face with a female who's superior to him in all ways. Strangely, it feels like a relief.

But then, all these people are so like Nature Girl. They truly live in the now, doing crazy things on the spur of the moment. Like the day they lugged a full length mirror to the Park Zoo and placed it in front of the caged orangutang who, in reaction to its reflection, began to jerk off in front of everyone, much to the disgust of all The Straights. Or like their spontaneous agreement to tear down all the doors in their commune — even the bathroom's— thereby zapping any residue of buttoned-up straight-world privacy so that they could all be free. Yes, they are, without a doubt, beautiful people. They've even gone ahead and prescribed his cure. Each morning, just before leaving to go pick fruit and vegetables which they'll later deliver to the various Alternative Food Shops in and around the city, they set out a plan for his day. Usually, they tell him to take a couple of apples and peaches and head over to the beach. Several hours a day of sunshine and silence, they prophesy, is all he really needs to sort himself out. He's convinced they're right. He trusts them completely.

Even Vic. Vic ... Curly Joe can't puzzle out what makes him feel uneasy around Vic. He's friendly enough, for sure. They even share a lot in common. Maybe too much. Almost like mirror images. But Fun House ones. Which could be the problem. Still and all, maybe it's just that Vic and Nature Girl almost certainly had something going before she turned her affections in Curly Joe's direction.

Whatever ... Vic can certainly rattle on. And on. And on. Doesn't seem to notice that others might have had enough of listening to him. Just keeps going at it, oblivious. For example: two nights ago, out of the blue, Vic made up his mind that Curly Joe needed to hear about all the alternative events Vic had been there for and which turned out to be crucial moments in the history of The Movement.

'I was living the life in San Francisco, man. Saw the beginnings of it all,' says Vic. He smacks his lips, takes another puff on the joint he's bogarting, and then he's off. 'Oh yeah, I was there all the way from the start. Things took off when this painter guy, Michael Bowen, and his wife, Martine, had this big dream of all the San Fran Freaks coming together in one huge happening. Which is how the Great Human Be-In came to be, dont'cha know?' Vic gives Curly Joe the hairy eyeball just to make sure that he does. 'Yep. Sunday, January 14, 1967. The Gathering of the Tribes. Something like ten thousand hippies, radicals and free spirits buzzing it up over in Golden Gate Park. Ginsberg was there. Gary Snyder. Michael McClure. A whole bunch of them Beat Poets, for sure. And the Bands ... Like, wow, man! You got *The Charlatans.* You got *Jefferson Airplane.* You got *Big Brother & the Holding Company (starring Janis Joplin).* You got *Quicksilver Messenger Service.* I mean, what else you gonna need, right? Even the pigs got into it. Oh yeah, pretended they couldn't see nor smell all the joints people were passing around. Aw, man! At one point, I thought I was hallucinating because I spied this fuckin' Hell's Angels guy helping some hippie chick find her lost daughter. Can you beat that? No way, right? But, hey! Turns out it was happening for real! Even the Hell's Angels were on board, man!'

Vic waits for the communal snorts and sniggers to simmer down, then moves on. 'So after that, the fuse was well and truly lit. All sorts of "-Ins" started happening all over the place. Next thing, New York gets in on the act. Gotta say, mainly thanks to Bob Fass over at WBAI. He got that "Fly-In" thing together over at JFK. Somehow brought out thousands of hopers and dopers on a freezing cold East Coast February weekend. Had 'em singing, dancing, toking, clapping at all the planes taking off ... the whole shebang. Mainly, it got everybody thinking "Hey! Like, this is something else! Let's do it again. But when it's, like, lots warmer, right?" Which they did. On Easter Sunday, too, no shit. Pal of mine wrote me about how they got as many Freaks to truck on over to Sheep's Meadow as we'd had at our Be-In over in Frisco. Ten thousand full-time and weekend hippies coming together — some of 'em taking that to mean *literally* coming together, if you catch my drift — shaking the *Big Apple* to its core.'

Vic burps, blows out some smoke. 'Gotta admit, those East Coast kids let their imaginations run riot after that. First there's this brillo idea by this guy, Emmett Grogan, to organize a "Sweep-In". Yeah, let's go and clean up the Lower East Side! Can you get your head around *that* scene? All them Diggers and Merry Pranksters armed with mops and brooms doing their best to turn a slum area into something bright and clean? Outtasite, right? Which means ... Cosmic Balance time! Here comes that "Soot-In" over at *Con Ed Headquarters.* Freaks throwing handfuls of ashes all over the place, landing on the Straights' jackets and ties, down their necks, making their point about wanting cleaner air. Real Yin/Yang stuff. And then, round about this same time last year, there was that anti-capitalist "Big Bucks-In" at the Stock Exchange where traders got showered with dollar bills. Remember that? Crazy!'

Vic stops to take another lengthy toke. 'Okay, so I wasn't at any of those. Not physically, anyway. But I did get to sneak across the border and crash the Monterey Pop Festival back in June last year. Stuck it out all the way to the end, too. *Jimi Hendrix. Otis Redding. The Who.* Even *Ravi Shankar,* for Pete's sake. And with Beatle George there looking on beatifically.' That reminds him. 'Speaking of which ... Who's to say that Monterey wasn't the inspiration for *The Beatles* to play *All You Need Is Love* one week later for that very first live worldwide satellite TV broadcast? Me and Nature Girl and the gang had to traipse on over to some other cat's house to watch it because we don't have a TV set. Don't want one, either. But, Hey! It was *The Beatles*, right?'

Vic's history lesson is going full steam ahead. So far, it's all been SIDE A. SIDE B is more of a bummer. Now he's jabbering on about heavy-duty riots in Detroit. Tampa. Buffalo. Newark. Minneapolis. Milwaukee ... Take your pick. No, Vic's not into rioting. He stays clear of all that "up against the wall" stuff that's going on everywhere from Paris to Hong Kong. Plus, you've got the USSR and China arguing over who's reading Marx in the right way. Greek Colonels making good on their military coup. The Middle East flaring up. Civil War in Nigeria. Cyprus. Philippines ... On top of *The War*, natch. That's all heavy shit, man. Nope. Protest marches is as far as Vic's willing to go where comedowns are concerned. Sure, he was there with the thousands and thousands of anti-war marchers in San Francisco. All of them in their bell-bottomed and tie-dyed uniforms that made them easy pickings for the pigs, for sure. But great recruitment adverts as well. Vic nearly got himself arrested, too. Just like good Ol' Dr. Spock. No, not the guy on *Star Trek.*

Vic wags an index finger. 'So much going on, it feels like everything's for the taking. Thing is though, as much as it scares the kittens out of us all, we also got to admit that we're getting a charge out of it, too. As if that "what happens next?" is opening up possibilities, stretching our ways of thinking way beyond the usual. Like with Love, for instance. Okay, so maybe it's gotten a little too V-fingered and sloganized, true enough. But that don't mean it's not still there. In thought and deed. Shining brightly.'

One more event Vic *didn't* attend: the death and burial of the hippie, in summertime 1967 San Francisco. Which is another reason why he pulled up stakes and relocated way up north here in Vancouver. Different flowers, but that Love and Peace vibe is still alive and well.

Listening to all that stuff, Curly Joe is impressed. But he's also feeling like he's being put down. Vic's done and experienced so much. What's *he* done? Just another seen-nothing, done-nothing, know-nothing Montréal hick. Which is probably why he's agreed to stick out his tongue like at Catholic Mass and get set to meet the godhead.

Curly Joe feels the acid working at last. The changes, curiously, haven't been all at once. When the initial distortions become more noticeable, he hears Vic blabbering away again. But now the words seem to echo and reverberate deep inside Curly Joe, some shrinking, some expanding, all of them unfocused and too full of noise. He feels himself talking back, but can't grab hold on what he's saying. The thought of this makes him laugh. Still laughing, he connects that he can also hear himself talking. Which makes him laugh all the louder. So loud, actually, that everybody else overhears him. Soon, the whole room begins to echo with laughter. At first, he enjoys all the caterwauling, dives into it to get the full-on experience. But then, right after he does, his head starts to feel very clear and real again and he's oh-so-calmly asking the others just what it is they're all in hysterics about.

The question stumps them. They can't explain. 'We thought that you knew!' the others shout back. They sound aggrieved. maybe even angry. That gets Curly Joe feeling stupid for having asked in the first place. The word stupid rings inside him, creating further mental bamboozlement. 'stupid. stu-pid. stew-pid. stewpit. stew-pit. there are 49 different varieties of campbell's *stew-pit.*' Curly Joe is overwhelmed by the profundity of his statement.

'my god!' Curly Joe yells, 'i'm tripping!' Which starts him up laughing all over again, unable to stop. Next thing he knows, he's rolling all over the floor. The rest of them see him and add up that what he's up to looks real cool. So, they too, begin to roll around, no excuse required.

All except Vic. Vic's the Trip Guide today. Vic hasn't taken anything in case one of them starts drowning and needs a lifeguard. Doesn't stop him from laughing as well, though.

Before Curly Joe knows it, it turns very dark. It must be late because the sun had set just after they'd dropped. They'd gone out to see it, but it had carried out its act too soon for them to *really* see it. So that's why they're indoors and not outside. Never mind, Vic is putting on a record. He says: 'Listen to this, you guys.' They all do. It's that *Country Joe And The Fish* album, *Electric Music For The Mind And Body*. It does things to them. They all just lie there and take it in.

Curly Joe finds himself playing with words again. He's noticed that he can just pick a word, or even a part of a word, and hold it in time. Almost. It never really stops entirely, but he can slow it down indefinitely. He enjoys doing this; it makes him feel somehow more linked to the sounds, as though he has a hand in creating them. He thinks he should ask the others if they mind what he's doing. Somewhere, his head throbs with a chorus of 'no, no. go on. we're enjoying it, too!' So he continues.

It seems a very long time before the record comes to an end. Truth is, he isn't sure if it *has* ended. Music still plays on inside him but he isn't too certain where it's coming from. It's only when he starts to swivel his hands to it like some mad conductor that he sees them start to disappear. Fingers first, then palms. He wasn't expecting that, and gets to worrying what's going on. In moments, an intrusive panic begins to take him over. What if it isn't just his hands that are disappearing? What if there's more to this new game? Much as he'd feared, as soon as he peeks, he's forced to confirm that his body is vanishing layer by layer, as though some vast army of flesh-eating termites is at work on him.

He thinks he might be screaming now. He screams again, just to make sure. The termites are up as far as his knees in no time, as well as around his elbows. Pretty soon ... He tries to leave the rest of the thought uncompleted. He doesn't want this; he doesn't want to disappear or die like this. He feels like crying, but can't. The terror's too strong.

Then he hears Vic's voice asking what's wrong. He can't explain since he has no mouth or tongue anymore. Can't the idiot *see* what's wrong? It's torture for Curly Joe to open the gap where his mouth used to be, but, somehow, he forces himself to form an 0 that he hopes will be understood to mean zero. As in: none of me left. That's all he can squeeze out of himself. The termites are just below his neck. He's nothing but a floating head now.

At the same time, from way above, where he can watch the whole scene taking place, Curly Joe thinks that what's happening is hilariously funny. But down there, where he's taking part in it, he's gone frantic, frozen into near catatonic shock.

Wait a minute. Vic's saying something again. Curly Joe tries to focus his hearing on the words, but it's difficult. Doing his damnedest, all he can pick up is: 'Look inside and enjoy.'

what's vic getting at? how can i look inside when i have no inside to look at? and how can i possibly be enjoying what's happening? it's a dead cert: vic must be as high as the rest of them.

That settles it. He's had it for sure; there's nothing left except his eyes now. Somehow (though don't ask him how), he can see them gaping, suspended in the air like two weirdo omelettes. They'll be disappearing any time soon, as well. He looks once more at where his body should be. Though it isn't there, he's somehow able to trace its outline.

Strangely, his eyes are still floating and visible. On their own, they focus upon his now nowhere to be found left hand. He feels them zoom in on the space as though they're microscopes. They're more than that, though. Not only are they zooming in, they're also shrinking, getting closer and closer to the no-space where his hand used to be. And then, something totally bizarre happens. His eyes shrivel down so small that what he'd thought wasn't there somehow starts to emerge.

Curious now, Curly Joe begins coming round to the view that he's not disappearing at all. He is, on the contrary, becoming more visible than he could have ever believed. He can see things about his body that he's never really noticed before. It's so large now, that nothing about him can possibly get missed. The hairs on his hands, for instance. Growing like wild, wind-swept forests. He walks inside them going deeper, further, falling into moon crater pores, swimming in lakes of tepid sweat.

And, with that, Curly Joe's *there*. He isn't lost at all. He's more found than he's ever been. He's a being who can turn itself into every possible size and shape. Bigger than the biggest fairytale giant. Yet, at the same time, somewhere on that giant is a minuscule, gnat-like Curly Joe, crawling and winding his way through a hinterland of hair and skin. And, as well, he's above these two beings, like some hovering presence, an all-benign, jolly god participating in a thoroughly divine way.

He blanks out after that. When he regains consciousness, he finds himself in Stanley Park plopped down on strange, jewel-like grass that tickles him. The others are there as well. Vic has a guitar and he's playing it. The grass likes the music. Curly Joe can tell that from the murmured vibratory hums that the grass provides each time a note's struck and reverberates into the night. He wants to tell the others about what the grass is doing, so he tries to focus his eyes on the colour-blurs that gurgle and speak around him. This is how he finds Nature Girl.

'Ah Rick, isn't this just ... just ... heavenly?'

For a moment, he's not sure who she's talking to and feels jealous. Then, thankfully, it comes back to him that "Rick" is the name they all know him by over here. He's uncertain why that is, then blows it off. What's in a name, anyway? No time for imponderables, he's got better things to focus on right now. Nature Girl's squatting there, eyes narrowed in such a way that he knows that she's already aware of all he wants to say, not least about the humming grass and all the other experiences he's going through.

'why?' he asks her mentally.

She smiles, shrugs, and then moves towards him haphazardly, her cut-out shawl dancing as she approaches. His left hand reaches out and catches at her hair. Like a thousand thread boas, it twirls and clings onto his fingers and palm. He's aware of her life, feels her beat. He knows in any number of ways how different it is from his. And yet, how compatible these differences are. The colours swim and dive around inside her, too beautiful to be spoken of. Life knows only Life.

Somewhere, sometime, they make love. All he'll remember of the event is the orgasm that wouldn't end, the sensation of feeling millions of homunculi of him eject themselves out one by one and enter her.

They fall asleep, spooning each other, on a beach towel Vic has laid out for them.

In moments, the sun will rise to warm and then awaken them from their acid dreams.

19. DEPARTURES AND ARRIVALS

A different kind of awakening is taking place for our Stooges. Separately, unaware of the current events in their private lives, each opens his eyes to the glum concession that the last few days of August are upon him. September stands in their way like some grimly ticking alarm clock that they rivet on in half-dismay, half-fascination, bitterly anticipating the buzzer which will chime at an all-too well-specified time.

McGill's in the ascendant; all thoughts turn in its direction.

* * * * *

Moe's last few days of freedom are passed waiting for the inevitable to happen.

The Gypsy's persuaded him to Major in what sounds like a possibly intriguing re-direction: psychology. He doesn't know anything about the subject, but he's already fired himself up into thinking that it'll give him the means to solve people's problems. Possibly, even his own.

He still sees The Gypsy every day but it's become clear to him that the time they pass away together is becoming more and more painful to both of them. The mystery of their growing alienation nags at him. What's happened that they could be slipping apart so easily? A month ago, they'd have agreed that they'd each found someone who offered happiness. Isn't that enough for her? No. He's being unfair. The question could just as validly be applied to himself.

If Moe could read them, he'd know how striking in their similarity The Gypsy's thoughts are to his own. She's as miserable as he is. She's trapped in the centre of the tug of war between the laid back security that Moe offers and the uncertain possibilities of individual freedom. Every morning she repeats her mantra: *Live, Don't Just Exist*. If only she could truly hear herself say it.

In their pursuit of reasons, both have forgotten that it was the very absence of reason which characterised their first encounter. But then, they're no longer those people. The Magic has passed them by.

Two days before Curly Joe returns to Montréal, Moe sees The Gypsy for the last time. Nothing traumatic happens. No shouting. No arguments. No secrets revealed. They simply pass away another agonizing evening, pretending that there's nothing at all the matter.

Unable to muster up the courage to tell Moe, The Gypsy has arranged to leave for Europe. Officially, it's only for a few months of travelling around taking in the Old World culture until her savings come to an end. She's not told her parents of other, much more revolutionary, possibilities. Her choice having been made through lack of choice, she'll walk out of Moe's life just as she'd come into it.

Unexpected and unforgettable, she'll always be Moe's personal embodiment of The Sixties. The sadness of her leaving cuts deep; though, when it comes down it it, not as deep as he'd expected.

Somehow, he doesn't quite feel that he's lost.

* * * * *

The car is zipping across the Alberta badlands. Tumbleweeds are blowing and Curly Joe thinks of what he's leaving and where he's heading for. Right or wrong, the choice he's made is irrevocable. There's no going back to Vancouver or the people with whom he's shared such a pivotal part of his life. They'd all known that when they'd said goodbye. As much as he'd wanted it to be, their trip isn't the one he's on. Though he wishes it wasn't, he's certain that, for some unknown and unwanted reason, McGill's pulling him back.

More clearly than anyone else, Nature Girl had understood that. That's why she'd given him her gift. Pale white, smooth and cold against his bare skin, it hangs around his neck. It's a whale's tooth. And it holds a legend. Somewhere in time, it began its astral journey from one *Evangelist of Love* to another.

According to the sloppily Romantic Myth built around it, possessors of the tooth are entitled to wear it only until they meet another who is recognised as worthy of its ownership and the title that accompanies it. This way, The Legend goes, the tooth will be passed onto the worthiest over the years, decades, even centuries to come.

The pseudo-Chivalric nature of the whole business has pleased Curly Joe immensely. Having been selected by Nature Girl in this way, he feels himself not only to be a different person but a holier one. And, with that, the feeling of strangeness about his life which has bedevilled him for so long has begun to make perfect sense. Now, at last, he knows. He's among the chosen. He *has* to suffer. It's his fate.

His lift up to Calgary ends and then he's alone on the road again. It dawns on him that Calgary reads too much like Calvary to be a coincidence. It's got to be another sign. Yes, it will be a hard and painful path he's on, but he's ready to suffer it for the cause of Love.

It isn't just another tired kid hitching his way along the highway this day. It's a new Redeemer come to teach the world the oldest of lessons.

* * * * *

On the night train to Montréal, Larry sits across from two industrial salesmen who are grimly triumphing in getting themselves drunk. Descending fog has delayed matters; the train's been stuck in Toronto for several hours. Not that he cares all that much. As long as he arrives in time to get to McGill by 2.00pm tomorrow and register.

His mind's still in Vancouver, in his shit-heap hotel, lying naked with Suzie Q. Again and again, passing the time, he recreates that scene. The look and shape and smell of her body. The way her eyes shut tight every time her climax took her over.

He has various drawings of her in his duffle bag. A couple of them, his first flings at drawing nudes. Suzie Q had agreed to pose only if he swore to never ever show them to anyone else. He'd agreed, but only because his efforts had been so dismal.

Mostly though, Larry replays their final moments together, she hurriedly dressing in order to be back in time for supper at Grandma's without raising questions. She's still, in some official designation, a virgin. He smiles at that. So absurd and yet so oddly beautiful as well.

He reaches into his jacket pocket and takes the photograph she'd placed on the chair — along with the necessary cash loan to pay for his cross-country train journey — just as she'd left. It's a picture of Suzie Q at the age of three. A tangle-haired, chubby, smiling urchin. On its back, she's written:

> *For he who has the gentleness*
> *to return me*
> *to that simple state.*
> *Je t'aime.*

He wishes he could show off the photo to his friends. But he knows he can't. That last night together, they agreed that their charmed Vancouver Time had come to an end and now they were both going back to take on board a Montréal reality where Curly Joe is Suzie Q's steady and Larry's best friend. Their promise to each other to honour that pledge was an indecently difficult one to make. But they are both resolved to stick to it, come what may.

An announcement tells him that the train is now ready to start its journey.

Close to tears, Larry puts the photo back inside his jacket pocket.

* * * * *

When the train reaches Montréal and discards its passengers, Larry's blown away to clap eyes on Moe and Curly Joe smiling on the other side of the gate.

The three of them, together again.

The Flacon roars out onto the highway while they laugh and turn the radio on. *Hey Jude* is playing. They thank *The Beatles* for releasing the tune at just the right time. Minutes later, song completed, throats dry from singing along to it, stomachs empty, they pull up at a drive-in to order hamburgers and french fries and onion rings and milk shakes.

Just as they begin their meal, Moe nearly chokes mid-chomp when he remembers that Science students with last name initials A to M are due to enrol in the morning and those with N to Z in the afternoon. Naturally, his is the former group. Already late, panicking at the thought of this latest of stamp of disapproval on his academic life, he hurries them and their meals all back into The Flacon, guns her motor and speeds them off back to McGill.

Having arrived now, stomachs queasy with undigested food, they split up to head for their separate Registration Centres.

Larry slowly makes his way to the McConnell Engineering Building.

Moe drives madly up to the Sports Centre on Pine Avenue.

And Curly Joe takes his time, soaking up the academic scene, waiting for the afternoon to happen and vaguely trying to guess what he'll do should he bump into Suzie Q.

It's another year beginning.

PART THREE: McGILL

SEPTEMBER 1968 — APRIL 1969

'The feeling we had in those days, which has shaped my entire life, really, was: we're making history. An exalted feeling — suddenly *we* had become agents in world history. Not an easy thing to process when you're only twenty-three years old.'

— Daniel Cohn-Bendit —

20. REVOLUTION IN THE AIR

It's black and white and read all over: eyes and minds are glued to the latest news. Holidays over and done with, day-to-day preoccupations with front-page events have been climbing the charts and getting ready to go through the roof. So here we are, a couple of weeks before Halloween, and TVs and daily papers can't stop grousing about the ghouls and goblins unleashed to prowl city streets. It's like that movie which came out at the start of the month, *Night of the Living Dead.* Except it's happening during daytime, too. What in hell has gone wrong with the world? *Out Demons Out!*

Everywhere you look and read these days, media exposés that once fussed over the pitfalls of placid hippie lifestyles are being ousted by blaring headlines and breaking news denouncing the soaring number of street-corner revolutionaries who are itching to pick any old fight with The Establishment. Just to make the point clear to everyone that The Summer of Love has given way to The Days of Rage, less than a week back, those poster child peaceniks John and Yoko got busted for drug possession. And wait until that LP cover of the two of them full-frontal buck naked comes out in November. *Two Virgins* my foot! *Out Demons Out!*

Looks like Flower Power has wilted. The Hippie has morphed into a Yippie and it's "Revolution for the Fun of It". No More V-finger. All Hail the Clenched Fist. Seems like every shape and shade of oppressed minority is hell-bent on raising its arm and vowing it's "Gonna Make Change Happen — Here and Now, No Matter How". Even the Olympics over in Mexico can't pull the plug on protesting athletes racing to catch the eye of global media so they can tell it like it is. And maybe oddest and scariest of all, here come the first scattered eruptions of what's calling itself The Women's Liberation Movement. Case in point: everybody's still jabbering on about those 150 members of the New York Radical Women Group who took it into their collective heads to stage a protest against the Miss America

Pageant. Yeah, you read that right right. The ever-so-cute and wholesome Miss America Pageant, of all things. *What? Why?* Who ever even heard of these people? They aren't anything like the adoring moms and happy housewives and chirpy teens straight out of *Leave It To Beaver, Gidget* or *The Donna Reed Show.* More like *The Addams Family* as Directed by Alfred Hitchcock! What's all this exploitation guff and nonsense about anyway? And while we're at it: liberated from *what? Out Demons Out!*

As to the regular news ... Oh boy! The Warsaw Pact has crashed the Czech party that's been going on since last spring and is busy making sure that all the lights are hammer and sickled off. Meanwhile, over in Derry, Northern Ireland a whole bunch of Peace Protesters' heads are being cracked open by Local Constabulary batons as a way of marking the official start to *The Troubles.* And hey! Let's not forget: LBJ's quit, so it's Triple-Heck Hubert Horatio Humphrey and Mr. Ed the Hoarse-Talking Muskie gearing up for a tag team match against Tricky Dicky Nixon and Shit-Spouting Spiro T. Agnew. *Boo! Hiss!* Plus ... As if all of the above isn't enough, how about getting in a sweat over the 1968 Flu Pandemic — the Hong Kong Flu, as it's being called — which is busy killing somewhere between one and four million people worldwide? *Out Demons Out!*

* * * * *

Swayed by the call-to-arms sounded by self-appointed radicals from all over the world, the McGill Student Body has responded by issuing black arm-bands, free copies of Chairman Mao's *Little Red Book*, a Manual on Birth Control, and, most indispensable of all, a complete list of the RCMP narcs who've infiltrated The Union Building.

A glorious time, then. Too glorious, for sure, to be wasted in being bored to tears with trivial studies. And anyway, side-by-side with the political and social revolutions being predicted by one and all, there are personal acts of revolt to be awakened to and shaken-up by.

Curly Joe, for one, has got a stuck record needle of a question driving him nuts: how's his future panning out? Already having switched to the Faculty of Science, he began the academic year with very vague and, on re-evaluation, decidedly warped plans to Major in Social Administration. Why? Because he thought it was a good idea for him to learn how to be a natural leader. Inexorably, his gambit has already crumbled to dust. How could it be otherwise? Having been informed that, economically speaking, "men are not pigs" and how a "guns and butter" graph curve is all that's needed to make accurate forecasts about the state of the world, Curly Joe can't avoid concluding that he's blown it yet again. Even if he is among "The Chosen", what's it going to take to find the right direction for his life to take? Maybe, scribbling down as many poems as he can come up with on a daily basis will present him with an answer. Recently, he's crossed paths with haiku. Here's his latest inspiration:

> _prophets_
> _in a world beguiled_
> _by perpetual merriment_
> _a prophet must cry._

And when even such deep thoughts don't provide the necessary clues, Curly Joe's rewardingly lustful encounters with Suzie Q have got him speculating if more of these are what he needs to set himself on the path to enlightenment. Not that it would be an out-and-out wasted effort if they didn't ...

As for Larry, since way back to the first week of his return, he's come round to accepting that the grotesque picture of Engineering that he'd painted during the summer months has, hands down, turned out to be a rather sympathetic one when compared to the reality he's thrown himself into. To make matters worse, he can't stop obsessing over Suzie Q. In spite of their shared agreement to end their _amour fou_, they've continued meeting up in secret, engaging in every sexual act imaginable other than total penetrative sex, then glumly going their separate ways, guilt-racked by their repeated betrayal of Curly Joe and swearing loudly that this can't ever happen again. Until the next time. In-between these encounters, they write to each other. Mostly, the letters read like one long stream-of-consciousness, page after page filled with minute details of the daily trivialities in their separate collegiate lives. Other times ...

From Larry to Suzie Q

Holding onto the darkness,
my upper hand like a vise
clamped round your neck
our searching eyes
melting into one another
silent lips breathing
the same breath
caressing tongues seeking
hidden crevices
no nether mouth too sacred
to remain unscarred,
                    'Je t'aime,'
                    I whispered.
'Fuck me,'
you screamed.

From Suzie Q to Larry

The other night, when you said:
'You know all there is to know about me.
But I ... What do I know of you?'
Your question made me smile.
Ah, Laurent! Mon très ardent Laurent:
When I smiled
— Quand j'ai souri —
That was my way of telling you
all there is to know about me.

This mishmash of French and English language missives has become a sacred tract for Larry to muse over. He dreams of one day assembling all their letters together so that they will form a wondrous book delineating the earliest chapters in their forbidden life-long romance. For now though, he stuffs everything away into a shoe box inside his clothes closet, safe from prying eyes who'd be too quick to judge.

And Moe? *Shock Horror!* Of the three, Moe's the one in best shape these days. Much to his bemusement, he's got to admit that he's honest to goodness enthusiastic about psychology. Sure, there's all the interminable lectures on animal learning, simplistic stimulus-response theories and the naive belief in an experimental doctrine that he keeps being fed by his over-enthusiastic professors. But there's something more — something of value — that he's also got wind of. Thanks to one of his post-grad tutors, Moe's learned that a radical movement calling itself Humanistic Psychology has sprung up with the aim of re-igniting those values of relevance and challenge to the status quo with which the profession had begun its life. Moe's eager to enlist. Mind racing, he can even imagine himself being in the vanguard of this newly-unveiled epic struggle over the mind. Granted, its main appeal is that being part of this particular revolution isn't likely to get him thrown into jail. But still ... As an added bonus, it provides the necessary allure to stop him from quitting university altogether.

And when that doesn't seem to be enough, there's always Emily.

Who?

Flashback time ...

* * * * *

Just to liven things up at the start of this academic year, the University Union is holding a Freshers' Dance, a questionable offering even at the best of times. Just the same, it retains that potential "Some Enchanted Evening You Will Meet A Stranger" September adventure which makes it worth trying on for size.

A couple of hours before they're due to rendezvous though, Larry phones Curly Joe and wimps out with some excuse about having to babysit his little sister. Not that he can tell his friend the truth. Which happens to be that his Vancouver tryst with Suzie Q is still so very much on his mind he's just *got to* phone her up to establish whether the enduring feeling is reciprocated. After that, he'll need a whole lot of time contemplating what they'll do if it is. Which it better be.

Suspecting nothing, Curly Joe doesn't think twice about Larry calling it quits. If he and Moe could think of anything better to do ... Aside from that, it's not raining, it's a Friday night and he can come up with a lot worse time wasters than the two of them twiddling their thumbs for a couple of hours while keeping an eye on what's happening over at The Union.

Speaking of which ...

Tonight, like most other nights, singles, couples and groups of varying sizes and genders are sitting and chatting on the large slabs of stone that form The Union's outer gallery. Further down, backs hunched against the adjacent concrete wall, several line-ups of assembled males hang around waiting for friends, eyeing up every new arrival, or, more and more these days, looking to score some dope. Nickel-and-dime dealers have at last hit Montréal in a really big way.

But let's nip indoors, shall we? Curly Joe and Moe are already there, sipping cherry colas.

Curly Joe's decked out in the sort of clothes he thinks a contemporary prophet should wear: a gaudily resplendent orange shirt with unashamedly oversized triangular collar, tight olive-green jeans reaching no further than his ankles, Indian sandals, an old barf-encrusted brown leather vest that has lost all its buttons, a gauze-like knotted-up red kerchief, and, of course, The Tooth. Still tanned from his Vancouver beach days, wild mop of hair not cut for months, and holding on to a moustache that keeps giving the brush off to growing bushy, he looks like someone straight out of a photo from *Rolling Stone Magazine*. Which makes him feel exceedingly proud of himself.

Moe's opted for his usual buff-jeans, blue sport shirt and tan desert loafers. He's not into challenging either tradition or comfort. He is, however, wearing a pair of cheap black plastic sunglasses because he thinks that they make him look like a super-cool blues harp player. Moe's on the prowl tonight. He hasn't made out with any female since The Gypsy went travelling and he's aching for some hot lips action. Only problem is, those sunglasses don't make it easy to keep track of any eligible contenders. And, just to add to his troubles, the cafeteria's subdued its lights to near dark levels, so that Moe finds himself regularly hitting the roof at the approaching sound of every unseen passerby. It's like a scene out of that wacky *Monkees* TV series he used to watch on Monday nights when he had nothing better to do. Which is why, when Moe fesses up to Curly Joe, it comes out like this:

Can't see her face
I ain't a believer
I wouldn't notice her if I tried.

Over on the stage overlooking the auditorium dance floor, a second-rate local band's trying to imitate *The Who*. Or maybe it's *Question Mark and the Mysterians*. They're kicking up an atonal storm reminiscent of a jackhammer cracking cement. They're also dying a well-deserved death even though a few tasteless couples insist on prolonging the agony by fidget-dancing to their demolition beat. Most other people stand or lean up against walls and tables trying not to listen.

So far, so boring. Not that they're willing to admit it, but both of them are secretly asking themselves if the sensible thing would be to finish up their drinks and go stake out what's playing at the downtown movie theatres. Or, even easier, just call it a night. Instead, minds made up — for now, anyway — to hold back any further thoughts of a quick escape, Moe and Curly Joe make a deal to split up, mingle, maybe hit the jackpot and catch some of the so far all too well concealed action.

After bumping into a couple of tables and knocking over several chairs, Moe reluctantly resolves to push up his sunglasses so that they're nesting over his forehead. Sure, it makes him look like a doofus but at least he's regained his sight. As a reward, within minutes he zeros in on two approachable females who, having traipsed into The Union as a pair, are rejecting any advances from single males.

Thankfully, Curly Joe's still close by. Moe rushes over to him, clearly mega excited. 'It's a dead cert, man,' he says. 'You can tell they're into a swinging group scene, dig? This'll be a night to remember.'

Curly Joe catches Moe drooling as he points out the Two Freshers to him. Okay, he'll be magnanimous. He'll even let Moe have first choice.

Dead set on making them sweat, the Two Freshers aren't initially all that responsive to their advances. They're hanging loose, just in case a couple of better options show up. So far, all they've given away is that they're Arts students. But more into Keats and Wordsworth than Burroughs and Corso. Well, at least they agree that the band is crap.

Not really caring how the evening is going to turn out, Curly Joe has a hunch that things are bound to drag on like this forever unless ... One blink over at Moe, and they're both on the same wavelength. It's Russian roulette time!

'jeez... the air's pretty dry tonight,' Curly Joe says, as though he's talking to himself.

'What's that supposed to mean?' one of the Two Freshers asks, raising her eyebrows, and smiling enough to showcase Bugs Bunny front teeth.

Curly Joe smiles back to her, thankful that she's Moe's pick. 'oh, you know. not much smoke in the air.'

Both Freshers take a good long look-see.

'There's lots of people smoking,' Bugs Bunny says.

'yeah ... cigarettes.'

For a few seconds, the duo are dumbstruck. Then all is revealed. 'Oh ... You mean ...' they blurt out together.

'you got it,' nods Curly Joe.

There's a long pause; it can go either way now.

'You saying that people do it out in the open? Like, really?'

the other Fresher takes up, eyes gleaming.

Curly Joe likes the way she says that. Main thing though: both of them are curious. Jackpot!

Sensing victory and already envisaging the end to his days as a virgin, Moe joins in on the game. 'Well, Rick here, he isn't used to the East Coast. He's speaking more about 'Frisco.' He pauses, then seals their fates by adding: 'Like, in The Haight? Where it's all open air, free and easy.'

'You're from San Francisco!' Now the Two Freshers are dazzled through and through.

Aware of the danger of a personality cult developing, Curly Joe chooses his next words with extra care. 'naw, that's just what a good pal from thataways told me. thing is, we've both of us just come back from a long trip out west. all the way to b.c. and back. we're just noticing the difference, is all.'

'How'd you get there?' the more suspicious Fresher asks.

'Thumb, natch,' Moe slips in. 'There and back. Even hopped a train. What other way is there to go, right?'

Just then, the band walks off and recorded music starts playing, much to everyone's relief.

'hey, listen to that sound!' Curly Joe says hoping to avoid further interrogation.

'Yeah! Wow!' Moe answers, 'My all-time favorite record of the week! Gotta dance to that!'

It's just some AM Pop. A *Gary Puckett and the Union Gap* Gag-arama. But, hey! The Two Freshers are following them to the dance floor, aren't they?

* * * * *

Not long past 9.00pm the band comes back on. No one seems to mind this time. Beer and whatever else have dulled away any residual good taste pretensions.

By now, Curly Joe has no idea where Moe is. He suspects he's doing the same thing he is, which is casually getting into an extended necking session with his willing dance partner. *probably not*, he thinks it over. *knowing moe, it won't be quite so casual as this.* Curly Joe's bored. He wants to leave and head back home, but it's too early to do so without busting up Moe's chances. So, instead, he keeps amusing himself by betting on how far his Fresher will allow him to advance. So far, she's allowing him a lot.

In fact, they're mouth-mashing hot and heavy when he first catches a glimpse of Suzie Q. He has to stop and look again before accepting that it *is* her, standing a few feet away, swaying in the sort of way that people do when they've gone beyond their alcohol limits. Way beyond it seems like, in this instance.

'hang on a minute,' Curly Joe says to his Fresher. Already forgetting her, he shoves his way towards Suzie Q. Up close, grabbing hold of her just in case she crashes to the floor, he catches a whiff of her breath. *Yup. Drunk as a skunk.*

'How could you hurt me so much?' Suzie Q's angry and miserable all at the same time. And now she's crying as well. Not getting any reply out of him, she repeats her accusation.

Pressured into saying something, Curly Joe hits back. 'hey! you got things the wrong way round! i'm the one who should be asking that very same question.' His words bring on a further effluvium of tears. Doing his best to calm her down, Curly Joe cuddles her. There and then, he's feeling alive again.

A minute into their extended caress, Suzie Q calmly remarks that she's going to be sick. Holding hands, they skedaddle out of The Union and into the cool night. Moments later, Suzie Q's retching up in front of the nearest tree. Curly Joe holds her tight to prevent her from keeling over. Immensely pleased with himself for not experiencing any revulsion by what he sees and hears, he's on a powerful groove of protection and affection. And then everything falls into place: this is, manifestly, the first test for his new role. The coolness of the whale's tooth up against his chest assures him that he's right.

After a while, Suzie Q stops gagging and whispers that she's feeling better. She's also wishing the earth would swallow her up but doesn't say so. Instead, she continues letting Curly Joe take care of her. It feels good to have him close to her again.

Then she thinks of Larry and his phone call a few of hours ago. How their agreement to meet up soon — in secret, of course — filled her with equal parts shame and longing. Right this moment, she wishes that she could erase the days she passed away with Larry in Vancouver. But then again, she doesn't really. Oh Lord! Whoever thought she'd have *this* to have to deal with?

Adding to her confusion, after Larry happened to mention Curly Joe's whereabouts, she'd been resolute about finding him. Approaching McGill, she side-stepped into one of the student-friendly bars for a quick alcohol booster. Or three. Or more. Thankfully, all these unsettling memories are pushed away as soon as Suzie Q hears Curly Joe tell her that they should take a walk around the block and give a verdict on how she's doing. Suzie Q thinks that's a great idea. It feels so nice when he puts his arm around her before they start off. Then she does the same to him. He shivers from the cold, but doesn't care. Minutes later, Suzie Q picks up on that and suggests that they go have a coffee somewhere.

Inside some bar called *The British Bulldog,* Suzie Q semi-lies and admits that she'd spoken to Larry earlier on and that he'd told her about the Freshers Dance at The Union. She'd headed over to it, frantic to sort things out with Curly Joe only to catch him making out with some slutty-looking girl. She'd concluded that this was his way of giving her the big brush-off and proceeded to get herself drunk.

All of this is pretty weird news to Curly Joe. Talking about big brush-offs, he reminds her of that phone conversation they'd had when he'd first hit Vancouver. What was he supposed to think she was trying to tell him? Which now leaves Suzie Q totally non-plussed. She wasn't trying to tell him anything except that she was happy to hear he'd arrived. Pushing back, she lets him know how broken-hearted she'd been with him disappearing like that and making no effort whatsoever at any further contact. Not even when they were both back in Montréal. What was *she* supposed to think, hey? If it hadn't been for Laurent ... Well, best to leave him out of the account for now.

They catch a bus to get Suzie Q home. All the way there, they never once stop holding hands. When they reach her door, they kiss silently and forever. Suzie Q's breath tastes of vomit, but Curly Joe doesn't let on.

At her front door, Suzie Q sighs and says: 'You've changed. I don't know how, but I can feel it in your kisses.'

Curly Joe smiles to hear her say that. *of course ... it must be plain as day to everyone who knew the old me.* Then, just to prove her right, he kisses her again with an urgency that leaves them both swooning.

In her bed, Suzie Q's fantasising Curly Joe doing all sorts of fabulously shameless things to her.

Except, it's not always Curly Joe. Laurent keeps popping up as well.

And sometimes ... Sometimes ... *Golly Gosh!* They're *both* there at the same time!

* * * * *

Moe's evening is turning out to be pretty significant as well.

After an hour of getting nowhere with his Fresher, he calls it quits and makes some half-hearted excuse that she doesn't seem at all bothered by. *Only thing she was interested in sticking down her throat was a joint. Still, at least ya got to touch up her tits, which is a helluva lot more than you've done for ages, Johnny.* Moe looks around for Curly Joe but can't locate him anywhere. Never mind. One last cherry cola and then it'll be time to hit the road.

Sipping away, sunglasses back on as they should be, he doesn't notice that there's an amused female sitting down across from him.

'How can you see anything at all when it must be so bleeding dark wearing your glasses like that?' he hears her ask him.

Amused, Moe pushes them down to the tip of his nose for a better look. Hmm ... Not bad. *And* she's alone and smiling in his direction. Before he knows it, Moe finds himself captivated.

In hardly any time at all, she volunteers that her name is Emily and that she's British. Maybe it's just the novelty of her nationality, but she's also no dimbo like that Fresher. For one thing, she knows as much about English bands as he does. She can even name the individual members in most of the groups. And ... She's been to a *Cream* concert! Mightily impressed, Moe introduces her to the addictive pleasures of cherry cola and they embark upon an haphazardly easy-going one-to-one. *Beatles* or *Stones?* Clapton or Bloomfield as the iconic guitar god? And by the way, what dullard came up with idea of getting that jerk Nixon to go on *Laugh-In* this week and tell one and all to 'sock it to me'?

It takes no time nor effort at all for Moe to have Emily giggling non-stop. Turns out, she's from some place called Guildford, in a part of England she keeps calling "The Home Counties". Doesn't ring any bells with Moe. What he does get, though, is that she's pretty lost in this New World her parents have brought her to and not sure she likes it all that much. Without exception, Emily tells him, Moe's the first new person she's spoken to who seems to want to make her time here something more than just plain awful.

Moe likes hearing her say that. And that accent when she says it is pretty damn neat as well. He's drawn to her strange new way of pronouncing words. Sure, she's cute and classy. But, oddly enough, he doesn't feel headlong attracted to her in any straightforwardly sexual way. If anything, it's more like he's meeting a possible new friend. Who just happens to be a woman. *Wow! Are such things possible?* Leaving any answer to that unresolved for now, he cheers her up by taking her phone number and promising to call her soon, show her the sights, introduce her to his friends. He's ready to bet that the smile she's produced in response to his offer is emphatically on the level.

Just to add to Moe's certainty, Emily's way of saying thank you is to stand up, go over to where he's sitting and kiss him. It's nothing more than a friendly peck on the cheek, but it's pleasantly unexpected and, if he's honest, it's much more memorable and tingle-some than any other Moe's gotten all night.

Driving home in The Flacon after having dropped her off at her place, Moe keeps repeating her name over and over again.

Emily.

He likes the sound of it.

Emily. Emily. *Very* Swinging England.

* * * * *

By the time it occurs to any of them that they're rarely together without Emily also being around, the very idea that this was once, and could still be, otherwise seems somehow to be both alien and wrong. What kind of existence would they be leading if they didn't have the certainty of knowing that, come lunchtime, Emily will be there sitting at their usual table waiting for them? Most days, her cool and casual presence is the only reason they bother to come into McGill.

Every so often, Suzie Q drops by as well. Emily doesn't like that. She sees Suzie Q as being unworthy of Curly Joe. But then, it must be said, she sees *every* female in that way. She wants none of the brotherly affection Curly Joe pours on her to be diluted by anyone else. Larry's the easier one to handle. Every chance he gets, he tells whoever's around that he's steering clear of new romantic involvements. Something about how he keeps saying that makes Emily suspicious, even if she can't for the life of her explain why. Just in case though, she's quick to remind Larry of his assertion every time it begins to look like his eyes might be beginning to stray. Which, oddly enough, they're more likely to if Suzie Q's joined them. How intriguing!

Even more noteworthy than that though, when Emily thinks about it, is how once upon a time she'd have adored to have Larry as a boyfriend to show off to the world. No longer. As with Curly Joe, she's gleaned that she prefers relating to him as an ersatz sibling. Someone she can joke around with, even nuzzle up against without a whiff of anything raunchy creeping into things. They can even talk about bodies and sex and topics like that and never once go all sweaty and woozy.

For some reason, it's Moe she's most attracted to. So there. Not that she can explain why that is to herself. Larry's definitely more physically appealing. And Curly Joe carries an intensity about him that makes him and what he has to say so thought-provoking. And yet, Moe's got something extra to offer. Something that, even in remaining ineffable, Emily accepts without hesitation.

They all do. Unequivocally.

Larry and Curly Joe have taken this as a great and good sign that life is finally on the upswing for Moe. Seeing him with Emily makes them aware of their own inadvertent role in placing Moe in the position of low man on the totem pole. They've got to admit it: Moe's regular failures with women made their own partial successes seem impressive. Now perhaps, they think, with Emily so irrefutably favouring him over them, he'll come out of his corner ready to take on the world.

How odd then that it should be Moe who continues to be the least convinced of the lot of them by this turn of events. Oh, sure, he *likes* Emily. When it comes to it, he also *trusts* her. But, then, as he so succinctly puts it: 'Trust ain't Lust.' For all that, when he's feeling lonely, or bored to death with his regular masturbatory rituals, he constructs a scene where he's hitting on Emily by slurring the supreme sleazoid tough-guy pick-up line: 'Old enough to bleed, old enough to butcher, doll face.' Jerk-off success guaranteed.

Most of the time though, seeking some kind of balanced compromise, Moe settles into musing: '*Que sera, sera*, Jim.' And then he chuckles like that *Looney Tunes* Tasmanian Devil.

* * * * *

Meanwhile ... Suzie Q's living it up fuelling Larry's and Curly Joe's fantasies while pigging out on her own. She knows that what they're all up to is insane, but ... Whoopee do! Even her usual Catholic guilt has gone on vacation. Risks, repercussions, consequences have all been analysed and rejected as not being significant enough to bring their discrete encounters to an end. People meet, fall in love, music fills the air. So what if it happens to be two different men at the same time who can induce a feeling of rapture like nothing she's ever experienced? Even telling herself to get real and rational hasn't changed anything. Reason's been relegated to the boondocks. It's a grand disease, this love. Or whatever it is.

With Larry, something opens up for Suzie Q that is naughtily freeing. Like the other night, when no one else was around at home.

She's made him wait on the other side of her bedroom door until she's ready for him. Then she hides so that when he's allowed to enter she can creep up on him from behind. All she's wearing is the white shirt she borrowed from him back in Vancouver and isn't ever going to return. It's all done up except for the top button, her long light auburn hair sliding over its collar, shirt tail whistling up and down in some sensuous flapper's dance of its own making. She is the vision of a holy prostitute, the whore-nun that poets warble on about, the Full Moon. She doesn't have the patience to watch him undress. Jeans unbuckled and unzipped, briskly pulled down to ankles along with white cotton underpants, boner already full flush and quivering, she doesn't think twice about kissing its tip and then going even further. The hot lava-sperm shoots out of Larry in seconds. And when it's his turn to repay the compliment, she traps his head between her thighs and won't let him stop until she can't tell the difference between pleasure and pain.

On the flip side of the coin, when it's Curly Joe who's the centre of her attention the erotic charge quickened in her is much more innocent. But just as God Almighty all-consuming. With him, Suzie Q can be the Princess she's always dreamed of being. What she's been astonished to latch onto is that doing Princess things like demanding that her every whim is fulfilled and that she never stops feeling adored can also make her act in very salacious ways.

Like when, much to Curly Joe's chagrin, she insists that he take her to the Annual Debs Ball. What a hoot of a pair they make: she in low-cut, bra-less, blue sky frilly evening dress and he tangled up in rented charcoal black tux, white bow-tie and blood red cummerbund. Even his scrawny moustache and hair not cut since last July look impeccable. They feel *so* close to each other tonight, bumping into Montréal notables while dancing old-fashioned dances they hardly know the steps to, sipping real French Champagne, nibbling daintily on finger food grabbed from passing waiters' trays. *Tres* romantic! And so hysterically funny to re-imagine the Princess Perfect absurdity they've thrown themselves into. As to the sauciness ... Oh Lordy! That begins with the moment when, sitting down facing each other, they — well, Suzie Q at first, but Curly Joe quickly joining in — get into comparing other women's boobs (Suzie Q's word) to her own. In a mad moment, eager to assist his evaluation, she leans over and tugs at the top of her dress so that his judgment doesn't have to rely on memory. The way his eyes bulge with incredulity start her digging into her memories as to whether Curly Joe has actually ever set eyes on her boobs before now. That thought remains so titillating that, even when once more appropriately covered, her erect nipples stay like that for ages. As does Curly Joe's "thing". And, for once, she doesn't have to take the lead after that. Locking themselves inside a convenient Changing Room, Curly Joe pretty much begs to see her beautiful breasts once again. Can you believe that! *Her* Curly Joe not holding back from making his desire for her so explicit. And after that ... *Oh My Good Lord!* She hadn't expected the soft yet fierce kissing and suckling that follows. She must have come a dozen times tonight and still wants more.

How long can this last? Suzie Q asks herself. Truth is, she's not really wanting any answer to her Once Upon A Time Fairy Tale question other than the unmistakable one: "And they all lived happily ever after."

* * * * *

Not that these various events, consequential as they are, have conspired to loosen the bond between our trio. If anything, they may have brought them even closer together. Though, come to think of it, their shared infatuation with the current music scene is a more likely candidate. And not just because they're devoted listeners, either.

One afternoon not much different to most others these days, the three of them are sitting around in Curly Joe's home yakking the yak. Curly Joe, as is his recent habit, is plucking on his nylon string guitar, riffing on various chords, trying out different melodies that just might turn one of his poems into a suitably mournful song. It's something they've all got used to and hardly even notice anymore.

Except, today, they do. And having noticed, a question drops into their heads: what if we tried playing something together?

Larry's got his own guitar, but, too bad, it's back at his place. Hey! So what! Curly Joe's got a second one — a steel string — some friend of his parents has passed on to him. Great!

And Moe? Moe's got his trusty *Hohner* blues harp in the key of D right there in his inside jacket pocket.

To everyone's amazement, unlike all the other times that they could have but didn't, they actually start to jam. And, like, whoa! *The Warthogs* are born! It's a raucous mess of a sound that they create. But, however brief, it has its moments of musical wizardry. Still and all though, definitely nothing worth recording. Except it is. Isn't that Curly Joe's *Grundig* reel-to-reel on the card table? And, look: the tape spools are already in place, the mike's plugged in and all that needs doing is to press down on a couple of control buttons in tandem ...

Most of the time, when they're not dream-talking about making it big as FM radio stars, their efforts start them laughing so hard and non-stop that they have to take turns making a mad scramble for the washroom. This regular exercise in laughter brings them to the collective conclusion that, as far as their lives are concerned, 1968 will forever more be known as the "Year Of The Laugh".

On the face of what's happening in places like Vietnam,

Laos, Cambodia, The Middle East, Northern Ireland, Czechoslovakia and Czechago, it seems to them that the world's become too raw, too terror-stricken, to deal with rationally. Which is maybe why it's mostly the comedians and funsters and musicians who are being censored on the public airwaves. It's their stand-up routines and songs and sketches that give shape to the slogans of the resistance. Why them? Well ... *Here come da Judge!* Because in crazy times like these, laughter's the only weapon left to push back against the enemy's onslaught. Even when that enemy might be yourself.

Thanks to that *Grundig* of Curly Joe's, something of their laughter-filled discourses on laughter still survives, decades down the line.

Here's a bit of one just to satisfy your curiosity:

- Laughing's like any other social disease: it's contagious.'
- Yeah! Like: Uhm ... Sorry to have to tell yuh this, but
   yuh caught a dose of terminal laughter, son.
- oh no! no way, man! how could i? i'm not that kinda —
- Did anybody ever tell ya a dirty joke, pal?
- no ... not once ... never ... but ...
- *But*? But what? Out with it, kid!
- well ... i sat on the toilet seat at the system theatre once
   and ... and ... i read the graffiti.
- Ah-ha! There ya go, Jim! That's it! All it takes is reading
   one line.
- gosh, doc. what can i do?
- There's only *one* watertight cure, son. But I hesitate to
   mention it because of its extremely painful nature.
- *tell me! i'll do anything!*
- Sit down, first. Yuh'll need to. The *only* thing that'll cure
   yuh is:
- *yes! yes! tell me! tell me!*
- Okay, ya asked for it, pal: It's sitting through an all-
   night festival of Jerry Lewis movies.
- *aaugh! no! anything but that!*
- Take it or leave it, son. It's either that, or it's "Dirty

Mouth" for the rest of yuhr life.

- sweet jesus, deliver me —
- Hmmm ... I had also better inform you: there *is* one possible side effect you should be aware of ...
- tell me! what could make things any worse?
- Let me give it to ya straight, kid: it *could* turn ya into a *French Film Critic.*

21. THE PLASTIC ICICLE EXPERIENCE

November already. *Blah!* What to do just to get through?

Curly Joe wakes up one morning and can't wait to let them all in on his outtasite brain blast. His nineteenth birthday's coming up. The final year of his teens. That deserves some formal recognition, doesn't it? So ... How about a party at his place?

But wait! Wait! Here's the best bit! It can't just be any ordinary sort of a party. Oh, no, no! This has got to be something really special. Something way extraordinary. A party like no other he or his guests have ever been to. *This* party is going to be a mega psychedelic blast!

He sits down with Larry and Moe later that day and, after a couple of hours of concerted discussion, they come up with the necessary ingredients to make the affair really mind-blowingly freaky.

Let's see now ... A strobe light or two! *Fab!*

Plus ... Shape-shifting oil-colour slides that beat in time to the music! *A gas!*

Don't forget that array of slide-projectors set on automatic blinking a barrage of iconic words and pictures up against every wall! *Heavy!*

And, of course, the latest vinyl sounds on offer by the very best underground bands! *Right on!*

How about *that?* Well ... Okay, so maybe that sounds real solid, but it's nowhere near all that new and radical enough as yet.

Okay ... How about *this* then? They'll cover the basement playroom's walls and ceiling in silver! *Oh Yeah!*

Rolls and rolls of aluminium foil stapled all over the large room until it's become their decorative answer to the *Cheetah Club* or the *Electric Circus*, or, even, the fabled *Factory. Now you're talkin'!*

And then ... *Oh wow! Get a load of this!* How about making the effect that much more stunning, by hanging different lengths of silver Christmas-tree tinsel on the ceiling so that everybody's heads will brush the tops of its strands while they dance beneath it! *Fabuloso!*

Hang on! Listen up! There's an outdoor side approach leading down into the room, isn't there? So what if they turn that into a sort of grotto for guests so that they take the stairs through it and then scuttle straight into this way-out world! *Too much, man!*

Which, when they come to think about it, kind of resembles an ice cavern, doesn't it?

Hey! You know what? There's a name for this otherworldly shebang: *The Plastic Icicle Experience!*

But first ... Curly Joe has to coax his parents into letting them go ahead with what less tuned-in minds might view as being a no-chance-in-hell kind of idea. Amazingly though, given that it's his birthday treat and all, Ma and Pa give him the green light. There's even a parental promise to shut themselves and doggy Diana inside their bedroom for the night and never once dare to sneak downstairs for a peek at proceedings. Overcome with gratitude, Curly Joe drags his two pals upstairs to add their thank you's. Which is when the whole deal almost hits the skids.

First, Larry brings up this new idea he's just had. He can borrow several buckets of dry ice from the Chemistry Department and set them up in the playroom so that they create this spooky floor-level smoke and cloud effect which, combined with all the flickering lights, will turn the place into something really unearthly. Neat, huh? Not on your life. Curly Joe's Dad has visions of the entire Westmount Police and Fire Department knocking down his front door should he agree to such a categorically lunatic notion.

Fine ... So what if, Moe offers as another possibility, right before the party starts we go buy a live pig — a really young piglet, not a fully grown one obviously — that we bring back and grease up and then let it run around the place while people try to catch it? Lotsa fun, no? Curly Joe's mother's reaction to this suggestion positively flummoxes Moe.

Realising what they're up against and, worse, what could be lost, Curly Joe does his best to return everybody's focus to the original agreement. Luckily for one and all, he succeeds.

* * * * *

It will become pretty famous as a party.

Respectably late arriving on the night, Larry drives over all on his lonesome. Just this once, his father's relented and allowed him to borrow the family car. Larry's thinking of Suzie Q. For someone who claimed not to know what "69" meant, she's sure learned fast. Suzie Q ... Suzie Q ... Natch, tonight she's busy being Curly Joe's steady — which she is, of course — so that's where it's at. Never mind, there'll be plenty of single women around to dance with. Which might even make Suzie Q jealous enough so that next time they're alone, she'll be open to the possibility of their going all the way.

Since he's got no one to embarrass other than himself, Larry makes his grand entrance stripped to the waist, a bullet-belt wrapped diagonally over his chest, and his grandfather's bayonet from WWI clenched between his teeth. Then, brandishing it in his left hand, he growls out 'Up against the wall, *motherfuckers*!' in exemplary South American guerilla style. For sure, everybody notices him. Some even clap, though they do so gingerly, just in case he means business. It takes Curly Joe's loud crow of approval, followed by a shoulder pat and bear hug to cool down any residual tensions.

Curly Joe's already pretty high on the evening's immediate success — over sixty guests and counting — and is rushing around everywhere with Suzie Q in tow playing at being the coolest of hosts. To make sure everyone can recognize them, they both wear little boy's cowboy hats — his white, hers red. Suzie Q's also placed these hippie mirrored glasses over her eyes to offset the strobe light's near-blinding effects. Their frames are slightly crooked, and, when the white light reflects off them, they turn her into Madame Medusa flashing freeze-ray beams onto nearby dancers.

Seeing Suzie Q so happy and carefree, Curly Joe's back to being in love. She looks gorgeous tonight and he's raring to let her know the effect she has on him. During *Dance to the Music,* he plasters himself tight against Suzie Q's body so that she feels his erection up against her belly.

'Naughty boy!' she fake chastises, then licks one of his earlobes.

She isn't expecting what happens next. Curly Joe sticks his hand under the back of her miniskirt and begins massaging her bum. Wide-eyed, downright shocked even, Suzie Q loses her balance and topples backwards onto the parquet floor taking Curly Joe with her. Which gets the other dancers around them clutching their bellies from laughing so hard. Not as hard as Suzie Q and Curly Joe though.

One of those people turns out to be Larry. His and Suzie Q's eyes meet for a second and then turn away. Still, it's long enough for lovelorn messages to be sent and received. *Oh-hum. Be grateful that Curly Joe's clueless to it all.* Wanting to steer clear of any further rummages through Suzie Q's and Curly Joe's antics, Larry joins a bunch of guests filing their way upstairs to the buffet that's been laid out. While he's at it, he spies Moe and Emily sitting by themselves on a couch in the furthest and darkest corner of the room. The strobe's been shut off temporarily, the music plays low and peaceful. Some new singer. Writes her own songs. Like this one. *Cactus Tree.* Joni ... Joni something or other. Mitchell! Yeah. Joni Mitchell. Squeaky kind of voice. Maybe she'll go places. Back to Moe and Emily. They're unmistakably caught up in something. Moe with one of his arms around her, Emily with her eyes shut and head leaning on his shoulder. They seem blind to anyone else's existence. In spite of his own situation, Larry smiles. Now he knows why he's hardly seen or spoken to them all evening. *At last,* he thinks.

Upstairs, a new eye-opener awaits: a couple of the guests have brought some pot with them. Larry's never been to a party before where people hike a nickel's worth of grass out of their jeans' pockets, roll it up inside a *Zig-Zag* and start to toke in public. However, just so nobody watching him would ever suspect this, he rushes to join the growing line of cool dudes and dudettes who are on the point of turning Curly Joe's parents' antique living room table into a resting spot for baggies and papers and pipes and even scissors and knives. A lot of the guests take in what's going down in stunned disbelief. For many, it's their first contact with such barefaced criminal behaviour. Some even begin to worry that maybe the cops will catch wind of things at any moment and arrest them all. Most, however, tell themselves that this is really groovy. They're revolutionaries now. Fuck the pigs and join the line-up.

Suzie Q, who's followed Curly Joe into the room for a drink and a nibble belongs to the nervous group. Curly Joe's already told her about how he'd dropped LSD over in Vancouver and she'd freaked out at the thought of that. She still believes the various newspaper articles she's read about what drug-crazed hippies get up to. She wouldn't mind if the reports of their all-night fooling around turned out to be true. But definitely not all that other mind-bending stuff.

Curly Joe, on the other hand, is euphoric. This party of his is going to lodge itself into lots of people's memories. Being host, he doesn't hesitate to jump the line and squat himself down next to the head felons. He takes two long drags on the badly-rolled joint a girl he's never seen before passes him, smiles his illegal smile, and then floats back to Suzie Q who gives him the one and only "how could you be so dumb?" look she'll throw his way all night. Even then, he finds something in her reaction to go on smiling about.

Larry waits for Suzie Q's exit before he starts to indulge. It's been nine months since his one and only blowout and he's uptight not to be taken for a novice. No worries. Even though he breaks into fits of painful coughing the first couple of times he inhales, he still makes sure to keep his place around the table until the two nickel's worth of *primo* weed are nothing more than hovering puffs of smoke. By now, Larry's feeling top of the world. He isn't going out of his head anywhere near like when he's drunk. Rather, the dope is expanding his mind's boundaries.

Which is why he can hear the music being played downstairs and the people stomping their feet in rhythm to it with such stunning clarity.

What's playing, just so you know, is the song that Curly Joe's been saving up all night. *Suzie Q* by *Creedence Clearwater Revival*. Larry's got to admit: it's an inspired blast. A sinuous, back-beat shake takes him over. Ready to rock 'n' roll, he turns to look at the now deserted table. Yup. That grass was something else. He's definitely up for further in-depth investigations.

* * * * *

Not long past 1.00am, the party's ready to call it a night. People study their watches, blanch, and yearn for All-Niter cups of coffee to wake them up enough so that they can go home to sleep things off or engage in parties of a more private nature.

One of the guests who's eager to get going more than most is a guy called Paul, who happens to be in Larry's Engineering Problems class. Larry has no idea why he'd invited Paul to come along. Probably because Paul's one of the very few students who hasn't completely written him off as a no-hoper. He's noticed Paul off and on during the evening doing his best to impress a disdainfully attractive female guest. He seems to have pulled things off successfully enough for him to have the moxie to cajole Larry into driving him and his impassively willing partner back home.

'A little back-seat action to end the party on,' Paul mock-whispers into Larry's ear. 'And, who knows? Maybe more!'

It's not what Larry had in mind, but ... He guesses that it's his night to be gallantly unselfish. His generosity pays off. Noticing Suzie Q all on her own and also getting ready to say goodnight, he soft-shoes his way up to her and makes her an offer she immediately jumps at.

Except ... A couple of seconds later, Curly Joe turns up as well and, hearing a censored version of what Larry and Suzie Q are about to do, he immediately invites himself to come along for the ride as well.

'But what about the remaining guests? Don't yuh need to be here to shoo them off?'

They can take care of themselves. Just to play it safe though, he'll have a quick word with Moe and Emily. They don't look like they're in any hurry to stop pawing each other. They can hold the fort until he gets back.

* * * * *

It's a clear and peaceful November early morning. As they drive, Suzie Q squished in the front seat shoulder-to-shoulder between him and Curly Joe, Larry slips into some kind of gentle wavy reverie. The high has worn away, but he's still getting haphazard flare-ups that keep him wide awake. Then again, it might just be the effect of Suzie Q's body brushing against his.

Everything changes in a split second. The splutters and groans accompanying the heavy necking session going on behind him come to a sudden halt. Looking into the rearview mirror, Larry sees Paul edge up to the car's nearest window, open it, stick his neck out, and begin to spew up into the darkness all that his unsettled stomach is no longer able to hold in. Which, because of the speed they're driving at, is a strategy that doesn't go according to plan. Instead, a large portion of Paul's gift to the world whizzes back inside and sprays itself not so much on him but onto Larry's jeans, Suzie Q's bare thighs and, worst of all, over Paul's new girlfriend's face and dress. In violent reaction, she shrieks in disgust, causing Larry to brake the car to an immediate halt.

Adding to the chaos he's created, Paul's unsparing feelings of shame taunt him to push open the car door and highball it out to the darkness of a nearby field where, according to his mind's drunken logic, he can escape into the silence and hide there until everyone goes away.

What are they going to do now? Larry's father's car is soaked with Paul's puke and already starting to stink. In its back seat, a flustered and angry voice whines on and on, threatening to start its own round of retching. Most bothersome of all, Paul's out there somewhere, dying in some farmer's field. Springing into united action, Larry and Suzie Q and Curly Joe leave the complaining woman to fend for herself and charge outside, the three of them shouting Paul's name. Seconds later, the near-freezing early morning weather reminds them that they're not dressed for this. Flapping their arms to beat away the cold, eyes still unaccustomed to the dark, they head off in ever-widening circles as much and as fast as they can bear, hoping that Paul will come round to responding to their calls.

In spite of the near-glacial chill, the pointlessness of their search and the frequency of any one of them slipping onto the damp and muddy ground, they can't resist breaking into sporadic spasms of laughter. This adventure's simply too absurd not to merit otherwise. However ... Some ten minutes gone by, the silliness of it all begins outstay its welcome. If things don't change soon, there'll be *four* frozen stiffs to be found out here later in the day.

It's Larry who, in due course, tracks down Paul. Admittedly, it's by pure chance. He has to trip over Paul's prone body for it to dawn on him who — not what — is lying there.

Paul's asleep, soaked to the skin with barf and sludge, looking vampirically pale in the moonlight. Larry's nudging wakes him up enough so that he can be led back to the car, shoved inside and propped up near an open window.

Totally uncaring, the by now clearly *ex*-girlfriend manoeuvres herself as far away from Paul as she can. Focused only on her struggle to clean herself with tissue paper, all she keeps repeating is that she wants this nightmare to end.

Fine. No argument there. They'll reverse direction and head to the other side of Montréal just to shut her up. But first, it's time to get Paul home safe and sound.

Some fifteen minutes later, parked in front of Paul's house, Larry and Curly Joe lug him to its threshold. Fumbling with the house keys for what seems like hours, Paul somehow finds a way to get the door unlocked. As soon as he's semi-pushed inside, he slumps back into unconsciousness. Never mind;

they've got him home. Paul can deal with what happens next all on his own.

* * * * *

So now, it's backtracking time. Crossing the Jacques Cartier Bridge, Larry and Curly Joe reawaken memories of last year's early morning adventure trying to cross it. Seems so long ago. Still, it's a good tale to recount. Suzie Q sure thinks it's funny. Even Backseat Girl pipes up with an inelegant grunt. At last, they can drop her off. She thanks them quickly, even somewhat icily, and makes a run for it. Maybe, with some sleep and a couple of showers, she'll come round to forgiving Paul. As if ...

Her unconcern over Paul gets Larry to thinking how lucky he is. Suzie Q would never react like that. Neither would Moe or Curly Joe. Emily, too. What makes them different is the honesty that binds them all together. *Whoops! Now why did he go and tell himself that?* Unable to erase the thought, Larry has to accept that he and Suzie Q have been playing fast and loose with the truth.

He turns to catch the look on Suzie Q's face. He's 100% sure she knows what he's thinking because she's thinking the very same thing. Before either of them can stop the other, they both start gabbing away to Curly Joe about what they've been up to.

'whaaaaaat? are you guys kidding me?' It's a dumb question for Curly Joe to ask. He has no doubt they're being totally straight with him. Okay. Deep breath. 'so how long's it been since this here "thing" between you started, huh?'

'Since Vancouver,' says Suzie Q. 'When you dumped me.' Well, that's true enough. It *was* in Vancouver when she and Larry had really embarked on their ... their what? Affair? Entanglement? Love Story?

'i didn't dump you,' Curly Joe answers. 'more like the other way round.' But still, somehow, being told it was Vancouver has calmed him down. It doesn't feel near as much like a betrayal. Maybe he'd have done the same if the sandal was on the other foot.

'I'm sorry, man,' Larry says. 'Yuh know I'd never want to do anything to hurt yuh —'

'Me neither,' Suzie Q says.

'It's just that ... Hell! Me and Suzie Q just couldn't stop ourselves —'

'so what do we do now?' Curly Joe cuts in.

Larry and Suzie Q share one big gulp. They know what they're about to give up. But they also know how much more they'd be giving up if they don't make themselves do the right thing. 'We'll stop,' they say in unison. 'It's not fair on you and we both love you too much to keep on —'

'wait!' Curly Joe says. He's tapping the whale's tooth, reminding himself who he is now and what that means. 'how about ... how about ... we just keep things going as they are?'

'Whaaaaaat?'

'look,' he continues. 'why should any of us lose out on something that feels so right and good? the only wrong thing about it was that you both found it necessary to keep things secret. but now ... if we all thought that what was going on before was beautiful — and it sounds like you guys thought that it was — just think how much more beautiful it'll all be once it's out in the open. get it? this is 1968, ain't it? if *we* ain't gonna be willing to do some radical experimenting then who the hell is?'

'Are you serious?' Suzie Q says.

'He is!' Larry's grinning like it's his birthday, too. 'Yuh really are, right?' He waits for Curly Joe to agree. 'Wow! Yuh are something special, yuh know that? Well, I'm up for it, man! None of this straight possessiveness, right? Freedom now!'

Curly Joe and Larry turn to Suzie Q. Everything's down to her.

'Are you guys sure? I mean, for me it's fine. Weird, but fine. No. More than fine. It's great! It's mind-blowing! It's —'

'it's honest,' says Curly Joe. 'let the honesty shine on us.'

Dazed by it all, still standing next to Larry's parked car, they embrace non-stop, not caring who might see them. Then, filled with the bravado of the new and dangerous, they clamber back inside, squeeze up against one another. Who starts things is hard to tell, but in no time flat Suzie Q's got two hands belonging to different people sneaking inside her underwear and causing delicious havoc while she, in return, plows away at both her lovers' jeans-covered cocks, driving them all to the finest dry hump of their lives.

* * * * *

Suzie Q delivered safely to her front door, Larry chauffeurs Curly Joe back to his house. Blessedly, the basement lights are still on. Inside, they find Moe and Emily sitting around finishing up any food and drink that's been left over. The smiles on everybody's faces answer all the questions worth asking.

Before Larry can drive himself back home however, there's the little matter of cleaning Paul's vomit from the car. Curly Joe goes off to find new clothes for Larry to put on and then, soapy water buckets and towels in hand, the four of them start scrubbing away.

The togetherness he's sure everybody's feeling while carrying out the task takes Larry flying even higher than when he was stoned. As far as he's concerned, the bond between them all, Suzie Q included, is at its height this early November morning. At last, simply and silently, what they've dreamed and longed for as a possibility, seems to have become their reality.

Wow! What a legendary party!

* * * * *

Later that day, it snows incessantly, and they all suffer from excruciating hangovers.

22. LOVE TALK

'I don't know *what* I felt that first night,' says Emily, looking into Moe's eyes and feeling the full flush of self-effacement that follows truth.

'Did ya like me?'

'Yes ... I enjoyed your company ... You were funny ... But ...'

'But?' Moe cocks back his neck in mock-incredulity.

'You won't be angry if I say?'

Of course I will, but you'll never guess. 'No! No way! What? Tell me!'

'Well ... You looked ... Uhm ... A little old-fashioned,' Emily offers, visions of Carnaby Street *Pop*-ing up in her head.

'Old-fashioned? Ya mean my clothes?' Moe takes a quick admiring peek at what he's wearing and confirms that today's duds really *do* look cool. It's just that Emily's not that into his Chicago Blues look. Good thing she loves the sound, though.

'Yes, mainly. You reminded me of some telly character from my childhood. Someone altogether seedy and dangerous.' She only half-succeeds in suppressing a full-blown laugh.

'Gee, thanks. Now I'm a dirty old man.'

'Don't be upset! You said you wouldn't be.' She squeezes his arm, then begins to gently stroke it.

Moe gives himself a second going-over. 'Maybe I *could* do with some new threads.' He's grooving so much on the feel of what she's doing, that he's ready to say anything just to keep it happening.

'It'd help a little.'

'Oh.... And do I *need* help?'

Now she pokes him in the ribs for wanting so much from her. 'Of course not, silly boy! Added to which, seeing as to where I am, it's an unnecessarily rhetorical question.' Emily looks around Moe's bedroom, deciding on the spot that her reaction to it is highly similar to what she's been trying to express about his clothes.

'Yeah ... Okay, I'll give ya that ... Uhm ... Did ya wanna hear what I thought when we first met?'

'Yes, of course, ' Emily half-lies.

'I thought ya'd make a really good friend. Ya seemed like a nice person to talk with.'

'That's all? A "really good friend"? That's *it?*'

'Yep. I was a real schlep. As usual.'

No longer mortified, Emily scrunches up her face to show that his daft way with words has left her totally stymied. Again. 'What's a ... schlep?' She emphasises the unsavoury word as if it alluded to some private bodily function.

'What it sounds like. A dope. A bozo. It's a Lenny Bruce.'

'Who?' Another exasperated face scrunch.

'A comedian ... A really great one.' Moe shakes his head. 'It's not important.' Well, it is, actually. But he lets it go. That's how much she means to him.

'So ... Why did they change?'

'What?'

'Your feelings for me, silly!'

'Oh, them! I dunno. They just did. Especially at the party. Ya just seemed so warm. I felt like ya were making me into the only person in your life.'

'I was. Cross my heart.' She does so — and winces — once again. 'Are you happy spending time with me?'

'Now *you're* the one being a schlep,' Moe answers. *Hollywood, I am here.*

'I'm not being a ... a ... schlup! I —'

'Schlep.'

'What?'

'A schlep. You said schlup. Which, come to think of it, I kinda like.'

'Fine! Schlep! Schlup! Whatever! It's just ... It's just that I have no idea. I need you to tell me.'

'I'm happy spending time with ya.'

'That's nice.' Emily hopes that he hasn't picked up the relief in her voice.

Moe wants to say what he really feels, but he's scared to. Time to change tack. 'Fill me in some more about your life before ya came over here. Ya hardly ever talk about The Motherland.'

Emily tenses up. 'Where do I begin?' Her attempt to evade truly answering him falls flat. *Oh well ...* 'To be honest, it makes me sad to talk of it, because I miss it so much. I love Britain, and this country's so bitterly cold. And I don't mean only weather wise.'

'Ya seem to be doing all right.'

'You and Larry and Curly Joe are the only three bloody Canadians I've met who've shown any semblance of being friendly! And you have gall to say *we're* meant to be distant and aloof!'

'Wow, I musta touched some nerve there.' Moe is already putting this info into storage in what psychologists like to refer to as his long term memory. Then, still in that role, he adds: 'Tell me about your childhood. School ... Ya know, that kinda stuff.'

Emily throws Moe her death stare, but capitulates. 'I went to a Girl's Public School — which means private over here — most of my life. I lived there all the time except for vacs.'

'Did ya like it?'

'Mainly. But we were so restricted! Always flocked together onto the same grounds. And no boys, hardly ever. We girls used to only see boys about once every three weeks.'

'Bet ya was happy then.'

'I'll say! We were all just so randy! Twisting our knickers, we were.'

Moe laughs at the sound of a potential new phrase for their private language. 'What the hell are knickers?'

'What? Oh ...' *Stupid damn language differences!* 'You know: underwear.' Emily points to the ones she's currently wearing, then shuts her eyes not able to believe she's just done that.

'Gee. You Limeys sure talk funny. Twisting your panties ... Geez ...'

'I can't think of a more repulsive word than "panties",' Emily cringes. Then, smiling wickedly to herself, she continues. 'We used to play kissyface in the woods all the time.'

'Play what? Kissyface?'

'Yes ... That was a game. Boys chased you until they caught you. And then they were allowed to do anything they wanted with you.'

Moe fakes a look of shock horror. 'Oh wow. You're joking, right? *Anything*?'

'Well ...' Emily thinks about what she and Moe have been doing. She turns her head to hide how hot and red her cheeks have turned. '"Anything" usually meant lots of kissing.'

'*French* kissing?'

'Possibly ... If the boy was, you know, sexy.' *Most of them were. Not that anyone cared enough to stop them from missing out on the fun.* 'Once in a while, if a boy was a really good kisser, we might let him touch our bras a few times ...'

'Touch your *bras*?'

'Well, we couldn't bloody well take them off, could we?' Emily's wishing like mad she could put the pair that landed on Moe's floor twenty minutes ago back on now. 'Added to which, most of us wore padded ones.'

'You're kidding!' He tries out his version of the Hollywood Leading Man giving the Hollywood Leading Lady a slow, up-and-down body scan. 'What did *you* need padded ones for?'

Emily's not sure if she should take that as a compliment. She decides she will. 'I'm not *that* big.' *Yes, I am.* And I had to develop —'

'Ya sure did.'

Emily tells herself that she's said enough.

'So that was it, huh?'

'What?'

'Ya got chased by these horny little Limeys and let them neck with ya. Didn't ya do any more?'

'No.'

'Nothing?'

'No ... Still a total innocent.' *Though a little less of one since you came along.*

'That makes two of us, doll.'

'Ho!'

'I ain't kidding, for Crissakes! You've probably done a whole lot more than I ever have!'

'Don't swear. And I've just told you: I've not done much of anything!' *Until today.*

'See! I said ya were more advanced!'

'I don't believe you!'

'I swear, it's true! I'll even swear it on a stack of *Playboys*!'

Is he pulling my leg expecting me to believe him? Not a snowball's chance in Hell! 'But you picked me up so easily! And... And ... Look at me now! I'm in your room, totally alone with you! We're both practically naked and lying on your bed! I don't even have the faintest idea how you manoeuvred me into agreeing to this. And you're telling me *you're* innocent!'

'But I am! Look, have I tried to get you to go all-out naked?'

'No.'

'See!'

'But you were going to soon. You were building up to it.'

'No, I wasn't.'

'You weren't?'

'Nope.'

'Why ever not?'

"Because I'm innocent. I've never done this before.'

'Done *what*? See? You're playing a game. That's how you get your women.'

'Jee-zus, Emily ...'

'Don't swear.' *Is he really is telling the truth? I don't think I want to go there right now.*

'Well, ya make me mad.'

So let's go here instead. 'Don't I attract you?'

Her question stuns Moe. 'Sure ya do. What's that gotta do —'

'Well?'

'Well?'

'What shall we play then?'

'What?'

'Shall we start with kissyface?'

'Do I have to catch ya?'

'I think you've caught me already, love.'

* * * * *

- Hello?
- Hiya, doll.
- Oh! Hello!
- Wanna chaw?
- What?
- Wanna chew the Ol' Cheroot?
- Moe! That sounds filthy!
- Okay. Be like that. I'll start again. Hi.
- That's better.
- How are ya?
- Very well, thank you.
- What'cha up to?
- Not very much. Trying to guess if you'll call.
- Me? Li'l Ol' me? For gosh sakes! Why wouldn't I?
- Well ... Maybe as you'd had your way with me last week, you might not be so keen any more.
- Are ya kidding me?
- I'm being entirely honest.
- You really think I'd act like that?
- I kept hoping that you wouldn't, but —
- Besides, we didn't go *all* the way.
- Oh! So you're hoping for more!
- No, I —
- You're not?
- Well, I ... Aw, shucks. Yer voice sounds so purty when yer talkin' dirty, little lady.
- Don't put on your funny voice to avoid my question.
- Why, its purtier than a magnolia blossom out there in the cotton fields where all the happy slaves are a-hummin' an' a-singin' an' chewin' tobaccki.
- Oh, hush!
- All right.
- Now ... Can you please talk sensibly?
- Yes, dear.
- Don't call me "dear".

- Fine, sweetie.
- Or "sweetie".
- Darling?
- No.
- Hon'?
- No!
- Doll?
- *No!*
- Tutti Frutti?
- *Piss off!*
- Chou-fleur?
- Uhm ...
- Ya like that, huh?
- Well ...
- Them Froggies sure can come up with crackerjack words. *Ah ma petite chou-fleur, tu me fais si horny!*
- What does that translate as?
- What? Horny?
- No! Chou-fleur, silly.
- Cauliflower.
- Oh, Moe!
- Couldn't resist it.
- Do I really remind you of that? A cabbage?
- No, not a bit. Chou's cabbage. Chou-fleur's a cauliflower. I just told ya that.
- *All right! Enough!*
- How 'bout love?
- What?
- Can I call ya love?
- Bloody hell, Moe! *Stop it!*
- Oh, oh ...
- What *did* you call up for?
- Uhm?
- Why are you calling?
- Gee ... Dont'cha like me to call?
- Of course I do, but —
- Am I bothering ya?

- No!
- Why are ya shouting at me then?
- *Moe!*
- I just wanted to make sure.
- My god.
- Are ya all calmed down now?
- Yes.
- Ya won't yell at me?
- No!
- Ya promise?
- Yes.
- Promise.
- What?
- Promise.
- I promise.
- You're not crossing your fingers, are ya?
- Moe ...
- All right. I believe ya.
- ...
- ...
- Well?
- Well what?
- Moe, will you *please* tell me why you called?
- Does there have to be a reason?
- Moe, if you don't tell me this second why you called, I shall put down the receiver.
- Did anyone ever tell ya, ya sound gorgeous when you're angry?
- Goodbye.
- Wait!
- What?
- Okay. I'll tell.
- I don't want to know now.
- ...
- *Tell me!*
- But ya just said that ya didn't —
- Enough. Goodbye.

- I phoned to tell ya that you're the first person that's made me feel the way I'm feeling now. Ya snuck up on me in the nicest possible way and I don't ever wanna lose ya. Ya make me feel free and relaxed and I can tell ya things like "I love ya" an' not even worry if that'll upset ya or anything because I know for sure it won't. So ... I called to say I love ya. Emmis.

- ...

- Hello? Ya still there? Have ya fainted?

- Moe ... I'm ever so touched ... But did you have to put me through Hell to tell me you love me?

- Well, a man's gotta be sure.

- Are you sure now?

- Ya passed with flying colors, kiddo.

- I was beginning to have doubts.

- I had faith in ya, doll.

* * * * *

And, for once in Moe's life, he's in a regular relationship that includes sex. And it's good sex, too. True, Emily's not on The Pill yet, and is adamant that she doesn't want to risk becoming pregnant, so they'll have to wait until that's sorted. Which, when Moe thinks about it, means that it's bound to happen sooner or later. For the time being, they've formed what Moe calls their Merry Mutual Masturbation Society. They have a routine:

They go into Moe's room, put an LP on automatic, move a table up to the door so that no one can walk in unexpectedly, and then begin.

Emily takes off all her clothes except for her "knickers" while he removes his shirt but leaves his trousers on. She lets him kiss and suck and squeeze her breasts and belly until it becomes too much for her and the whimpers begin to escape from deep inside her throat. That's the signal for Moe being allowed to palm and finger her crotch until the flimsy cotton barrier to her sex turns wet and all she can think of is how much she wants him to enter her. At that point, she hurriedly undoes and tears at his jeans and underwear until they fall below his knees leaving him helpless and so blatantly erect. Wildly pumping his penis, and, while going at it, being oddly reminded of holidays at her uncle's farm where she'd been taught how to milk cows, she brings them both to teeth-gritting orgasm.

At first, Moe had to go through with the last part of their act by himself because she was too shy to do anything other than marvel and flush bright red out of a combination of bashfulness and flagrant carnality. Moe had been shame-faced as well, but the need to ejaculate easily won over any qualms concerning possible social improprieties. As far as he knows, the book that provides the final word on masturbatory manners and the etiquette of orgasm has yet to be written.

After a few times watching him, curious and on fire, Emily shoved his hands aside and took over, exhibiting a natural expertise which half-convinced Moe he should ask her for tips that he could put to practice when on his own. Best of all though, Emily's coos of pleasure while tugging away at what she keeps calling his "Willy" make her own arousal evident. A couple of times now, she's whispered to him how everything just quivers inside her when the unmistakable result of her ministrations finally happens and she feels the mad rush of his sperm emerge in spastic spurts to spray onto her belly and breasts.

All in all, such sumptuous promiscuity is more than enough to keep both of them satisfied for now.

After all, they each have their adolescence to catch up on.

23. ANYONE FOR SATORI?

Sages of every kind enjoy reminding whoever will listen that all journeys begin with the first step.

Our Stooges first step on the path to the Mystic East begins somewhat lamely. It is Emily who convinces the three of them to get on with it by giving yoga a go. To be more precise, she shames them into it. The way she puts it is that yoga is a series of exercises whose purpose is to keep one's body fit and supple. After that, she pauses dramatically and points out how noticeable the effects of their long-term addiction to cherry colas have become. Agreements obtained to deal with this *pronto*, she herds them over to the Union's Events Bulletin Board where they take turns signing the *Interested* column to the McGill Campus Yoga Beginner's Class. The appeal of anything with an Eastern slant — even if it involves weird body-stretching exercises — is singularly enticing to Larry and Curly Joe for them to want to try out its possibilities. The cheap thrill of leching over Emily in leotards is enough of an inducement for Moe.

At the start of their first class, a slightly pudgy, middle-aged woman named Wanda Ripley — 'but call me WR' — introduces herself as their instructor. Then she proudly proclaims that, due to yoga, no one will ever guess her true age. To prove this, she passes her eyes over her seventeen new devotees searching for the model candidate. Pointing to Moe, WR asks him to estimate how old she is.

'Forty-eight,' Moe guesses, only to be told by WR that she's actually forty-five and that she always welcomes a good joke. At the proper time.

Not long later, in retaliation, she makes Moe strip off his shirt in order to demonstrate the effects that years of adopting an improper stance can have on human bone structure. Which brings about a rapid end to the journey for Moe.

After a further four lessons, Emily falls by the wayside as well. WR's too much for her. The way she goes on and on to the women in the group about not being ashamed to release one's sexual energy and mastering ways to flex one's *yoni* in order to achieve optimal orgasms is a step too far. Being invited to envisage herself carrying out WR's detailed instructions back home and *in the nude* while in the same room as a group of complete strangers, as well as Larry and Curly Joe, is definitely not what Emily signed up for. Her *yoni* works perfectly fine just as it is, thank you very much. To cap things off, as if all that malarkey wasn't enough, WR makes matters even more intolerable by positively insisting that the class spend half its time engaged in candle meditation and chanting. Both activities which, as well as being diabolically boring, make it abundantly clear to Emily that this training has nothing whatsoever to do with keeping fit.

Naturally, candle meditation and chanting are the very things that keep Larry and Curly Joe coming back week after week. The results of focused contemplation sound pretty cosmic to them. Not that they've yet achieved a breakthrough into the transcendental realm remotely akin to what WR swears they will experience anon. Still, what foretastes they've convinced themselves they've had are tantalising enough to keep them trying. Or should that be "trying not to try"? Or maybe even "not trying not to try"?

Except ... Larry starts to notice that his move towards "The Heavenly Joy That Is Satori" is having an undesirable effect on his ability to remain fully attentive to both his own and Suzie Q's more carnal needs. Worse, he's begun to suspect that Suzie Q is becoming noticeably aware of this as well. Looks like The Absolute will have to wait its turn. As if to prove him right, while scanning the Bulletin Board for something else to keep him busy, Larry's found a Beginner's Class in Painting that's only just started up and is still open to newcomers. Sounds like fun. With that, and the need to make room for composing new material for *The Warthogs,* Larry's got the convenient excuse to drop out as well and keep his focus on the sort of divine happiness he's more used to.

It's left to Curly Joe to keep at it and follow things through to the point where he can now sit in a full lotus, carry out the complete Sun Cycle, and even give himself a weekly nasal douche without wincing too much at the thought of doing it. It is, however, mostly the meditation that's seduced him. Sitting cross-legged, eyes riveted on the candle in front of him, he concentrates on its flame until he can see a rainbow within it and then, if he's celestially ready, zone in on what WR has told him is its aura. Way far out! Better yet, WR's hailed him as "a natural" at meditation.

It's the finest compliment that Curly Joe believes he has ever received in his life.

24. CHRISTMAS CRACKERS

Life's strings tug on. It's the end of the current semester in a week's time. Exams will begin and go on for a week after that. And then, a whole month's reprieve. If you can call a time that includes Christmas and New Year's a reprieve.

The Stooges have no idea how it's possible for the autumn months to have passed by so rapidly. What have they been doing with their lives? But ... It's not just them anymore, is it? There's now also Suzie Q and Emily to throw into the mix. As a last defence against their daily grind, they have taken to indulging in the crazies. Inspired by Emily's tales of what the Brits get up to during the upcoming Holiday Festivities, Moe dubs these activities *Christmas Crackers*.

A couple of days ago for instance, the three of them with Emily tagging along as the Fourth Musketeer used up nearly five dollars worth of savings mugging and hamming it up inside the one-minute Photo Booth over at *Woolworth's*.

Yesterday, they rode the elevator to the top of *Place Victoria* just to show Emily its majestic skyscraper view of the city. Noticed by some on-duty building cop, they were summarily kicked out. But not before they bought each other long-stemmed roses.

And today? Today ... Well, the impetus to what they are up to today has come about through their noticing that the Union has begun selling a strange new food. Something called *yoghurt.* It comes in a couple of fruit flavours — strawberry and blueberry — and you can have it either as your breakfast or lunch. The claim is that it's good for you. They're not sure about that. And they're also not sure if they like the weird gooey feel it instigates as it slips and slides down their throats. But ... That's not the essential thing. What the introduction of this mystifying concoction has got them to realise is that way too much of what they usually pile into themselves is unadulterated slop. So, in protest, earlier this morning they all trotted off to *Dominion's* in *Place Ville Marie* and chose ingredients for a much more nutritious lunch.

Curly Joe bought four thick slices of freshly roasted chicken.

Emily added some "just out of the oven" rye bread and questionable "Real English" shortbread squares to have for dessert.

Moe opted for four Red Delicious apples plus a jar of French mustard to spread onto the sandwiches.

And Larry topped it all off with a chunk of camembert. And a genuine coconut.

For drinks, it was a quart of apple juice and a maxi-sized bottle of fizzy water.

Now back in the Union, Moe puts on this Parisian accent and pretends to be a Maitre d', turning the event into a public spectacle. Fellow students are stopping in their tracks to gape and nail down what drugs these loonies are on. Especially when they're figuring out how to pry open the coconut. In the end, they have to borrow the nearest thing to a hammer from the kitchen staff. Naturally, the coconut splits apart into dozens of pieces and sprays their table and shirts with sticky juice. Also, they establish that none of them are all that keen on fresh coconut.

* * * * *

There's another side to Christmas Crackers. One that Moe knows all too well. But since Emily hasn't heard it a thousand times like Larry and Curly Joe have, he volunteers to tell her.

'Listen,' Moe says, setting up the routine: 'Why do I hate Christmas so much? Okay, I'll tell ya. For one thing, it's so phony. Several million dullards wingeing on about how they're gonna "Love Their Neighbor" for one whole day in the year and let's not be spoilsports by reminding ourselves of the other 364. Or 365 to be precise, as this happens to be a leap year. Now where's that at, Johnny?

'Ya wanna hear what Christmas is like for me? Yeah? Well, it starts with my parents having a full-scale brawl because the old man won't let a Christmas tree into the house. Why not, ya ask?

Because, Jim, as far as he's concerned, he's in mourning. What's he in mourning about? Just that when he was growing up as kid his parents were too poor to buy him presents. Which got him deciding that Christmas was a load of crap. That memory is so strong that he still can't see it any other way. Which gets him depressed. Then he gets even more depressed because no one else is depressed over all this crap. And *after that*, he gets depressed that he's depressed that no one else is depressed. And *nothing's* more depressing, let me tell ya, than to be depressed that you're depressed that no one else is depressed over what you're depressed about than to have some crummy Christmas tree staring ya in the face.

'So, what can he do except get drunk? Which is when things start turning really, really awful. After a bit, he reaches a point when he looks up, starts laughing his head off, shouts "Ahh, what the hell ..." and makes up his mind to go out to the stores to buy everybody some presents. Except by that time it's too late. Or else everything costs too much. Or just *looking* at other shoppers blows him back into depression. Which leads to him blaming my Mom for not telling him that he's been acting like an idiot all along. And then, when she tells him exactly that, he plows into her. And the screaming match starts up all over again.

'And *that*, to sum things up, is what I've gotta put up with every year. Which is, to return to the start of my argument, why I *hate* Christmas. *And* why I wish we was Jewish! *Emmis*.'

* * * * *

Now that their three-way romance is out in the open, Larry and Curly Joe and Suzie Q have found a pattern to satisfy them all. Each couple is guaranteed one date every week. The other days are up for grabs, depending on who feels like what and when. Some social occasions, like a movie or a music event, they might all go out together. Smooth sailing all the way. Moe and Emily mostly come along too, even though their views on the experiment judge it to be beyond bizarro.

What's really curious, though, is that so far there's been no hint about wanting to take the experiment any further and contrive for the three of them to get sexual together. They don't even talk about that possibility. Okay, so there was that first night. But everybody had kept all their clothes on. And they were in a car, right? Passersby could have caught them at it! And besides ... Besides what?

Well, Suzie Q knows for certain that if they were to, you know, all get in the same bed together, then there's every chance she'd give up her virginity to one of them. But she'd have no choice as to which one, would she? And she *wants* to have that choice. Really and truly. And, for now, the trouble is she *can't* decide. So thank goodness no one's rocking the boat. She isn't even *dreaming* of the three of them together any more.

Curly Joe? Curly Joe's not saying a word because he keeps imagining the different erotic combinations that such an event might open him to. Him and Larry, if he's honest. Yeah, their main focus of attention would still be Suzie Q. But still ... What if their hands or mouths slipped over and ... And what if they *liked* it? Talk about challenges!

And then, of course, he replays his Kitimat experience over and over again. How he and that other guy had made sure to steer clear of any accidental contact with each other. What did that feel like then? And, don't forget, that was with a complete stranger. This is Larry we're talking about. That same Larry who keeps wanting to lock himself up in a room with Curly Joe and two guitars and not come out of there until the twelve greatest songs ever to be put onto vinyl have emerged.

Which is such a *worthy* desire. But if their friendship turned into something more complicated, would Larry still want to? Would *they* still want to? And is that possibility worth the risk? Nope. Curly Joe doesn't think so.

As to Larry ... Here's a paragraph or two from one of his latest letters to Suzie Q.

Yup. Even though things have changed, he still keeps on writing them.

I live on dreams that no amount of money can buy.

I live in a world where doing things like engineering because "there's money in it" are just not allowed.

Due to all this, my work suffers. But then, it's suffered since September, since the day my train pulled into Montréal and I popped myself out of a dream and into this academic nightmare.

Most days, I walk the streets alone. I meet people who pretend they don't see me. I want to dance for them. Smile. Laugh. Shout. Even grit my teeth and squat down like a female dog pissing. I want to bite their ankles.

All because of you.

I want you. I have eyes for absolutely no other.

I need you. As simple and downright easy as that.

I. Need. You.

Everything else is nothing but a blur.

Like this letter.

Reading between the lines, what Larry's not saying — as much to himself as to anybody else — is that he sees an endpoint to their experiment. And that endpoint will be one where the triad reverts to being a couple. And that couple will be him and Suzie Q. Permanently. But he knows he can't think that way. He's not allowed to. It ain't with it. Too straight. And that's not who he is. Or wants to be. Right?

* * * * *

Unlikely as it may seem to Larry, his no-chance dream is just about to come true. Curly Joe's sitting outside the Union, waiting to meet Suzie Q. It's his turn for a one-to-one date. He's just finished writing another poem. He's going to need to buy a new hard-covered black book soon. The poem ends like this:

> *drifting*
> *drifter*
> *drift.*

He's not sure where those lines came from. They've startled him with their honesty.

Curly Joe looks around himself. He notices the consequences of the latest snowfall of the season and frowns. He knows only too well that Suzie Q will look at the same scene and jump for joy. Because snow means skiing which is, for Suzie Q, one of the unequalled thrills in life. Curly Joe doesn't share her devotion. Even at the best of times, he's not much of a sports guy, and the thought of tearing down mountains while trying to keep his balance creates nothing other than unmitigated terror. He thinks back to last year, just after he and Suzie Q had started going out together. He'd given in to her insistence and agreed to put his life on the two lines of wood. All he'd wanted to know was how to make yourself stop. Suzie Q couldn't explain, mainly because she was unable to see the point to his question. *Why would you want to stop skiing unless you absolutely had to?* Outcome? He'd passed away the day falling forwards, backwards and sideways. So, yeah. She'll be yearning for her little Laurentian village. For the mountain slopes and chairlift to their top. For that second before the body pushes and the skis take command.

Somehow, all these thoughts bring Larry to mind. Okay, well ... Larry will want to get up there and give things a try. Larry's more ... More physical. Set free, Curly Joe's imagination spawns multiple pornographic movies of what Larry and Suzie Q get up to when they're on their own. With the added enticement of a family mountain cabin, and frozen lake and snow ... Shit! Suzie Q's parents even own a skidoo! More movies: Larry and Suzie Q breezing along, a silent moonlit night, both feeling hot regardless of the temperature ... *Hey! Wait a minute!* If Curly Joe didn't know better, he'd say he was feeling jealous. Jealous? How can he feel jealous when he's an Evangelist of Love?

Naw ... It's more that for the next few weeks he's going to be seeing less of Suzie Q than he's gotten used to. It's airtight: the holidays are right around the corner, which means that they'd have had a lot more free time doing things together. Except now they won't. Still, on the positive side, it looks like they'll all be spending New Year's Eve over at this old girlfriend of Moe's — Chastity — who, it turns out, went to the same high school as Suzie Q. That unexpected connection has flabbergasted everybody, probably Moe and Chastity most of all. But, there it is. Weirded out or whatever, Chastity's still gone ahead and invited all of them to come along. Which will be fun. So why does it continue to feel like everything's gone to shit?

Suzie Q shows up minutes later. The casual brush of of his hair and mouth-to-mouth kiss she gives him not caring who might see them cheers him up. As Curly Joe's predicted, she's in a festive mood. And here comes another prediction he's also certain he'll get right:

'*Eaton's Pet Store?*' she says.

yup. nostradamus, eat your heart out! Suzie Q loves going there to fuss over the various animals on display. It's become one of their rituals.

Walking down Peel Street, Curly Joe can't get over how so many people are running around like thousands of ants whose sense of direction has gone haywire. The gift-buying fury of Christmas in close-up. At least the pet store isn't swamped with hordes of last-minute shoppers who have convinced themselves that pet chinchillas are the "in" thing to give someone this year. Thankfully, *Eaton's* doesn't stock chinchillas. Not live ones, at any rate. Funny little furry things called gerbils are about as exotic as *Eaton's* is prepared to go. Still, they're fun to watch.

Afterwards, they take themselves over to *Dunn's* for some onion soup. Time to sit and chat. Then figure out whose home is more likely to be people free so they can fool around as much and as far as they want.

'where'll you be over the next few days?'

'I've got to study for exams, so I'm gonna be out of action, sorry to say.'

'same goes for me.'

'I'm driving up to St. Therese as soon as I've finished the last one.'

'oh.'

Suzie Q doesn't like the sound of that "oh". 'You can come up, if you want.'

'naw. i don't think so. i'd be in the way.'

'I've got a Ski Club on the first day. I'll be at the cabin all on my own that night because my parents won't make it over until the night before Christmas Eve. You could stay over before they do.' *How flagrant do I have to make it?* Suzie Q asks herself. She's reached a momentous decision. Curly Joe's the one she wants to rid her of her virginity. Yes, Laurent would probably be more exciting, but Curly Joe is bound to be gentler and more attentive. And, size-wise, his is smaller. And, admittedly, cuter.

All the same ... While everything's still wild and fun with the three of them and she's in no hurry to change things, Suzie Q knows that, in time, this mad experiment of theirs will come to an end. Oddly enough, she sort of wants it to. Not now. Not right away. But down the line ... Maybe it's her Catholic guilt building up. Or maybe it's just the natural order of things reminding her. After all, finding *a* partner — not partners plural — and being a couple is what everybody wants. What *she* wants.

Suzie Q gives Curly Joe a good long pout just so he gets the point. 'Doesn't my invitation sound all that appealing to you?'

'yeah, of course it does.'

'So ... Say yes, then.'

Curly Joe can't shed light on why he's hesitating. Something about the snow and skiing. No, more than that. Those things are pointing out the differences between them. What drives them. What they want from their lives. Okay, so like his poem reminded him, right now he's just drifting. Doesn't have the foggiest as to what he wants. Or maybe even *who* he wants. Suzie Q. He knows he loves her. He knows she loves him. But is that enough? Is each of them the lover-of-a-lifetime for the other? Maybe. But ... That song from *Blonde On Blonde* intrudes. *Most Likely You Go Your Way (and I'll Go Mine)*. Is that —

He's hesitated for far too long.

'Have it your own way,' Suzie Q says. Right now, she hates

him for making her feel like such a ninny.

Curly Joe misses all that. He's reeling to the echo effect between him thinking of the song and Suzie Q's words. Is this the answer he's been on the lookout for?

Suzie Q's struggling to hold back the tears. 'You can be incredibly cruel sometimes.'

'i'm not trying to be. i —'

'Never mind. Forget it. I'll find out if Larry's up for it.' *There! She can be cruel as well!*

Suzie Q's words make Curly Joe's blood run cold. It's the end-game that he reads into them. Everything's changing in an instant. No, he's not yet ready to accept that. 'so when are you coming down for the new year's eve party?'

'I don't think I'll be going to it.'

this is turning out worse than vancouver! 'what? why not?'

'I think it'll be nicer in the countryside. I wouldn't enjoy the party all that much anyway. I don't feel like seeing a bunch of people that I knew when I was in high school. You and me and Larry and Moe and Emily can have our own party when I get back. Maybe we can all go out for an expensive meal somewhere. That'll be fun, won't it?'

'yeah, but ...'

'I'll talk to Larry. See what he thinks. One of us will be in touch.'

* * * * *

Larry's more than up for a night in the Laurentians alone with Suzie Q. He's *way* up. In every innuendo of the word. And Suzie Q feels so let down by Curly Joe she assures herself that she'd been wrong all along and Laurent is unquestionably her preferred choice as the man in her life she'll always remember as the first to make love to ... No! The first to *fuck* her. Yes, she avows, it's high time she makes that happen.

Except ... The day before they're due to drive up to the family mountain hideaway, Larry catches the worst feverish flu he's had in years.

Suzie Q takes it as a direct message from On High.

Larry? He's tucked up all alone in his bed, coughing and sneezing too much to care.

25. "NEW YEAR'S EVE" EVE

Having nothing better to do, Curly Joe settles on going to Chastity's New Year's Eve Party. What's he got to lose? He'll head over to it on his own, catch up with the others when he's there. It won't be the first time he makes the scene without a date. Likely won't be the last, either. He's doomed to such things. No, not doomed. More like chosen. And, who knows? Suzie Q might throw a curveball and show up. Good enough reason to be there, just in case.

Unfortunately, New Year's Eve doesn't start off all that great for Curly Joe. In a moment of seasonal *bonhomie,* he gives in to his parents' prompting and heads over to the local barber shop. It'll be several years into the future before he'll repeat such an act.

'a trim and some minor reshaping, nothing drastic, leave more near the front than in the back, please', is what he asks for.

Instead, the barber responds to the request by taking it as his opportunity to express all the pent-up frustration he feels over the new longer-length styles threatening his business. Paying no attention to Curly Joe's instructions, he razors and hacks away at the chaos of curls until his handiwork culminates in what during the dreaded 1950s would have been admired as a near-definitive example of a "bean shave". Even Curly Joe's carefully nurtured side-burns are now a thing of the past.

The litany of curses howled by Curly Joe as he stomps away will, in time, be instrumental in bringing down a great many barber shops, not least the one that "did a Delilah" on him.

Pleading guilty for having contributed to the molestation her son has been subjected to, Curly Joe's mother partially saves the day through the creative combo of *Aqua Net Hairspray* and roller brush so that what's left of the front becomes a bristly wave which, for a few seconds, might fool a half-blind drunk into believing that Curly Joe's hair is longer than a gnat's prick. A gnat's *flaccid* prick, to be more exact.

By the time everything's straightened out — or rather, waved

— all that's left for Curly Joe to fuss over is what clothes he's going to wear. As far as that goes, he opts for a casual, blend-in-with-the-crowd look. Clean cream jeans, honey-coloured turtle neck and his favourite black V-neck cotton sweater. And, oh yes, The Tooth. To complete his appearance, he slips his feet into a pair of rust-coloured moccasin-style loafers. No heels, all the better for dancing. The way he sees it, everybody's going to take one look at him and wonder why Chastity has invited this Vietnam Grunt on leave to her party, so he might as well make himself as comfortable as possible.

Ready at last, he pulls on his winter boots, buttons up his camel hair coat all the way to the top, ties a checkered-scarf around his neck, covers his nearly-bald head with a black wool hat and begins his trek to the 102 Bus Stop. It's not much past 8.30pm. The party's due to start in half-an-hour. Of course, most people won't arrive until 10.00pm, or later. By bus, it will take him around forty-five minutes to get there. Maybe a bit longer. Plenty of time to amble to the bus stop, breathe in the cool breeze.

In keeping with his run of bad luck, the year brings matters to an end by disgorging blasts of viciously gelid air that rip right through Curly Joe's coat and numb every inch of his face. So much for the leisurely stroll. No bus to be seen, he runs on the spot while standing in line just so he can still feel something of his body. Curly Joe stage whispers a new set of blasphemous oaths until the 102 finally arrives. It's a short ride to the next bus. *Hallelujah! A break at last!* There it is, tuning up the motor and getting ready to depart. This one, like the first, is also nearly empty of passengers. He plunks himself down in a seat near the back. The bus follows most of the same route that takes him to Suzie Q's house. Now that she's on his mind again, Curly Joe starts to feel boneheaded appearing at a party full of Suzie Q's friends without her being there as well. For one thing, they'll be studying him through shifty eyes, thinking how hard up he must be showing his face on his own. He nearly gets off the bus. Twice. Only his dumb pride keeps him on it.

He reaches his stop earlier than planned, but so what?

There's a couple knocking on the party front door. Curly Joe scuttles over to stand behind them. The door opens. Chastity.

'Ooh! How amazing you came! Come in! Come in!'

'uhm ... thanks. and thanks for the invite. you're looking great.' Wasted words. Chastity's already moved on, gabbing away non-stop with the couple. Fine by him.

Now indoors, Curly Joe settles on playing it Vancouver suave and streetwise. Following Chastity's footsteps into the main party room, he's greeted out of nowhere by some woman he's never met before who insists on telling him that she's Chastity's best friend. Then without further ado, she gets him in a clinch and kisses him passionately, tongue straining against his teeth. Her extravagant behaviour is so unsubtle that its message is too barefaced for even Curly Joe to miss: she's ready and willing to take over from wherever Suzie Q's left off. Flushed with this unsolicited reassurance that he's not a total write-off, all the same his response finds a way of communicating that he's not ready to jump into new commitments. Resolution noted, they exchange another minute's worth of trivialities and jointly agree to hang loose together later on and rap some more. As if.

Just as he turns away, Curly Joe spies Moe being greeted at door. He and Chastity hug. Old pals. Then Moe introduces Emily. Both women take their time giving it a good long look up and down, each thoroughly mystified as to what Moe ever saw in the other.

Curly Joe glides up to them, allowing Chastity to make a quick escape. An odd thought passes through his mind: perhaps — no, certainly — he'll be kissing Emily at midnight. How will they both feel about that? And when it comes to it: why is he obsessing over these possible scenarios? He leaves his question behind and offers to take them to the room that's been set aside for people to leave their coats. They kibbitz among themselves for a couple of minutes and then head off to mingle for a bit, get a feel of the action.

Just before they do, Moe takes Curly Joe aside, and quickly asks if he's all right. Curly Joe nods yes.

'Good. And, on a different note,' Moe adds, 'who scalped ya?'

It's the first time that Curly Joe can laugh at this ignominy. Good Ol' Moe.

Making the rounds, Curly Joe bumps into a guy who he vaguely recognises. Turns out, they'd both been in the same Second Year Class at Heebie Jeebie High. All he remembers about him is that as a big fan of *The Who*, he'd scotch-taped a miniature plastic electric guitar with its neck broken onto the inside of his desk and then printed "Pete 4 Ever" beneath it. The act had struck Curly Joe as being so lame-brained that it had formed his lasting opinion of his classmate. Now however, his judgment is undergoing major re-evaluation. Astoundingly, this poor deluded Townshend-worshipping caterpillar has turned into an alluring dope-dealing butterfly. And just to prove it, he's dangling the offer of free joint samples professionally tucked into a *Buckingham Cigarettes* pack.

Curly Joe's awed by this dramatic zigzag to the night's festivities. A turn-on at Chastity's party! He wishes that Larry would hurry up and arrive so he can tell him the great news. He'd tell Moe right now if he thought for a minute that Moe would be interested. Would he be? Moe's loosened up a little about drugs, true enough, but now there's Emily to contend with. She's over-the-top negative on the subject. Even worse than Suzie Q. Maybe he'll keep the information to himself for the time being.

As it turns out, becoming a butterfly hasn't made the guy any less boring. They try to chat over old times, but their memories are from different worlds so that all they keep returning to are the twenty sticks of instant enlightenment ready and waiting to be lit. Run out of things to say, they grin stupidly at each other.

While he's working through various strategies to make a getaway without exiting empty-handed, the only woman Curly Joe's seen so far tonight wearing T-shirt and jeans cruises by, stops, and then picks her way toward him. Her identity a mystery, she exudes an unmistakable West Coast hippie-trippy stance.

'Off the wall, huh?' she casually asks, not bothering with

introductions.

'what?'

'This party. These people. Pretty oddball scene.'

'oh ... yeah. weird's the word.'

'What brings you here, man?'

'what?'

She throws him a look that says 'is "what" the only word that you got a grip on?' Then going all charitable for her own arcane reasons, she adds: "I mean, you look pretty hip. What brings you to this here shebang?"

what is this woman on? she's gotta be out of her tree if she can go around calling anyone that looks like i look tonight "hip". Curly Joe wipes his hand automatically over his scalp, then cringes. 'nothing much else to do. i'm playing it by ear. winging it, you know?'

'Yeah. Same here. I'll hang around a bit longer. Then see which way the wind blows, get my drift?'

'sounds good. well, let me know if anything better comes up. maybe we can, you know, catch the wind together.'

For some reason, that makes her laugh. 'You hitting on me, man?'

'no! i —' *i was hoping to!*

She laughs again. 'I gotta give it to you. You are one far-out cat trying it on right in front of my old man!'

her old man? what? oh ... oh shit. mr. butterfly! 'hey, no! i was just ... you know ... i'd never —'

Now Mr. Butterfly butts in. Good to see he's grinning. 'Easy, man. No harm done. We're open-minded. Anyhoo ... Me and the wife have gotta go and mix with the mixers. But, don't forget ... ' He pulls out the *Buckingham* pack again. 'Offer's still there when you're ready for a taste. We'll have to toke outside, of course ...'

'sure. no problem. we'll catch up.'

'Come here! Give us a cuddle, Mr. Swinging Cream Jeans!' Butterfly's wife says.

Curly Joe obeys. It feels like something more than a friendly clinch, but he's not going to point that out.

'Well, hope to see you later, man. If this scene don't improve, we can go somewhere and make our own. Stay with it!'

Too many mixed messages. Time to indulge in some of the free booze. Sitting on his own, his drink slugged down rather than sipped, Curly Joe's got his head cushioned between his hands while staring at his shoes. Every couple of minutes, he sneaks a quick look at the other revellers. What secrets lie behind the facade of middle-class normality? Take Chastity, for instance. Busy being "the hostess with the mostest" and acting all grown up as if that's who she really is. And maybe that's so. But what would he see if he could inch his way into her mind? Maybe something a whole lot scarier than what's on show. Which reminds him of Nora. And what he did to her. *Oh hum.* Back to his shoes.

Not long later, Curly Joe feels the weight of someone plunking themselves down on the couch. *His* couch. At least they're keeping their distance. Not bothering to look up and face his neighbour just yet, he angles his head enough to zone in on the intruder's chosen footwear. There's a pair of shiny, ink-black, patent leather kitten heel shoes nearby, but they're lying there on their own! She — whoever she is — has taken them off and is happily stretching her tights-enclosed toes. Well, she's certainly got more than enough *chutzpah*; you don't wear blood-red pantyhose underneath a black miniskirt unless you're out to be noticed. Distracted enough to be moved to action, Curly Joe sneaks a peek at the rest of Miss Red-Legs. Her face is pretty, not beautiful. It's rounder than he'd like but far from undesirable. Also, she's short, too short for the large size of breasts. All in all, though, it's still the hose that would be the first thing to catch somebody's eye. Just the same ...

'They don't smell, do they?' she says.

'huh?'

'My feet. I'm sorry if they do. But I just had to set them free. I hate those shoes! I don't know why I thought it'd be cool to wear them. I can't anyway. And dancing in them! I ask you: why would anybody want to try to dance with semi-high heels on? It's ridiculous! And dangerous, as far as I'm concerned!

Now you, however ...' She makes a show of appraising Curly Joe's moccasins. 'You made a much more sensible choice to dance the year away.' She shakes her head. 'Sorry! I'm just babbling. Pay me no mind. I apologize. I've disturbed you.'

'no! no! you haven't! i was just —'

'Contemplating the world. I like doing that, too. Especially when there's lots of people around and I'm bored with being sociable.'

'yeah, i guess.'

'Are you?'

'am i what?'

'Bored with being sociable.'

'not any more.'

'Goody!'

Her name is Eve ('As in "New Year's"', she jokes), she drinks screwdrivers, studies zoology, and — *Yippee!* — is all on her own. Curly Joe becomes even more entranced. They talk non-stop for what seems like hours. Their only pause-points are to refill glasses. When they eventually get in the mood to dance — Eve staying shoeless, of course — they are so free and energetic that all the other boppers keep their distance. And the music's passable. The better part of Top 40 1968 and earlier is being played. Even Dylan's in there somewhere, luxuriating in his vitriolic contempt for the people he sings about.

While strutting to a *Rolling Stones* song from their latest album, Curly Joe notices that Larry's in the room as well. They wave at each other in greeting but go no further than that. *larry's been acting kinda funny of late. almost like he's doing his best to avoid me.* Curly Joe thinks. *must be that flu he had. maybe i should go over —*

He'd play with further possibilities, but before he can Curly Joe feels a tap on his shoulder.

'Hey! What happened there? One minute we were in a groove and in a zip I'm all on my lonesome. Have you lost interest in me?' a voice says.

He turns, half-expecting to see a sorrowful Suzie Q. Instead, he finds himself looking down into Eve's searching brown eyes.

He smiles, nonplussed by the realisation that he's happier to see her there than anyone he can think of. Even Suzie Q. 'how could i ever forget about you'?' he answers her, and, saying this, he bends down in total calm assurance and kisses her.

Like the other kisses he's given and received tonight, it's uncontrolled and probing. She welcomes his tongue unhesitatingly, offering hers in return. They press closer. He feels her breasts on his lower chest and grows a quick erection. Eve's kisses become even more torrid. Encouraged, Curly Joe's hands slide lower until they touch the base of her spine. He shocks himself at his boldness, but she doesn't show any signs of being offended. They stay like that for ages, entwined and swaying in tune with the beat coming from the record player. Then, all of a sudden, Eve turns pale. Sadness splatters itself over her face.

'what's wrong?'

'I think you and I need to have a talk.'

Cryptic as it sounds, Curly Joe is already positive he knows what she'll say. He feigns confusion in the hope that she'll prove him wrong. They head for the top of the stairs where it's darker and more quiet.

Eve looks morosely at him. Her lower lip begins to quiver. 'I have a steady boyfriend. Matter of fact, we're engaged.'

got it in one.

'I just didn't want to lead you on, or hurt you.'

Inside himself, Curly Joe's asking over and over again why he has to be so doomed. Outside, he shows hardly any emotion. It's tough being a man. And an evangelist, on top of that. So he puts on one of his regular performances of a lifetime. 'you couldn't hurt me. you're not capable of it.' *now for the bigger lie.* 'thing is, you beat me before i could say something similar. i was getting worried i might hurt you. you probably know my girlfriend, suzie q? the ski nut?'

Eve wipes her eyes, believing him. 'Yes. Yes. I know her. Not very well though.'

'you're both pretty different people. but ... uhm ... why are you here all alone on this "night of nights"?'

'He works in Ontario. If he stayed there, he'll get two and a half times his normal pay. So he'll be coming down the day after next with a pile of cash. We added up that it'd be better that way.' She plays that over in her head. 'I guess we got our sums wrong. I hadn't really thought out all the implications.'

'who ever does? i'm here all on my lonesome because she has this big skiing competition somewheres or other and she had to leave to practice. she won't be back for a few days.' It's another passable lie.

There's a long silence after that. Giving in to the unspoken, Curly Joe puts his hand over her left shoulder and encourages her to sit closer to him.

'Two lonely people,' she whispers.

'not so lonely as they *could* be ... what's his name, by the way?'

'Who? Oh ... Bill,' Eve says, It throws her to sound so apologetic.

'well bill, wherever you are, I hope you know how goddamn lucky you are.'

Eve allows her tears to erupt freely. She's not entirely sure if they're for Curly Joe or for Bill. Either way, she's letting them both down.

'i'm sorry, i shouldn't have said that.'

Eve stops crying, looks up at him wild-eyed. 'No! No, I'm the one who's sorry. I was trying to imagine what it'd be like if I'd met you before Bill. I'm half-ashamed for thinking it, but I *am* thinking it.'

'i was just thinking the same,' half-lies Curly Joe. Or maybe he's speaking the truth for once. 'the responsibilities of love ... maybe we take it all way too seriously ... it oughtta be so liberating! don't seem to be, though.'

Eve totally gets what he's saying. She's sure now that they're kindred spirits. Maybe even soul mates. 'What you just said reminds me of something in a book I read a couple of months ago and keep going back to. I fell in love with its author. Maybe you've heard of him? He's a Lebanese writer called Kahlil Gibran. For some reason, your words made me think of him.

The book's called —'

'*the prophet,*' Curly Joe completes for her. 'i read it, too. loved it. it's hard to follow its teachings, though.'

That book's already like The Bible to Eve. She quotes from it every chance he gets, much to Bill's irritation since he isn't into all that hippie-dippy-trippy stuff. 'I think you could do it, though,' she says. 'You sound like you've understood what he's driving at. You *could* do it! I know for sure you could. You even look a bit like him. Maybe you're one of his followers? An Evangelist. Or something like that.'

Curly Joe tries to tell himself that it's only another coincidence. Evangelist isn't that uncommon a word these days. But any reasoning is useless. She's said the words and the questions he'd been asking himself before are answered. Of course! Once again, the reminder of who he is and that, therefore, what's happening tonight is necessary. All these different people offering up their bodies, their drugs ... Themselves. They've been telling him something that he's only now truly wised up to. There's always going to be such offerings. But, for one reason or another, they're never going to be enough. Not for him. Oh yeah, he'll be able to get close to people, does so already, but there's always going to be a gap. Something that he can't put words to as yet. Something about his Calling.

He turns to Eve and recognises her as The Messenger he needed. Some mythical angel come to guide him through his period of temptation. Even though he hardly knows her, he's sure that in another time or place, if things were different, Eve would be his perfect partner. The First Prize. But ... She can never be his. The search is over. Even if he's emerged empty from it, its completion brings on a peace of sorts.

He feels The Tooth bump against his chest. Close to his heart. He's certain: he doesn't need it to remind him anymore. He's been wearing it all these months, yet it's only now, in the act of removing it, that he begins to truly divine its message. Placing it around Eve's neck, speaking reverentially, he repeats its legend for her.

While he's doing that, Eve thinks to herself how silly everyone is for not accepting something breathtaking that happens, like this right now, because it goes against memories of the past or expectations of the future. She decides to listen to herself for once, to let herself be with him, allow them to take themselves as far as they both want to go. She'll regret it, probably, in the morning. But, at the same time, she's caught hold of one single powerful truth: the only real regrets we have are those of refusing to carry out an action that everything inside us screams is absolutely right to want to carry out ... Whatever comes of it, it will be forgivable.

It's dark and she'll listen to no counter-arguments. She wants him now, not in some all-too-unlikely future when any Bill or Suzie Q's been discarded or forgotten. It's probably not even for forever. Just now. This moment. Tomorrow she might want Bill or maybe still this almost stranger. And it shouldn't matter. But it does. Or, people *say* it does. Well ... To Hell with them! Unrestrained, her hands begin to mangle the swell between his legs while his fingers make their way into her shirt and over the cotton cups that cover her breasts. Strange fingers find her nipples. She whimpers as they grow in reaction to his touch. Then she urges him to go further.

Sometime later, not sure how long they've been cut off from everything except the all-consuming turn-on their bodies' experience, they silently agree to stop. Far from satisfied, maybe even still frustrated, they're left with no doubt that what they've given and taken of each other is certain to be forever stamped on their memories. Midnight and 1968 have come and gone. The acceptable time for the party's guests to kiss friends and strangers free of excuses has passed. Eve and Curly Joe have needed no excuses. They have revelled in their freedom. People trying to edge past them have leered in admiration and jealousy. Tongues will wag wildly. Let them.

When the festivities come to an end, a stranger caught up in seasonal love for his fellow human beings offers to give both of them a ride home. In the back seat of the car, Eve won't let go of Curly Joe's hand. Like him, she smiles and cries all at the same time.

Eve is the first to be let out. They kiss fiercely, then let each other go.

'Goodbye,' she whispers. 'Have a wonderful life, okay?'

'i'll do my best. you, too. i know you will.' Curly Joe pauses. He wants to say more. 'maybe ... in the future ... who knows?' he says.

Her back to him, unsure how she'll ever explain all this to Bill, or if she even has to, Eve is already too far away to hear him.

* * * * *

On the evening of the First, in the new year of 1969, Curly Joe comes across a crunched-up slip of paper with what looks to be a phone number on it. Flashback time: someone coming up to him and Eve asking for their numbers so that they'll be invited to next year's celebrations over at her place. As soon as Eve finished scribbling hers down, Curly Joe snatched it away and stuffed it into his pocket.

'i'll call you,' he'd joked. Or words to that effect.

It's taunting him now. He heads over to the nearest phone and dials the number.

He hears Eve's voice. She says 'hello' twice, and then he hangs up.

After that, he's left with no doubt that he couldn't be anything else but an Evangelist.

* * * * *

Next day, Curly Joe dials a couple of more numbers. Larry and Suzie Q. They agree to meet in a couple of days, when Suzie Q's back in town. Just the three of them.

When they do, he somehow finds the will power to let them in on his irreversible conclusion. The experiment is over. He stretches the truth to its limits and points out that from what he's seen of how Suzie Q and Larry get on with each other, he's been made all too aware that the lovers' bond between them is so true and luminous that he can't continue to stand in their way by staking a claim at something that, clearly, doesn't come near it.

It doesn't take much argument to sway them.

Now, all three holding each other's hands, they tell themselves that what used to be a triangle has become a circle. No matter what, they will always, always be the very best of friends.

26. REPERCUSSIONS

Eyes laying bare everything he feels for her, Larry is mystified by his mind's spontaneous recalling of the early years in his life when the myths of the Church had most entrapped him. He'd believed in Guardian Angels then and had even named his very own personal Guardian Angel "Doug" because that was his best friend's name. Only, his best friend had moved away and he missed him. Doug. He'd talk to the new Doug most nights, tell him his problems, play games with him, ask him what it was like in Heaven. The thing that Larry was most curious about Heaven was whether you still had to go to the bathroom or not. Doug had said yes. Angels don't lie. Larry snaps back pronto. How absurd to be thinking of Doug right now! And then he looks over at Suzie Q.

Suzie Q's slipped the winter sheets and blankets over her. She's wearing that shirt of his again. Nothing else, of course. It's two weeks into 1969 and they have successfully made it to the Laurentians. On their own. A couple now. Getting ready for her "awakening". At last, their lovemaking will be total and complete. If it hadn't been for Curly Joe's declaration ...

And how does Suzie Q feel about that? After all, everything began with Curly Joe. He was her boyfriend. Her steady. Maybe she should be sad that things didn't turn out as expected between them. And she is. He was fun, in that oddball way of his. But it's not as though she feels dumped or anything. Not like in Vancouver. They've moved on. They're still friends. Which is heartening. And honestly, though she doesn't want to admit it, she feels oddly grateful that their experiment has ended. As much as she'd enjoyed it — loved it even, especially all the attention she got from it — there was something ... something ... *Go ahead, say it!* There was something sinful *(There, I said it!)* about it all. It broke one of the Ten Commandments, didn't it? She's not sure which one.

Suzie Q nearly squeals. She's been so busy thinking about her sinfulness and how on earth she could ever get herself to talk about it at Confession, that she hasn't noticed Larry sneaking into her bed. *Talk about sinfulness! But at least it's more normal.* She slides herself close to him, bodies touching, making it all too evident that he's got nothing on. *Oh Lordy! It's really gonna happen!* She's about to give up to Larry what she'll never again be able to give up to anyone else. This physical act bonding them numinously forevermore.

They have prepared for this moment of merging. All potential obstacles have been accounted for, not least the most basic. It took Larry ages to raise it.

'Uhm ... About ... Yuh know ... Precautions. I guess I'll have to bring some condoms, right?'

His unexpected bashfulness gets her laughing non-stop. 'It's about time we brought the subject up.' She waits until his unease becomes too agonising to allow to continue. 'You — we — have nothing to fear. I've been on The Pill since September.'

Larry's relief is quickly overtaken by his curiosity. 'How did yuh pull that one off?'

'It was no problem! Mom came up to me one day and said "I don't want to know if you have sex with someone. But I *do* want to know that you won't get yourself pregnant unless you want to. So we're going for a visit to the family doctor, okay?" And that was it. Easy-peasy.'

'Like, wow!' Larry says. *But why did yuh never tell me before? Uhm ... Probably best to let that thought bury itself.*

Back on their bed, Larry begins unbuttoning the long column of stays one by one until the shirt parts totally. She wriggles out of it and tosses it away, fluttering into the night-light room and landing in a ruffle, its buttons chinking as they hit the oak floor. Unclothed and vulnerable, they turn on their sides to face each other, their kisses impatient to move on. They know their bodies so well now, not that the familiarity has diminished the fervour of their encounters. Quite the opposite. And soon ...

Larry's on his knees now, facing her. His hands encircle Suzie Q's ankles, spread her legs wide apart so that he can inspect that most secret part of her. His desire to look has little to do with any pornographic gaze. What propels Larry is his worshipful awareness that this swelling of flesh is the terminus to the canal through which human life emerges. Talk about Big Bangs! Weeks ago now, awestruck and inspired, he won over Suzie Q's initial reticence to allow him to draw her exposed *chatte* (as they've jokingly named her vulva) again and again. Once she'd become more used to his fascination, she'd consented to trim her pubic bush so that he gained a less obstructed view of her mons. And how was she to know that the remaining bristle would become such an itchy irritant? Astonishing herself, Suzie Q even pleasured herself in front of him thereby providing visual access to the unfolding of her labia, the distending of her clitoris. Convinced that he could see changes in hue and shape as she progressed through her monthly cycle, he was eager to sketch her while menstruating. Suzie Q drew the line at that. As detailed as Larry's close-up drawings are, their purpose is not illustrative. Rather, for Larry the aim is to produce a replica of such perfection that it will, in some mysteriously mystical way, provide him with the total re-experience of his own journey into life. Why he desires this is not a question he bothers to ask himself. Not least because its answer will only emerge once the re-birth has been achieved. And now ... Now a different opportunity is about to become available. The act of penetration will fuse their beings, temporarily recreating a conjoined state akin to pregnancy. And then ...

Suzie Q has more down-to-earth ambitions guiding her thoughts. Larry's visual obsession with her cunny has made her aware of how limited her own explorations have been. Perhaps, following his example, she should awaken her own desire to look "down there". But then, it is touch, rather than sight, that is her dominant means to arousal. In line with this, Suzie Q allows one hand to stray until it finds her lover's hardened penis. No matter how many times she's fondled it — with hands and lips and soles of feet — this "manhood" of his remains unfathomable. So different from the smoothness that is the rest of him. So much its own creature. So sinuous ... So ... As if on cue, an image of The Serpent in The Garden surfaces. Yes! Of course! No proffered apple nor any other fruit is necessary to understand Eve's choice. The Serpent itself was inducement enough. So be it. Perhaps all women are subjected to that same temptation. Suzie Q has no doubt that she is.

Suzie Q tightens her hold of Larry's hard-up cock. He groans. Her fingers snake up and down the staff, lingering at its crown to squeeze just enough so that he's ready to erupt. *No! Not now! Stop! It's too soon!* Freed from her grip, Larry pushes himself far enough away. No time for pencil and pad adoration today. Instead, palms under her bum, he lifts her lower back so that the target can't be missed.

Eyes open now, Suzie Q takes in this strange human kaleidoscope of two lovers about to become. All bedclothes scattered and tucked down the bottom of the bed, nothing in their way to impede their union. She shakes like a leaf *(from the Tree of Knowledge?)* in response to his blind search for a point of entry. It's a strange sensation, more uncomfortable than painful. The slippery smooth head probes, begins to push, stretching her opening to what feels like its straining point.

Suzie Q asks herself if she'll be able to hold back the cry that she's certain she'll feel the need to utter. Will it be like this all the time? Will future sensations of his imminent entry persist, indelibly fixed onto her thoughts as a result of this soon-to-be moment? She squeezes her eyes shut and attunes herself to Larry's breathing. He sounds as though he's in pain as well, frustration shivering through his teeth.

Then it happens. Suzie Q feels her lining drenched with his sticky substance and immediately thinks lunkheaded thoughts of having wet her pants like a little girl who'd waited too long. *Silly Moo! You've got no pants on for you to wet!* Her self-contained hilarity is shattered by his actions.

Already rolled over onto his side next to her, he utters curse after curse all the while repeating how sorry he is about his pathetic lack of control. She can't get up to speed as to what's happened.

'Laurent! What's wrong?'

'I came! That's what's wrong!' he nearly shouts.

Yes. Of course. The wet. His contribution to life's creation. But not inside her. He's not entered. She's still ...

Suzie Q loses herself in her state of happy sadness. Sadness for him; happiness, strangely enough, for retaining her virginity. But hadn't she wanted ... Dreamed even ... Yes! Yes, of course! But still ... She can't deny her relief. Perhaps she hadn't really been ready yet. Maybe they'd hurried things too much. She tells herself it's wrong to think like that. She'd wanted to as much as he had. Yes, she had. And yet ...

'We can try again,' Larry says.

'Are you sure?'

'Are *yuh*?'

Unable to contain herself, Suzie Q hugs him. 'Ah, *mon amour,* you look so dejected. A little boy lost. I love you so, so much in this gloriously heavenly moment —'

'I don't think I share yuhr —'

'You are beautiful! What happened is beautiful! It's *us!* It's who we are! What happened — and didn't happen — is what makes our love so special.'

They agree that they will recall this night in future years. They are so blessed to have such reminiscences. So much better and so unequalled by any ordinary de-flowering account. They proclaim that she's officially a non-virgin even if her hymen still throbs and protects the entrance. And so, of course, there are no further attempts made this night.

She is still pure. Still a virgin in the eyes of God.

27. DOOBIE DOOBIE DOO

So much shit is going down in 1969 that if ever there was a time for mind-blowing, get-out-of-your-head drugs, this is it.

As of 20th January, Nixon and Agnew have been making themselves at home in Washington, DC. One's in the White House, the other has a whole suite waiting for him any time he wants to make use of it at some fancy hotel calling itself *The Watergate*. Talking their forked-tongue version of "Peace In Our Time", they are busy gearing up the Vietnam War so that it extends, if still secretly, into Laos and Cambodia. Immediate result? Hawks vs. Doves. Hard-Hats vs. Hippies. True-Silent-Majority-My-Country-Right-Or-Wrong-Patriots vs. Drug-Dazed-Brainwashed-Commie-Bum-Gook-Peacenik-Sympathizers.

From London to Tokyo students are on the march pretty much against anything and everything. One of them, Jan Zajic, an ordinary Czech student living in extraordinary times, has just set himself on fire in protest of the USSR-led invasion of his country. He will never be forgotten.

Further East, God only knows what's happening in China. Chairman Mao's come up with a movement all his own: the "Up to the Mountains and Down to the Villages" travel plan that's sending all those city students off to the countryside for a period of unrest and re-education. Turns out, the teen-aged Red Guards have taken the idea of a Cultural Revolution so far, even The Great Helmsman has got the jitters.

Not that it seems to be stopping anyone from marching to a rebellious beat. Can't avoid its vibe. Even Pope Paul VI is in on the fun and games. He's just gone and cancelled all sorts of names of Saints from the Roman Calendar. Including Valentine. And guess what date he chose for his proclamation from on high? Looks like the Pope's heralding the end of Love.

As to the music ... Jimmy Morrison's been arrested for indecent exposure during a *Doors* concert. *The Beatles* gave their last ever live performance rocking out on Apple Records'

Oxford Street rooftop. *The Stones* are sympathising with The Devil. And — gasp! — The Voice of His Generation himself is just about to release a shit-kicking country music album titled *Nashville Skyline.* No wonder John and Yoko have hightailed it over to Amsterdam and snuggled themselves down to a bed-in.

Even in sad old Montréal, Quebec's homegrown liberation radicals, the *FLQ,* having bombed the Stock Exchange, are right now busy considering the potentials in political kidnapping. And, even better, events are building up to that merry day in February when nearly all of Bishop Street is littered with a rain storm of computer data cards and private records of students attending *Sir George Williams University* — the result of self-styled "grades are gratuitous" guerillas hacking and burning the academy's corporate computer to death.

The world is holding its breath, waiting to exhale.

* * * * *

Having had a taste of the brain-zap potential that a well-packed joint has to offer, Larry and Curly Joe have buddied up with an exclusive group of like-minded aficionados who keep on truckin' through life following the dictum "Take The High Way To Happiness".

Irresistibly, barely a day passes by without them making a couple or more brief, paranoia-fuelled visits to Student Union toilets gripping their nickel bags of Panama Grass and Mexican Maryjane in order to toke up and then engage in hours of mental gymnastics.

Seeing his two pals having so much fun, Moe has to admit that he's intrigued. Lately, he's been kicking around this idea that now that he's getting closer to deciding to Major in psychology, maybe he owes it to the profession to open himself to the mind-blowing experience. Purely for the advancement of science, natch.

Moe's initiation takes place one early March night in Curly Joe's basement playroom which, still adorned with by now torn and dirty aluminium foil walls, all agree is the definitive setting.

As the event is nothing less than historical, Curly Joe sets up the portable *Grundig* reel-to-reel and presses down on RECORD. Then he turns on the hi-fi and starts to play *Child Is Father To The Man* by *Blood, Sweat & Tears*.

And away we go!

(Taping starts)

- Is it rolling?
- yeah. it's on.
- Is the mike working, guys?
- yeah, sure. you wanna say something, larry?
- I think Moe should.
- yeah. you're right. moe? c'mere. talk into the mike.
- Okay ... Hello? ... Uhm ... This is Moe. I ... Uhm ... I'm sitting in a friend's basement right now and I'm about to lose my virginity. No, not *that* virginity, ya thilly thavage! I'm saving that one up for the Holy Ghost. Ma, I've fallen in with a bad bunch. A couple of psycho derelicts have talked me into smoking some ... ah ... Merry Giuana. They tell me it's good stuff. I'm scared. And I know I shouldn't be doing this. But ... Ah, what can ya do, hey? They got a starving hungry white Peace Dove ready to peck away at my heart if I don't ... So, anyway, assuming I don't make it through, I hereby donate my complete jerk-off collection of magazines to the Heebie Jeebie High School Library. Have fun, gang! All my other stuff, ya can send to the Father Flotsky Fan Club. Well Ma, Pa, so long and goodbye. And all ya fuckers out there, ya won't have Moe to kick around anymore ... That's it. I'm done. That's all I wanna say. Let's get on with it.
- Right.
- okay, larry, you wanna comment while i light up?
- Sure ... Well ... It's an exciting day, ladies and gentlemen. Here in this typical Anglo upper middle class bourgeois pig abode, we're about to hear the rantings and ravings of three thoroughly doped-up loonies. And now ... Yes! Yes! The

moment is upon us! The *very* nicely rolled joint is being placed between a pair of lip-smacking lips. Recently tooth brushed teeth are holding it in place in a truly expert way. Always a sign of a pro at his best. I see that the *Zippo* is being thrust forward! Yes! This is it, ladies and gentlemen! The lighter *has* been lit! It is now moving towards the doob ... Closer ... Closer ... *Contact!* A prolonged intake of breath. A look of incredulous astonishment. Comment! Comment!

- wow!
- Yuh heard it first on —
- What happens now, huh? What happens, Larry?
- Now it's yuhr turn, Moe.
- Oh.
- mmmmm. wow! was that something else!
- Good huh, Curly Joe?
- wow. yeah.
- Okay, come on, Moe. Puff!
- Mmmmmmmmmmmmmmmmm ... *Augh!*
- No! No! Don't breathe out! Keep it in!
- *Augh!* It burns, for Crissakes!
- Come on ... Look! Look at me do it.
- yeah. watch larry.
- It burns though, ya know?
- you just have to get used to it.
- Ohhhhhh ... *Shit Lamarr.*
- damn fine weed, huh?
- *Alouette! Gentille Alouette!*
- here, try it again, moe.
- Mmmmmmmmmmmmmmmmm ... *Augh!* Was that any better?
- yeah! yeah! see? it's easy.
- I don't feel nothing, though.
- Well yuh just took one little puff, Moe.
- Yeah, but everything looks the same.
- Give it a bit of time.
- Give me that thing, Curly Joe! Hey! It's gone out! Where's

that *Zippo*, huh? Who's got it?

(20 minutes later)

- Gee, has it started yet?
- yeah, sure. my head's swimming.
- Well, I don't feel no different.
- Yuh don't feel different?
- Nope.
- whadda you mean?
- where's all the visions I was expecting to get?
- Visions? *What* visions?
- No visions? Gee, I thought that's what this was all about.
- no visions, moe. not unless you smoke all six joints in one go.
- Aw. What a raw deal. What about all the lights then?
- *what* lights?
- Ya know. All the twinkly-colored lights ya see. Like in lite-shows.
- Like in lite-shows? Oh, wow! God, Moe! Like, where'd yuh get all these dumb ideas from?
- I dunno. *Life Magazine. Look. Ladies Home Journal.*
- c'mere. puff on this.
- Yeah. Puff on that and forget all about *Ladies Home Journal.*
- Okay. But I gotta tell you guys, all I'm getting is one major sore throat.

(15 minutes later)

- *Augh!* How much more of this shit do I have to take? My mouth's wrinkling up!
- shut up and puff, moe.

(8 minutes later)

- *Wow.* Enough.

- yeah. my head's spinning non-stop.
- That music's fantastic, man.
- yeah.
- Hey! I feel like I've been gypped!
- What's wrong now, Moe?
- Nothing's happened!
- aw ... for god's sake.
- Look Moe, what were yuh just doing?
- Nothing.
- what do you mean, *nothing*? you was dancing!
- Oh, that. Yeah. okay. So what?
- well ...
- Well, what?
- well, when have you ever danced like that with or without someone else?
- Huh?
- Yeah. When, Moe? Yuh were spinning like some goddamn Dervish! And yuh were pulling faces.
- and trying to do handstands.
- Uhm ... Well ...
- Never.
- Never?
- Never.
- Guess you're right, Larry.
- so you're stoned, you bum!
- Stoned?
- yeah. c'mere!
- Oh! Oh wow! *Wow*!
- What is it? What's wrong, Moe?
- *Kee-rist!*
- what's wrong? you feeling sick?
- Aw, Jesus. No. No. It's just ... Oh ... It's just ... When ya went to reach out for me ... Holy Shit! Curly Joe's hand just *grew,* Larry! I swear —
- What?
- It *grew*! Like, way, way *huge*! Goddamn!
- He's stoned.

- yeah.
- Aw, go on. Gee, this is a real downer. All the visions that ain't there —
- shut up, moe. let larry light up some more so's you can go back to dancing.
- Fuck. Do I have to? Where's that stuff, then? Hey, put on some Paul Butterfield, will ya?

(10 minutes later)

- is this tape still turning? yeah, okay. what I wanna say is that there's this castle. it's very real in my head but larry and moe can't see it. nobody can see it, in fact, except me. i see it. the drawbridge is closed. it's big and brown and silver chains hang down from its sides. it's slowly opening up .... it's slowly opening up .... and it's even more slowly descending ... lower and lower ... the chains rattle. now it's opened up all the way. but there's another drawbridge behind it ... black. yeah, black. and it's closed up. but this one's slowly opening, too. slowly falling down ... lower and lower ... and still another drawbridge appears. blue, this one is. blue and dark. somehow, menacing. it opens, too. it creaks, but it falls, and exposes a red drawbridge. a big bright red one. it falls as well ... the slow long thud of wood on wood. and now, green. a green drawbridge. it stands. and then it falls. oh. a yellow one, now. it opens. falls. then ... wow ... a white drawbridge. nearly invisible. transparent. it also falls. and then ... nothing. nothing but space. and ... and ... a hand ... appearing. long and scraggly. beckoning. it's pointing to a door. it's closed. it begins to open only to reveal a brown drawbridge which is closed ...

(18 minutes later)

- Hey.
- what?
- What's Moe doing?

- where is he?
- He's up on the chair over there, leaning over to the *Wingate Paine* poster on the wall.
- what?
- He's —
- what? what's he doing?
- Look!
- what?
- He's getting it on with the woman in the poster!
- *what?*
- I don't believe this!
- moe's doing what?
- Now he's licking her between her legs!
- *what? moe?*

(5 minutes later)

- I got hair caught in my teeth, gang.

(14 minutes later)

- I'm wrecked.
- why? what are you doing?
- Tracing a picture of Suzie Q onto the foil.
- oh, yeah. i can kinda see that now.
- Do yuh think it looks like her?
- yeah, i guess. i've never seen her completely naked before. uhm... not all at once, i mean. only in bits and pieces.
- Bits and pieces? What are yuh going on about? Yuh wanna sing some old *Dave Clark Five* song?
- *(mutual laughter)*
- i dunno. I mean ... I've seen all of suzie q's body. but not all
- at the same time. same goes the other way around, i guess. i mean, she's seen all of me but not like in one go. anyway, not in such detail. especially her ... uhm ... you know ...
- What *are* yuh going on about now?
- *(more mutual laughter)*

- fuck knows. something about seeing suzie q completely
- naked. uhm ... like you obviously have. otherwise, you wouldn't be doing such a great job.
- Don't tell her, okay?
- tell her what?
- What I'm doing.
- sure. but ... why?
- Why what?
- *(another round of mutual laughter)*
- okay, read my lips: why are you tracing her?
- I'm trying to draw her out of the walls.
- is it working?
- I think so. But it's hard.
- you want some help?
- No. I've got to do it by myself. Thanks, though.
- okay. anytime. hope you guys make it.

(24 minutes later)

- *Woo-hoo*! God ain't this music great? Put on the other side, Larry, quick! Hey, I'm having fun! I take it all back, you guys. This is fabbo! Hey! Let's smoke some more, huh?
- Aw, Moe —
- i've had it. that's it for me.
- What?
- Curly Joe's right. I'm gonna hit the pit, too. I'm wrecked.
- Aw ... What? You guys gonna flake out?
- Yup.
- Aw, god. You bums are no fun.
- Hey!
- what?
- The tape recorder!
- it's okay. it's still rolling.
- What? It's still going?
- sure it is. i've been checking it.
- I'll go turn it off.
- yeah ... hurry up. i wanna hit the sack.

- Hey, Larry? Uhm ... After ya turn it off, can we have just one more —

(Taping ends)

28. CURSES! FOILED AGAIN!

Even though this new "Friendship Circle" thing between Larry and Suzie Q and Curly Joe seems to be going smoothly, in reality they haven't teamed up as a trio since ... Well, since Curly Joe dropped his bombshell back in January. There's the ready-made excuses, of course. Essays to write, looming exams to study for, timetables that spurn all efforts to match up. But excuses is all they are. So what's really behind their avoidance? Simple: the three of them are super-jittery about how they'll react when they do meet.

When it's only the two of them, Larry and Curly Joe are doing just fine. Making music and smoking dope are all they require as enticements for a get-together. Every week for instance, they have their *Warthogs* jam. It doesn't seem to matter that the quality of the music that emerges shows no sign of improving; what's fundamental is that it reminds them of who they are and how much they mean to each other.

During those times, Larry talks freely about how his relationship with Suzie Q is progressing. He makes it sound like everything's snow white. Always. To which Curly Joe responds by congratulating him and feeling more and more laid back that he made the right call in letting go of Suzie Q. He definitely misses her company, though. They've bumped into each other a few times over at The Union and when they have, they've rabbited on as easy-flowing as ever. Maybe even more than when they were going steady. But these encounters have been infrequent and brief. Too infrequent. Too brief.

And ... Well ... Curly Joe regrets losing out on the sex. Especially as Suzie Q's looking so great these days. She can still turn him on just by standing there. Not that he can show it. And why would she want to know? She's bound to be looking the way she does because of what she and Larry are getting up to every chance that comes their way.

If Curly Joe only knew! Yes, sex is still something that both Larry and Suzie Q get into in a big way when it happens. But something's stopping it from happening as often as it used to. And ... *It* hasn't happened yet. Not since Larry's one and only failed endeavour. They don't even talk about *It*. *It* is for their someday future. Larry wishes things were different. To feel himself inside her — he's not talking just his tongue or fingers — has become a craving that nearly cancels out his enjoyment of all the other gratified desires Suzie Q's ministrations can call forth. Happily, the drawings are still coming along. Goddamn, though! He still loves her and wants everybody to know it. Suzie Q most of all. But, flaky as it sounds, Curly Joe knowing as well comes a close second.

With that last thought in mind, Larry comes up with a plan for a fun-filled Circle Reunion. *Yay! Let's sweep away the cobwebs of winter!* Why not all meet up on Moe's upcoming birthday? It's a date that providentially suits every Circle member's schedule. Suzie Q's up for it. So's Curly Joe. Moe and Emily? They're bound to be as well.

Wanna bet? Before Larry can get a word into Emily's ear, Moe gives it to him straight: Nothing doing. Plain and simple, he isn't up for it. And Emily won't be, either. Any other night, yeah, sure. But this particular birthday night is going to be a momentous, and ultra private, extravaganza. He and Emily are going to be alone in Moe's house while his parents conveniently disappear for a few hours. Moe doesn't have to spell it out but does anyhow: this is going to be a birthday that he and Emily are celebrating in their birthday suits. Got it?

Okay. Larry calls it quits; his suggested scenario can't compete with that. Well then, The Circle's Round-Up will have to go ahead with just the three of them. Maybe that's no bad thing, right? Yeah! Why not? So he and Curly Joe pool together a pile of cash they've saved for something special and agree to treat themselves and Suzie Q to a splash-out meal at an Old Montréal seafood restaurant. Then, after that, they can head back to one of their homes and finish off what's left of their dope stash. If Suzie Q will let them.

Maybe Suzie Q's feeling guilty about her continuing unwillingness to sort *It* out. Or, just as likely, she's now heard too many of her friends go on and on about how eye-openingly divine — but in a very sexy sort of way — the effects of smoking pot can be. All previous reservations set aside in favour of conformity and curiosity, she agrees not only to watch but also to join in. 'It's my debut as an outlaw,' Suzie Q titters. *And maybe,* she tells herself, *getting stoned will put an end to this ongoing guilt trip of mine.*

* * * * *

Over at the western end of Montréal, Moe's getting more and more psyched-up. He can't stop hovering between being thrilled and scared shitless. Right now, he's re-reading several key chapters in a sex-technique book that he borrowed from Curly Joe. Taking in the scope of what he's expected to achieve, he's going to make sure he's beat the meat at least twice before Emily arrives. Sensing that even this may not be enough to mellow himself down nice and dandy, he sneaks into his parents' bedroom and steals a couple of tabs of *Valium*. *Relaaaax*. After that, he tidies up his room so that everything's arranged just right.

Then he selects three appropriate records to make love to and sets them up on the turntable of his *RCA Victor* portable stereo. He'd put on more but the machine only takes three in one go. Hopefully, by the time the last one comes to an end, they'll have better things to do than worry about turning over a bunch of LPs. Thinking of LPs pushes Moe's addled mind to start humming a tune from this steel-string, redneck album that *The Byrds* released last year. *Sweetheart Of The Rodeo,* it's called. The song playing in his head is evidently something Dylan wrote and then forgot about. Already, Moe's playing with the lyrics to suit the occasion.

Ooh-wee, unzip my fly
Today's the day my gal's gonna cum and cum
Oh-ho, we're gonna fuck ourselves dry
Before we come up for air.

Well ... It's not one of his better efforts. But who's going to hear it, anyway? Back to business. What's left? Oh yes ... Sort out the right clothes to wear. Everything has to be immaculately clean. That way, when Emily rips them off him, she won't be put off by any unwanted odours. Which reminds him ... Body. Moe smells himself with clinical detachment. He's already showered in the morning, but best to do so again, nearer the time of her arrival. He'll soap and scrub every bit of himself. Especially ... The thought of Emily up close and getting a whiff of his prick and balls persuades Moe that jerking off a third time makes a lot of sense.

* * * * *

Back at her place, Emily is going through pretty well the same motions that Moe's acting out. As she soaks in the tub, she can't stop from asking if this first time is going to hurt. Shooing away such undesirable thoughts, she forces herself to adopt a more level-headed focus on the expected sequence of events. *Will Moe make sure to test those rubbers he bought in a public loo? No, wait! Perhaps he shouldn't test them. Oh, stop this silly worrying! They're totally safe. After all, that's what people here call them, isn't it?* Emily wishes she was on The Pill. Maybe soon, she won't need her parents' written permission before being allowed to start on it. *Bloody savage pig-ignorant country!*

* * * * *

Arrangement slightly altered because they can't be bothered to walk all the way to Old Montréal, The Circle seats themselves down at *Chez Pausé*. *Des Jardins* would have been the ideal option, but it's too expensive. Not that it matters much, any seafood is sure to induce gourmet delectation. They order an *aperitif*. Then snails as a starter, followed by lobster (cooked in three different ways for a multiple shared taste experience) and rice and vegetables to bulk things up. A bottle of

Beaujolais, naturally. And in complete agreement, for dessert they each have a rum baba, and *Cognac* to digest everything down. By this point, the thought of dope really turns them on.

They lurch their way back to Curly Joe's home bound together arm in arm. It's still early evening but the night's already come down. Street lights point the way for them ... Although they don't voice it, each individually questions why they'd ever worried about how they'd feel being together. This is *so* good! Friendship taken to perfection.

Later, huddled next to Larry while Curly Joe rolls up the second doob, Suzie Q finds herself laughing staccato-style for no reason at all. Not that she minds. She isn't sure if it's the liquor or the drugs affecting her like this. Or maybe the company. *Something* sure is, though.

* * * * *

Emily's due to arrive after 8.00pm. Moe's masturbated for a fourth time just to be absolutely on the safe side. Thoroughly washed and dressed just right, he's about to pop his *Valium*. A drop or two of *Johnny Walker* wouldn't hurt, either. Looking at his reflection in the bathroom mirror, Moe starts making faces and hissing until he stops to question what he's doing. *Probably just nervousness. Maybe another shot of that there JW will do the trick.*

* * * * *

'Hey!' Suzie Q's waking up from a trance wherein Larry had mysteriously altered into a ladybug crawling up her arm, '*Ou est Moe?*'

Disturbed from their own flights of fancy, Larry and Curly Joe snort in unison.

'Moe! Where is he? *Je veux Moe! Toute suite! Ici* and now!'

'moe? moe's at home with emily. you can fill in the blanks.' Curly Joe belly laughs to see Suzie Q's red-faced reaction.

Larry joins in. He's time-travelled back to the two-hour pep talk he'd had with Moe this morning. Then another thought breezes by, bringing on uncontrolled cackling.

'Qu'est ce qu'il-y-a, mon amour?'

'I was just daydreaming how hilarious it'd be to go say hello to them. Wish Moe a Happy Birthday.'

They all think Larry's idea is hysterically funny.

'oh boy,' guffaws Curly Joe, 'wouldn't moe love that?'

'Yuh, and Emily as well, ' Larry agrees.

'Alors! Allons-y!' Suzie Q says, cutting off the laughter.

'Now? ...We can't go ...'

'Pourquoi pas? We'll only be there to sing him "Happy Birthday" and then leave again. Wouldn't that be nice? I'm sure that Emily would —' *Would what? Clap her hands? Go ape shit? Insist on celebrating her joining the "I'm No Longer A Virgin Club?" with them all? Unlike ... Unlike ...* Suzie Q leaves the rest of her sentence dangling.

They agree to drag things out a little longer before making a move.

* * * * *

The music has stopped playing. All they can hear is Moe's mother's white canary, Perry Como, chirping away for all it's worth in his kitchen cage, as if he knows what's up. Not that he can though, can he?

Moe's miscalculated because they both still have their underwear on. Just. Everything looks set for the moment where Moe's at the point of removing Emily's and she gets to work on his. This is it ... The Moment's upon them. Time to get down to it. Moe kisses and licks her appendix scar because this has always turned her randy in the past. Randy. Another word he's picked up from her. Ready to go, his hands find their way to the rim of her knickers — *I'm becoming an Anglophile! Pip Pip, Matey! Cheerio!* — and begin to pull down as gently as possible. Emily wriggles and giggles when Moe's new, executive-style, moustache slides along her bare skin. She helps him by arching up her back. The material slithers over her thighs and down her legs. *Oh my God!* she thinks. *I'm entirely exposed in front of a man for the first time in my adult life! And I'm not ashamed!*

Not knowing why, Moe starts humming some tune he can't put lyrics to. *What the hell is it?* Something in his mind keeps hinting that it's this song by that English group. *Traffic.* Yeah, *Traffic.* Why's he thinking of ... Oh! Now he's got it! *Here We Go Round The Mulberry Bush!* But why — *Oh, wow! Of course! Emily's bush!* Not wasting any more time, Moe sweeps his left cheek back and forth along her mound. Emily clearly likes that. Then he takes the plunge and dampens it with his tongue.

Oh! So good! So nice! Yes! There! There! Emily flushes, inflamed as she's never felt before. One hand massages Moe's neck. The other reaches over and draws down his underwear until they don't get in the way. Now she's stroking his phallus. She likes that word, not so icky as the others. D.H. Lawrence comes to mind. Is Moe her Mellors? *Oh please, please let him be!* But wait ... Something doesn't seem to be quite right ... Emily turns, inadvertently pushing Moe away. She has to make sure.

'Moe! What's wrong?'

Moe's non-plussed. Nothing's wrong. What's she going on about?

'You're ... You're ... *soft!'*

Moe's confused. *Is she saying she wants me to go down harder on her?* Then he sees the light and looks between his legs. *Come out! Come out! Wherever you are!*

Emily is distraught. Surely, there must be something wrong with her. 'Don't I ... you know ... get you going?'

Where did that crazy idea come from? 'Of course ya do! You're a total turn-on!'

Consoled to hear him say it, Emily considers another possibility. 'Have you already ... Uhm ... You know ... Spilled your seed?'

Moe's got to laugh. 'Spilled my seed? Where'd ya get that —' Oh! *Now* he gets what she's driving at. Should he tell her about his "preliminary arrangements"?

Emily's not wasting any more time. She didn't think she'd be up for it, but now ... She pins Moe down so that he's flat on his back stretched across the bed. Then, before she can think through what she's about to do, she takes him inside her mouth. Moe can't believe that he's actually getting a blow-job. Talk about the best birthday present ever! Better still, Emily's impromptu initiative overrides the effects of the alcohol and *Valium* and everything else. Up and at 'em success!

Now what? Emily wavers. *Do I continue until he ... he ... comes? And if that happens will he be able to get hard again after that? Because he has to if they're going to — Wait! What if ...* As she's on top of him already, maybe she'll take charge and ease herself into him at her own pace. *Yes! Why not? Give it a whirl. If it bites, you bite back.*

'The rubbers!' Emily shouts.

'What?'

'The rubbers! Where are the rubbers? Put one on, quick!'

Moe has to wriggle around to get to the 3-Pack he's placed under one of the pillows. Doing so, his engorged penis hits up against Emily's mound, feels her pubic hair tickle. *So good! Maybe he'll just rest here for a sec'.*

'Hurry up, Moe! What's taking so long?'

Okay. Okay. Thankfully, he'd thought ahead so that the packet is already open and he can get his hands on one of the johnnies. *Kee-rist! How do you put these on? Should have practiced.*

Emily feels Moe fumbling around, getting more and more frustrated. So is she, but in a different way.

'Is it on? Have you got one on?'

'Nearly. Damn thing's really tight though, ya know? Maybe I should have bought Super Size.'

'Dream on, dear.'

'Ha-ha. Very funny. Okay. I'm covered up now. Ready for action.'

Moe's not sure if what's happening is normal for a "first time" scenario. It's as if they've skipped straight to "advanced class". Still, he's not going to argue. He's got Emily's beautifully bountiful breasts dangling provocatively above him. And those nipples! They're begging him to suck away at them. How's that *Steppenwolf* song go?

Let 'em hang low, baby.
Sucky. Sucky. Sucky.

As soon as they hear it, they both jump, uncoupling just as Emily's about to take the plunge. The front door is getting a heavy pounding. Even Perry Como's gone silent.

'What's happening? Moe!' Emily whispers, white-faced, near-hysterical.

'Somebody's at the door. Maybe I better go answer,' Moe whispers back trying his best not to jump out of his skin.

'No! Don't you dare!' hisses Emily.

'No? But —'

'Moe, I'm scared!'

'It's just someone at the door.' *Yeah, and they're using a battering ram to get our attention.*

'Moe! You have to do something!'

I was gonna! But ya stopped me! 'Let's wait it out for a sec'. They'll go away when they realize there's no one home.'

'But what if they come in?'

'How can —'

'What if they find us here! Like this!' Acutely aware of her nakedness and, therefore, unquestionably guilty in the eyes of her unknown intruder, Emily starts hopping around like a demon possessed, wildly searching for clothes to cover herself.

'Quiet! They'll hear you!' Moe yelps, he too now scrabbling for his own clothes.

Then, mercifully, the knocking and banging abruptly end.

'They're gone,' Moe says, able to breathe again.

'Who? Who was it?'

'We'll never know.'

They're on the brink of laughing now. Danger over, something might yet be salvaged. Moe can't take his eyes off her. 'Ya look — ' He's about to say 'gorgeous', but the scraping and clattering he hears coming from the back balcony puts the rest of his sentence on an extended lunch break. Somebody's definitely bursting to get into the house.

'*Kee-rist!*' Moe screams.

'Who is it, Moe? What's he doing?'

'This guy ain't gonna stop until he makes it inside.'

Emily's certain she knows who it is. 'My *father*!' she screeches. 'It's my father!'

What? Can't be! 'No way!' argues Moe, half-believing her.

'Who the bloody hell else then?'

'I dunno!'

They hear more scraping and rustling. Then ... laughter. And after that, a woman's voice that Moe recognises right away shouts, 'Moe! Moe, *mon cheri*!'

A moment later, The Circle erupt in a cacophony of whoops and hollers, that segue onto a Happy Birthday sing-along.

Moe recognises those voices as well. 'Those bums. It's those bums,' he whines, gritting his teeth.

'Who?'

'Those assholes I thought were my friends.'

'*What?* What are they — '

'Who cares,' Moe sighs, trying not to pay any attention to the shouts that continue to come from outside the house.

'*Moe! Let us in! Or we'll huff and we'll puff and we'll blow yuhr house down!*'

'Are you going to answer those oiks?'

'Nope.'

'Oh ... I want them to go away!'

'Yeah,' answers Moe. 'And not just for tonight, either.'

* * * * *

The Circle are on a bus to Curly Joe's house eating blackballs and jujube babies they've found in a Corner Shop straight out of their childhoods. They break up again and again at Curly Joe's description of Larry's determination to scale the balcony like some frustrated Romeo.

Back at home, they each savour one good puff from the dregs before getting rid of any evidence. Suzie Q's got to get back to her place so she can hit the books bright and early tomorrow. Taking that on board, Larry accepts Curly Joe's offer to stay overnight. All three together allow themselves a long goodbye huddle. None of them wants to let go.

If they both wanted me now, Suzie Q thinks, *I would give myself to them. Without a second thought. Maybe this is why I've been holding back —*

Curly Joe breaks the circle. Seconds later, Larry, too, shifts aside.

Good Night!

Sleep tight!

Oh, well ...

* * * * *

Moe takes Emily to a nearby café for a cup of tea. She's still shaken and highly strung. The liquid calms her enough that she starts complaining about how these bloody Canadians don't even know how to brew a proper cuppa. Still, there is no way on earth that she'll go back to his house after what she's just gone through.

Afterwards, Moe drives her home. At last, back in his room and piecing together what's been happening over the past few hours, Moe can't believe it: after all that, he's still a virgin. As if to put the boot in, Perry Como starts warbling away real loud. Which makes it so disheartening, Moe can't even be bothered to masturbate.

* * * * *

Next morning, Larry and Curly Joe phone Suzie Q to sound out how she's doing. She feels just great! Hasn't slept so well in years! And she's getting on just fine with her revisions. Just for the hell of it, they go catch this new flick, *The Prime of Miss*

Jean Brodie. In honour of Emily.

Emily? She's laying low in her room for the duration. She's bloody furious with them. And, when it comes to it, with Moe, too. For having such pillocks as friends.

Moe's stuck at home as well. He's waiting for the telephone apologies that never come. Box turned on, he's casually tuning into this cartoon, *The Adventures of Rocky & Bullwinkle.* There's *Dudley Do-Right of the Mounties* putting the kibosh on *Snidely Whiplash's* latest evil genius plot.

And what's that Ol' Snidely always says? Oh yeah: 'Curses! Foiled Again!'

You and me both, pal.

29. TURN! TURN! TURN!

How is this possible? Exams around the corner. Their futures one big question mark. Another McGill year just about gone by. It's all a bit too much like pepper dope: the buzz it offers lasts only a couple of minutes and then you're right back where you started.

Moe's first up to confront the awful reality. Too bad; he'd started off so well, too. What happened? It's a little too convenient to blame matters on his new-found fondness for drugs. Even if they *have* played a role for sure. But, let's not jump into easy-reach conclusions; nobody can really say how big a role that's been. The bottom line is that Moe's come round to accepting that his academic road's irreversible. Even psychology, which he'd pinned all his hopes on, has fizzled to less than zero. His meet-ups with some of the aspiring revolutionaries have been such a let down. All they kept going on about was how inspired they were over something called "encounter groups" and how they're going to change society from the inside out. Okay. He was willing to give one a try. Half a dozen sessions completed and what it feels like to Moe is kids with popguns facing up to a howitzer. They're singing along to *Street Fighting Man* but all they're really doing is *Dancing in the Street.* Or how about if Moe just reads out some of the song titles off his favourite *Paul Butterfield Blues Band* album? *Pity the Fool. One More Heartache. Droppin' Out.*

Come the end of March, the most intelligent course of action Moe can think of is to quit university. Maybe not forever, but a year for sure, maybe more. Find some job that'll stuff cash into his pockets every month. Put some proper focus into mastering the secrets of blowing the blues out of his harp. Get in The Flacon and take himself and Emily places. Moe's idea isn't entirely crazy. The absurd logic of The Academe argues that it's wiser to re-accept a student who's feigned illness and dropped out before any end of semester exams get written than to allow some sucker who took the exams and failed them to give it another try. The principle seems to be that it's better to be a quitter than a loser. Go figure.

Naturally, Emily's not taking this lying down. Not that she's taking much of anything lying down since *birthday night.* She makes it clear that she wants to be going out with a *student,* not some company wage slave. She wants lunch times at the Union spent chatting with her boyfriend and getting his undivided attention and then bus rides home with him at any old time of day they feel like because they're both free from a fixed clock-in/clock-out attendance system to be able do such things. Added to which, she's rattled by the all-too-likely parental reaction. She's getting more than enough stick as it is having Moe as a steady.

'Play the field,' her mother tells her.

'It leads to trouble. I know what young men are like,' her father reminisces.

They'd both be screaming the effing roof down if they suspected that their precious only daughter is regularly engaged in reciprocal *gamahuching* with a soon-to-be drop-out.

Driven to prevent Moe from taking this drastic step, she's threatened, taunted, pushed, ridiculed and nearly broken Moe's heart so many times that, in the end, Larry and Curly Joe have had to butt in and tell her to lay off a bit and leave him be. Feeling unheard and betrayed, she'll never put her trust in them as brothers again. Still, all her efforts having failed, she's had to give in. But only under one condition: her parents are not to know anything. As far as they'll be aware, Moe is taking a year's break to get some real-world work experience before completing his degree. They will, she's certain, settle for that. Possibly even approve of it as a sensible manoeuvre taken by a disciplined young man.

Agreement made and treaty signed, on Monday March 24th, 1969 Moe makes his way to the Registrar's Office and hands in his Student ID as well as a medical doctor's report that this particular undergrad is incapable of experiencing any more academic pressures for the time being. He is told to get well soon and come back fighting next year. As a way of marking the event, taking a goodbye tour of the university — with periodic side trips to nearby washrooms — makes a goofy sort of logic. Larry and Curly Joe lead him to the *Redpath Museum* so that Moe can admire the stuffed animals before they lose all of their stuffing. After that, they sneak him into the fabled *Iron Ring Room* to show him what Engineering's all about. As Moe stomps out of the Union's glass doors, they break out into their gender-altered version of *She's Leaving Home* in their very best McCartney melancholia.

In less than a week, Moe lands a job as a sub-accountant in one of Montréal's larger insurance companies.His studies in psychology have, for once, turned out to be of some use. Moe's gotten sensational scores on the company's personality and motivation tests by guessing the responses its analysts are sure to rate most favourably.

In fact, Moe's done so well on this task that he's got everyone believing they have a Boy Wonder on their hands. He's bound to work his way up in no time. Vice-Presidency by forty-five. Moe's happy to let them think what they want. What matters most to him is that the work's a dawdle, he gets free parking and the money's good.

Better still, having given in, Emily now makes sure she comes to meet him after work every day. As an added bonus, she doesn't hesitate to cling to him with all the passion of a girlfriend who's been separated from her partner for weeks. Once inside The Flacon, she's even developed the habit of unbuttoning the lower part of his shirt and curling her fingers around his belly hairs. Her efforts always succeed in both flustering and turning Moe on at the same time. She loves the effect so much, she's become an expert in the art of button-popping.

All in all, hanging in there with his plan to quit McGill just goes to show that the oft-repeated link between Darkest Hour and Dawn continues to hold true.

* * * * *

As to Curly Joe, he's got himself fired up enough to want to make it through his academic year one way or another. And with reasonable grades, thank you very much. But then, he has to if he wants to remain a student. His one cause of concern continues to be Economics, though even it, regardless of its absurdity, isn't going to be that difficult to pass. Galvanised by the conviction that his mission in life is to be an Evangelist of Love, he's gone so far as to write up all of his end-of-term essays so that each deals with the topic of martyrdom in some form or other. And, because his efforts are different enough from all the others that his bored lecturers have to plow through, he finds himself being awarded B+ grades — even the exceptional A — for his efforts. One of his readers was impressed enough to add a handwritten message in the margins: *Hang in there! You've got something to say that needs saying! Power to the People!* Well ... it *is* 1969 after all.

And then, of course, there's all that yoga mystique he's still into. Mainly, it's the candle meditation that's he's immersed in. Curly Joe's so busy staring into the abyss, he doesn't notice how the abyss is readying itself to stare back. When it happens, he's all on his own at home sitting cross-legged on his "meditation mat" up in the third floor room he uses as study. Like every other night, he's concentrating on connecting with the aura of a solitary candle whose light is blazing away a million colours per second. Detached from any bodily sensations, all that exists in this moment is that light and the hum Curly Joe can hear emerging from its core. And then ...

Unexpectedly sucked into that light, floating freely, Curly Joe is bombarded by a series of tableaus that the candle's aura is goal-kicking straight into his mind. Some of these are highly surreal and preposterous. Most, however, have an everyday, mundane reality feel to them. In some cases, the scenes involve his friends and people that he knows; typically, however, they focus on complete strangers. Whichever, they are all saying and doing the most ordinary things. When the visionary spectacle ends in the early hours of the following morning, Curly Joe's left with a jumble of question marks about what he's been experiencing. Still and all, he hurriedly writes down as much as he can recall.

A couple of days later, still thoroughly puzzled by it all, Curly Joe waits until the end of yoga class to catch WR's attention. He's hoping that she can throw some non-candle light on what happened. When he shows her the hurried notes he'd scribbled down, she humours him and begins to read. Moments later, WR blanches and has to sit herself down. Several of the descriptions of people and events that Curly Joe had witnessed are strikingly similar to those from her own life. There's even one of WR's husband singing their private language "I'm feeling sexy" song, *Ain't Misbehavin'*.

Satisfyingly, after a week's worth of resolute investigation, she unearths enough information to verify that a hell of a lot of Curly Joe's visions are highly accurate reflections of events that have really happened.

Next meeting, much to WR's stupefaction, Curly Joe's reaction to her near-breathless revelation is to panic. He doesn't want to know these things, he bawls. It's too spooky. Too much like he's been thrown into some *Twilight Zone* episode. Being an Evangelist is supposed to make you feel like you're special, not like you're some space oddity. If this is where meditation is leading him, he wants nothing more to do with it.

Watching him exit her class for the last time, knowing she can do nothing to argue him out of his insistence, WR shakes her head. Why are such remarkable abilities wasted on the young? 'Innocents are the world's greatest egotists,' she concludes. Then, considering what uses such powers might be put to by more advanced beings like herself, WR turns back to her remaining students. Maybe, from now on, she should concentrate more on the physical benefits of yoga.

As if all that isn't enough to shake-up Curly Joe's view of candle meditation, something weirder still is waiting to happen. Another week later, he bumps into Suzie Q near the University Library concourse and they agree to take time out for a catch-up chat. At some point, she casually asks him how his yoga stuff is going.

'it's not. i quit.'

'What? Why?'

In reply, Curly Joe launches into this scary tale about the near-supernatural occurrence. Which immediately fascinates Suzie Q all the more. As he's got his trusty Thought Book on hand, Curly Joe shows her what he'd written down that had freaked him out so much.

Part way through reading them, Suzie Q comes to an immediate stop. 'Hey! I'm pretty sure that this is Edna you've been writing about. Here, I'll copy what you wrote and send it to her. See how she reacts.'

'edna? who's edna?'

Oh! Right! Curly Joe was away when Edna came to Montréal and everything started up with Larry. So Suzie Q gives Curly Joe an edited version of who her friend is and what they all got up to during her visit.

But what's really, really strange, when Suzie Q comes tothink about it, is how her talking about Edna right now is a majorly odd coincidence. It turns out that just yesterday she'd received a letter from Edna informing her that a summer job teaching water-skiing on Lake Huron had come up and wouldn't it be great if Suzie Q applied for it because she'd be sure to get it and then they could spend the next few months together again. Spooky!

And spookier still ... Four days later, Curly Joe receives a postcard whose message reads: *Stop peeking into my life! I don't know how you did it, but your "vision" of what I was doing was 100% accurate. Still, I don't like being spied on. So stop it right now! Peace, Edna.*

Irritated as he is by the tone of the communication, Curly Joe is more than happy to comply.

* * * * *

Suzie Q's jubilant announcement that she's got the job and is heading off to London, Ontario almost right away after exams for training purposes is yet another stab to Larry's heart. The worst one yet, to be sure.

More immediately though, Larry's got his academic woes to keep him company. He damns himself for his stupidity in staying on in Engineering and not having walked out of it last year along with Curly Joe. Just setting foot into the McConnell Building makes his stomach wobble. He's become a joke there; everyone knows he's flunking out. All that needs to be clarified is by how much. So when it reaches crunch time, Larry turns himself into a *kamikaze* pilot aiming his plane for the big, up-in-flames final flight. There he is, sitting in on his Physics exam. The question he's reading strikes him as having been written in Urdu-Hindi. *Compared to the next two exams I've got to get through,* Larry thinks, *this one's a cinch.* So far, his answer booklet is a total blank. Twenty minutes later, it's still the same. Like his mind. Which, when he links the two together, is truly hilarious. It's so amusing in fact, he has this brilliant idea: he's going to write his professor a poem.

> *'My dear Professor Gormley:*
> *It's bad enough when you force me to sit*
> *in Physics Lecture Theatre A*
> *each Monday, Wednesday, and Friday*
> *at 3.00 o'clock in the afternoon*
> *just to watch you spurt out your physical excretions.*
> *And, it is a sad state of affairs When I*
> *— and several hundred others —*
> *must each bow down to you*
> *and beg to wipe your ass with our note paper.*
> *But, Professor Gormley, why do you act so shocked*
> *when I begin to retch and vomit*
> *Just after having been told that*
> *I must now eat up and digest your turd?'*
> *ps. Thanks for a great class!*

Proud as he is of his effort, Larry also knows that he won't be so inspired again. So why bother showing up for all his other exams?

* * * * *

Talking of anal excretions ...

Curly Joe's writing an exam as well. His favourite subject: Economics.

His certainty that, at worst, he'll manage a bare Pass has been challenged by an overactive bout of diarrhoea that came on last night. So here he is in a packed room trying to concentrate on the questions while the only thing that's on his mind is whether his bowels will hold out long enough for him to finish before he shits in his pants. It doesn't help matters that every question he reads sets him to thinking thoughts that release memories of his condition.

The one silver lining to this state of affairs, however, is that his incontinent fears have awakened a full-flush creative inventiveness regarding economics the like of which he's never experienced before. Dazzling himself, he rushes through his paper producing three booklets worth of economic theory that will bowl over his examiners for its lucidity and speculative power. Not far down the line, several articles will be published in Learned Journals, their primary arguments having been illicitly "borrowed" from Curly Joe's unadulterated *taurus caca*. All Power to the Anus!

At last, alone in a toilet stall, flatulently discharging his not-quite-solid gift to the world, Curly Joe calls to mind one last fact obtained from dubious sources: no less a personage than Martin Luther had conceived his entire religious philosophy while perching on his privvie. In his case, however, Curly Joe recalls, the complaint had been constipation. *uhm* ... he ponders. *who knows what theses would have been nailed to that Wittenberg church door if he'd been suffering from the opposite affliction?*

* * * * *

Moe's sitting at his office desk sharpening pencils. He tries to make their points as super-fine as possible so that he can note down the digits in his numbers column just right. So what if he can only write one digit at a time before the lead point cracks and turns unacceptably dull? He's gone through a dozen pencils in four days and has only got as far as filling out two and a half pages worth of total sums. At this rate, he'll bankrupt the company if he doesn't watch out.

The thought of that makes him smile and grab hold of his pencil-sharpener for another twist of the blade.

* * * * *

Exams over and done with, they've got some heavy duty catching up to do.

'Curly Joe and me got jobs for the summer,' Larry says.

'Oh yeah? You guys gonna wash dishes again?'

'Naw. We're working for FUCK.'

Time out for some free and easy guffawing all round.

'What?'

'yeah, man. we're *the men from fuck.*'

'What the fuck are ya talking about, for Crissakes?'

Okay. Enough. Time for an explanation. 'FUCK. F.C.C. *Foundation of Catholic Charities,*' Larry spells out.

Now Moe's definitely impressed. Maybe even a little bit envious. 'Ya got a job with the *Foundation of Catholic Charities*? How'd you guys pull off that trick?' *Yeah. And why didn't I think of applying there?*

'we just called them up and asked. they want to give us money to figure out how many parishioners pay their dues and in what church.'

'Fuck!'

'Exactly. That's what we said. And, oddly enough, the initials fit.

'That must be one of the most phenomenally toe-fat jobs I've heard of.' *And it should have been mine!*

'Yuh, but we don't waste much time on doing it, either. Mainly, we go there to write songs and they throw cash at us for it.'

'Yeah, pull the other one.'

'no, really! see,' says Curly Joe, 'they let us keep to our own hours. so they leave us to ourselves. which means that while we're pretending to slave away working out the grand total of parishioners over at saint rita's, we're actually scratching our heads trying to come up with the world's greatest lyrics.'

'Either that, or reading *Mad Magazine*,' Larry adds just to throw in a smattering of truth.

'But ain't they catching on?'

'Nope. See, they've given us this calculator that broke down and nobody's bothered to repair it so far. So we're hypothetically doing everything by hand. But —'

This is so good that nothing's going to stop Curly Joe from butting in. 'what happens is, every once in a while we just take some data to McGill and get one of these computer whizz-kids to do pretty well all the calcs for us and then we copy everything down on paper and hand it in a bit at a time.'

'Yuh!' Larry finishes. 'And we keep complaining that we're disappointed we're doing it so slow because of not having a calculator. They love us for being so dedicated!'

'But ... Wait a minute! If you guys can come up with a way like that, why can't they just do all this computer stuff by themselves?'

Larry and Curly Joe shake their heads in unison.

'Oh no! Yuh see, they've got to have all their sums done by a certain date.'

'So?'

'So ... There's all sorts of people like us who've got jobs until that date. But if they were to computerize it all, it'd get done too quickly and then all of us would be out on the street. Including the guy in charge of the project. Get it? It's all "Michael Row The Boat Ashore, But Don't Yuh Dare Rock It".

'hey! that's pretty good. i'm gonna write that one down.'

'Let me get this straight: you guys are getting paid for doing something that ya don't do but rather get done by some computer guy who does it in a quarter of the time that you're not doing it in except nobody's gonna let on that he's doing it because then a lot of people are gonna be out of their jobs?'

'Yup. Yuh got it. See, nobody gives a shit about who does what where. That's just an excuse for everybody to go on not working and get paid for it.'

'pretty mind-blowing, right?'

'Wow. That takes the Father Flotsky Prize for sure.'

'Well, me and Curly Joe reckon that Catholicism has fucked us pretty bad in the past, so we're fucking it right back.'

'Yeah, well ... Give 'em one for the Ol' Gipper as well.'

'yeah, we will. the only boring bit is when we gotta share the office with this woman who's been working for fuck for years and years. so we're not sure if we can trust her. good news is that when she's there, all she seems to wanna do is plaster ten pounds of make-up on her face. that's so she can give larry here the eye. he's on easy street.'

Larry grimaces. 'Ever since she found out I'm *Quebecois*, she keeps handing me boxfuls of pencils and pens to take home. She just says *'C'est un Anglais'*, referring to the main boss.'

'*Jee-zus*. A regular smoked meat on rye.'

'yeah. sometimes she types. that's when we have to do some analyses because it's impossible to think.'

'Listen, ya don't have to tell me, Jim. I'm a working man too now, remember? Offices are such dumps. Chairs, desks, coffee table, telephone, bulletin board. Every one no different from any other. They give me the creeps.'

'how you getting on with everything work wise?'

'Me? Oh, I got a really top-priority job. *Kee-rist*, I hesitate to think what'd happen to this country if I didn't show up one morning to add up my set of numbers. You guys have no idea what it's like having all that responsibility. I mean, I get a hard-on thinking how me and the other nineteen dullards I work with hold Canada's economic balance in our hands.'

'yeah, you're pretty vital.'

'You bet, Jim. Why, lunch hours are such a drag. People gotta chuck me outta my desk so's I can get some grub into me.' Now Moe's on a riff. 'Listen,' he says, 'Ya know how at Elementary School there used to be this invisible line in the playground and how all the boys stayed on one side and all the girls on the other? Well, it's like we're all back in Elementary School at my office. All the secretaries cluster around one end of the employee's caf' and all the junior accountants and exec's stay on the other. Typical mind exercises. All the males talk about is sports, booze and joy-juice. Mainly sports. They're still partying over the *Canadiens* fighting it out with the *St Louis Blues* for the *Stanley Cup* second time in a row.'

'Good Ol' *Habs.* '

'Yeah, well ... And if it ain't that, it's how the *Montréal Expos* are showing the Yanks how to play baseball.'

'exciting or what? too bad the *alouettes* ain't got nothing to brag about.'

'What stimulating company, though. So much to discuss! I bet they're gasping to engage in the impact on our lives brought about by the recent successful implant of an artificial heart.'

'yup. for sure. they're all singing along to "you gotta have heart."'

'They sound like delightful folks, Moe. I bet all yuh want to do is spend every second of yuhr time in their company.'

'There's no avoiding 'em, Jim. Part of my salary's deducted for lunches whether I eat 'em or not.'

'you kidding or what?'

'Wish I was. The claim is that these caf' lunches are being whipped up by an expert dietician who knows what food's best to get the most out of us. And before ya ask: the meals are really buff! The food looks and tastes like any other cafeteria slop except there's less of it.'

'What about the secretaries? What are they like?'

'Aw, God! They're just the same as the male inmates. I played dumb once and went to sit with them for lunch. They talked about make-up, office-movie-TV gossip and oblique joy-juice. On top of that, they treated me like a superior even though I'm earning no more or even less than a lot of them there. I could have said anything and they'd still have answered something like: "Gee, that's interesting."'

'Hey, look, my weenie's just sprouted wings!'

'gee, that's interesting.'

'I can't even get any private time to myself! I bring in a book, ok? So some putz sees me reading it and right away it's snap synopsis time, gang. Which is then followed by: "Why have you got your head into this crap when, instead, you could be doing some one-handed reading of the latest Harold Robbins?" The only thing that works a bit is my listening to them and then making some kinda cryptic comment that's really confusing and gets 'em backing away. Like, the other day, I picked a real winner. I said: *Who looks outside, dreams. Who looks inside, awakes.* That one kept them outta my hair for hours and hours.'

* * * * *

Without any warning, the bar they've been sitting in for a couple of hours starts reeling out of control.

They've never been in it before, but, out of some sick sense of gratitude to the *Foundation of Catholic Charities*, Larry and Curly Joe insisted that they pass by Heebie Jeebie High and pay it proper homage. Once there, they found a secluded corner so that they could piss on its lawn as a warning to leave them be once and for all. Then they'd skipped their merry way over to the nearest bar — the very same one that's now reeling out of control.

A few faces seem familiar. Variant age versions of the traditional Heebie Jeebie look. But who cares? They're only here to drink and get drunk. Larry and Moe are guzzling beers. Curly Joe's into rum and Coke.

'Here's to the year,' mumbles Moe.

'Some year,' answers Larry.

'correct yet again,' retorts Curly Joe, who's heard this same exchange since the early afternoon and is getting pretty sick of it. 'another year gone. so long, mcgill. see you in september,' he adds, hoping he can bring their refrain to an end.

'*Yuh* will. But I might not,' whimpers Larry.

'Come off it, Larry. They'll let ya back in if ya switch courses. Now me, I'm just the reverse ...'

Aside from the jobs they've found, what back-and-forth there's been all day has focused on the twin topics of Larry's failure and Moe's lack of courage by running away when he should have stayed and fought the good fight. The two of them keep arguing about who's in the worst position. Curly Joe acts as referee. His willingness to commiserate is declining steadily. Even though he knows how they feel because he's been through something like it himself, he's reaching his saturation point. Pretty soon, he assures himself, he's going to waste the both of them.

Across their table, two German construction workers who, for some vague reason, have gotten it into their heads that Larry and Curly Joe have just passed their Medical exams, are singing Bavarian drinking songs to them. They can't take on board who Moe is or where he fits into the celebrations but since he's the one who sings *In Munchen ist ein Haufbrau House* along with them the loudest, they like him anyway.

Larry's smoking a cigarette that he bummed off one of them. This is a danger signal. Whenever Larry starts to smoke cigarettes it means he's too far gone and is about ready to start barfing all over the place. One beer later, he is. He doesn't quite make it to the nearest open toilet seat in the men's can. There he is spewing out putrid yellow goo all over his cubicle's floor so that it seems to Curly Joe, who's rushed in behind him, as if raw egg-yolk's flying out of Larry's mouth. Fighting back the tightening up of his own stomach, he tries to get Larry to bend over the bowl. They both slip and end up ass-wiping the vomit. Then Larry starts to up-chuck again.

Elsewhere in the main lounge, Moe has started cursing his life detail by detail. Oh well, if nothing else it succeeds in getting the Germans to shut up.

Twenty minutes later, they all think it'd be nice to go bowling.

This, too, is part of their shared Heebie Jeebie past. Every Annual Heebie Jeebie High School Party, the classes would be treated to an afternoon of bowling. Year after year in the same place just to play out three free games each. An all-male high school turn-on.

So here they are at *NDG Lanes*. It's large and plastic and almost right next door to the bar. Larry's in the can heaving up a little more just to make sure there's nothing left inside him. 'Some year,' he huffs, as he flushes the toilet. It's past 11.00pm, which means that the only people in the place are bowling fanatics who, as a rule, are fat, crew-cutted men gung ho on shouting 'Yahoo', or 'That's the one, baby!' every time the ball does something right. And when it doesn't, they gripe 'Ya scumbag!' or meekly hack out a 'Jeez ...' Some even wear T-shirts with team names on them; all of them chew gum and rub their towels over their foreheads, looking very, very committed to making this their mission in life.

The Stooges opt to play ten-pin because the targets are easier to see. So are the balls. They haven't rented special bowling shoes. They're supposed to, but cash is running low. The shoe counter guy gives them the okay; they can get away with just wearing socks.

Larry hits two gutter balls, grins, and throws up all over his lane. Then he goes berserk. Why him? Why now? Hasn't he gone through enough already? He hears the Lanes Assistant screaming, and starts to feel ill again.

Moe and Curly Joe are laughing, but they grab up their and Larry's shoes and hurry him out of the place.

'you can sleep on my floor tonight, larry,' Curly Joe suggests.
'Thanks.'

'that's ok. we can all go back and blow some smoke.'

'Hey, good thinking, Jim. Let's do just that,' smiles Moe, perking up.

'Why not?'

'yeah. it'll be a gas.'

'I can't believe it's over,' whines Moe. 'Here's to the year!'

'Some year,' bleats Larry.

Curly Joe stays silent and walks between his friends, hands on both their shoulders, as they go through their ritual. Still silent, he makes a wish that they won't repeat this dialogue again.

Not that they know it yet, but this April meet-up will be the last time the three of them are going to be together for several months.

The Full Moon shines, and there's one final exchange:

'I've wasted a whole fucking year,' croaks Larry.

'Kee-rist, Larry, I've wasted a whole fucking life,' answers Moe, thinking of dope.

PART FOUR: FREEDOM

MAY, 1969 — AUGUST, 1969

**It was like a flying saucer landed. That's what The Sixties were like.
Everybody heard about it, but only a few really saw it.**

— Bob Dylan —

30. LARRY

Over to his right, Larry pinpoints two Asian-looking guys sitting in a red light stalled bus, clutching cameras, peering back at him. He scrunches up his face and does a circle hop for them. Exposed, they grin, secure a quick snapshot each and then stick out their tongues. The light turns green and their bus moves on. A brief encounter that captures Larry's mood. Everything is transitory. And unpredictable.

People heading in his direction deem it wise to steer clear. His growing hair now reaches beyond his shoulders and is being blown everywhere by the wind. He's wearing a grimy T-shirt and jeans. He hasn't shaved for three days.

He passes by a popular Italian restaurant and stops in front of its window to mug at the people inside. When the party of six notices him, they all go nervous, their forks missing the food they were meant to spear or losing direction so that they go wide of their intended target and, as a consequence, mouths chomp at the empty air. The effect he seems to be having on people amuses Larry. Then he reminds himself he's only eaten an apple all day and trudges on.

The driver who'd picked up a hitch-hiking Larry earlier that evening was a South Shore Straight ready for some horizontal action, all dressed up and ready to swing. They'd made an odd couple. Still, the guy had been decent enough to stop and ask Larry where he was heading. As it turned out, they were both going downtown. Joe Not-So-Cool was on route to a party he'd been invited to. Larry was welcome to come along if he wanted. That sounded too much like a replay of Kitimat, so he begged off. Larry got out of the car at Peel and de Maisonneuve. His chauffeur wished him happy hunting. Then, as an added extra, showing off his credentials, the would-be man-of-the-world volunteered the name of a tonic to use in case Larry ever got the clap. Something to keep in mind.

Now, a couple of hours later, Larry's back on Peel. He's just finished watching a movie, *The Illustrated Man.* Its message, as far as Larry can puzzle it out, is that people shouldn't want to know about the future ahead of time because they will, as a matter of course, live to regret it. Could be right. Who can say? What Larry *can* say is that it was painful sitting by himself inside a Saturday night theatre full of couples who'd held hands and waited anxiously for the lights to go down. What he can also say is that it was a boring movie; no idea why he ever chose to go see it by himself rather than pass the time away with his friends. No, make that friend. Singular. Curly Joe's done a disappearing act. Another mystery to deal with.

Suzie Q left Montréal two weeks ago, the day after Larry's birthday. She's a permanent guest at her friend Edna's family home in London, Ontario and will be there for the whole of the summer making good money teaching people how to water ski. They've played around with the possibility of Larry coming over to visit, but, in the end, both saw that it would be too complicated and frustrating. Edna's home doesn't have additional rooms to put him up as well and it's not worth fantasising that her parents would give the go-ahead for Larry and Suzie Q to share the same bedroom. Larry could shack up in some nearby motel of course, but that would be so sordid and Edna's family would see through what they were up to in no time. Better that they wait things out until Suzie Q gets some days off so she can make the trip to Montréal and stay over for as long as possible. It's a sensible arrangement but that doesn't stop Larry from feeling rejected and just plain miserable. The situation resonates way too closely with what he went through with Angel, a lifetime ago. Even reminding himself of Suzie Q's written reassurances doesn't help to kick that connection out of bounds.

Would you believe me if I told you that I'm only going because I have to? Will you ever forgive me? I couldn't earn anywhere near as much as I'm being paid doing some more ordinary summer job. Laurent, Laurent, qu'est-ce-que je peux te dire? You've won me, Laurent. Mon amour, mon Quebecois, si gallant, si serieux, si ... Je t'adore. But I must leave you, my

sweet darling. I, too, have "promises to keep". Do you understand? Will you? Here is a very big and naughty secret I will share with you and only you: every night, when I go to bed, I wear the shirt I stole from you back in Vancouver. And sometimes, sometimes Laurent, I remove it, lie nude with it on top of me. And I pretend. I make believe the shirt is you and allow it to travel over my body. Everywhere. Caressing my chatte. I go wild. I whisper your name ... And later, I feel like a fool. Like a hopelessly love-sick little teenage virgin. Et je suis ça. Oui. Tu le sais. Please, forgive me. Please, tell me you see the sense in my going. Will you allow me to visit you as soon as that becomes possible? Will you? S'il vous plaît, laisse-moi. Une autre fois: je t'aime, Laurent. I love you. You must believe it. Tu dois! Once more, forgive me, s'il vous plaît.
The flower-child you plucked,
Suzie Q

Larry has memorised that letter. It's already filled him several times (as it does now, reading it again) with a joy so absolute, that tears overtake him. But, too bad, it's still not enough to assuage his hurt pride. To make matters worse, although Suzie Q swore to write to him every single day, it's been two days now that no mail has arrived. All of which sets that "too much like Angel" alarm bell ringing non-stop.

Stupidly, he didn't remind Suzie Q to let him have Edna's home phone number. To get it now, he'd have to contact Suzie Q's parents and ask them for it. Which he's uneasy about doing. Larry's pretty sure that Suzie Q's parents aren't all that pleased she's going steady with him and they'd probably start asking all sorts of awkward questions. Or worse, simply refuse to give him the number. He'll have to make sure to ask her for it next time he writes.

So here it is, Saturday the 24th of May, 1969, nearly 10.00pm, and Larry's walking all by himself down St. Catherine Street. The window display at *Classics Bookstore* is showing off its latest literary gems. Among them is a book entitled *The Teachings of Don Juan: A Yaqui Way of Knowledge*. Since it is in hardback, very few of the people who, in the fullness of time, will turn its author, Carlos Castaneda, into a worldwide mystery shaman are as yet aware of its availability. Tellingly, if the dates of subsequent events in Castaneda's life (as recounted in his later books) are accurate, it's doubtful that Castaneda himself is, at this current moment in time, the least bit concerned about how the sales of his first book are doing and who its readers might be. He's too busy discovering that the separate reality Don Juan is patiently leading him toward goes way beyond anything that *mescalito* has on offer.

Not that Larry's giving the book much notice right now. Probably because he's too busy taking it in that, as with his experience in the movie theatre, Montréal seems to be full of couples promenading arm in arm. Larry puts his hands into his pockets and continues walking. On the corner of University, a little ways into the approach to a darkened passageway, he takes in a plastic hippie girl adjusting her beaded headband. Flustered by his accidental presence, she eyes him up suspiciously. Larry picks up on her unease and flashes her the Peace Sign. Smiling now, she answers it back, and then moves away into the shadows. Another passing moment.

A few yards further on, three student types are leaning on a *Mustang*. Then a fourth comes over.

'Did'ja get the stuff?' the first three ask.

The fourth one nods, then points to the side street Larry's just been gawking into, and pulls out an aluminium foiled dime of hash. They all pile into the car and make off into the night.

Oh ... So that girl's a dealer and ... Never mind.

Less than a block later, Larry comes upon a line-up of people waiting to be ushered into a fancy-looking discotheque. He's never been inside this particular one and, seeing the ties and jackets and smelling the money, he knows why.

More couples pass by. A car with New Hampshire licence plates pulls up beside a Montréal cop.

'Hey, man, where's *The Lido* at?' one of the car's passengers shouts.

The cop doesn't understand.

'Don't jive us, man,' the driver yells, leaning out of his window and displaying a bald head that's as round as a cue-ball.

At that, the cop, still not catching on, gauges that he's irritated enough to start asking for licences.

'You'se a mean motherfuckah!' shouts another of the passengers. Then he jumps out of the car, looking ready to kill. The woman who's been sitting next to him tells him to hush and get right back inside quick, before some honky pig ruins their vacation.

Leaving them all behind to continue glowering at each other, Larry shrugs and tells himself that what's just gone down is a textbook example of the race problem that everyone's so busy decrying or denying. Just as easily, it could be the French/English Language problem Canada's needing to deal with. Lesson over, Larry putters on.

Three drunks from The Main greet him, adamant that he's someone named Trixie. Larry tells them that Trixie's in a near-by tavern. They thank him and skulk their way inside a nearby Hot Dog House.

A few minutes later, another drunk, peg-legged and holding on tight to the waist of a streetwalker he's picked up, nearly bumps into Larry.

'Love, man,' Larry says.

'Yeah! Sure will,' the drunk answers while his partner laughs, making all too visible the terrible condition her teeth are in.

On Park, Larry turns off St. Catherine Street, heading for darker places. A man with a very Yiddish accent walks by with his wife in tow gabbing about how the best business to have in Montréal is a shoe store since Montréalers are, according to him, shoe crazy. 'In Toronto, it's real estate. In Miami, it's dentists. Here, it's shoes. What can I tell ya?' he expounds, sighing the sigh of a man who's come upon such vital information too late in his life.

Ten minutes later, Larry picks out a young greaser and his girlfriend deep into a heavy necking session. He feels a pang then, and in that moment, vows to write Suzie Q the angriest, most hurtful letter he can think to send her just to let her know the full extent of his sacred pain.

He passes away the entire *Metro* ride back to his home composing it.

Hello Suzie Q,

00.00am ... Hell, what time is that?

Hey! I'd tell you the tale of the Gypsy mandolin player and the French horn but it speaks too much of reality and I'm sick of telling it.

What have I been doing today? Let's see ... Oh yeah! I shot up some smack, sniffed a salt shaker full of coke, ate two pounds of hash, smoked 51 joints, chewed and gobbled 347 assorted pills and died so totally I was reborn again in seconds. Does that grab your attention? It's all a lie, of course, but then, as Johnny Cash keeps asking: what is the truth?

The next thing that Dylan's going to put out, so Curly Joe tells me, is a six album collection of grunts that he's been performing since 1961. Leonard Cohen will back him up here and there with a selection of good old Montréaler farts. It'll be called either "Rhymes for the Times" or "Cleopatra Spreadeagled". Other than that, there's nothing earth-shaking happening in the record business.

The new birthday blue jeans you bought me are still new and blue. I've already run out of half the acrylic paint in each of the twelve tubes my parents gave me for my birthday. No brushes, though. Used my fingers which are now stuck onto the canvas boards. My life is in no one's hands. Whatever happens next depends entirely on if the number 3 or number 17 bus comes first.

And that's no joke.

There's so many earth-shattering things to say! A new cop is standing on the corner. Somebody's crying right now. And the world did not end a second ago. I haven't eaten mayonnaise for two years.

Hey! Can you guess how many nudes are on Paul Butterfield's "In My own Dream" album? Here's a hint: two less than all the ones I've drawn and painted of you.

I've quit McGill in a cloud of dust and a hearty Hi-Ho Silver! I've turned into a tin-horn gambler with a stacked deck and a derringer up my sleeve riding a Mississippi paddle-wheeler with my faithful butler, Jeroboam.

It is now night time, twenty years later. But don't let it get around.

Speaking of which,
why haven't you
written?

An Island of Madness
in a Sea of Reality

and ps:
What's your London home phone number?

Have you ever stood on your head on the grass, seen life upside-down and realized that this is the way it should be? I asked Emily that the other day but all she could do was look coy and answer she was too shy to try anything like that because then her "knickers" would show. What's wrong with that, I retorted, to which she attached a bowling ball to her big toe and proceeded to pound my head out.

To Moe, everyone has become a Barney. We are all Barneys walking the earth in search of a piece of individuality or a piece of ass. Too many of us seem to settle for the former.

Maybe Curly Joe's become a Barney, too. All that his parents can say is that he's traveling around some unknown somewhere and keeping in touch through collect calls to let them know he's still alive.

I am just about to walk up to the first woman I see on the street and ask her if she'd be willing to curb her poodle, throw off her mink stole, shrug off her Coco Chanel mini, remove her Vidal Sassoon hairpiece and stomp down Sherbrooke Street with me in search of a root beer popsicle. Just my good fortune, no women seem to be around right now.

But don't forget: re-arranging is only the illusion of changing. And, we are all, all of us, masters of illusion.

My goddamn sandals keep falling off.

I've moved out of the family home. I now live on a little street near a fish market on The Main flying the Jolly Roger and being forced to compete with alley cats for rotten fish. I sold my eyes to the eye-bank, filled up 42 quart bottles with sperm, sold 7 1/2 pints of blood and shaved myself bald so that somebody can have a wig to wear. I'm sick of revolutionaries, peanut butter, Mad magazine, ice cream cones, unread books, hot 7-Ups and black and white TVs. I crave the ultimate cherry.

The wind is blowing East and I fear it's taking me with it.

I've never been to Newfoundland and I have a feeling I know why.

Once I could stand in front of a tree and hear it breathe. Then I would breathe. Now, all the trees do is couph. (How the fuck do you spell cough?) And I couph along with them. Don Francks said that. I wrote it.

And I've figured out why "What The Butler Saw" is called "What The Butler Saw" and not "Gardening, Gefilte Fish And You." Do you know why? Take each letter and reverse it so that A would be Z, or B would be Y, or M would be N. A very clear and distinct message will appear. At first, it will read like gobbledegook. But repeat it backwards quickly enough and you will certainly hear "The Pope Smokes Dope".

This pen isn't writing down what I tell it to. It's a very disobedient pen. It's got a mind of its own. Sick, perhaps, but still its own. It's untrainable. It's a constant struggle for me to try to make it not make any sense at all. I think I'm succeeding.

There! I've said enough.

I'd tell you about the Gypsy mandolin player and the French horn but I think you've heard it all already.

Sincerely,

Larry (the guy you said you love)

He feels proud of his letter. It makes him smile in self-congratulatory jubilation at the thought of the confusion and anxiety it will almost certainly produce in Suzie Q when she reads it. She'll never be able to see through it, nor even appreciate any of its humour. Probably no one would — except maybe Curly Joe. Not that Curly Joe's ever going to see it.

* * * * *

Next day, Larry mails the letter and begins to wait for the apologetic reply that he's certain will arrive soonest possible. He almost gloats over the thought.

His wish comes partly true. Tuesday night, after he's come home from a day's work at FUCK, there's a telephone call for him. It's Edna on the line and she explains that Suzie Q hasn't been able to write to him over the past few days because of the water skiing accident that messed her up.

'She's still in hospital and will be there for another few days longer so that the doctors can confirm that everything's okay. She asked me to tell you that she wants to write you a letter but her right hand is still too sore. She'll phone you as soon as she's allowed out. She also wants you not to worry. The nurses have told her that the scars will almost totally disappear over time.'

Edna makes the news sound as if she's been talking about the average rainfall for this time of year.

All at once catching on to Suzie Q's silence, Larry thinks of the content of his last letter and proceeds to go to town on self-loathing. After that, he feels like he's going to puke any second now. As a counter-measure, he lays out all the money he's earned over the past few weeks, then stuffs the amount into a spare pair of underwear. His hash stash, paint tubes and drawing pencils get thrown inside last summer's duffel bag along with a couple of shirts, socks and his brand new pair of jeans.

Now to tell the parents ... Not to alarm them, he'll say that he's planning to be gone a week, or as long as it takes for Suzie Q to be back on her feet. Grateful that their worst fears aren't being confirmed and that their son hasn't gotten his girlfriend pregnant, Larry's *père et maman* offer to pay for his train journey there and back so that he'll arrive as soon as possible.

Everything settled, he phones Moe and puts him in the picture.

- Suzie Q's had an accident. I'll die here not knowing what's happening. I've got to make my way over there. I'll likely stay a while depending on what the job scene is like in London. Write. I will too. And tell Curly Joe what's going on when he gets back, okay? Love to Emily. Okay, gotta go now. Bye.

* * * * *

Larry's train pulls into London mid-morning on the last Wednesday in May. He hasn't slept properly since Edna's phone call and, on his last legs, feels totally unprepared to visit Suzie Q in hospital. When he's permitted to enter her Ward and make his way to the side of her bed, he finds himself shaking in fearful anticipation of how awful her injuries will be.

Suzie Q is sleeping. The flowers he's had delivered to her are on the bedside table next to similar bouquets dropped off by other visitors. There's one large square bandage covering her right cheek and another smaller one across most of her forehead. The bruises around right eye make it look as if she's been involved in one god-almighty barroom brawl. When Suzie Q turns on her side, Larry sees the extensive bandaging wrapped around the lower half of her right arm and the whole of her hand. He counts the tips of its fingers and thumb. Yes, they're all still there. Grateful that things don't look anywhere near as horrendous as he'd dreaded, still and all Larry wants only to be out of the room, out of the hospital, out of London Ontario itself. But he can't move; Suzie Q's injured body is enough to root him to where he stands.

A nurse enters to take Suzie Q's temperature. 'You must be Larry,' she says, giving him a quick inspection. Before he can confirm his identity, she adds: 'We're all extremely grateful that you were able to make it over here. Your girlfriend has been sobbing on and on about how you'll never want to see her again.

From the moment she heard of your imminent arrival she's become a model patient. We all love you here.' As one memorable mind reading trick to leave him with before moving on to her next patient, she forecasts that Suzie Q should be allowed to go home in a couple of days. Maybe even as early as tomorrow. Then, clicking her tongue, she disappears.

Left on his own, Larry finds a pencil and pad and begins to draw. He concentrates on Suzie Q's bruised and bandaged face, determined to make it look as beautiful and desirable as he feels it to be. None of the sketches works. He rips up multiple pages before calling it a day.

Not long later, Suzie Q wakes up, and, although still in a druggy haze, manages to make out who's in the room with her. She begins to cry and Larry rushes over to cradle her. When she's able to speak, all she can say is that she doesn't think she'll be paid for the time that she's taken off from her summer job.

For a second, Larry wonders how something as mundane as money could become one of the first things anyone would worry about just after coming to in a hospital bed. That said, he works out how to calm down Suzie Q by convincing her that, as soon as he leaves the hospital today, he's going to track down a job for himself and that he'll make up whatever amount she's lost with his take-home earnings. So nothing to worry about.

The smile that spreads across Suzie Q's face is more than enough to put Larry's mind at rest that what he's just offered to do goes some way in earning her forgiveness. Might even be noble.

* * * * *

The grim reality is that the one job Larry can find real quick is work in a grimy factory on the edge of town. A part of him sinks to think of what a miserable fate he's resigned himself to. Another part feels incandescently proud to have straightened everything out so rapidly.

After a restless night semi-sleeping on a bench at the cross country Bus station, Larry is eager to find a place to stay. This turns out to be no hassle either. Asking around, a couple of street people point him in the right direction. Before long, Larry's paying cash — one week in advance — and moving into a small, rather dumpy room in a two storey bungalow on William Street. Bumping into a couple of its other occupants, he pegs down the place as a boarding house for the washed-up and weary. Still, its rates don't stretch his savings too much and, to add to its allure, a railroad track runs by next to it. Best of all, his room's window is only feet away from a rarely-used railway tower.

On his first night there, Larry stays awake well into the early hours drawing and listening to the occasional freight train speeding by. He's hooked on the sound each makes and how that spurs a strange kind of romantic devotion in him. Acknowledging the room's seediness, nonetheless he feels he could live quite happily where he is. He surveys the curling, stained wallpaper and the double bed that sags and the lone desk and chair on which he'll write his poems and letters. One way or another, he'll come up with a stand that can act as his easel. There's bound to be somewhere in London where he can buy a cheap frame and canvas. Starry-eyed thoughts lead him to adopt the room as the first of many in which he'll pass away a substantial part of his life.

Even so ... Returning to his room in the evenings, only drugs can drown out his feelings concerning the factory he works in. Every day, five days a week, he's expected to screw in a specific type of screw into a designated hunk of metal that rolls down a conveyor belt along with a hundred other identical hunks of metal all of which require the same type of screw to be fitted into them. He has no idea where his handiwork goes to or what it becomes at the end of the line, since nobody's volunteered any information except to hint that vehicles of some indeterminate kind are the outcome of their efforts. After a while, he decides that there are probably very few people in the place who have any idea what they're busily constructing. Perhaps they, like he, simply prefer not to know.

* * * * *

And here it is: the game called "being in love" begins again.

The first couple of days, Suzie Q won't leave Edna's family's house. Setting foot outside is too much of a challenge for her. They are mainly reduced to phone calls that play out in pretty much the same way each time.

- How are yuh?
- Uhm ...
- Don't yuh feel better with the bandages off?
- Uhm ...
-What's the matter?
- ...
- Hey! What's wrong?
- *I look horrible!*
- Don't be silly!
- *It's not funny!*
- I'm not being funny. I've seen yuh. Yuh don't look horrible. Yuh're —
- I'm *ugly!* My face is terrible! I've got this *huge* scar across my cheek and my nose is crooked now!
- Aw, come on, Suzie Q. Yuh're beautiful. Those scars aren't gonna stay there forever —
- *Yes, they will!*
- No they won't. Yuh heard what the doctor said. They'll virtually disappear.
- Virtually isn't the same as entirely! I'll be ugly the rest of my life!
- Yuh won't! And in case yuh've forgotten, yuh're beautiful already. Yuh could have scars all over yuhr body and yuh'd still be the most beautiful girl in the world as far as I'm concerned.
- Stop being so nice.
- I'm not being nice. I'm being honest.
- ...
- I am.
- Uhm ...

- I *am!*
- Are you really?
- Of course. I love yuh. *Je t'aime.*
- *Moi, aussi.*
- So stop being silly and tell me what'cha been doing.
- Sleeping. Eating. I can't read because I can't turn the pages easily. Mostly, I watch stupid, boring TV. Mainly, though, I just think of you.
- Me? What's there to think about me?
- Lots of things, dummy!
- Like what?
- Like ... Uhm ... Your hair!
- My hair? What about my hair?
- How it's getting so long and wild!
- I'm getting comments about it at the factory.
- From all the girls, I bet!
- No ... How about we change subject?
- Okay. So what did *you* get up to last night?

* * * * *

The way that Larry sees it, he'll only ever totally convince Suzie Q of his feelings when they are alone and naked on his bed, making love. Then she'll know for sure.

Distressingly, when the day arrives that Suzie Q feels brave enough to meet Larry outdoors, when she gets to see his dingy room at last, when she notices all the drawings and even a couple of paintings of tracks and trains passing by his open window that he's scotch taped onto its walls, when he sits her down next to him upon the hard mattress and begins to caress the scarred skin on her face and arm, she remains strangely reluctant to accept the truth he offers her. Instead, she throws feeble excuses focused on her body's wounds in their way. Nothing he says or does will sway her. Only once she ascertains that he's given up on his demands for the time being, does she offer the promise of a *"demain"*. But they both know that it is an uncertain tomorrow whose coming cannot be measured by the passage of time from one day into the next.

On the first Saturday night after her release from hospital, Suzie Q is invited over to Larry's room for a meal he spent half the day slaving away at in the boarding house's communal kitchen. Shrimp Cocktail as appetiser, followed by Quebec salmon and *glissands* as Main, and Maple Syrup Pie for dessert. First thing she notices when she arrives is that a few more drawings and paintings have appeared on his walls. Where does he get the time? Does he ever sleep? She comments on how much she likes them, how he's turning into a real artist. It pleases Larry to hear her say this, even if he, himself, doesn't agree. Not yet, anyway. The dinner goes down well. For once, Suzie Q isn't nibbling away at her food; she even agrees to a second portion of everything. Enjoying themselves, it doesn't take long after they've finished eating for them to get blissfully stoned. Suzie Q seems more relaxed, more like her old self. Stretched out on the bed together, shirts unbuttoned, zippers unzipped, Larry whispers that he thinks it's time at last.

Saying nothing, her silence affirming her ambiguity, she watches Larry strip off. At first, apparently leaning towards agreement, she responds to the explicitness of his desire for her with teasing squeezes and caresses. But when it's her turn to undress, her earlier hesitation quickly turns into a total freeze-out. Unable to move, all Suzie Q can offer as explanation is that she doesn't want her gift to him to be so pointlessly wasted. When she's healed enough to feel pure once again, then she'll offer him everything. Until then ... Well ... She's happy to provide a service of relief. Disappointed and close to offended by her offer, Larry agrees that they can wait until the time is ideal for them both. It's enough for now that they can be with each other. Reproaching herself for demanding such patience from him, Suzie Q asks Larry if he'll teach her to draw.

'Yuh want to draw?'

'Yes! I want to draw you!'

'Me?'

Suzie Q lowers her face so he can't see her grin. 'Yes! I want to draw your ... you know ... your snaky cock!' *There, she said it without bursting into bashful laughter.*

'Yuh wanna draw my cock?' Now Larry's laughing as well.

'Yes! Fair's fair after all! You've drawn *ma chatte* all you've wanted. I should have equal rights! And don't worry, I won't show my drawing to anyone. I'll sneak it home and sleep with it next to me.'

Larry shakes his head. 'Uhm ... Okay. But only if yuh'll let me draw yuh again. It's been a while ...

Well, Suzie Q thinks, *at least that part of me hasn't been scarred.* 'As long as you promise not to tape it on the walls,' she agrees. No longer ill-at-ease, she invites Larry to help her remove her clothes.

Walking her back to Edna's home after their drawings have been completed and the June sun has set, they stop to kiss at every street corner they come upon. The act pleases them both; it reminds them that their love is steadfast, as strong as ever.

Passing by a church, they pause to contemplate its locked door. For a second, Larry gets it into to head that he could ask Suzie Q to marry him. And then, just as quickly, he rejects the ridiculous notion as being nothing more than the effects of too much grass. Their love doesn't need some old-fashioned formality to shine bright and true. Suzie Q, too, finds herself thinking absurd thoughts. It isn't the first time in the past couple of weeks that she's considered them. But now, standing in front of the church, unable to enter, a message she can no longer avoid nor dismiss settles in and makes itself at home.

* * * * *

Once again in his room all by himself, Larry hears a train whistle blowing. He thinks of Moe in Montréal and of Curly Joe off to parts unknown, and imagines the three of them as tuneless drifters separately inhabiting cheap dilapidated rooms such as the one he's in. The whole of his body trembles. Things would be so much more bearable if the three of them could be together. Aching to be rid of this dreadful loneliness, he unzips his jeans and begins to masturbate. He stares at his latest drawing of Suzie Q's cunt while reminding himself how much he loves her and how he wants to place the very same flesh he's currently pawing inside her every orifice, fill her up with its seed. Then, catching himself, he's forced to accept that, once again, his seed will fall on barren ground. The memory of the Biblical tale of Onan enters his thoughts. He looks around and down to the crumpled bed sheets, the towel nearby waiting to be used again to cleanse him of his sins. He tells himself that, in this moment, he *is* Onan. Unwillingly, disturbed by what his mind evokes, he imagines a whore upon a creaky bed being fucked by one more stranger who feels compelled to whisper 'I love you' in her ear while, at the same time, calculating whether she's been worth the price. Trying his best to rid himself of the image, Larry's turns his attention back to Suzie Q once again. Too slow, for a heartbeat, he he hears himself ask if she, too, is worth *her* price.

* * * * *

At approximately the same time, Suzie Q's begun to question whether Larry will ever begin to take in how much he's asking of her. Although they're not lies, the obstacles she's placed in his way haven't been the entire truth. What she knows for sure is that the accident has changed everything, and her adamance is a reflection of that. No matter what anyone says, she has no doubt that she came very close to dying. Like it or not, she's no longer able to shrug off this persistent fear of the unknown that her brush with death has brought about. Suzie Q accepts it as a warning: get your life in order and make sure it stays that way.

Because of this command, which she feels duty-bound to follow, Suzie Q has re-connected with her childhood desire to embrace purity. It's for this reason that, unknown to Larry, she's taken to going back to Mass. But the church, as she now wants and needs it to be, is dead. There's only lifeless ritual, bereft of even the minutest hint of joy, being carried out in front of near-empty pews. It is as closed off to her as the chapel she and Larry had stopped at.

Just the same, Suzie Q knows that God is calling her; it's just that, as yet, she can't locate Him.

* * * * *

After some two and a half weeks of escalating frustration at the factory, Larry reaches his breaking point. Before he can talk himself out of it, he gets up from his bench and makes his views regarding the mind-numbing, dehumanising nature of the repetitive task he's been called upon to carry out brutally clear to his foreman. Minutes later, accused of being a namby-pamby university ingrate, he finds himself outdoors, taking in the sunshine, his job at the factory now a thing of the past. And good riddance to it! For a moment, he feels free and high, exhilarated by the moral correctness of his act. Too bad it doesn't last. Already, Larry's begun to worry about how easy it will be to find another job and how Suzie Q will react to this change in his financial life.

Thankfully, Suzie Q isn't all that upset. She tells him that it's worth it just to see him so happy and smiling once more. She even plays down the difficulty of his finding something else that provides a salary. After all, she's back at work now, and Larry's generosity has more than made up the loss of income during her recovery.

Which means ... They have something to celebrate! How about, Larry urges, they go and see what *Paradise* is like? *Paradise* is the fantastic new dance hall that some of the heads in Larry's building have been getting all worked up about non-stop. It has the latest underground sounds and its light-show is said to be finer than anything that even Toronto has on offer. Best of all, it's been designed specifically for freaks and has a policy of not hassling anyone who just goes there to dance and listen to music. They don't even sell liquor in the place. You just pay your two bucks at the door and then you can do what you like. Even play chess if that's what turns you on.

At first, Suzie Q is reluctant. She still can't get used to the scars on her face and how people will react to them. At work, she's far less bothered because it's her expertise that's on offer and which her Beginners focus on. Here though, it's who she is and what she looks like that will be scrutinised. But then, seeing how uplifted Larry is by the prospect of being with "real" people again and feeling indebted toward him, she agrees that it'll be a great idea for them to go. Hopefully, his gratefulness may stop him from exerting his usual pressure on her.

* * * * *

They've been in *Paradise* for only ten minutes when someone passes Larry a joint. The gesture isn't even guarded as if meant to be transacted under the table. Larry looks around; nobody seems to be uptight, everything's out in the open, as casual and tolerant as all the people here. Flattered to have been accepted as a fellow freak, he takes a long drag and passes it on.

In spite of all its rave reviews, *Paradise* is still only half-completed and almost sleazy in its decorations. Yet, it throbs with a life Larry's never felt in discos before. It may not be the perfection demanded of a true Paradise, but it is still a heavenly place. Maybe even somewhere similar to that fabled *Sgt. Pepper Land* some dopers have browbeaten themselves into believing is real. Beyond the coloured lights and strobes and supersized speakers, it's a people show. Long-haired, jeaned, tie-dyed T-shirted and bra-less, free people are dancing and shouting, revelling in their chosen expressions of liberation. They make Larry feel like he's found his home at last.

And the music ... Wow! The finest there is. Marvin Gaye singing *I Heard It Through The Grapevine*. *The Youngbloods* urging everybody to *Get Together.* Best of all, there's this never-ending *Sly and the Family Stone* instrumental called *Sex Machine*. It winds down with a drum beat that eases up slower and slower until it seems as if the drummer's died on them right then and there. The volatile silence that follows is broken by this ugly, wise-ass record-voice that comes on like a shot to sneer: 'We blew your mind!' And then everyone who's been dancing in *Paradise*, now tired and stinking of sweat, yells back: 'You sure did, man!' and waits to catch up to the latest acid beat forming inside.

Larry zeroes in on this dancing couple and is mesmerised by them. The guy, especially. Flat-out high, his long mane of blonde hair waving free and wild, he appears to be totally loose and relaxed, jumping and swinging all around the room, as if he's the only person in it. Thing is, he's so totally involved with himself that it feels to Larry like he's connected to him as well and, that by following him around, he's become part of the dancer's abandonment. Spontaneously opening up to the experience, he's possessed by a burst of acceptance that is as welcoming and open as he's always wanted to believe love should be. Unlimited to any political cause or particular person, not even Suzie Q, it's allegiance is to Life itself. Larry has no doubt that this is where he wants to be. Deep breath taken, he asks if there are any jobs available. The groovy couple he's approached think it over. Yeah, they can use someone else to help out at the fruit juice stand. The pay is minimal and the hours are weird but, the way Larry sees it, he's ready to pay *them*.

* * * * *

Once again, days turn into weeks and Larry shaves while staring into his cracked mirror. He sees himself doing nothing but searching out ways to keep alive until eight at night when he opens up *Paradise*.

Suzie Q visits him every day after work. She wakes him up each time with a kiss and then pulls out the snack-of-the-day she shares with him. They talk, laugh, even gaze silently into each other at times. And the late-sun afternoons somehow speed by.

As there's hardly any money, when the weather's nice they go to Victoria Park where they sit and watch the people or else lie down on the cool grass and snooze. It's a simple life. For a while, Suzie Q was cooking a full-blown meal as well, but food's expensive and he's allowed to sneak sandwiches and cakes from the *Paradise* counter he works behind. Most evenings, having walked with him to *Paradise's* main door, she's taken to kissing him goodnight and then going back home for a family supper with Edna and her parents.

Suzie Q only joins him at *Paradise* on Saturday nights now because, she says, she still tires easily and, on reflection, she wants to cut down on smoking so much dope. Larry doesn't mind too much. Sundays and Mondays are his days off. They talk each week of escaping from London during that time but, invariably, there's always next week for that.

They don't really even meet up with other people. Suzie Q's water skiing work is demanding so she hasn't had much opportunity to form close friendships with the other staff members. Edna is still her only real one and she rarely accompanies Suzie Q for visits to Larry's place. Maybe, Larry thinks, she's never quite forgiven him for not paying her much attention when she came over to Montréal. As to Larry, he's gotten to know and chat with several *Paradise* regulars whom he likes but nothing approaching a friendship with any of them has developed as yet. When it boils down to it, what brings them together is smoking dope. It's hard to tell if they share any interests beyond that. Fair enough. As Suzie Q keeps reminding him, they don't really need anybody else anyway. Their world's too personal for others to intrude on.

As to their love, well ... Though neither doubts their own or their partner's continuing devotion, it remains incomplete. Suzie Q says that she loves Larry as much as ever. More even. And Larry believes her. He also believes that she has no doubt that he loves her. So what's the problem? For one thing, Suzie Q keeps passing on staying overnight at his place. Her reasoning is always the same old one: what would Edna's parents think? But they both know that's bullshit. The real reason is that if she agreed to spend the night with him they'd be bound to try once again at ridding her of her cursed virginity. And, for some reason Larry can't untangle, Suzie Q doesn't want that to happen. Larry has tried telling her what it's like for him to want to express that love in this most intimate of ways. And always, she responds by insisting that she feels the same, wants the same. And yet ... When it comes to the point of doing something about it, she backs away, blocks him off with trivial excuses: it's not the right time. Or place. Or mood. Or moment.

Still, dissolute and unsatisfactory as it is, sex does still have its place in their relationship. Many afternoons are spent lying in bed together, both of them nude, as their hands and mouths explore and caress their separate bodies. Their actions bring on the desired orgasm but it feels solitary and only achieves some sort of near-release. Unable to understand it herself, much less explain it to Larry, Suzie Q's nonetheless unwilling to change her mind; and that's that. Larry, in turn, pretends not to be bothered and, for a while, is convincing enough to dupe them both. Then again, most times he masturbates after she leaves. Unhappily, the relief provided is short-lived, and, all too often, leads only to disgust.

As a consequence, little by little, Larry is beginning to feel himself gone mad, obsessed by sex. The memory of his times with Pattie Pubes plagues him. He relives those encounters, embellishes them, dreads them, and, when he's being honest with himself, opens up to his yearning for them. *Paradise* is no help. Beautiful women casually strut by, passing him suggestive looks that make it clear that they fuck and enjoy indulging in such activities with whoever they want.

He hates his thoughts. He hates his dissatisfaction with all that Suzie Q gives him. He wishes he didn't want everything at once. He wishes he could wait. He wishes his prick would wait. But he knows otherwise.

* * * * *

July 10, 1969

Hiya, Moe:

Larry here. I don't know why I'm writing again as I've got little new to tell you. I feel like writing though, because I'd really like to see you now and this is the next best thing. Though it's not really enough.

Like I said, little new is happening. The Paradise job's still splendidly beautiful — though financially unrewarding. But, blow it off, as you'd say ... Every night is just fantastic. I've been meeting all sorts of weird and wacky characters. London's crawling with street people, children of the revolution.

Something really IS happening, Moe. You can just see it in the love and brotherhood that circulates naturally in this place. It's another totally different world Paradise people are living in. A much more innocent and peaceful way to be. It's very alluring, and I find myself becoming more and more a part of it.

It reminds me of the dream we all used to have about setting up a fairy-tale island commune. It could come true, Moe. Except it wouldn't just be an island — it'd be the whole world! It's got a chance, Moe. 69's a weird year. Things are happening fast.

I read the papers less and less because they just bring me down. Eldridge Cleaver on the run in Algeria, Brian Jones dead. Like somebody said to me the other day, 'It's a bitch just trying to remind yourself that life ain't the pits.'

Have you noticed how the last two paragraphs totally contradict each other? I guess that's where my head's at. So ... Enough of this. Have you heard anything from Curly Joe? I haven't gotten a thing from him since he left. I worry about him at times. I also wonder if I'll ever see him again ... If any of us will.

Which brings us to ... London, Ontario! Like everything else about this quasi-rural southeastern Ontario city — not least, it's very name — London is one sick joke. I'm betting that Emily would laugh herself silly over this place. People here all seem to be trying to sound as though they were living in London, ENGLAND. Maybe they really think they are. Even the pigs try to "talk English" when they're busting in on street people. And they go around wearing bobbie hats! Dig it! And ... There's even a stretch of water, little more than creek in size really, that snakes its way across a section of the city, and calls itself "The Thames". Put that in your pipe and smoke it! If anything,

London's a university town. Very affluent and very, very, dull. It is officially called "The Forest City" for the natural wilderness that its presence destroys. Unofficially, it's known as "The Drug Center of Eastern Canada" due to its proximity to Detroit. It is also referred to as Canada's typical city. Which, in a way, it is. Yeah, I know: another contradiction.

All in all, London's a pretty buff place, in spite of the heads at Paradise. There's a lot of money blowing around. THE MALL's where it's happening. THE MALL. It's like a waiting area in front of a shopping center only it's completely covered with people sitting and taking in the sun or on the make thinking that they're real cool dudes and dames even though they're really just backwater hicks.

It's such a weird place, though, Moe. It's like, I was walking down this long stretch of road called Windermere Road that's really almost like it's out in the country. Dig this: I was exercising my legs out there all by myself and out of nowhere I had this horrifying feeling that I was being spied on! I could see that there was no one around, but I still couldn't get it out of my head. So I looked all over the place and the feeling wouldn't go away. And then it hit me that what was freaking me out was the trees! Trees! I mean, Moe, this sounds crazy, but London trees are like no other. They're HOSTILE! I thought they'd start moving, chasing after me any second. Then I got into thinking that London's also called "The Forest City". Now this might be an explanation as to why I get such strange vibes here. Maybe it's the trees creating this wall of weird energy that totally closes in on London. Maybe the trees aren't really trees at all! Maybe they're space invaders waiting to take over the world one place at a time! And they've started with London, Ontario. Which would explain the kookie behavior of the people here. Did you know they put paper sacks on window display dummies when they undress them so as not to offend anyone? THAT'S what I mean.

Oh ... I forgot to mention the bugs. If you thought Montréal was bad ... London's got bugs the size of golf balls — I kid you not — that crash in the millions against doors and windows then lie there on pathways and sidewalks waiting to be crunched to death by shoes or, far worse, bare feet. June bugs, they're called. Except it's July now and they don't seem to be going anywhere.

Fuck London. How are you and Emily? A purely rhetorical question, since I know you're both okay. No, more than that: I know you're both great. Wish you could come down one weekend in The Flacon. It would be inspirational.

Did you make it over to the Pop Festival in Toronto a couple of weeks back? Some of the freaks I spoke to went to it and said it was a blast. All sorts of bands played, including The Band itself. Procol Harum. Charlebois. Dr. John. Even your favorite, Tiny Tim! I tried to talk Suzie Q into going, but she wasn't into it enough. I wasn't too bothered. Between you and me, being in Paradise feels like being at a pop festival all the time!

Thankfully, Suzie Q's getting better and better every day. The scars are nearly invisible now and she's no longer too upset at being seen by other people. And her work is going great guns. She's a natural born teacher according to everyone. She gave me a summer present yesterday. A bright pink ribbon to tie my hair into a pony tail. Yeah, it's gotten THAT long, would you believe? I'm a full-fledged, high-flyin' freak now!

Unlike me, for reasons that keep passing me by, Suzie Q loves being in London. I've seen her reading some brochures about maybe switching from McGill to over here at Western University. Which has got me to thinking about starting over at Western for my degree, too. It's a really nice university and Suzie Q and I could maybe live together somewhere. Study together. It's a bit late for applications and things but I'm going to go see somebody in a few days ...

Still... if I DO get in, it won't be the same without you or Curly Joe around! But maybe we'll really start doing some work for a change. Anyway, like I said, it's not at all definite yet but it IS a possibility ...

I tried to be light-hearted a couple of sentences ago, but I'd be lying to you if I kept on. It'll be TERRIBLE to go to university without you and Emily and Curly Joe. The thing is, if

Suzie Q does switch, I just KNOW I couldn't take a year of writing letters, and waiting for weekends that are just too quick to fly by. It's too much of a hopeless sort of life, Moe. I've lived through that scene once already with Angel, and we both know where THAT got me!

On a more positive note, I've been looking into the possibility of studying at an Art College. The other day, I took some of my paintings and drawings over to this place to see if I had a chance of getting in. The guy who interviewed me took one look at my work and deemed it to be primitive rubbish! Yeah, really! I was ready to crawl my way out the door and give up on any further attempts, but then he added that in spite of all that he could see a possibility in my style which maybe some dedicated work on my part could turn into something worthwhile. I'd have to start over and take a basic training program.

Talk about going backwards! I'm still seriously thinking about it, though. It feels so right in contrast to my pointless ambition to become an engineer.

Whatever happens though, I (we) decided I HAVE to go back to school. I don't know WHY but I know it's necessary. All too many people with things to say and do that go unheard, or who give up trying because they ain't got those letters after their names. Christ, okay. Play the game to get beyond it. Get the insignificant letters and become something more than significant.

There I go again.

Whatever happens, I'll be down by the end of August to either spend a few days with you and Emily (and, hopefully, Curly Joe) or to sort myself out for the onslaught of another year at McGill ...

Well, I better get myself ready for Paradise. I'll write again soon.

Happy summer to you and Emily.
Love.

— Larry —

* * * * *

There is a good deal missing in the letter. Things that Larry finds he's unable to write down. He tells himself that he'd be more than willing to talk about them if that was possible. It eases his guilt. What he wants to say is that Suzie Q has changed a lot since her accident. She doesn't laugh nearly as much as she used to. And she's gone mysterious in some ways. And more distant.

Plus, there's the new development: Suzie Q's stopped having orgasms. She insists that it's just temporary, the after-effect of her accident. Well, that's possible. But then she adds that she doesn't need to nor really misses them. That her primary pleasure lies in witnessing his pleasure. In return, Larry claims to accept and refrains from arguing back. But what he repeats to himself is that he has become an unsatisfactory lover and, worse, that what arousing beauty she once saw in him is being seen no longer.

But this can't be. Their love is spotless and forever. Isn't it? Left to think out such thoughts on his own, Larry struggles and screams and curses.

The voice that welcomes you to Hell can only be your own.

* * * * *

One Saturday, making their way to *Paradise*, they agree that they've had enough of London for a while, and so, first thing tomorrow, they will hitchhike to Grand Bend, sleeping bag away the night, and lie out on its beach for a couple of days.

Grand Bend is London's most accessible summer place-to-go. Located right on the edge of Lake Superior, a mediocre, Canuck hick version of places like Atlantic City, it is, at any rate, the nearest thing to a resort area that Southern Ontario can offer. Grand Bend is full of amusement arcades, fun-fair rides, cheap fast food restaurants, trailer parks, run-down motels and guest houses, screaming kids, local chapters of the Hell's Angels and Satan's Disciples, loud vulgar AM muzak, and long stretches of sand dune beaches that offer expansive and free sleeping accommodation so long as you find the means to avoid the special night patrols who roam about ensuring that the area is protected from invasion by hordes of hippies who'll give the place a bad name. Basically, Grand Bend is the pits.

On the positive side though, being the only choice available in the area, it's quick and easy to hitch a ride to it or back to London. When there's little money available, a visit to a place like Grand Bend becomes something to get yourself enthused about. Which is why, less than two hours after having set out on their brief retreat, Larry and Suzie Q find themselves saying their goodbyes to the middle-aged, motherly woman driver who'd picked them up. Then they gather up their hidden sleeping bag belongings and traipse off to the beach.

All day, they swim and eat the sandwiches they've brought along with them, soak in the sun, buy each other ice cream cones, read novels and relax. Satisfyingly, everything seems as natural and soothing as the lapping of waves along the shore-line.

The spell lasts until sunset. Arm-in-arm, still clinging to their shared sensation of renewed peace and direction, idling their way casually down the main strip, they are confronted by a couple of recruiting agents from some sort of Christian Commune that's set up its summer residence in one of Grand Bend's motel lodges.

As soon as Larry sees the fervent followers and figures out who they are, he feels a deep revulsion easing its way up his throat. As far as he's concerned, having anything to do with old-style religions like Christianity in 1969 identifies you in no time flat as someone who just doesn't have the vaguest clue, much less anything relevant to say as to what's going on in the world. Likewise, it's their clean-cut presence more than anything that repels him. He'd be more than happy to turn his back on these jerks and then go back to the beach to smoke some of the dope he's brought along.

To Larry's dismay, Suzie Q doesn't allow this imagined scenario to become reality. She's right in there talking animatedly with these sickos, and seems thoroughly absorbed in hearing them spout on about their dubious beliefs. Even worse, when they're invited to go back to the commune to listen to some folk music that'll be played by a few of the Brothers and Sisters, Suzie Q jumps the gun and agrees without once considering what Larry might think. Probably just as well, since all that's floating through Larry's mind is the many different ways he could tell these Jesus Freaks where to get off.

They are led to a cabin that has a banner reading *Jesus Loves You* stretched across its front entrance. There must be around thirty followers gasping to welcome them and perhaps a handful of outsiders who've come to witness the festivities. Larry hates the whole set-up from the start. He tries to sway Suzie Q to leave with him right now, but she snubs his entreaties point blank, telling him not to be so narrow-minded and make an effort to notice the similarities between what these people are preaching and what hippies are trying to achieve. Larry can't see any long hair or smell any dope or hear raucous rock music. Conclusion? Whatever similarities there might be can only be superficial. But Suzie Q won't listen and chooses, instead, to pay attention to the group's Leader who has appeared unannounced to welcome all the visitors and rap about what he and his acolytes are into.

As soon as he hears these well-practiced lines, Larry becomes certain of the correctness of his earlier intuition and turns off to the pre-arranged lecture the man begins to deliver. But wait! He can't quite take the wraps off what's driving him back in to listen. It's not so much what the man says that's compelling, but more the way he arranges his words together. This guy's got some power going for him, Larry's got to give him that. And ... Although he's no predictable show-off, the range of material he pulls out to make his points is, undeniably, pretty impressive. Poets, novelists, philosophers. Damn! He's kept up to date with the current music scene and can quote lines from songs. Dylan's most often. Eager to probe further, Larry studies the man more carefully. There's something about him ... He keeps thinking of Curly Joe even though the two don't bear the slightest resemblance. Now why is that? *Hey! Wait a minute! Could it be ... No! Impossible!*

Suzie Q, too, is hanging on to every pronouncement that emerges from the man's mouth. It feels as if he's speaking directly to her and her alone. And what he has to say rings true with what she's been feeling but hasn't found the means to express it. He has the words she's been searching for. He blesses his audience for being part of a generation that asks questions, seeks answers, concerns itself with the major issues in life. He sympathises with their disenchantment with traditional Christianity and its old ways of putting people in touch with God. He agrees that there are good reasons for the churches being empty. And then, he exclaims that these same churches aren't empty because people have lost their faith in God, but because God has moved out of them and now lives on the streets, the airwaves, the communes. He's even smiling when reminding them all of how some people are going around saying that God is dead, when it's as plain as day that He's more alive than ever if you look in the right places. And when the preacher ends his sermon by proclaiming that God is Love pure and simple, Suzie Q feels that she's at last understood what her heart's been trying to tell her for months now.

Afterwards, when the man's doing the rounds, pressing palms with one and all, and urging everyone to call him Brother Zeke, Larry's bouncing up and down ready to spring his question. Noticing him, Brother Zeke makes himself available.

'Hey there, Sinner!' he says. 'You look like you've got angst in your pants.'

'Are yuh Prof Guggenheim? From McGill?' No small-talk, Larry's straight in there. *Bingo!* Brother Zeke's reaction satisfies him he's got it right the first time.

'Who wants to know? Are you some newshound looking to cause a stir?'

'No! Nothing like that. It's just that yuh used to teach a good friend of mine, Curly Joe? He thought yuh were great!'

Relieved by Larry's mention of Curly Joe, Brother Zeke turns on the charm. He owns up to being — or, more accurately, that he used to be — Prof Guggenheim. But now that he's found his Way to Jesus, he wants nothing more to do with his past life in academia. 'Don't look back, right?' he says.

Contradicting himself, he's curious to know how Curly Joe's faring. But when Larry isn't able to tell him much about that, his interest level plunges. Maybe he's done enough of these things to tell that Larry isn't likely to be ready as yet to receive The Lord. Unlike the young woman Larry's with. Now *she* is clearly open to being saved. If he could, Brother Zeke would turn all his attention on her. But Larry isn't going to be easily brushed aside. He wants to know how and why Prof Guggenheim made the switch to Brother Zeke.

'Okay! Okay! All shall be revealed! But later, when I'm finished greeting everyone. After that, we three will have a good, long chat,' Brother Zeke says, then he winks at Suzie Q just in case she'd missed the emphasis he'd put on "three".

Brother Zeke keeps to his word. Meeting up a little over an hour later, he guides them to an outdoor cafeteria where they're not likely to be disturbed. Sitting around now, glancing up at the stars and out to the lake, a tale of loss and redemption is told in-between chocolate milkshake slurps.

The Hero, Guggenheim, finds himself cast adrift, thrown out of his cloistered university world because he dared to criticise and challenge those who governed it. Worse, it seems that he's been blacklisted as "unsuitable and problematic" so that no other university he applies to will even bother to invite him to an interview. Defeated, alone, on the wrong side of thirty, he suffers through a dark night of the soul that lasts several months. Most of that time, he owns up, remains a blur viewed through a haze of alcohol and drugs. And that's exactly how this Hero wants to keep it.

What matters is that at his lowest point, when everything is looking like it's heading for the final countdown, he finds himself on his knees pleading for salvation. Which is nothing like what the Hero would have expected. Sure as can be, it's fucking amazing! Not least because up until this point, the Hero was convinced that he'd rid himself of all that superstitious "opiate of the masses" nonsense calling itself religion. *Any* religion.

Furthermore, as if what he's found himself doing now isn't unnerving enough, a million times more astonishing is that The Lord hears him. And then He speaks to him. Yea, verily! The Lord deigns to speak to this little lost pissant self-declared atheist, as if he matters. How awesomely insane is that? And why is a *Christian* God wanting to have anything to do with a non-observant Jew? No way, right? Except ... Jesus was a Jew, too, wasn't he? *And* he was also the Son of God. But why would the Son of God choose to become flesh and blood in order to free us of our sins *as a Jew*? Why not a Roman? Or an Egyptian? Or Greek? Or whatever else? Why make it so tough on Himself?

Asking that question electrifies the Hero. In that moment, all the confusion and uncertainty that has characterised his life zaps its way to a shining clarity. And in that moment as well, the Hero who used to be known as Prof Guggenheim dies, and Brother Zeke is born.

Brother Zeke calls himself a Messianic Jew. Yeshua, or Jesus as most prefer, is the Messiah prophesied in the Old Testament. No ifs, ands or buts. Everything He says, as recounted in the New Testament, is The Truth, The Law, The Power and The Glory and overrides any earlier Rabbinical Rules. And The Messiah's Message? Nothing but Love, Love, Love. But just make sure you love Him above all else.

'That's what we're up to,' preaches Brother Zeke. 'We want to bring Love into people's lives. We're gonna change the World like nothing else ever has. Communism. Socialism. Capitalism. Radicalism. Pick whichever "ism" you want. None of them have worked, nor will they work, because they've all lacked that special, unique missing ingredient. And you know what that is? Yeah, Love. That Supreme Love that Yeshua offered to the whole world through His Crucifixion and Resurrection. That very same Love whose vibes continue through the ages and resonate in each and every one of us.

'It's the Lost Chord we're all searching for. And it's playing our song. That tune you'll never get tired of hearing once you've opened your soul to it. That's what this group we formed, *Children of Jesus,* is all about. We ain't preaching, man! We're on a Never-Ending Tour to Heaven on Earth. And we'd love to have you hop aboard with us!'

* * * * *

Later, when they've landed upon a suitable beachside patch for them to sleep, they zip up their sleeping bags together and ease their ways in. The night is silent and dark, only faintly illuminated by stars and moon. Keeping their clothes on, they make do with what's possible. The uncertainty and danger of being caught not only sleeping but canoodling outdoors adds a special secret ingredient to their shared excitement.

Unfortunately, Larry brings everything crashing down when he rather stupidly muses aloud if 'all that love talk crap they had to sit through means that those jokers are allowed to fuck each other.'

Before he knows what's happening, Suzie Q's pushed him away.

'What is it? What's wrong? Did yuh hear something?'

'Yeah. I heard the sound of infantile gloating.'

'What? What do yuh —'

'Listen to yourself! You can be so insensitive sometimes! Why can't you allow yourself to consider for just one second that Brother Zeke and his followers might be good people who are doing no one any harm. And you know what else? It seems to me that they might be doing a lot more good than all the stoned-out hippies you like to hang out with. What if the *Children of Jesus* have something to say that could actually teach you something? But no, that's too far-fetched, right? How could they *possibly* be right about anything?'

Larry can't believe what he's hearing. Overcome by his awareness of the chasm that has opened up between them, he refuses to try to bridge the divide. 'That's crazy! Those people are even more fucked-up than The Straights. And "Brother

Zeke" is the most fucked-up of the lot of them! I don't know what's happened to him. Curly Joe used to think Guggenheim was some sort of god. And maybe he might have been when he still had a brain. But now, Guggenheim's the one who's gone and convinced himself that he's been turned into this Supreme Being. He's on a power trip that is one major downer. What's he got to say that's so revolutionary anyway? Just the same old —'

Edna's scream interrupts his rant. 'Oh grow up, Larry! Try listening to someone else other than yourself for once! What's it gonna take for you allow God back into your life, hey? What? You tell me.'

The several minutes of silence that follow are broken by their simultaneous and profuse apologies. They cuddle, and tears are shed and more apologies follow. But the spell is broken.

The next day, after a less-than-tranquil sleep, they both agree that Grand Bend's a waste of time and that they'll be happier back in London. It's a lie, of course, and they both know it. But it's a lie that serves to hold back a far more deplorable truth.

* * * * *

There's a young hippie woman who works at the snack counter over in *Paradise*. Larry's begun to take staunch notice of her. He's attracted to her but he tells himself that the attraction lies in how free and easy she is with whatever comes her way. He'd like to learn how she does that; perhaps she can teach him.

Her name is Billie and she's small and her dark skin makes plain her Middle Eastern roots and she's always friendly towards him. The easygoing greetings and goodbyes she offers at his arrivals and departures reflect her openness, her spontaneity. Being around her, Larry can forget all his worries about Suzie Q and his friends and the uncertain future. He knows that Billie has a boyfriend, so nothing dangerous is ever going to happen, right?

Afterwards, having fucked themselves silly, Larry's baffled

to note that he feels no guilt or shame. Still, out of a desire to keep things honest, he tells Billie that he hopes what they've just done won't affect her relationship in any threatening way. That makes Billie laugh out loud. Her boyfriend will be really happy for her that she had such a fun time at work. They're not into any kind of buttoned-down-world relationship. No jealousy. No restrictions. What just happened between her and Larry has got nothing to do with anyone else. They like each other, right? And they let their bodies express that liking. No headache. Maybe it'll happen again, maybe it won't. In any case, why turn it up to heavy-duty level? Nothing's really changed between them except that now they both know what the other looks like without any clothes on. Did Larry like what he saw? Billie hopes so because she sure liked what she saw.

Larry's straining to accept everything Billie's saying. He keeps telling himself that he does. But he can't deny that he isn't as free as Billie. But then ... When he and Suzie Q were part of that Triangle with Curly Joe, he didn't feel hung-up about that. Or, at least, he doesn't recall feeling so. On reflection, that time was probably when he and Suzie Q were at their happiest. Which, when he comes to think about it, makes Billie's case all the stronger.

Except ... There's no way on earth he'd be dumb enough to tell Suzie Q about Billie. She'd never accept her sharing him with another woman. Just like, to be honest, he'd never accept sharing Suzie Q with another man. Not even Curly Joe now.

What happened? How come their relationship has suffered such a setback? What's turned their love into something so fragile? When did their saying "I love you" turn into a set of rules that now seem so unfair?

* * * * *

Suzie Q, too, has her own secrets.

Since Grand Bend, she's been visiting the *Children of Jesus* at their communal house. Nobody knows. Not even Edna. And definitely not Larry. This is something exclusively for herself.

Having initially assumed that they were headquartered in Grand Bend itself, she'd been dumbfounded to bump into a couple of them spreading The Word in front of The Mall. Which was when she found out that they were primarily based in London. So now, most afternoons, on her way back from work before heading over to Larry's, she calls in on them.

They make her feel so welcome. Brother Zeke as much as any of them. He's been so kind and attentive. Always careful not to prod or pry but at the same time letting her know that he's there to listen to whatever's on her mind. She's told him so much already. About how she feels that her whole life has been one long search for something she doesn't even know, can't point to or name, but is certain she will recognise it as soon as it presents itself.

In return, he's divulged that he, too, has been on a very similar journey that continues to this day. Reconnecting with the Divine Word Made Flesh has provided his calling with a direction that hadn't been clear to him before. It is The Way, he's certain of that, but the Ultimate Goal hasn't as yet been reached.

And then he adds, as if it has just now been made manifest to him: 'But maybe ... maybe ... I'm beginning to think that we might not be able to reach that Goal all on our own. By ourselves, I mean. Maybe it's only possible when there's others — or, *an* other — who's walking that same path you're on with you. And, if that's the case, it seems to me that our paths have reached a common junction point and we're maybe going to be on the same path at least until if and when our roads diverge once again. If I'm right, I'd be happy to walk along this path beside you. If you'd like the company, of course.'

Suzie Q doesn't know what to say to that. She feels so honoured that this Holy Man has offered to be by her side. She wants to hug him but stops herself because the act is too physical, all too easily open to being misread. Instead, no doubt crossing her mind, she kneels in front of him, bows her head and whispers 'I've been so lonely, waiting for a true spiritual companion. At last, God has led me to you.'

* * * * *

On the Sunday night of July 20th, Larry is invited over to Edna's home so that he can watch the Moon Landing on TV. Everyone is welcoming and friendly and Larry is on his best behaviour, polite and grateful for every soft drink and snack offered him.

He and Suzie Q sit next to each other, bodies barely brushing, yet something has changed. And for once, it's for the better. Unlike so many other recent times, right now they feel charged enough to generate jolts of erotic electricity that can't possibly go unnoticed. And when the fuzzy, distorted televised shots of Neil Armstrong taking that one small step appear, and everyone in the room holds their breath before emitting a communal 'whooo!', those jolts go into supercharge mode. Faces flushed, Larry and Suzie Q share the groove of what each has so spontaneously experienced. It has nothing to do with Moon Landings. Much to their amazement, the sexual heat of their love has begun to blaze full force once again.

Once a decent amount of time has gone by and the broadcast moves to continuous replay, Suzie Q comes up with the most minimal of excuses to notify everyone that she's accompanying Larry back to his house. 'Don't wait up for me,' she adds. 'I probably won't be back till late.'

Holding hands, on fire, they sprint their way from block to block until they reach Larry's room. Door securely locked, they waste no time undressing. Even their foreplay is dispensed with. There is no need for questions as to whether this might be the time at last. Both of them are as ready and as certain as they'll ever be.

And when it happens, the penetration is swift and effortless. Feeling no expected stabbing pain, instead receptive to the novel sensations being experienced, Suzie Q's body picks up Larry's rhythm such that who thrusts and who receives rapidly becomes too debatable to tell. Brief as it is, their union is euphoric. Responding to the invader's eruptive spurts, Suzie Q's vulva tightens it grip, squeezes, then initiates a succession of involuntary spasms unlike any other she's experienced before that leave her breathless and trembling. Disentangling their bodies, they stretch out on the bed, overflowing with joy and relief.

'We did it!' Larry crows. 'At last!'

'It's too good to be true,' Suzie Q agrees. 'Thank you, *mon amour*.'

And she is, truly, feeling grateful. Even blessed. Although ... The strange thing is, while thankful that she suffered no pain, Suzie Q also feels a little bit disappointed that she didn't. All these years of agonising and playing out possibilities ... There doesn't even seem to be any blood on the sheets! It forces her to query whether physically she was *ever* a genuine virgin.

Chattering away now, they talk about doing it again, but worry that this would diminish the specialness of their experience. Besides, Suzie Q insists, she must be heading back. It was awkward enough having run out on everyone and making it all too unmistakable as to the reason why. And, when it gets down to the nitty gritty, though she keeps it to herself, Suzie Q is desperate to guess what God thinks of what they've just done. Her happiness is unfeigned but that irritating speck of uncertainty outright refuses to be brushed away.

* * * * *

At last! All barriers to the full expression of their love removed, Larry and Suzie Q feel as if their romance is once again in its earliest moments of becoming.

Their passion for each other seems unquenchable, their delight like nothing they've experienced before. Their love is at its pinnacle They have it all.

The trouble with having it all though, is that you still want more ...

* * * * *

For Larry and Billie, staying on a little longer in *Paradise* once it has shut down at night has become a regular occurrence. It's not the most inviting of places to fuck in, but they don't seem to mind. In fact, some of the fun comes from their experiments in trying out different locations and items of furniture. The floor or counter are just about bearable when their chosen position demands that they both are able to fully stretch out in some way or other. Most often though, it's Larry sitting or squatting on an armless chair with Billie astride him, face to face or back turned, that does the trick.

Some late nights as well, when her truck driving boyfriend is on extended hours, Billie accepts Larry's invitation to drop by, stay until the morning if she wants. Saggy and grungy as Larry's bed is, it's way softer than their usual options. Staying over gets Billie's vote; according to her, her orgasms are so much more massive when she can tune in to the sound of a train rumbling by.

Larry's not going to argue with her about that. *Whatever turns yuh on ...*

One thing he's noticed, though: each time, after Billie leaves, Larry finds himself thinking how come he's letting this happen. He's already fucking himself crazy with Suzie Q. What's he needing Billie for? Sure, he likes her, has fun being around her, but it's nothing close to what he and Suzie Q have got. Probably same goes for Billie and her boyfriend. So why? Is it wanting to be free like Billie is? But does he want to be?

Pointless questions. Larry knows he's not going to change his mind.

* * * * *

Usually, they will first kneel together face-to-face, each lost in private communication with their God.

After that, they talk. Because they both find it so easy to talk with each other. The topics can be almost anything, although they usually focus on a passage from The Word and explore its possible meaning and implications. By and by, apparently without knowing it, they will turn towards more personal concerns centred around their dreams and hopes.

That's when Suzie Q will ask for guidance about her relationship with Larry. The funny thing is, ever since they've gotten through "the sex barrier", she's noticed herself feeling different about Larry. Oh, she's enjoying what they get up to. All the different positions, the sheer excess of it all. And she's climaxing again. Can't stop, in fact. It's just that their meetings are always so exclusively physical. Like they're only bodies, nothing more. And Larry seems to want that. He's like a little kid with a new toy. Oh, she's certain that she still loves him. But now that she's talking about it, it occurs to her that she no longer adores him. She can't. It feels blasphemous for her to adore any being other than God.

And Zeke — they've gotten close enough to dispense with his title — he'll furrow his brow and then admit that he's probably the last person on earth to give advice on relationships between men and women. He's had no success in such affairs. He's come round to thinking that maybe God wants him to give up on hoping to find that special person in his life.

Each time he affirms this to her, he follows it by going silent. Best to allow the intimation to settle in its own way. At which point, Suzie Q always wants to throw herself on him. But she doesn't. Instead, she tells herself that she must surely have misunderstood what Zeke seems to be suggesting.

And the common desire will fester and agitate both dreamers' dreams.

* * * * *

It's another Saturday night at *Paradise*. Suzie Q smiles across to Larry. Billie has the weekend off, so no sweat about any worrisome encounters and revelations.

Every once in a while, Suzie Q sneaks behind the counter to give Larry a hug. She keeps saying sorry and how much she loves him. Larry's not at all clear what she's so sorry about, but he's not asking any questions. Maybe if she's sorry enough

Suzie Q will agree to stay overnight at his place.

The music being played is loud and emotional: peace and love interspersed with rage and revolution. Everyone in *Paradise* is a part of it; they're all in tune with one another.

Except for Suzie Q.

Tonight, in spite of all her efforts, she feels cut off from this community. She's come to accept that she's not like them. They inhabit a world of drugs and music and what they call personal freedom. And, for a while there, they'd lured her into this fantasy as well. But it's tearing her apart now. She doesn't want it anymore. It's no longer enough. Right this moment if she's being honest with herself, these people strike her as being rather pitiable. Just how free are they really? They have to behave in a certain way, dress in a certain way, think in a certain way. They wear their uniforms as blindly as their parents wear theirs. And they're slowly killing themselves off with chemicals whose effects no one knows anything about except that they alter people's heads into some uncertain direction.

Suzie Q's pity is mixed with a level of contempt so powerful that she wishes she could simply disappear. It feels too much like being a guest at some secret society gathering: too many "in" phrases and jokes who's secret messages are appreciated only by insiders determined to remind you that you're an outsider. Nobody but Larry ever really speaks to her, or asks her to dance or is curious enough to want to get to know or open up to her. They pass her dope. This is as far as they go: the offer of dried leaves that send her even further into herself.

Suzie Q catches Larry laughing and joking and has to accept that she feels sorry for him as well. He's so driven to fit in. And yet, he doesn't either. Not really. And *they* know it, too. If Larry wasn't so scared of losing them, he'd also come round to admitting that they share as little of value with him as they do with her. But Larry's not strong enough for that. Nor will he be, until he has The Lord on his side. It's odd; Suzie Q becomes aware that, for once, she's understood something before he has. Studying him, she concludes that she was correct in identifying him as a little boy. Such a beautiful, light-haired little boy who's trying for all he's worth to be a part of the gang.

Suzie Q's crying now. But she doesn't mind because it feels like a release of some sort. She knows that she's not going to come here ever again. It feels nothing like the welcome she experiences with the *Children of Jesus*. With Zeke. There! She summoned his name. Zeke. How she longs to touch him physically. Not just soul to soul. But hand in hand. Mouth to mouth. Belly to belly.

Turning to look her way, Larry notices the tears. He comes over, wraps his arms around her, asks for explanations that she's unable to provide. Seeing him brought down so low, racked by the guilt of her imagined unfaithfulness, she offers him something close to the truth and confesses that she's been spending time with some of the Christians from Grand Bend. She enjoys their company. They've helped her re-connect with her own Christian values and beliefs. And, because of that, she's not enjoying being here. Honestly? She's finding this to be really, really boring. And crude. And false.

Hearing herself, Suzie Q gets to grips with what she's really been trying to say. It's not *Paradise* or its community that she can no longer pretend she's part of.

Not yet grasping her deeper meaning, Larry's had enough of a jolt trying to unravel how Suzie Q can get depressed in a dreamworld like *Paradise. She's one of us!* he insists. He negotiates a few minutes off from his counter duties and leads her outside to late night London. Now that they're alone, she starts to relax. When he asks her to come back to his room tonight, he's momentarily thrown when she puts up no resistance and agrees straightaway.

* * * * *

Later, sitting side by side on his bed, Larry takes hold of one of her hands. 'Now,' he speaks solemnly, 'tell me what's wrong.'

'It's like I said: I can't go back there anymore.'

'Why? Were yuh bothered? Did someone —'

'No! Nothing happened! I'm just not right being there! I'm

just ... Oh, Laurent. You know what I'm trying to say. And I can't say it. *C'est trop pour moi. C'est trop.*'

Larry turns away, Outside his window, he hears a freight train in the distance moving closer. A part of him feels detached enough to take everything in: the night, the stars, the train, the room, and two lovers leaning delicately upon his mattress. The white heat of the moment burns into his memory leaving him with the certainty that this will be one more indelible scene in his life. *Now* he's clear as to where all this is heading. And worse, he unwillingly accepts, he's powerless to alter its direction. But still, he has to try.

'Hey ... '

'Uhm?'

'It's late. Why don't yuh stay and sleep here tonight?'

'Oh, Lord! Haven't you understood? I *can't* stay!'

'I just want yuh to get some sleep, that's all!'

'I can't!'

'Why *not*? We're supposed to be two people in love, can't we act like it?'

'I can't pretend anymore. I won't. It's not about you, or what we had or who we were. I'm just not that person now. We ...' Suzie Q's sentence hovers incomplete. She knows she's hurting him. But she also knows that she'd hurt him even more if she were to let him in on the truth. That it's Zeke she want to make love to. That giving in to Larry would be a sham. She won't allow herself to treat Larry like that. Accepting that, she wrenches her hand away from his, then stands and heads for his door.

Larry watches her stomp out of the room. Miserable as she feels, she still makes sure to shut his door as silently as possible so as not to irritate his neighbours. So much like Suzie Q to worry about others. Not that Larry's really thinking about Suzie Q. He's time travelling back to another place. Another woman. Another "love of his life" who turned out not to be. The scene's too similar to bear. The freight train he'd heard earlier passes by and the room shakes. Larry wishes he was on that train. Next best thing? Sit by his window and draw that desire.

* * * * *

Contrary to his expectations, he's slept pretty well and right through the rest of the night. Could it be that everything he remembers happening was just some dream? He figures that the best thing is for him to stay in bed and try to work that one out. Ten minutes later, Larry's asleep again.

He's awoken by a knock on the door. His watch says that it's late afternoon. He should be heading off to *Paradise. Fuck it. I'll call in sick.* 'The door's unlocked,' he says.

A moment later, Suzie Q's standing there. 'I wanted to give you these.' She holds out a bundle of letters. *His* letters to her. 'They're too beautiful to destroy. But I can't live with them.' There! She's found the courage to say it, even if she feels herself being torn up inside. Is she doing the right thing? And if it is, then why does she keep trying to fight it off? Deny it?

'Yuh came back here for that?' Larry asks, almost offended.

But Suzie Q's already most of the way down the stairs and doesn't hear him.

Larry weighs the bundle, planning on hurling it out the open window onto the train track below him. Just as he's about to, he drags his duffel bag over to him with his feet and then stuffs the blue-ribboned stack into it. He can't bring himself to destroy their love letters either.

Challenge dealt with, Larry begins to feel strangely detached from everything. He resolves to lie low and hole up in his room for the next few days. Like some criminal on the run.

Transistor radio switched on to the local FM station, a couple of tunes get played and then it's time for some British group with the goofy name of *Cupid's Inspiration* to take their turn. Their song is called *Yesterday Has Gone* and they're playing it just for Larry. Its message is too catchy and repetitive for him to avoid: the life you had is in the past, it's gone. Don't waste your time looking back, focus on the present.

Larry starts to cry. He knows that every word he's hearing is true. Life's too brief. So live every present moment to the full, minute by minute. Next thing he knows, he's laughing non-stop that it took listening to some dumb pop song to remind himself of something so obvious. How sick-making is that?

Having no satisfactory answer, Larry switches off the radio and goes back to sleep.

* * * * *

She runs to Zeke because he's the only one who is sure to empathise with what's happened. She knows that there will never be a man like her Laurent in her life again.

Hearing her words, Zeke intones: 'Only God can be God.'

All doubts erased, Suzie Q rushes to clasp herself to him. Because he's right. Because she's certain he's ready to receive her.

As good as the sex is between them, when they're lying side by side on Zeke's king-size bed, Susie Q feels confused. She's being flooded with memories. There she is noticing Curly Joe that very first time. And now, they've got as far as to start talking. And here's Larry being introduced to her. And their first wild kiss. And Vancouver. And The Triangle. The Circle. How it felt to have Larry inside her. And who'd have ever guessed that it would feel so different with another man? With *this* man?

She bathes in the heat of his body. She has so much to learn from him, she knows. But right now ... Right now, she doesn't have the first clue as to what on earth that could be.

* * * * *

Larry knocks on Billie's apartment door.

'Hey, hi! Where ya been? I haven't seen you in ages!'

'I've been in my room. In bed.'

'Why? Have you caught some bug or something?'

'No, nothing like that.'

'Then what? Something wrong, man? You okay?'

'It's finished between Suzie Q and me.' Larry tries his best to sound relaxed.

'What? No! Aw ... Shit, what a drag, man. I don't know what

to say. I mean, I hope I didn't have anything to do with it.'

'No. No, it was ... something else altogether.'

'Ya wanna smoke?' she offers, getting up, heading for the cookie jar that hides her stash.

'Uhm ... Not really, thanks.'

'Well, what are ya gonna do now?'

'I dunno. Hang around a while longer. Go back to work at *Paradise* tomorrow, I guess.'

She looks at him as if he's just this second grown another head. 'Hey! Ain't ya heard, man? *Paradise's* been shut down!'

Larry hasn't heard anything about anything for the past four days. The world could have ended and he wouldn't know it. Maybe it did. 'What? Yuh're kidding! How?'

'No joke, man. Yeah ... We got busted a couple of nights back. Pigs caught some freaks dealing so they revoked the licence. It's finished. *Kaput!* Maybe we'll get another place set up in September. If the stars line up in the right way.'

'I can't believe it.'

'That's the way it is, man. Reality's a bad trip. Fuckin' pigs.'

'Shit ... I just can't take it all in, you know?' Larry truly can't. The uncertainty of his future strikes home with a vengeance.

'What're ya gonna do now?' Billie repeats.

Unable to speak, he shrugs in response. He's too proud to do anything other than leave her to come up with the various possibilities.

It's now Billie's turn to shrug. Then, she adds: 'Shit, I wish I could help ya out, man. I mean, I'd really like ya to stay, fool around a bit, turn that downer you're on into a great big grin. But Dan's getting a little heavy about us and I'm not so sure he kinda wants me to be seeing ya right now. Ya know how it is.'

Larry picks up on the edge in her smile. *So much for freedom.* 'Listen, don't worry. There's really nothing to hold me here, anymore.'

'Naw. I guess not,' Billie agrees quickly, unable to stop herself from sounding relieved. 'Sure ya don't want a goodbye smoke? It's Colombian. *Primo* shit, trust me.'

Larry shakes his head no. 'Well ... It's been good knowing

yuh, Billie. Take care.'

'You too, Larry. Peace.'

Billie gives him the sign, but keeps enough distance between them so that any suggestion of physical contact can be deflected. She has nothing to worry about.

'Yeah. Peace,' Larry answers back. 'Whichever way yuh spell it.'

* * * * *

Monday August 4th, 1969

Moe,

This'll be brief. I'm heading back to Montréal just as soon as I've straightened myself out a bit more so that I can face the train ride back. Things have happened that I'll tell you more about. Suffice it to say Suzie Q and I have gone in different directions. It's all right. Just, please, don't leave Montréal over the next few days. I need you. Soon.

— Larry —

* * * * *

Turning his back on London Ontario, Larry vows never to set foot on its boundaries again. Something burns inside and he's ready to cry in joy when the train he's on pulls away from the station, heading for Toronto.

It's the Sixth of August; an envelope containing most of his earnings is addressed and in an Ontario mailbox. There's no letter of explanation; both he and Suzie Q know that none is needed.

For a moment, Larry tries to reconnect to the person he was back in May when he'd first arrived. Not a chance. All that comes to mind is the unshakeable awareness that here he is again, suffering the consequences of yet another dreadful mistake. What is it with him and women? Angel. Suzie Q. They used him. No, he allowed himself to be used.

And then he thinks of Pattie Pubes. Maybe Billie, too, for that matter. The simplicity and straightforwardness of their time together. They didn't use him. Well ... Maybe they did. But he used them, too. It was interchangeable. They all got what they wanted. No bullshit. Feeling the tightening of his stomach, the taste of bile on his tongue, Larry raises a shaky fist to the skies. Why didn't he see that?

Larry catches a reflection of his face in the train's not-quite clean window. Unlike his typical reaction, today he can accept how attractive — beautiful, even — he is. And, with that, a heart-stopping realisation sinks in: he can have any Pattie Pubes and Billie on the planet just by letting them see that he's noticed them. And is that what he wants? Yes! Yes, it is. That and to persevere with painting and drawing. Getting better and better at both. That's *all* he wants.

So yeah: yesterday has well and truly gone. Goodbye, Angel! Goodbye, Suzie Q! He'll never again allow himself to be used in the name of Love. Like the song goes, love is just another four-letter word. He's got the letters and the memories to remind him of that.

31. MOE

It's already the last Thursday morning in May. Moe wakes up earlier than he wants to so that he'll clock in at work on time. Showered and dressed, it occurs to him that it's almost summer. He thinks back, somewhat idyllically, to how he used to live out his days on the basis of "school time" and "holiday time" and that, under those rules of perspective, by now he'd be well into a regime of freedom and laziness. Dream on!

Rushing to The Flacon, combing his hair in its rear-view mirror, Moe tries to come to terms with the new reality he inhabits. Here he is, along with millions of other suckers, on an unvarying round of a "five days on, two days off" kind of life. Stuck inside an office, it makes no difference at all whether the sun shines or snow falls. As to time ... Well, as far as he's concerned, the only time that really matters is when the hour and minute hands on the silent mounted wall clock reach that life-saving 5.00pm configuration which gives him permission to pack it in and crawl his way home.

No kidding, Moe isn't enjoying his current working week lifestyle one teensy-weensy bit. Still, there's no denying he made the choice. Not that that's stopping him from giving it his best shot at playing victim just the same. Maybe it's all the instant coffee he's drinking to keep himself awake that's bringing on the shakes.

But probably not.

* * * * *

Moe's at his desk now, bum on seat, passing his eyes over to the expressionless faces trapped in the room with him. He asks himself how these people can go through their lives without complaining about the repetitive conditions their workaday world demands of them. And then, some damn voice inside his head points out that he's in the same boat, going through identical motions just to stay afloat. Which gets Moe speculating: *Maybe somebody else in here could be giving me the eye this very minute and banging on his brains trying to get wind of what keeps me doing what I'm doing. Hey! Maybe every single Barney in the room is noodle-scratching over that exact same question right now! Whoa! And none of us is doing a goddamn thing to switch the channel!* With that thought in mind, Moe lowers his head, musing on sackcloths and ashes.

What's mostly bothering Moe about his job is that it has shot his TV habit to hell. He can't get home in time to hear Paladin's latest philosophical pearls of wisdom. Worse still, every time he's stayed up late to catch up with Johnny Carson, he's slept straight through the alarm going off in the morning. Tough luck for Moe, VCRs are still a decade down the line.

And to top it all off, he's been left behind by both his pals. Curly Joe took a hike over a week ago and now Larry's headed off to Ontari-ari-ari-o. Which leaves Moe with nobody except Emily to shoot the breeze about all the really pivotal news stuff going down.

Like *The Who* putting out this new LP, *Tommy,* that they're calling "a Rock Opera". Whatever that means. Or how *The Beatles'* latest single, *Get Back,* seems to have settled into the #1 spot and is planning on staying there for good in spite of the efforts of some piece of bubblegum shit, *Sugar, Sugar,* by — I kid you not — an animated cartoon band named *The Archies* which has stuck itself onto everybody's brain so that they can't stop humming it. Oh! What about that Mark Volman guy falling off the stage five times altogether while *The Turtles* played the White House? Probably did it because he was shamefaced for being there in the first place. And let's not forget all those pretty pictures of Earth that *Apollo 10* just sent out from space. Plus, there goes *Gomer Pyle, U.S.M.C.* bowing out after five hilarious seasons. Couldn't possibly be because of all the rumours going around that Gomer's been dating Rock Hudson, could it? *Nah!* Uhm ... And let's see, what else? Oh yeah! Trudeau's House of Commons majority just voted to legalise abortions. That, too!

Most definitely, having to keep all this stuff to himself

makes it cold turkey time. With one exception. Moe's relying on dope more and more regularly as a way of papering over the ever-enlarging cracks in his willingness to endure the restrictive regime that his office life has imposed on him. As anxious as he still is about being made "Today's Poster Boy" for the Montréal narcs, he's got to admit that he's enjoying the soporific effects that the weekly dime of grass has on him. It's already become his after work ritual:

1. Make it back home.
2. Change clothes to casual shirt and jeans.
3. Place chair against the door to bedroom.
4. Put on a blues album and play LOUD.
5. Furtively light up and start dragging on that joint.

He doesn't mind keeping his parents in the dark but Moe wishes that he didn't have to hide his new-found lifeline from Emily as well. There's no denying it though, she'd surely freak at the thought of his criminal activity.

Periodically, when he's a little more stoned than usual, Moe allows himself to fantasise his pulling out a freshly-rolled doob in front of everybody while at his desk, taking a toke or two, and then passing it on to the Head of his Division. Now *that* would be too much!

That he's even bothering to play around with such possibilities gives a pretty good hint as to another ongoing problem Moe faces in the office: the other inmates have started steering clear of him as energetically as he does his best to avoid prolonged contact with them. Oddly, the reasons for this are the same in each case: both sides think that the other is dangerous to their mental health. And, for once, they might all be correct in concluding so.

As to the work itself that he's being paid to carry out, it's a piece of cake. Not that that's stopped it from going stale on him. All that Moe's mostly required to do is to add up numbers. However, because he finds such activities risible, as soon as he starts up a series of sums, his mind begins to generate totally unrelated thoughts. A Paul Butterfield riff might suddenly loop through his head until it becomes necessary to stop his additions and, instead, try to pin down which LP track the tune comes from. Or an apparition of a bare naked Emily might pop up challenging his memory to mentally paste on her various birthmarks and freckles in all the right places. And, of course, by the time his overactive his mind is put to rest, whatever calculations he'd begun are entirely lost to him. Twice already, he's been caught daydreaming by the floor sergeant and told to shape up or ship out. In retaliation, he's devised outlandish tortures to inflict upon this cretin. Which, of course, have now become another focus-point for Moe's escapist repertoire.

Moe looks around his desk with its pens and adding machine and scraps of paper and the photograph of a radiant Emily. He peeks out the window to a warm and sunny Montréal. And then he crooks his neck to pore over all the other desks around him and their occupants who work as slowly as allowable, and he feels ... Actually, the problem is that he feels less and less. Emptied out, it takes a lot to get Moe back into some emotional zone that he can access.

And these days, the only way he seems capable of doing this is to tap into gloom and doom possibilities. The main one being that since Emily took on a summer secretarial job, there's been some horny corporate lawyer boss sniffing her backside who just might beat Moe in the "Let's Get Rid of Emily's Virginity" Sweepstakes. At least the jitters that this horrifying possibility precipitates make turning back to number crunching something a lot more bearable. Even if it is, still and all, just one great big drag that can only be offset by taking a mind-bending after work drag or two from his dope stash.

* * * * *

Having just spent the best part of his day lost in a daze of sadistic fantasies, Moe rushes home to wash up, change clothes, and ready himself for a weeknight date with Emily. Oh yeah, a couple of tokes before heading out are bound to help. They're meeting in a bar that Emily insists on calling a Pub. Because of that, it's probably best to leave The Flacon behind and catch the *Metro* instead. Maybe one more toke's required to help face the joys of public transport.

A fish and chips meal and a couple of drinks too many later, Moe now finds himself sitting next to Emily inside a homeward bound 104 bus. Emily's doing her best to change the topic, but all Moe hears is the latest ploy on the part of her increasingly arrogant boss to pretend that he's not dead set on seducing her.

'That Barney's gonna have to be put straight!' Moe protests, interrupting Emily in mid-sentence and causing the French-Canadian *grand-maman* sitting behind them to grumble 'tsk, tsk' while frowning in righteous anger into the back of his head.

'Oh don't get mad, love,' Emily assuages, while smiling conspiratorially to the old dear.

'Well, *Kee-rist!*'

'And don't swear,' Emily adds mechanically.

'I'm *mad* enough to swear! Here's this jerk-off making hairy eyeballs at ya all day and —'

'But he *is* my boss, Moe.'

'Big shit! He pays ya for your work not your tits and ass!'

'Moe!' Emily yammers in reproach.

The 'tsk, tsks' start up again.

'Well that's the unvarnished truth, ain't it?' Moe answers, lowering his voice in response to the clucking sounds behind him.

'You *could* have said that in a nicer fashion.'

'Why? He's a shifty little creep.'

'But we're on a bus ...' Emily half-smiles, then gestures in the woman's direction with her neck. 'Other ears might not wish to hear,' she half-whispers, then does her best to recall when she'd first heard that injunction being uttered.

'Well, anybody listening in oughtta mind her own business!' Moe blusters on, failing to drown out the ever more urgent tongue-clicking that emanates from the irritated senior citizen's mouth.

'Oh, hush! You're only angry because we had to use public

transport instead of your car,' Emily's trying her best to veer him off the track. At least her efforts succeed in silencing their listening-in neighbour.

'Yeah, the Ol' Flac's gonna be mad at me. She doesn't like being left out of any fun events.'

'Honestly!' sighs Emily in stereotypical mystification, 'How men can take a pile of metal and address it as though it were alive and female is beyond me!'

'But she *is* alive,' answers Moe, matching stereotype for stereotype. Then, putting on a tough Texan accent, he continues: 'Whya, she's mah Flacon. Purtiest thing on four wheels West of the Pecos, honey pie!'

'Oh *do* be quiet!' Emily laughs, then mouths a silent apology to grandma who, in turn, has suddenly gone both deaf and blind.

'Maybe you're right. Maybe I *am* taking it out on Snot-Face because of The Flac.'

'He's a terribly nice man, really,' Emily offers before she can stop herself.

'He just wants a feel of the goodies.'

'Oh Moe!' *Here we go again.* Then, attuning herself to the agitated shuffling taking place behind her, she turns her eyes heavenward, her patience rapidly spinning to its end.

'He does though! I know his type!'

'But you've only met him once! And that was only a passing hello.'

'Once is enough, trust me! He's trying to be with it and cool wearing those apache scarves and paisley shirts and his hair tickling his ears. I betcha he even comes in wearing a Nehru jacket sometimes!'

Emily, for a moment believing in ESP, says nothing.

'What did I tell ya!' boasts Moe, glorying in his intuitive abilities.

'Oh ... Maybe he has done, once or twice. But, so bloody well what?'

Not unexpectedly, a new round of unamused and imperious 'tsk, tsks,' begins.

'So what? *So what?* So he's a phony, that's so what. I mean, there he was, flexing his arms every couple of seconds just to show off he's one of the Vim Boys —'

'He's very athletic!'

'He's a grade-A jerk-off, is what he is!'

'Tsk, tsk!'

'Why? Just because he keeps himself in shape? What's wrong with that?'

'I've got nothing against people keeping themselves physically fit. But there's ways and there's ways. Any way that turns ya into a slime-ball dullard like your boss is the wrong way, Johnny. Believe you me!'

'*Tsk, tsk!*'

'You're jealous!' laughs Emily, hoping that, in poking one of Moe's primary sensitive spots, she'll shut him up at last.

'Me? Come off it! I'm just pissed off that he acts like such a slob over you,' Moe tries not to, but he can't stop himself from squirming.

Sensing success, Emily becomes suddenly conciliatory. 'Well, perhaps you're right. Still ... It *could* be worse. He could have been a dirty old man.'

It takes Moe nearly a minute to process the implications in this statement. 'What did ya just say?' he asks somewhat aggressively, setting off another fusillade of 'tsk, tsks'.

'I *said* that he could have been a dirty old man,' Emily answers. *What could possibly be the matter now?*

'Oh, wow!'

'Tsk, tsk!'

'What's wrong?'

'Tsk, tsk!'

'what'cha just said!'

'Tsk, tsk!'

'*What* did I just say?'

'*Tsk, tsk!*'

'He turns ya on!' Moe accuses, while wiping spittle from the back of his neck and giving his attacker the evil eye.

'Tsk, tsk!' she responds, unperturbed.

'No, he doesn't!' squawks Emily, answering his accusation with a look that wishes to ask: 'How could you think such of me?'

'Yeah, he does! Ya just said so!'

'*No!* All I stated was that, thankfully, he's not an dirty old man.'

'Exactly!'

'Tsk, tsk!' the woman continues, though noticeably less obtrusively since she's now intrigued by the evolving plot.

'*So?*'

'So, ya got preferences!'

'Well, of course I bloody well have got preferences! If someone's going to slobber all over me all day long, I'd prefer it to be him rather than some ghastly old man!' Overcome by an unwelcome — and unfair — feeling of guilt that she wishes to be rid of right this instant, Emily turns around to confront their tormentor once again. 'Would you kindly stop making that fatuous noise, please?' she asks firmly with a frozen smile on her face. This nearly causes grandma to faint. Holding up the crucifix which hangs on a chain around her neck as though warding off demonic forces, she recovers herself enough to offer a passably redemptive and, mercifully, final response by getting up and changing seats.

'I can get that some old guy would be needing it more than Hairy Harry!' Moe continues, noting none of this exchange.

'You are *so* wrong there! Harry has difficult problems with his relationships.' *Oops! Now why did I slip that in?*

'Yeah, I bet he does. And I bet he just loves telling ya all about them! But that still don't change the fact that if he was some guy two whiskers away from Heavenly Acres you'd have told him where to shove himself and his tales of woe, long ago. Am I right?'

Emily demurs from answering him.

'Am I right?' Moe insists.

'Uhm,' she allows.

'Tell me: am I right?'

'Maybe.'

'Maybe,' Moe parrots.

'Yes, *maybe*. I think we ought to bring this topic to an end. Right now.'

'Yeah, ya could be right,' Moe replies. Having won some sort of moral victory, he can afford to be gracious.

'Now tell me: how did *your* day go?' Emily asks, picking up the thread of a conversation that had been abandoned what seems like light years ago.

Her query has the desired effect. Moe's off and running. 'Well, it started out as being one of those rare mornings when I managed to wake up on time and leave the house all pepped up to get into work early just to show the zombies that I mean business. *But*, instead, when I waltz in, all I get is the word that everyone from the Company President down to the Hungarian lady who cleans the toilets is so bursting to see me that they all came in extra early and had to wait until I arrived. So what that according to the clock I was sitting at my desk fifteen minutes early! There I am being told off for not coming in even earlier just so's they didn't have to hang around, frowning at their watches! And then, to make it a vintage morning, I kept being reminded of how there are hordes of people waiting, wishing they could have my job and that someone could pretty well get it if I didn't shape up. After that, it just went back to normal: sitting through a day of calculations and listening to the bozos in their cages whipping themselves off. Adding things up, I'd say that, all in all, I had a pretty good time.'

'Ha. Ha.'

'Riot, ain't I?'

'Tops,' Emily agrees, snuggling into him.

'Thank God it's Thursday. One more day left to go.'

'I've come up with something novel for us to do this Saturday.' Emily grins mischievously, pleased to be able, at last, to hint at her secret. 'I have to say that I'm mighty proud of myself for having thought of it.'

'What is it?'

'You'll have to wait and see.'

'No! What is it?'

'You just wait.'
'C'mon, tell me.'
'Not until Saturday.'
'Any guesses?'
'No.'
'Hints?'
'No!'
'Will I need my pyjamas?'
'Moe!'
'Ya got reservations for the bridal suite at the Queen E!'
'No!'
'The Sheraton?'
'No!'
'Your parents are lending us their bed?'
'Enough, Moe.'
'Tell me then.'
'No! It's a surprise!'
'C'mon. I won't sleep from trying to guess what.'
'Oh! You're terrible!'
'You'll tell me, then?'

'Yes, Moe, I'll tell you.' Emily catches her breath, makes him wait, pleased to be able to reveal all at last.

'What? What's your secret?'

'We're going to go kite flying on Mount Royal!'

Emily's revelation works; Moe's completely buffaloed. 'Kite flying,' he replies after a substantial pause, still sounding more than a little suspicious.

'Yes! Won't that be fun?' She's studying his reaction, on pins and needles for signs of approval.

'Uhm ...'

'Aren't you mad keen?'

'Yeah.'

'You don't look it.'

Sensing that he's being churlish, Moe changes manoeuvres. 'I'm getting my head used to the idea. Yeah, I like it,' he submits, trying his best now to sound enthusiastic.

'We'll take a picnic,' Emily adds, offering what she hopes

will be seen to be a bonus.

'Sure. Why not?' answers Moe, thinking of ants and other insects. 'I'm looking forward to it already.' He's hoping that didn't come out sounding as though he's just gone public to a particularly vile sin.

'Good! We'll take your car then. So that "she" doesn't feel left out.'

'Of course!' Moe says, brightening at the thought of the weekend. Then, to play it up, and to dispel any lingering doubts she might have, he puts on an old-world Yiddish accent. 'Don' vorry mein littul shiksa dollink. Lenny put zum gefilte fish in duh radiator an' all vot's gonna be fine. Emmis.'

* * * * *

The wind is blowing as though it thinks it's March and not the end of May. Mount Royal — already the natural habitat of dope dealers, still illegal same-sex couples, elusive bird spotters and single line processions of Ultra-Orthodox Jews — has been invaded by the tourists who take pictures of Beaver Lake, or ride in horse-drawn carriages (or sleighs when snow's on the ground) along pathways to the scenic Lookout Point or even all the way to the northeastern peak Cross.

Thankfully, avoiding this hurly-burly takes no great shakes. Numerous out-of-the-way paths and trails are easily found on Mount Royal. Once taken, they rapidly lead explorers away from both throng and noise. Having picked one and followed its winding track, Moe and Emily have ended up looking out onto a large stretch of flat, open land. About a fifty feet below, they can make out the tops of a forest of young, new leafed elm trees. Eye-catching as they are, they pose a potential problem to their enterprise. Still, what with the wind and the distance between them, there should be no likely danger of getting the kite getting itself caught in the trees' branches.

The kite itself is ready-assembled, plastic and purchased by Emily at her local *Woolworth's* for the grand sum of 99¢. It's not the most original or sturdy kite in the world but it has a drawing of an eagle on it and, most important of all, it is theirs. Unfurling it, they're both excited little kids again, taking in this near-majestic mountain world that couldn't possibly be at the centre of the bustling city, yet which somehow is.

Kite launched, it takes no time for the wind to take it flying clear up into the sky high as the string will stretch. Keeping a tight hold, Moe feels its breeze weave through his hair forever threatening to push him off-balance on the slippery ground. Sensing this, Emily presses herself against Moe's back and wraps her arms around him. Exhilarated by the feel of Emily's body up close against his, Moe begins to turn to face her but is promptly commanded to keep his eyes on the prize. As an added, if confusing, enticement that he do just that, Emily lowers her arms so that her hands fall below Moe's waist and begin to pet and probe as if innocent to the engrossing effect her ministrations have on him.

Sharing an unbroken contentment, connected as one, they feel themselves to be part of a strange, stretched-out umbilical flying machine. There's something so powerfully relaxing in their link to the kite; a surge of low-key energy vibrates from it so that its current rips straight through them, tugging at their lives as much as it pulls the kite ever skyward.

The cool and silent peace that hovers affects one of the thousands of friendly squirrels that live on Mount Royal so that it stands on its hind legs and points its paws towards its chest in a flawless caricature of a person asking 'Who, me?' Sniffing, it creeps closer and it, too, is overtaken by the languid energy that envelopes the scene. At last, the squirrel stands motionless, as if frozen, not in fear or distrust, but in total harmony with all around it.

Just like that, the wind dies down for a few seconds and they each respond as if the sun had been suddenly blotted out of the sky. The lovers skip a beat. The squirrel regains its wariness. And the cheap, plastic kite with its eagle emblem dips and ensnares itself in the tendril-like branches of one of the saplings below.

Rather than express irritation, Moe laughs and slips and

slides his way downhill determined to rescue their kite. Next moment, he loses his footing, nearly falls full-force flat onto the hard ground. Emily screams out a combination of fright and hilarity. Then, assured that he's safe and sound, begins to tease him. Remembering, she pulls out her pocket camera and snaps away. Moe's hair is flying wild in the air and the kite tangles itself up even further. To all appearances wishing to offer assistance, the squirrel skips after Moe then suddenly halts and quickly changes direction, disappearing into safer brush land.

Emily manages one more photo. It will become her favourite picture of Moe. Here's this skinny runt of a tree and, all around its topmost branches, is string and flapping plastic. And below, Moe swears in a resigned sort of way as he tries furiously to climb up it without damaging the newly-budding elm. He's just about halfway there and has grabbed hold of The Eagle when the camera captures that split-second in time. Right after that, Moe slips again and, in doing so, ends up enmeshing the kite even further. Calling on Emily to stop laughing and come down to help, Moe bends the nearest reachable branches towards her. Patiently, she tackles the unsnarling until most of the kite's string is let loose. Minutes later, Emily's struggles prove themselves successful and The Eagle is free to soar once again.

When the wind picks up so that they feel its chill, they agree that it's time for them to bring the ritual to its concluding phase. Reaching into her coat pocket, Emily hands Moe the nail scissors she's brought along. He passes hold of the string to her while he stretches and snips at it from as high as he can reach. Their end of the string gone slack, they look up to see The Eagle, now totally free, flying higher than it's ever done before. They keep their eyes turned skywards until they can no longer point to the kite's location.

They know it's almost certain that the kite will get caught up in other trees, or that, if the wind suddenly dies, it's bound to plummet far too quickly to save itself from destruction. And yet, there's always a chance of a different future. Perhaps it will fly for ages with all the freedom of the bird sketched upon it. Perhaps it will avoid the pitfalls, the false rushes, the luring of trees and ground. Perhaps it will make it.

They've done all they can. Whatever happens next is out of their control. Seizing hold of a sudden shared awareness, they begin to tease out a deeper understanding. *They've let go.* And, with that, they've kindled a happy-go-lucky acceptance of whatever awaits in their future. The wind blows through them and they nearly swoon from the certainty that there's more in the balance here than 99¢ and some poetic fantasy. Moe puts his arm around Emily and she, slowly, casually, leans her head on his shoulder. In that moment, cut loose to fly as they will, they, too, are truly and timelessly free.

* * * * *

Next day, on his way back to work, Moe stops in his tracks because the guy making his way into the *Queen Elizabeth Hotel* looks suspiciously like one of the Smothers Brothers. The funny one. *What's he doing over here?* And then the imaginary lightbulb above his head switches on: *Oh yeah! John and Yoko have been holed up in one of the suites since last Monday doing another "bed-in". Rock on!*

Too bad that Moe doesn't hang around longer. If he did, he wouldn't miss Allen Ginsberg, Dick Gregory, Timothy Leary and who knows how many other notables come dropping by ready to join in on a sing-along of this new tune, *Give Peace A Chance,* that's being recorded right then and there.

Another stake to the heart.

* * * * *

Tuesday, June 10, 1969

Hiya there, Larry boy:
How's the ol' roll of tarpaper, huh? Things down here at the homestead are just fine ... Keep all them cards and letters pouring in. And could you maybe send one to The Flac? The little nipper's dying to hear from you.

Seriously though ... I'm sorry I haven't written as often as I'd have liked to, but this job of mine is HEAVY. Pushing a pencil all day is a helluva lot harder than serving soft drinks and rolling you-know-whats, let me tell you! Not near as exciting, either.

Wow. I've just realized why I haven't written you yet, Larry. I haven't got a single thing to say! Would you believe I've pretty well exhausted all the news? Pretty buff, huh?

Let me see, there MUST be something ... Oh yeah! I peed twice already today! How's that for earth-shattering news? Pretty nifty, huh gang? Okay. Enough with the inanities. I haven't heard from Curly Joe since that letter from New York with the leaves in it. That's it. So my guess is as good as yours. To be honest, I'm a bit worried about him, too. Still, he's a big boy now, I guess.

Speaking of which, a couple of nights ago, we took in this weird new Dustin Hoffman movie, Midnight Cowboy. Ol' Dustin plays this hobbling doofus who ain't anything like Benjy-Boy from The Graduate. He is truly something to behold, take my word for it! Emily's made me swear not to let on to her parents that we've been to see it because it's been given an X rating and, according to her, with all the sex and swearing and nudity, it's the closest thing to a porno film that she's ever sat through. Keep it to yourself, but I haven't mentioned us sneaking in to watch I Am Curious (Yellow) last year.

Other than that, Emily's doing just fine. She comes over to my office building every afternoon since she gets off earlier than me. Her boss is this real putz who's dying to show her his schlong, so he lets her get away with anything she wants practically. Maybe at the end of the summer she'll touch it once with her pinky and he'll "pop his clogs". That's another of Emily's Limey phrases, in case you hadn't guessed. Weird, but a keeper, right?

Speaking of weirdos ... there's sure a hell of a lot of them around, boy. And during the daytime, they all seem to be locked up in the same building as I am! Confession time: this job I've trapped myself into is getting to be a real bum rap. I never knew I had it so good at dumpy Ol' McGill. I'm even kinda starting to think that it might not be a bad idea if I went back there in September.

Reading what I just wrote, I'm not so sure I know what I'm doing anymore. Okay, not that I ever did. But boy! I've been eating too many Planters Nuts! Yum, yum! Or, as Curly Joe would be sure to remind us Mr. Bob sez:

"When your head's got nuts in,
  You got nuts in to lose."

... Or something like that.

Anyhoo ... Weekends are the only things I'm living for these days. Other than Emily, natch. We're gonna get the Ol' Flac down to Lake Champlain now that it's officially summer and it's getting warmer. Visit our Amerikan cousins. Join them in an anti-war protest march or two. Breathe in some tear gas. Go on a picnic with some of them Weathermen kids. I hear they've got a great sense of Marxist humor they picked up from Groucho. Or maybe it was Zeppo.

Mostly though, we usually jump into the Ol' Flac and drive off somewhere on weekends. Up to the Laurentians or just out into the nearest countryside. It's still pretty quiet now, other than the mosquitos. And the green is just fantastic. I've been thinking of getting a good camera. Emily's got this little box-thing but it's more or less a laugh and a half. No, tell your dirty-minded mind that I was referring to Emily's CAMERA.

But ... Now that you've got me writing about Emily's box, guess what? I'm STILL pure! Yep. Bet you thought I'd never make it, huh? Bet you thought I was going to fall into the devil's clutches just like the Heebies warned us and get my berries to turn purple and green. Well, fooled you!

Not that that little serenade you played us on my birthday night didn't help keep me on the straight and narrow. Emily won't come to the house even when my parents are there, she's in such a blue funk about the place.

There's nowhere else for us to go, though. Her home is so

small and cardboardy that somebody farts three houses down and you can smell it in their living room. So you can imagine us trying anything on over there!

And there's no way she's gonna get into a motel. Not that I'd be Mr. Suave in that sort of situation either. More like Ol' Dustin again with Mrs. Robinson.

So what's left? Maybe if we find a totally secluded place in the country ... Just our luck though, we'd get caught bare-ass in some farmer's field. Wow. Now there's a picture that's just burned itself into my mind.

Truth is, Emily's convinced herself that safes aren't guaranteed safe and that, anyway, she wants it to be skin-on skin rather than feel rubber rubbing. If that makes sense. Anyway, the good news is that she's managed to get an appointment with a friendly gynaecologist who's agreed she can go on The Pill. Bad news? Emily wants to wait it out a couple of months and get her body used to things before playing "hide the boner". Which is probably the right thing to do. August seems like a hell of a long time away, though!

The way I look at it, I guess I'm doomed to be a virgin for life. Who knows? Maybe they'll turn me into a TV show. VIRGIN FOR HIRE. What sorts of jobs could a virgin do, though? Hand out towels at a Women Only Sauna Bath?

Enough. As long as there's an unused tissue lying around, I'll get by.

This is starting to sound depressing. How's Suzie Q? Has she totally recovered from her accident? I really hope she's all right and happy. With you there, she must be.

I'm really over the moon for the both of you. You're truly an ideal couple. You're both just perfect. I feel honored to have you as my friends.

Well, maybe if we get some extended time off for good behavior, Emily and I'll come over and visit you. The Flac is dying to be tested again.

Better still, why don't you guys come here? Montréal misses you.

I promise to write again soon. Or as soon as I hear word

from Curly Joe.
 All my best to you both. Be happy and don't forget to write.
 Love and wishes from Emily.
 And from me, of course.
 Emmis.
 — Moe —

* * * * *

The minute they cross over the Champlain Border, they know they've left behind the drab dreariness of Canada for something altogether different. Even the land seems to change: everything's greener, lusher, wider, louder. Most clearcut of all, are the differences in the billboards that line the highway. Their unilingual enticements tell it all:

HAVE A SCHLITZ - THE BEER THAT MADE
MILWAWKEE FAMOUS!

REVISIT THE OLD WEST - COME ON OVER TO
FRONTIER TOWN!

NATURE'S WONDERLAND: AUSABLE CHASM!

ARNIE'S - PLATTSBURGH'S COOKING AU FINESSE!

As a child, these signs, (and hundreds of others of similar sophistication) lining the autoroute to hallowed theme parks and beaches like colourful professional emblems, had electrified Moe and every kid like him.

Crossing over into the USofA, he couldn't help feeling that this — not that staid and bilingually proper land mass he lived in — *this* really was the promised land.

Like so many other kids his age growing up in the grey 1950s, Moe's recurring dream had been to wake up one morning and find himself upgraded to an *American* junior citizen.

Once on the other side of the New York State border, various nearby New England States — Vermont, New Hampshire and Maine — tantalised visitors to head for places like *Storybook Village* and *Land of 1,000 Animals* for a fun-filled family visit. Young Americans got to read their month's worth of Superman Comics a week earlier than their Canadian counterparts. And there were usually *five* TV channels to choose from.

Best of all, Americans had the Lake Champlain beaches to romp on during summer. No doubt about it: once you crossed the country line, you entered a better world. Probably, the best there was.

This childhood feeling still finds a way of hitting Moe full blast. Even now, as he crosses the border with Emily and their lunch basket in The Flacon, he feels that utopian happiness ooze over him. Sure, he's all too well aware of how sick and twisted the United States can be these days. *The War.* The race riots. Student protests. Nixon and Agnew. CIA assassination plots and covert activities. All of the above, and more, are grim reminders of what Amerika is really like. And yet ...

In spite of all that, some sort of powerful, pull-you-in illusion prevails. The come-ons and proclamations that everything here is bigger and best are such splendidly beguiling lures that, each time he visits, put off as he is, Moe feels like joining in and becoming part of the Great American Dream whose history he knows so well. At times like these, somewhat guiltily, he embraces all the arrogance and crassness involved. The way Moe sees it, just to have *something* to be crass and arrogant about is enough of a thrill.

As to Emily, it's like that brilliant moment when the bedtime fairytale being read to her became real and she could thrill to the magical world she found herself in. Except now, that moment happens every time.

Which is why here it is the weekend before the Fourth of July and here they are in fantabulous downtown Plattsburgh. Plattsburgh is a tourist town. It lives entirely, it seems, on Canadian weekend refugees. It even handles their money as its own. Every store and restaurant proudly displays the same message:

CANADIAN CURRENCY ACCEPTED AT PAR!

What better way of attracting more Montréalers to drop over and spend their Canuck dollars? And besides, nobody minds that prices have been hiked up by a few cents to soften the blow of any currency exchange losses. *Everybody's* happy in Plattsburgh.

Plattsburgh's other great attraction is its lakeside beach. Once, long ago now, when it was more peaceful, Mohawk and Iroquois Indians had paddled on the waters of Lake Champlain in search of new trading posts, or just in order to survive. Then the French and their guns came. Followed by the British. Wars were played out upon the lake and by its shores. People were shot and drowned. But still, it never stopped being cool and clear. True, these days the waters have taken on a distinctly murky colour. Might even be polluted. As to tranquility ... Well, it's hard not to hear the unending noise emanating from all the hotels and beach villas and trailer courts that have arisen nearby. Worse still, speed boats are busily making waves which add an oily slick to the lake's surface.

Current visitors sizing up the place are likely to get the drift that it's the beginning of the end. So far though, it hasn't stopped tourists from coming back regardless. Whatever its state, the water's warm and the sun continues to shine bright. The give-away priced liquor also helps to keep the truth at bay. Certainly, Moe and Emily both still fall for it all: the slow-burn New England accents and the hot sand to sit on and the squawky-speaker drive-in movies. Despite everything, it's still close enough to a dream or a fairytale come true.

Usually, they leave Montréal early Saturday morning and return in the pre-dawn hours of Sunday. They'd prefer staying there overnight but that's a no-no as far as Emily's parents are concerned. It's enough, to their minds, that they've reluctantly allowed her the better part of a whole day on her own in Moe's company. Such tyrannical conditions grudgingly accepted, upon arrival Moe and Emily park The Flacon as near to the public beach as they can get. Then they walk along the shore until there's a stretch that's relatively free of people and garbage where they can remove their outer clothes, lie out in the sun until lunchtime, eat their picnic, and then lie again or swim until it starts to get cooler and it's time to drift back to the car, drive into town for supper, and maybe catch an outdoor flick. Then, it's a drive back across the border and to their separate homes.

The part of the ritual that they both enjoy the best is protecting themselves from the sun's rays. They take all the time they want spreading lotion very, very slowly over each other. Intent on avoiding either one of them being sunburned, they make every effort to smear the ray-shielding goop smoothly over every exposed part of their bodies. Just to see to it that the job's done right, they spend a good deal of added time and attention creamily caressing those parts of their bodies the sun isn't all that likely to shine down on.

Emily always makes certain to wear a skimpy bikini which squeezes together — rather than fully covers — her breasts, giving off the impression that they're even bigger than they measure out to be. When she bends towards Moe, providing him with a knockout view, he invariably obliges her with the silhouette of an erection pressing against his trunks. Which, naturally, makes her smile, or, more likely, squeal with naughty delight, before rewarding its appearance with a quick tweak of its crown.

In spite of these brief sojourns into the world of sex, most of their day is passed away engaged in much more innocent pastimes. They build shoreline castles, play "I Spy" or bury each other until only their heads stick out of the sand.

It's only when they're both swimming, their torsos obscured by water, that Emily's pursuit of the utmost turn-on takes on a much more erotic focus. Always keeping an eye open for the unheralded appearance of strangers, she tries out every lascivious possibility she can imagine to turn on Moe until he begs for mercy. By this point, equally highly stimulated, Emily then dives underwater to pull at his trunks with such a yank that they are round his ankles in two shakes. Then, leaping up, she greets him with her top pulled down so that her erect nipples disport themselves tantalisingly before him. Having secured the desired effect, she sinks her hands so that they grab hold of Moe's exposed manhood and begin to rub and tug wildly until, almost in agony, he whimpers as an explosion of sperm bobs up to the water's surface. As to her own entry into depravity, she'll wait until later, when, drying out on the beach, she covers her lower body with a blanket so that Moe's inquisitive hands can pull down her bikini bottom and do their best to return the favour.

Ah, America! Truly The Land of Opportunities!

* * * * *

Emily is sitting at her office desk, sipping her morning break cup of coffee. *At least the java over here tastes better than that Camp swill we used to get at Tesco's.* A half-eaten muffin — which the shopkeeper insisted on calling a crumpet — keeps tempting her. *It tastes all right, but ... These heathens can't even tell the difference between a crumpet and a muffin! So hopeless!* She wonders if the French have similarly shocking tales to tell when they make their move from the homeland to this ... this ... She remembers Vicky, her best friend back home, informing her of how Canada got its name. 'It was Portuguese sailors, see?' Vicky explained. 'When they reached the Canadian coastline, they took a quick look and said: *"Cá nada."* Nothing here worth stopping for.' They were both in stitches over that one. If only it hadn't turned out to be so true!

Emily misses Vicky. And Sally. Ruthie. Even smarmy Dennis, her first real boyfriend. He'd dumped her when she'd told him her parents were determined to pull up roots and start a new life over here. Thank Gawd it wasn't Australia. Or ... Who knows? Maybe it wouldn't be any worse. And she'd only have to deal with *one* new language. *Who's Dennis going out with now? Hope it's some slag who let's him go all the way and then announces that she's preggo! Serves him right.* Not that they got up to much when they were dating. Sloppy kisses. Sweaty hand pressing on her clothes-covered boobs. Enough for them to fantasise about afterwards, on their own. Bet Ol' Dennis would never guess how far she's been willing to go with Moe. Probably have a seizure realizing what he's missed out on.

In point of fact, Emily can't quite believe it herself. When one of her pals had first told her that men expect their partners to suck on their willies, she'd nearly gagged at the thought of it. Now ... Well, now Moe doesn't even have to ask, does he? Okay, so maybe he begs for it. That almost makes her fall down laughing and want to bite him. Not that she'd ever come out and say it, but she quite likes Moe's willy. It's so ... so ... *there.* And when she's grabbed hold of it, it makes her feel so powerful. If only they could find a way for them to be somewhere nice and all alone so that it could wriggle its way inside her. *Soon* ... Thanks to The Pill she takes every day. She is totally bored with being a virgin. She wants to feel like a woman now, not some silly little teenaged know-nothing. But what can they do? Maybe they should rent a motel room, like Moe's suggested, next time they go to Plattsburgh. But then they'd need to lie about being married! And what if they're asked for some sort of proof? Also, they'd have to leave without spending the night there! And who's to say that next time they're in Plattsburgh someone from the motel or a regular guest goes and recognises them, puts two and two together, points them out as despicable fornicators to everyone? Out of the question! She'd never live that one down!

But Moe ... Poor Moe. He's being so patient. He says he's happy enough with what they get up to. More than happy. Emily believes him. She unreservedly trusts Moe. Maybe even more than she trusts herself. He's so loving and attentive and always flat-out eager to please her. Not just sexually, but in everything. And he does his best to be a gentleman, even if his language is non-stop rough and ready. And she doesn't always make much sense of what he says. So many slangy references to people and phrases that don't mean much of anything to her.

All these weird actors and comedians he obsesses over and tries to imitate without success as far as she's concerned. Flies right past her. And *she's* expected to guess right away who he's pretending to be! He even has a way of confusing her with famous stars she knows about. How was she meant to ascertain, for instance, that this *Marlon Branflakes* character Moe kept going on and on about was meant to be *Marlon Brando?* Well, *now* it seems so glaringly obvious. But at the time ... And, true, Moe did make her chuckle when he recited that "I could have been a contender" speech in this squeakily effeminate put-on voice. Once she does get his jokes, she can appreciate how funny Moe can be. But it's a struggle a good deal of the time. Still ... Moe knows how to make up for it. He's even told her that she looks so much like that actress who plays Mrs. Peel in *The Avengers.* Diana Rigg. Moe couldn't possibly compare her to someone so beautiful and sexy and self-assured. But he did. And he stuck to his guns about it, too! Lovely boy! At least he didn't think she resembled Hattie Jacques!

What a lucky girl she is to have Moe as her steady. Maybe one day they'll find a way of travelling together to the UK so she can show him all the places that she can't stop jabbering on about because she longs for them so much. Moe would simply love Guildford. So supremely *English!* She could take him on a wander along Farnham Road to her old home in Onslow Village. And they might go boating down the River Wey. Feed the ducks and swans. Then promenade along the High Street. Go window shopping. Afternoon Tea with cucumber sandwiches, jam and buttered scones, loads and loads of properly brewed cuppas. Oh! And foraging for wild mushrooms in nearby forests! Boletus! Chanterelles! Yummy! Not forgetting London, of course. A short train journey to Waterloo Station and then a double-decker into the West End. The clubs. The music. *Carnaby Street ...*

Emily's meditation is brought to a sudden end with her employer's abrupt entry. She rapidly makes herself look busy. Offering Harry a friendly smile, she twigs that something's not right. What's he looking so upset about?

* * * * *

- Hello?
- Howdy.
- Hello, love. What can I do for you?
- Well ...
- Oh! Silly Moo! I let myself in for that one, didn't I?
- You're learning fast, doll. Actually, the reason why I called was to ask what'll we do Friday night?
- Oh! Well ...
- Uh, ho. This sounds ominous.
- It's not! It's just that I forgot to tell you —
- Tell me what?
- Now don't be angry, Moe.
- What are ya talking about?
- All I'm trying to say if you stop interrupting is that I'm busy Friday night.
- Oh ... Okay. So what's happening?
- Don't go all tense, Moe.
- *Kee-rist*! Will ya just tell me what's happening?
- Harry's taking me out. And *don't* swear!
- Harry? Harry your boss? Hairy Harry?
- Yes.
- Oh, great.
- Moe ...
- Fantastic. Just fantastic.
- Moe!
- He made it. That scumbag made it.
- Moe! Come on now ... It's —
- How could ya do it? More to the point: how could *he* do it?
- He ... He asked if I minded working a little later on Friday night.
- What? *Jee-zus*! The oldest trick in the book. 'Would ya mind working a little later?' And she falls for it.
- Well, what could I say? He's so nice to me ...
- Ya could have said: 'No dice, Jim.' Ya could have said ya was busy.

- Well, I couldn't.
- Why not?
- Because he'd asked me earlier in the day what exciting things I had planned for this weekend and I'd said nothing special.
- He set ya up! That sneaky cocksucker ...
- Moe!
- Well, he did.
- All right, perhaps he did. But you can see that there wasn't any opening for me to get out of it.
- Wait a minute. Working late is one thing, but how'd he find a way to get ya to go out with him?
- Oh Moe, let's not argue. What's done is done.
- I just wanna know. Tell me.
- Oh! You can be so irritatingly obstinate! Fine. Have it your way. The plain and simple fact of the matter is that it was all so offhand. About an hour or so after I'd agreed to work later, he came back to my desk saying that he'd just been speaking to his girlfriend and she had a bad temperature and wouldn't be able to go out with him tomorrow and here he was with two advance tickets to see *A Lion in Winter.* Which, as you well know, I've been dying to go to but a certain person who shall remain unnamed has, instead, insisted that we pay good money to watch a squirmy film about male prostitution.
- Oh *Jee-zus!* Ya fell for *that?*
- I didn't fall for anything! It's entirely within the realm of possibility that that's what really happened.
- Yeah, sure. And maybe Nixon's really a warm and caring human being.
- Well ...
- Well what?
- Well, what can I do? I've committed myself. I can't back out of it now.
- I dunno.
- Come on, Moe. You know I can't. Don't take it that way ... It's not as bad as all that.

- Yeah, sure.
- Come on, love.
- What?
- It *isn't* that bad, is it?
- Whadda ya think?
- It's only my boss.
- He can still get it up.
- Moe!
- That's what he's after.
- Well he shan't get it from me!
- Tell *him* that.
- I bloody well will if he tries.
- Sure.
- *I will!*
- Okay.
- I will, Moe.
- Yeah, fine. Look, I'm sorry. I should have more faith in ya.
- Yes, you should. Anyway, it's only for Friday night.
- Yeah.
- We'll have the whole weekend! Shall we go to Lake Champlain again?
- If it's nice.
- Good. You're not angry with me?
- No ... But just don't go doing nothing funny in the theater because I might be sitting right behind ya.
- You wouldn't!
- You bet your sweet bippy I would.
- Oh Moe, that would be so hilarious!
- Yeah. If he tries to give ya a peek of his joy stick I'll just —
- Moe! Don't be so rude! But ... Would you really do that over me?
- Yeah. Of course I would.
- You're precious.
- Just dumb, really.

* * * * *

Emily is anything but dumb. She's seen through Harry's manoeuvres pretty much from the start. Despite that, she's felt unable to do anything other than accept and pretend ignorance. *Now why should that be?*

Some of it has to do with Harry's age, which Emily mistakenly equates with maturity. He's travelled everywhere. Done so much. Even been mountain climbing in Wales. And he's so assertive, so used to getting his way. She's discovered that she likes that in a man. There's something very pleasing in all the lavished, well-calculated attention he pays her. Even if it's so manifestly like stalking prey, waiting for the kill.

Emily's busy asking herself if she's been too easy. If he expects her to give everything up to him, allow herself to be seduced like probably hundreds of others he's charmed out of their knickers. But she'll fool him. She'll be the one to show him up, teach him that *she* isn't some dumb little secretary he can have his dirty little way with on the first night. Won't he be nonplussed then? Just wait for him to make a move.

Except ... He doesn't.

Instead, after the movie, he takes her out to dinner at a luxurious North African restaurant where he seems to be known by everyone there. And he doesn't make her feel silly by asking which of the strange dishes she'd prefer but, instead, suggests that he order for the both of them since he knows "what's palatable". And, when a flower girl comes by, he buys a beautiful big red rose for her to admire and play with. And the wine's heavenly and the food scrumptious, like nothing she's tasted before. As to their small talk, it flows so easily. She could happily sit still and listen to him detail what he thinks was good and bad about the movie, not least what was and wasn't historically accurate because he seems to know so much about British History. And when he insists on hearing her views and opinions, he really listens to what she has to say, treating her comments as equal to his own. Best of all, Harry sympathises with Emily's continuing homesickness and accompanying conviction that she can't ever see herself truly fitting in and feeling at home in Canada. As reply, he makes a point of introducing Emily to the only authentically English Tea House in Montréal where the tea doesn't come in bags and the pots have real cosies placed over them.

Further dumfounding her when he drives Emily home, Harry even seems shy about saying goodnight so it turns out that it's she who, without prompting, leans forward to kiss him. And was that really a slip, or was her tongue eager to touch the tip of his?

Afterwards, alone in her bed, Emily feels guiltier than if she'd allowed Harry's sweaty hands to grope every inch of her body in the back seat of his car. Miserable, ashamed, she forces herself to admit that her anguish has got nothing to do with what happened and what she is now conjecturing could have happened. Paradoxically, her not feeling the least bit guilty about Harry taking over as the focus of her longing is what keeps on stoking her persistent guilt.

* * * * *

Hoping to put Moe's mind at rest that their relationship is as strong as ever, and, as well, to rid herself of the interminable bad conscience engulfing her, Emily has volunteered to tell him everything about the date. Well, nearly everything. However, having just been asked to repeat the previous night's events for a third time, she's rapidly losing what sympathy for Moe's need to know that she's had up to now. She's trying her best to remind herself that there is a point to all this, not least by imagining all the lecherous acts they will carry out once this inquisition is over and done with. That, Emily tells herself, will surely put them back on even keel.

Regrettably, the venture doesn't work. Moe keeps coming up with more and more questions that feed his ravenous insecurity but never satisfy it. He's plainly flummoxed by Hairy Harry's behaviour. From what Emily's told him, the creep's acted in a totally opposite manner to what Moe had expected. He's forced to concede that his rival just played out a super-sharp move. He's underestimated him. Okay, but now what Moe needs to figure out is the rest of the prick's game-plan. It's definitely got to be something really sleazy.

Watching Moe unable to stop torturing himself — and her, come to that — Emily's begun to wish she'd just lied to him in the first place and told him she had a cold on Friday night. Oddly enough, his jealousy doesn't please her. *What's he got to be jealous of?* she asks herself. Pausing to answer this markedly facile question, she catches herself with the image of Harry her mind replays for her yet again. Right then and there, much to her shock, something shifts. Emily looks over at Moe and wants him to be different. She's never thought like this before. That naive gaucheness that had so appealed to her now feels irritating in ways that create an unforeseen gap between them. She so enjoyed being attended to by Harry — someone with experience, who assumed it his right to take the lead, who wasn't always so gratefully adoring of her. *So why hadn't he wooed her?* Rattled by this reaction in herself, she's left puzzling what all this means. It's as if she's been thrown into the middle of one of those silly *Mills & Boon* Romance novels she and her mother used to devour.

Noticing Emily's agitation, Moe picks up a perhaps hint of what's passing through her mind, and registers, not really knowing why, that there's no time to hesitate. Leaning towards her, he offers her an all-revealing hug. She, in turn, responds to the gesture. Sadly, their attempt to rekindle their passion fails. They find themselves going through the motions of concentrated seduction. Disconnected from their bodies' stimulation, instead what they both experience is unrequited misery on the shore of Lake Champlain.

Giving up, Emily restrains Moe's left hand from continuing its distractingly annoying massaging of her inner thigh. 'I'm sorry. I guess last night tired me out more than I'd thought.'

Moe pulls a face, not quite sure what to make of it all. 'There's just something weird in what you've told me,' he insists. 'I can't quite —'

'You don't believe me, do you?'

'Believe what?'

'What I've told you happened last night.'

'With the mugwump ya mean?'

'His name is Harry.'

'I know what that mugwump's name is.'

'Well?' Emily huffs. 'Do you or don't you believe me?'

'Sure, I believe ya. I don't think you could invent such an absurd story. Besides, I think I've got my head around his M.O.'

'His *what*?' Emily's not so sure she approves of Moe's conviction that she's incapable of constructing complicated scenarios.

'His M.O. That's cop talk for *modus operandi*. His plan.'

'Oh. What *plan* is that, then?' Emily asks, trying not to sound too eager to know.

'How he's gonna get a handful of fur-burger, of course.'

She nearly slaps him then. 'Why do you have to be so revolting? Is sex *all* that's on your mind?'

'Naw, it's all that's on the mugwump's mind,' Moe retorts.

'Then why didn't Harry try anything?' she taunts, sidestepping her own inability to sort out why he hadn't.

'That's part of his slime ball master plan!' Moe explains. 'See, he's smart enough to work things out that you're not gonna let him get his rocks off on the first date because that's what he figures ya figure the date's all about. So he does nothing. Totally above board. So what does *that* do? Well, right away, you're shaken up because ya can't work out what he's got going on in that sick-o brain of his. And getting shaken up already wipes out half your defences. So now, if he's played his cards right, all he has to do is to get ya to agree to a second date and that'll be it. He can move in for the kill anytime.'

'Drivel,' Emily's wanting more than anything to remove that self-satisfied smirk on Moe's face even if he has hit the bulls-eye. The only part of his analysis that he's definitely on the wrong track about is that she's far too uninteresting for Harry to invite her out again.

'No, it ain't. I gotta hand it to Ol' Mugwump, he's got style.'

'Which is a lot more than you have on most occasions!'

'Thank God.'

'Why on earth do you have to be so antagonistic to such things? It wouldn't hurt to have a little bit of style, would it?'

'It's bullshit. Hell, Emily, what style do ya want me to have? I'm not a swinger. I don't know a bunch of fancy names to stick on meals. I couldn't even make out the difference between red and white wine if I couldn't see the color! I'm not into that sort of stuff. I ain't out to impress.'

'But you'll need to Moe, if you want to succeed.'

'Succeed in what?'

'Your life, for one thing!'

'I don't need that to succeed. Look, I'm no genius but I know my brain's not defective. I can run and see and hear and talk and all that malarkey. The ol' ticker's okay, too. I've got two of the finest people in the world as my friends and I've got a beautiful young woman as my lover. To me, that's pretty successful.'

His account comes close to reawakening Emily's desire for him. 'You're such an idealist.'

'No, I'm not. I'm a pessimist; Curly Joe's the idealist. And Larry's the Romantic, just in case ya wanna know. '

She pays no attention to his joke. 'Well, it's not enough.'

'Why not?'

'Because you need money. Prestige. A good job ...'

'Crap.'

'You *do*! Do you honestly think your friends or some future wife would stick around if you didn't make anything of yourself?'

'Sure. One-hundred percent they would, if they were really my friends.'

Emily shakes her head. *Why does he have to be so clever-clever when all I'm trying to do is to remind him how the world works?* 'Oh! I do so wish you'd grow up just a little bit, Moe. You can't live on love. You need money to be happy and to let love continue to flourish. Love isn't the answer to everything, you know.'

'Ya really believe that?' Moe asks, thrown by what he's hearing.

'Yes, I do. I truly do.'

'Well, okay. You're right. Love isn't the answer to everything. I agree with you on that. But the thing is, there aren't any answers or lives worth a bean without love at their heart. But maybe ya think I'm wrong about that, too. I don't believe I am. Not yet, in any case. And if I am, I guess I'll find out at some point or other.'

'You'll destroy yourself is all you'll do!'

'Maybe. Maybe not.'

'Oh Moe, don't be so blind! Look around you! I mean, I love all the optimism that's been in the air for the past few years. Love and Peace works for me too! I want it as much as anyone else. But —'

'Do ya think any of these people we work with five days a week are happy running around like maniacs, killing themselves off, fighting tooth and claw to get the key to the Executive Washroom, and thinking of buying huge houses with their own swimming pools just to show off how much they've got? Ya wanna know what they've got? They've got nothing, doll. Nothing at all.'

'They've got salaried jobs and nice houses with swimming pools.'

'Wow. What else is there to live for?' scoffs Moe. And just like that, The Gypsy springs into his mind. *Oh! So that's what you were going on and on about! Now I get it! Thank you.*

'And what the bloody Hell is wrong with having things like good jobs and nice homes?' Emily cuts in.

'Nothing! Nothing's wrong with it. But it's not the most now or never thing in the world. Fuck, don't ya think that if I had the money to take ya to a fancy place and drink the best wine and buy ya whole bouquets of roses every single day, that I'd do it like a shot? Don't ya think I'd *like* to do that? But I can't. I don't have the money. But that don't make me a nobody. Like I said, I've got other things: my friends. My life. You. And you matter a thousand times more to me than all that other stuff ...'

In spite of herself, Emily re-experiences now, why she'd fallen in love with Moe. She's ready to beat herself up: how could she have ever forgotten? 'I'm sorry,' she says, on the verge of tears.

'What's there to be sorry about?' grins Moe.

'The way I've treated you.'

'S'alright. I'm still standing.'

They burrow into each other. And, unlike before, now it's for real and how it ought to be.

* * * * *

Moe's breakdown of Harry's scheme is, of course, totally correct. However, being Moe, he's failed to see its culminating game plan. True, Harry *is* simply waiting for the moment when the prey's positioned into a checkmate. Moe's mapped out the moves that far. But what he hasn't foreseen is that Harry's ruse is to get the prey herself to demand ritual murder.

Two more Friday nights for Emily to spend time with him is all it takes. And then, to no one's great surprise other than her own, Emily finds herself behaving like a witch on Walpurgis Night, slavering and grinding herself onto him as they shuffle through hollow early morning St. Catherine Street. Something has possessed her. Some primal inner physical force has taken over so that her body is forced to writhe in Spanish-fly abandon. She explodes time and again, internal bombs going off in some slow, painful, time-denying outpouring of pleasure.

Throughout her madness, Harry's control continues to be total and indisputable. Even when she forces his face to turn towards hers, even in that wild moment before the look in his eyes is shut out by her tongue's searching, he is still the Master. Inviting her back to his apartment, his offer isn't posed as a question. It's only when he begins to enter her that he meets any resistance. But even this is not of her doing. It hurts her very briefly, like the momentary pain felt in the fingertips when snuffing out a candle flame. And then the animal comes back again and she's lost to urges she'd never suspected resided within her.

Throughout the act, he remains unmoved by the sounds of her coming orgasm. He fails to notice the dampness on his neck brought on by her dribbling lips. He pays no heed to her loud uncontrollable sobs. He knows, as she knows, that what he does to her is all she's ever dreamed of or desired. More, perhaps.

But, when it's his time to peak, when his cock increases its pumping and drives even deeper inside her about to erupt, Emily is shocked to realise that all she's really wanted is the life-force that has driven him, and which now drives him no longer.

* * * * *

On the night following Emily's giving up of her virginity, a car deeply side-swipes another parked car and drives away before anyone notices.

Staring at The Flacon, gouged and maimed beyond any feasible repair, totally uninsured against such unprovoked and cowardly attacks, Moe walks back home in silence and weeps. It is, corny as it might sound, as though a friend has died. It's all that.

He's had The Flac for just over a year. She's taken them to NewYork and back and all over Montréal and so many other memorable places. She wasn't a beaut of a car, but, she was unpretentious and cheap and large enough to fit into and feel easy with. And she's a wreck now. Mashed up and mangled, lying in death, stinking up the street.

It shakes Moe hard to see such a major part of his life suddenly become the past. It spells out something grim.

* * * * *

Well here it is, July already. Streetwise Montréalers have begun to notice the growing number of fly-posters making it known that a massive outdoor concert is to be played out on a farmer's field in upstate New York. So far, reactions are devoid of any burning enthusiasm. Moe sees such postings here and there, notes that Paul Butterfield is due to play, and then forgets. The distance, strictly speaking, is much too real for him to contemplate the possibilities for long.

Right now, as it turns out, Moe's lying on his bed smoking his third joint of the afternoon, vaguely listening to a John Mayall LP. A week earlier, he'd bought himself a new *Hohner* Blues Harp and now he studiously blows into it trying his best to duplicate the sounds he hears.

His office work — if it can be called that —seems to be at a habitual stand-still. The way he's going on, he won't be able to keep the sick joke alive for much longer. Already, he's been labelled a wipe-out by his fellow workers. To prove them right, he's taken to shaving only every third day and making his — dependably late — appearance wearing the same old grungy brown suit that's so worn down it shines. Though he won't admit it yet to himself, he's clearly looking to be fired. If only in his thoughts — so far, anyhow — what Moe most wants to do is to tell these people what impossible things they can go and do with themselves.

But this isn't really what's bothering Moe. What's of far greater concern is that, recently, Emily seems to have joined their ranks in his mind. He has nothing to point his finger on since Emily hasn't yet told him about Harry's success. But Moe's got his suspicions. Just the fact that she's agreed to go out yet again with the bastard — and on a Wednesday, would you believe — is enough to pretty well prove to Moe that she's either taken him for a ride all along or else she'd felt pity for him once and has now grown bored.

What the fuck, he thinks. *Blew it again, Jim. When am I ever gonna learn?*

Moe looks into mirrors and blames everything on his face, his hair, his body, his clothes. Anything, in fact, that will make everything clear to him, even if only for a few minutes. A conspiracy of "maybe's" is taking over his life. He inhabits that twilight world where all is certain yet nothing's specific. With false swagger and bravado he's trying to assure himself that it doesn't matter. Except, it does. Day in day out, he can't stop feeling so depressed that all he wants is to escape. Easiest way? He's turning more and more frequently to dope. And, in reaction, he's edging, slowly but surely, towards a lifestyle where flying sky high out of your head becomes the only thing worth living for. As well as something equally worth dying for.

One day, exceedingly stoned and just as deeply depressed, Moe convinces himself that it'd be groovy to push things as far as possible before meeting up with Emily. That way, he reasons, she'll get around to seeing the light and maybe deign to take the lid off on what she really feels for him.

Seeing Moe, shaken by the evident abuse of drugs he's indulged in, Emily's confronted with yet another dishonourable secret she's kept from him. Harry's taken that virginity from her as well. But Harry never lets the drugs affect them like this. And, besides, they're different drugs. The kind you snort through your nose with rolled up $10.00 bills.

When Emily hears Moe ask her his slurred question, all she can say is that she doesn't really know how she feels anymore. It would be a lie to say that Harry hasn't affected her at all. For one thing, her body's never been so perplexing to her. Without a doubt, Harry's brought her out so far, it makes Moe's attempts at seduction seem clumsy and naive. She yearns for the uncontrollable eruptions of unfettered lust when Harry takes control of her body, for the electricity that charges through her. But that's all. Afterwards, seeing the instrument of her fervour dangle between his thighs, wilted and ashamed, she turns to the man for rest and condolence. But it isn't the right man. Worse, it may not even be much of a man at all. That's when she wants Moe there next to her more than anything.

She wants to tell this to Moe. She can't deny the craving that Harry has set loose in her. But, more important than that, she needs Moe to hear how, more than anything now, she wants the same — No! Even better! — to happen with him. To achieve this, she believes, they'll have to investigate what their their bodies are capable of together. And separately. For the moment, Harry's helping in that way. Moe should bloody well understand that. And, more to the point, how much he means to her and that it matters they come through this together.

But Emily hasn't counted on the depths of Moe's fear. As

soon as she begins to explain, he interrupts her and asks, flat out, take no prisoners, if Harry's fucked her yet.

And there it is. The all-consuming question. Emily wishes she could have waited until they had some privacy and then allowed Moe to fuck her. Yes, fuck her. Not make love. Because Harry fucking her is what set off all this wailing and gnashing of teeth. It's nothing more than a contest as to who's first to stuff his almighty prick inside her. Nothing else seems to matter. Moe's either forgotten or dismissed the fact that he was the first adult male to set eyes on her pussy. To rub and finger it. To kiss and lick it. Wasn't that enough so that all this contest crap could come to an end? No, clearly not. All this fuss over what? Her virginity. And what does that mean, by the way? She'd bled all over Harry's sheets. That had surprised him. Well, he'd never even stopped to ask if she was still ... Not that she is now. Funny thing, after he'd gotten over his shock, Harry had seemed pleased. Didn't mind about the sheets. Not at all. And is that what all this is about? Blood? What on earth makes men get so obsessed over virginity? Did it matter to her whether Moe and Harry were or weren't virgins? Would she have hooted at her success in taking Moe's virginity? Had she been disappointed that Harry hadn't been one? No. Not a jot. Stupid, stupid men!

Disgusted as she is by Moe's question, she knows it's too late for any other options. Even if she stripped off in front of him right now and begged him to do it, he'd still be wanting to know. Having no alternative that comes to mind, Emily answers him directly and honestly. She sees his face flush, his body go tense.

'I guess there's nothing else to say then, is there?' Moe asks, feeling faint, itching for more drugs.

She wants to shout 'Yes there is, you idiot! You dumb, stupid *man!*' But Emily's pride has been too bruised to say it. Swept away by what's happening, all she can answer is 'I guess not.' A moment later — pride be damned — she pleads: 'I do still love you, you know. In spite of what you are almost certainly telling yourself right now.' Equally infuriated and deflated at receiving no reply from Moe, she adds: 'Fine, then. I'm off. Don't bother calling me until you've grown up.' Defeated, feeling like not ever again giving a shit about anything or anyone except her own happiness and material wealth and all those things that she knows can't possibly hurt her, Emily scurries away.

* * * * *

Moe's dreams have turned curiouser and curiouser. In the latest one, he's been transformed into a worm and is quickly caught, baited and submerged under water. He sees a shoal of nosey fish begin to circle him. He even knows which one will be the first to bite. It reminds him of Hairy Harry. As it opens its mouth, he screams and awakens.

A whole series of sweaty nightmares, as upsetting as this, have been tormenting him night after night. As if this weren't bad enough, there's a real doozy of a recurring one that's first in line in scaring up the worst palpitations. Just as drowsiness begins to overtake him, Moe feels another force trying repeatedly to drill itself inside his head, hell-bent on achieving overall possession.

He's tried and failed to make out what this entity is, but it's definitely evil and the only way he can prevent it from fulfilling its goal is to make sure he doesn't fall asleep throughout the night.

It's a regimen that he's so far kept to but which has its own problems. For one, his parents aren't all that keen on being kept awake by a sleepless, shambling Moe who thinks it's okay to make himself breakfast at 3.00am.

Even worse, his "Stay Up All Night To Beat The Demon" gambit succeeds in getting Moe fired from his job. Arriving at work unshaven, hissing oaths to anyone who dares come near him, looking and acting more and more like a zombie, it doesn't help his case any when his one and only act of the day is to fall asleep at his desk.

What floors Moe the most though is that it turns out to be the other desk-slaves who rat on him. A mass protest letter, signed by one and all, gets circulated pointing out Moe's various abuses. Next day, he's swiftly booted out. *Good riddance, too! Couldn't have happened to a nicer asshole! These goddamn university know-it-alls think they can get away with anything!* Not that Moe cares. He could have argued his case, but why bother? Even the thought of trying to screw a bit more money out of those camp counsellors isn't enough to motivate him.

Having no commitments left, Moe severs all contact with the world. He stops going outdoors, barely eats, can't see much point in getting out of bed. He's even given up masturbating. All of what's left of his energy is being channelled towards the nightly struggle with his unknown invader.

Driven crazy in his desperation, he's given in and sold himself on the view that dope is his only remaining worthwhile weapon. He arms himself more and more thoroughly each day with what's left of his stash. Nice try. It's clear to him that the battle's being lost; each night sees him giving up a little more of his resolve to win the war.

As a last-ditch stand, he takes steps to revise his time-cycle through and through. Soon enough, he's rearranged his life so that he drops off to sleep right after dawn and wakes up around 4.00pm in the afternoon just in time for a re-energising dose of Paladin.

If his parents didn't welcome his bustling around the place in the early morning hours before, the added discomfort of hearing their son snore his way through the best part of the summertime day only adds to an escalating combo of concern and downright irritation. Even poor old Perry Como's gotten so confused, he's stopped singing altogether.

Case in point: what's left of Moe's eating habits is playing havoc with his mother's weekly mealtime menus. Having initially tried to accommodate to his whims and make sure he eats one decent meal a day, she's reached her limits and left him to fend for himself.

At the same time, his father, pinning everything on some primal rationality, has been coming up with more and more agitated suggestions that Moe goes out and gets himself a job as a night watchman. It's a sensible argument. But Moe isn't into logic. What he knows with 100% certainty is that he doesn't want to work. Work requires energy that he can't afford to waste right now.

Before long, Ma and Pa decide to leave Moe alone until he gets over Emily. 'It's part of growing up. Things'll get back to normal at some point or other,' they assure each other.

Then, as an added consolation, they remind themselves: 'Well, at least we know where he is.'

* * * * *

Nearly two weeks into his new regime, and Moe's getting quite used to it. The only bothersome element is that doing nothing usually leads to long bouts of trying not to think. Mostly, he tries not to think of Emily.

The fantasies he does his best to erase usually place her in bed with Harry, both of them going at it like no tomorrow, letting off nonstop fireworks as his ever-erect prick fucks her or is being sucked by her oh-so-proper British lips. Worse than that, he daydreams Emily whispering revelations about Moe's sexual ineptness into the creep's ear. He pictures and hears them splitting their sides at her accounts of his bungled efforts and feels sick to his stomach. To add to his woes, he imagines the bastard taking all this stuff to *The Gazette* and convincing them to run a full page spread on him in its Society Pages. THE WORST LOVER IN THE WORLD. Or something like that so juicy that every other paper in the country — No! The World — wants to publish it.

Intermittently, Moe's hatred of Emily feels so over the top that sweat pours out of every orifice and his teeth scrape hard against each other. If she were to appear at such times, he'd certainly do his best to strangle her and not let up until her next-to-last breath.

And then one afternoon, something in what Paladin pontificates upon before shooting the bad guy dead, has such a greased lightning effect on Moe that, at last, it rouses him into asking what he's been doing to himself.

* * * * *

Monday, July 20, 1969

A letter?

As if the moon landing wasn't enough to go crazy about, the never-ending speculations on what happened when Ed Kennedy left a party, drove off a bridge at Chappaquidick and got his female passenger killed as a result have become too much to sit through. As a result, I ended up on St. Lawrence Blvd. The Main. A street full of pimps and whores and Jews and Greeks and Italians and French-Canadians and junkies and derelicts and lesbians and homosexuals and garbage and barf and fresh fish. My kind of place.

Is this where you predicted I'd end up?

Good guess.

Looks like you get everything and I get nothing.

But what's it matter?

Nothing is everything. Everything is nothing.

Take your pick, doll.

I offered you everything, but to you it was nothing.

I thought you were offering me everything, but what you truly offered was nothing.

So we both ended up with everything and nothing while too confused to recognize which was which.

Think about that one.

The trap was set and we waltzed right into it.

Who by, you ask?

Naw ... Knowing you, you'd say: 'By whom?'

What am I trying to say?

I wish I could forgive.

I wish I could forget.

I wish I could be funny Ol' Moe again.

Cheerio!

                    -Moe-

* * * * *

Although Moe sees no point in mailing his letter, it still changes everything. Mainly, what it does is allow him to start breathing again. And, with each breath, Moe feels more able to fight off and ultimately gain release from that invading disembodied force. It's the first good night's sleep he's had in ages. To prove it, next day he feels strong enough to take himself outdoors, let the sunshine in. Without planning it, he's wended his way over to Westmount Park. He doesn't expect to meet anybody he knows there and, when that turns out to be the case, is grateful for it. Being around strangers is one thing; meeting and greeting still feels like too much, too soon. The main thing about being in Westmount Park is that it brings back memories of those times when he and Larry and Curly Joe used to tootle over here together hoping to shoot the classic 8mm film which they still haven't completed, or, just to goof off.

Sitting on the knoll near the park's tiny waterfall, Moe notices a group of teeny-boppers horsing around, playing tag or hopscotch or happily camped out on the lawn chattering away. Their raucous jabber and loud yelps of unconstrained laughter aren't winning the hearts of most passersby. Not that these kids are going to do anything about it. Odds are, they'd be shocked to hear that people are being bothered by their going all out to have a good time. Moe is captivated by them. Their lack of concern reminds him of how self-centred the young can be. Unless they decide it's in their interest to do so, the only voice they're willing to listen to is their own. *Was I ever like that?* Moe chuckles. *Maybe I still am. And maybe I should be more so. Regain some of that power and freedom which comes with selfishness.* Moe's well aware that he's creating another Golden Age castle in the air. Taking that on board, he still wants to hang on to the illusion. Reality — his simpering reality, anyway — is way over-rated as far as he's concerned.

As a special added attraction this summer, the City Fathers have deigned to recognise the existence of teenagers and allowed them to set up a Music Booth right up close to everybody's favourite Westmount Park garden path. Much to the dismay of the Powers That Be — who'd never really expected their offer to be taken up — the Music Booth has become a great success. It seems as though every disaffected youth from the area is bringing favourite singles and LPs to play as loud as possible throughout the day. For good measure, what the municipal council Straights have failed to sniff out is that their efforts have also encouraged a now thriving dope trade which has set up its invisible shop right next to the music venue. The kids are being extra cautious to make sure that that particular cat isn't going to be let out of their nickel and dime baggies. As vigilant as they're being, to those like Moe who know how and where to look, the sight of teens and even pre-teens guardedly toking up behind the park's trees or hidden by low-lying bushes comes as an unnerving revelation. Until now, Moe had assumed that only college types ever toyed with the options offered by drugs. And yet, here's these ... these ... *children* flying eight miles high right in front of him.

Unnerved, Moe takes the wraps off his memories of being twelve or thirteen, when he was still more absorbed in playing with his *Dinky Toys* than with the dinky that hung, limp and unused, between his legs. As to drugs, they were totally unknown to him except as medicine his mother gave him when he was ill. *Who would have wanted to sneak off and take medicine?* The most he'd ever done was to try out cigarettes, and he hadn't done much of that anyway because he hated lighting matches. And yet, in the space of only some six years, here comes a whole generation that is totally something else. *Kee-rist! And they probably fuck already as well! What the hell are they gonna be like when they reach my age? Assuming they can be bothered making it that far.*

Still, he's drawn in. Behind all the bravado and tough talk on display, the innocence in their eyes gives them away. And it's there in their faces, as well: taut bright new skin with no hint of the scars that will be sketched onto them soon enough. Maybe deep down, Moe guesses, they're not all that different to how he was at their age. They're just being guided by a different set of illusions.

* * * * *

After a couple of days of hanging around the park, Moe starts to get noticed. At first, all he receives from the kids are hesitant nods of recognition. Not long after that, some of the feistier ones start offering him guarded hellos or some equally tolerant form of silent greeting. Eventually, concluding that Moe poses no danger, a few of them even deign to engage him in chitchat focused on the music being played. The fact that Moe hasn't shaved or cut his hair for weeks, and that he changes clothes as rarely as possible, has helped no end. This "bum look" is about to make it big in Montréal and Moe looks to be one of the innovators of the style.

Once Moe is allowed to start talking, he has most of them instantly enthralled. His hip patter, encyclopaedic knowledge of modern music and his passion for Electric Blues further teases his audience to the point where some eagerly invite him to bring over a couple of his own records so all can hear what he's so excitedly going on about.

And with that, adoration sweeps in; Moe's their newly-anointed guru. *If they only knew!* But what's the harm in basking in such an ego-boosting role for a while? And who's to say that what they're looking for from him is completely off the rails? Could be, he might have something worthwhile to offer. If nothing else, he's turning them on to sounds that make musical mincemeat of the predominantly Plastic Pop they've been playing.

* * * * *

What the fucking fuck is going on? Sweaty hands are snaking up his jeans, causing Moe's prick to respond in the most expected of ways. He has to keep reminding himself that no, he's not dreaming. This is all too unreal for it to be a dream.

Truth is, Moe's a guest at a party being given by one of his newfound followers. He accepted the invitation on an impulse to tag along as a not quite squeaky-clean paternal presence.

Twenty minutes into the performance, Moe's mind has been blown so far away, he's given up trying to be anyone except who he is: the oldest kid in the room having the time of his life.

The wealthy Westmount family Moe-worshipper who's throwing the bash points Moe to the trays of snacks and sandwiches laid out in the kitchen. Moe takes a look and feels ravenously hungry.

Music's playing turned up to the max on what seems to be the most expensive piece of stereo equipment going. He's never heard *Beggar's Banquet* sound so clear.

No sign of any alcohol. But dope is riding high in the charts. Everyone seems to have brought their own. Except for Moe, of course. He hasn't brought anything. But then, keeping to the status accorded him, he wasn't expected to.

He hasn't dressed up like everybody else, either. Which is, as well, exactly what everybody wants.

From time to time, one of the kids comes up to ask for a private audience. Moe consents, of course. The variety of topics and concerns being presented staggers him. Clothes and hairstyles. Irritating parents. High School dramas.

Music's in there, too. One kid's found the courage to invite Moe to come along and give a listen to the "Montréal Blues Sound" he and his bandmates are messing around with. Maybe he might even find it in his heart to jam along with them?

But then, some of these half-pints are worried about things Moe's hardly even thought of, much less experienced. Predictably, pimples and acne are a common concern. But so too are questions dealing with what to do about coming too soon or what the proper way to go down on a girlfriend or lick up a boyfriend's semen get thrown in as well.

Doing his best not to blush, nor to tip off anyone of his ignorance, Moe is creative enough to provide fanciful answers that, much to his relief, seem to satisfy his questioners.

Plus, the comedian in him resurfaces so that, in minutes, he's got an appreciative audience he can amuse with his latest song scrambler:

What becomes of the broken-hearted?
He bent to kiss her but then he farted.

That has them all in stitches. Hardly surprising, really. What junior high school kid doesn't still think fart jokes are hilarious?

In gratitude, if not adoration, joints are handed to Moe for lighting. He denies no one. Inhaling deeply, never coughing, as a Master would be expected, he takes his time before passing the doob to one of the many wide-eyed admirers, all of whom appear to be experiencing cherubic enlightenment just watching Moe get more and more blocked out of his skull. Now and again, Moe even sees fit to nonchalantly ordain that one particular specimen could be categorised as "pretty good". Not that he's in any way capable of rational judgement.

Either minutes or an eternity later, disco lights start flashing and eager couples get up to show off the latest mover-and-shaker mode.

In no time at all, what looks to Moe to be a mob of single female boppers take turns to shyly shuffle up to him in order to enquire whether they're worthy enough to be granted a dance.

This is jailbait, a minute part of Moe's mind warns. But the hesitant faces, like the music, are too seductive for him to pay it much attention. Besides, all he's going to do is *dance* with them.

Way too many dance partners later, wiped out by the hyperactive boogieing he's grooved on, Moe is more than ready to sit things out again.

Fat chance. The most unexpected in this long line of unexpected events is about to happen.

Someone (possibly the host) shouts above the din of music and talk and broadcasts the start of something he names as "Group Grope Time". Loud cheers erupt for the revellers. 'Turn off the lights, then!' they shout until their command is obeyed.

Finding himself suddenly in the dark both literally and metaphorically, Moe skulks his way toward a corner of the room and crouches down low. Scrunched up on his own, hearing gasps and cackles and even the intermittent satisfied rasp taken to its overexcited limit, his mind races to its furthest reaches doing the best it can to re-awaken reminiscences of playing "show me/show you" games as a kid.

Not having uncovered much to wax nostalgic about, Moe's search is cut short when he feels a determined hand grab hold of his knee. Its pressure awakens him to the reality of his situation.

'Wait!' Moe whispers. 'How old are you?'

His question is met by a bemused snicker. 'Sixteen,' the voice answers.

Whew! It sure sounds like it's a she, Moe thinks. 'Don't lie. I need to know the truth.'

'I'm not lying! I'm really sixteen.' A pause. 'Only —'

'Only what?'

'My "Sweet Sixteenth" was three weeks ago. So I'm only just sixteen, I guess.'

Only just sixteen, Moe repeats to himself. *Well, at least it's legal. Just about.*

'Do you wanna, or what?' the girl asks. 'Because if you don't —'

No hesitation. 'I wanna.'

'Neat!'

Before Moe can change his mind, he hears his partner whisper that he should remove his shoes. As he begins to follow orders, Moe worries whether his feet might smell. He leaves all such concerns behind him as soon as he feels the weight and pressure of her body squatting astride him. In response, Moe's open hands reach upward to cup her still-covered breasts. *Yes! No doubt about it. She is most definitely a she.*

Prying and poking, they allow their mouths to meet, silken tongues curling and straining to their limits. Wasting no time, his partner's adventurous fingers wedge themselves inside Moe's unzipped jeans and slither under the elastic band of his briefs. At about the same time, Moe rather clumsily prises apart the catches to her cotton brassiere so that it gives way and his palms fill up with pliant putty flesh.

'Tit for tat,' she laughs as her hands find their desired goal and free it from all restraints.

Okay, then ... Moe turns his attention downwards, unclipping her jeans.

'Should I take them off?' the mystery girl asks, sounding almost apologetic for not having thought ahead. 'And what about —'

'Yeah, sure, everything. Take it all off,' answers Moe. *Keerist! Ya only live once.*

She leaps off him while he listens, not needing to imagine what comes next. Moments later, as she begins to squat down on him again he reaches for her, pawing her already aroused sex. For a second, he thinks of Emily and how he loved to hear her responsive purrs when he did the same to her.

'Ooh! That feels really, really nice! Don't stop!' the girl interrupts his thoughts. *So long, Emily.*

Finding the approximate location of one of her ears, Moe whispers: 'Are ya a ... virgin?' Then he blushes, grateful for the room's darkness.

'No! Definitely not!' the girl answers, sounding offended.

'Three minutes!' a voice shouts out of nowhere.

'Shall we ... You know ...'

'Fuck?' she says.

'Yeah, I guess.'

'Oh! We can't! It's not allowed. Only groping. Maybe if we meet up again, later?'

'Oh, right. Okay. I didn't know.'

Sensing disappointment, Moe's rule-bound companion swoops down onto his still swollen member, encases it between her lips, then begins to suck while fondling his balls. Dumbstruck by her keenness, he comes in seconds. *Goshwowboyoboy!* Moe's lost all contact with anything approaching ordinary consciousness. His mind inspires visions so ecstatic they make the apocalyptic anecdotes of St. John seem like the jottings of a bathos-filled adolescent. Before he can come back down to earth and rationalise what's happened, Moe feels lips kissing his and tastes himself.

'One minute to go!' the unknown MC's voice calls out.

Leaping off him, Moe's already ex-partner picks up her scattered clothes, dresses herself and then disappears.

When the lights are turned back on, were it not for the all-too-prominent grins of sexual satiation, everything regains the appearance of social gathering normality. Moe looks around, eyeing up each female in the room, trying to guess which one ... Then a hand offers him a joint.

* * * * *

Back at home, next morning Moe finds Larry's letter waiting for him. When he finishes reading it, he has no doubts that their summer is flat out over. So much has undeniably happened to Larry. Probably to Curly Joe, too, wherever he is. And, it goes without saying, something significant has happened to him as well, though he can't quite think up too many words to explain what.

Moe lights a joint and thinks back to the teeny-boppers' party. In spite of her offer, he'd seen no point in seeking out his mystery partner for further fun and games. *You're still a virgin.* He cracks a smile in spite of himself. *One more chance of a lifetime down the drain.* And, with that, he promises himself he won't be returning to Westmount Park for a while. Although ... That other kid's offer to drop in on his band's rehearsals could be a gas. Probably a waste of time but ... He smoothes out the scrap of paper with the address and phone number. What else has he got on the cards anyway?

Assessing his state, Moe's got no doubts that he's not anywhere near being happy with his life. If anything, he's more confused than ever. He'll take that confusion with him when he goes to re-register at McGill. Thing is, he kind of liked hanging around with those kids. They listened to him. More, they trusted him. *Kid Protector.* Might be, there's a degree in something like that. Maybe he's finally got a handle on what he wants to become. One more toke, and Moe feels ready. Ballpoint pen in hand, blank sheet of paper on his desk, he begins to write:

Hi, it's me again.
I think I've grown up.
If you're "chuffed" enough to want to see if you agree, let me
know.
Love
— Moe —

This time, he'll make sure he mails the letter.

32. AND CURLY JOE

Unable to dismiss its message, Curly Joe's decision to hit the road is all down to this dream he had three nights ago and still can't stop it from jangling his brain. It was an absurd re-enactment of Jonah and the Whale, with Curly Joe in the leading role. Curly Joe doesn't usually have much of an interest in Biblical tales so he assumes that the dream must be pointing him to something more current. Actually, it's a breeze to interpret: it's got to be about the whale's tooth. So what's he going to do about that? He doesn't regret passing on the tooth to Eve but since having done so he's lost the clarity he once had about what he's meant to be up to. Which, he's certain, has to be the point of the dream.

Alone in his backyard, toking on a surreptitious joint, it comes to Curly Joe that he needs a Guide to set him back on track. Yeah! That makes sense! And, basically, there's really only one candidate he can think of who fits the bill. Which is why heading out is the only option he's got.

It takes Curly Joe another couple of nights to set things in motion once and for all. He's sitting at Moe's kitchen table, talking about this and that, when he overhears himself let drop that he's got to leave Montréal. Maybe for a week or a couple of months. Can't say for sure. He keeps the destination to himself as well. Moe might try to argue him out of it, or maybe even ask to come along. Forget it! The mission he's embarking on has room for only one volunteer. In any case, Moe has a summer with Emily to look forward to and Larry and Suzie Q are bound to cook up ways of spending time together as well. *Let the happy couples get on with it,* Curly Joe's newly-regained resolve whispers to him.

First thing next morning, Curly Joe resigns from FUCK. Luckily, it's one of those days when Larry isn't around so he doesn't have to go through another round of explanations. It's going to be difficult enough putting his parents in the picture without them going bananas over his mental state. Mercifully, they're relatively laid back about it. Could be because he's made it sound like he's off on an extended camping trip that will get him outdoors, breathing in the fresh country air. Agreement to keep in regular phone contact made, he's home free and ready to roll.

* * * * *

Sleeping bag and backpack. *Check.*

The $200.00 he's saved up hidden in various items of clothing. *Check.*

Quick detour to the corner magazine shop on Greene Avenue to buy a brand-new Thought Book. *Check.*

Hopping onboard at Atwater Station, Curly Joe rides the *Metro* to its South Shore endpoint and then tramps over to the thruway leading to AutoRoute 9. Behind him, in the distance, he can still make out Montréal's skyline. He has no idea how long it will be before he'll see it again. Not wanting to think about that, he sticks out his thumb and begins to hitch.

A little over twenty minutes later, he's picked up by a Black couple heading back to their hometown, Newark, New jersey. They have fun teasing Curly Joe by only referring to him as "The Honky" and take turns drinking from a bottle of bourbon that they've stood up between them on the front seat. They are as disinterested in exchanging their life histories with Curly Joe as they are in sharing their liquor. But still, they're friendly enough and, being honest about it, he isn't all that disappointed not to be offered either gift.

They drive non-stop to the Champlain Border where a bored American guard goes through a predictable and uninspired routine before waving them on. The Black couple whoop with satisfaction at being back on American turf, pull out the bottle of bourbon that they'd hidden under the front seat, and get on with their celebrations. They drop Curly Joe off near the SAUGERTIES exit. As a token of comradeship, they ask him if he'd like a quick taste of their liquor. Not really looking forward to it, but feeling an odd sort of obligation that comes with hitching a free ride off strangers, he nods in assent. They hold the bottle upside-down so he can see that it has been drained to the last drop.

'So would we, man!' the male guffaws, 'Boy! Betcha ya got the taste for it now ain'tcha, Honky?'

They all slap palms to show that there are no ill-feelings, and then the couple drives off.

Upbeat, pleased to have gotten so far so quickly, Curly Joe gathers together his belongings and scoots down the artery road. After over a half hour of covering ground, not quite sure where to go and getting nowhere fast, he comes upon a road sign pointing to WEST SAUGERTIES. Of course! This is the solution. According to the record sleeve he's studied countless times since buying their LP, West Saugerties is where *The Band* hang out and record their music. All he has to do is to find *Big Pink* and then ... They're bound to know where Dylan lives. And they'll tap into how urgent it is that Curly Joe meet up with him, even if only just to offer birthday greetings to his sure-to-be-willing Guide.

* * * * *

A couple of hours later, looking all around unfamiliar and unwelcoming countryside, Curly Joe is asking himself if he's crazier than he'd thought in having embarked on this half-baked pilgrimage of his. He notices the blood-orange sun setting down below what must surely be Overlook Mountain. Momentarily calmed by the tranquil scene, he plops down onto the verdant grass and focuses on the darkening sky. Taken in by the glory of it all, he totally gets it as to why so many ancient traditions dedicated themselves to the veneration of the sun. Hell, right now, he's ready to start a tradition of his own. On the spot, Curly Joe recalls the series of yogic exercises that make up The Sol Cycle. Maybe he should try to enact them. His attempts at worship are woeful and remain uncompleted due to his cracking up with self-effacing laughter part way through. Nothing to get hung up about. Ol' Sol won't mind. Hands down, all that does matter is that it's early evening, the 22nd of May, 1969 and he's sitting cross-legged all on his own somewhere on the outskirts of the small town of West Saugerties, in the State of New York. Re-invigorated now, Curly Joe renews his pursuit.

Another hour passes by. One more trail gone cold, he chances upon a tumbledown wooden shack. Curious, peeking inside, he notices that half its roof has blown off and, judging by its state of disrepair, it must have happened some years back. Plus, the structure stinks of rotting timber and unbaled hay. Still, on the positive side, there are no apparent signs that anybody's currently making use of it. Almost sold on the idea that he's found the perfect place to sleep for the night, Curly Joe throws himself into dragging piles of hay to where he guesses is sure to be the most sheltered section of the hut. Cosy mound now plumped up and waiting, he unfurls his sleeping bag over it and takes the weight off his feet. He lasts about five minutes before the stench of dried grain and shit becomes unendurable. Maybe hunking down outdoors makes more sense ...

Curly Joe earns himself a couple of hours of sleep before stirring. It's scarily dark and way past chilly now. The shack, and the protection it offers, regains its earlier attraction. By chance, he finds his previous resting place. He pretends to have gotten used to its stink. It helps to bury his head all the way inside the fully zippered sleeping bag. Curly Joe allows himself the briefest of smiles. His passing thoughts lead him back to last year's cross country trip. Moe would go insane now. Not that he's doing all that great tonight, either. *no! come on, you're doing fine!* He sniffs his underarms. Uhm ... Hopefully, he'll find somewhere to wash in the morning. *oh, for the pleasurable luxury of my bed and bath back at home. stop! enough with the self-torture!* Settled on comforting himself that his plan is both right and necessary, at last alert to the signs of sleep descending, Curly Joe shuts his eyes once more. They stay shut for the rest of the night.

* * * * *

He awakens with the dawn, feeling stiff and hard up to wash himself. Not too far from his manger he finds an idyllic burbling stream. The water is cold and clear and Curly Joe wonders if anyone would report seeing a naked male jumping into it. Resolving not to worry over such matters, he strips off and wades in. Nearly ten minutes later, he's back on land a little bit cleaner and drying as quickly as the sun will allow. Now much more willing to face the world, he makes his farewells to his overnight home and moves on.

A local farmer driving a station-wagon loaded down with Hessian bags full of compost sees Curly Joe dawdling along not sure where he's going and stops to offer him a ride into Woodstock. Well ... Since that's where everybody thinks Dylan camps out these days, it's probably sensible to give up on his search for *Big Pink* and head straight to the source. Good odds that *The Band* will be making their way over there as well so they can join in on tomorrow's birthday bash.

Hanging out in Woodstock, working through what to do next, Curly Joe keeps overhearing animated discussions between its resentful citizens about some threatened music festival that nobody seems to want to happen. Why are they so against the idea? This *is* an artists' colony, after all. And, bottom line, if it's okay for Bob, it's got to have something right going for it. Come to think of it, if this local musical shindig does take off, he's bound to be performing at it, right? *Wow!* So what's the problem? Well, okay. The place looks a little bit over affluent and self-satisfied with it. Not all that eager to be hosting a summertime jamboree. But still ... If it means that there's a chance that Bob'll be back on stage ...

Funny thing is though, even that possibility doesn't allow Curly Joe to wave away the inexplicable unease that keeps nagging at him. Being so close to having completed his quest, he should be glowing by now. Instead, he's full of fear and trembling. Something just doesn't feel right. Maybe he should stop for a moment, settle himself down on the stretch of grass alongside the path he's on and try to figure things out. Alarmingly, this strategy only succeeds in triggering added levels of anxiety. *maybe it's hunger,* he half-convinces himself. Bound to be lack of food and drink; he hasn't eaten anything now for nearly twenty-four hours. Happily, there's a General Store up ahead. That should sort things out.

Inside, armed with some home-baked bread, cheddar cheese slices, a small jar of *Skippy Peanut Butter* and a quart of milk, Curly Joe notices something that almost makes his heart stop. Right there, hanging in a row behind the friendly smiling salesclerk, are over a dozen whale's teeth that look exactly like the one Nature Girl placed around his neck. *How is that possible?*

The shopkeeper catches Curly Joe poring over the display and half-turns to admire them himself. 'Pretty nice, ain't they? Popular, too.'

'are they whales' teeth?'

'You betcha. *Sei* whale, they tell me. Come all the way from Maine. Massachusetts too, maybe.'

'and people just come in and buy them?'

'That's what I've got them whirling in the air for. They sell real quick, like I said. Mainly youngsters like yourself. Hippies. Yippies. Freaks. I don't know, whatever you kids go around calling yourselves these days. Hard to keep up, lemme tell ya.'

Curly Joe's stomach is quaking, though it isn't from trying to remind him that it wants feeding. 'but ... are there ... do any messages come with them?'

'Messages? What sorta messages? You mean like jokes?'

'no ... like... uhm ... to say they're special? or something like that?'

'Special? I guess them teeth were special to the whales afore they had 'em pulled out!' the shopkeeper laughs. 'You looking to make one of them your own?'

* * * * *

Outside again, too dizzy to keep standing, Curly Joe somehow makes it to a nearby bench and flops onto it, clutching his bag of groceries. *so if the whale's tooth is just a fashionable trinket instead of a one-of-a-kind beacon, then what does that say about* ... He can't bring himself to complete the question. Instead, he turns to the food he's just bought and orders himself to focus on that for now.

Only problem is, he can only go through the motions. He's got Nature Girl on his mind. Did she know? Did she make up that Whale Tooth Legend for some stupid crazy reason or other? Maybe she was trying to inspire him. Or ... Or ... Was she just having a laugh, weighing up how naive he could be? He feels the worn red gauze bandana that he keeps wrapped around his left wrist and sees himself stealing it from her rag-bag the day he'd left her and Vancouver behind. It occurs to him that, somewhere at the back of his mind, he's held onto a romantic vision of Nature Girl glumly hanging around Vancouver awaiting his return. Which is, he knows, about as far from any likelihood as you can get. There's no going back to people like Nature Girl. She looked so serious when she'd given him that Tooth, though. If it turns out that she was conning him all along ... *she better not have! because if she has, i hope she gets her karmic comeuppance!*

'Hey, man! Are you okay?'

Curly Joe is so taken up with his free-flowing imagination, he hasn't noticed that someone's come over and perched himself on the bench next to him. When he makes himself look up, he nearly upchucks the cheese sandwich he's been chewing on. The stranger sitting next to him ... He looks so much like —

'No, I'm not who you're thinking I am,' his bench mate says. Then he laughs the laugh of a man who's been through this joke more times than he cares to recall.

Giving him a closer once-over, Curly Joe accepts that the guy isn't putting him on. 'sorry,' he says, 'it's just that at first glance, i was ready to bet you were dylan.'

'No problem. It happens to me all the time. Especially being here. Believe it or not, Bobby and me have bumped into each other a couple of times now and I gotta tell you that we don't look nothing alike. Yeah, we're both similar in size and build, see? And my curly hair helps too, I guess. But the thing is, he's gone and cut most of his off! He doesn't look like he does on them album covers anymore. But there you go ... People see what they wanna see, I guess. Mostly, I take it as a compliment.' He grins. 'And it usually helps in opening up relations with the ladies. Not that I'd ever out-and-out lie to them, of course.' A two-way smile, a moment's pause and then the stranger gets back to more immediate issues. 'I didn't wanna interrupt, but you looked to be on edge and sort of arguing with yourself. I couldn't catch more than a couple of words of what you were saying. Something about karma?'

Curly Joe shakes his head. 'yeah, something like that. sorry to have —'

'Hey! No sweat! You know what they say: "My karma just ran over your dogma." Or maybe it's the other way round.'

Mutual chuckles completed, Curly Joe's in for one more didn't-see-that-one-coming twist. It turns out that this Dylan look-alike who's down for the summer to attend some music classes is, of all things, a McGill student, too. Not that Curly Joe remembers ever seeing him around. Still, having found something else in common, they each conclude that the other's an okay guy and worth passing away a bit of time with. When Curly Joe mentions that tomorrow's Dylan's birthday and he's come all this way to celebrate the event, his new-found pal rewards him with the information that he thinks he knows where Dylan's home might be. Directions given and scribbled down, they swear to get together again when they're both back at university. Then, wishing each other a great summer, they head off in different directions.

If nothing else, this quirky meeting has calmed things down for Curly Joe. Rudimentary map in hand, he's in the groove again. But not for long. About a quarter mile down the road he's been shown to take, the memory of that string of whales' teeth waiting to be sold jostles its way once again to the front row of his awareness. The questions it raises segue to an even more pressing one: why is it such a life and death issue to meet with Dylan?

duh ... easy. because he'll provide the answers, of course.

except, wait a minute! answers? what answers? don't i have all the answers already? aren't i an evangelist of love? yeah, but ... only because you were given the whale's tooth. and if that's all bullshit, then ... what if i'm not? never was. never will be, either.

dylan's sure to see that. and when he does, and adds up the truth of the situation, he'll just laugh me away, tell me to grow up, just like he did to the student in that movie, don't look back. what's more, he'll have every right to.

Something's happening here. And Curly Joe's trying his best to assure himself he doesn't know what it is.

* * * * *

(from Curly Joe's Thought Book)

may 24
happy 28th birthday, bob. all good things from a fellow human being who loves you and who's traveled this far without knowing why.

until now.

i wanted to bring you a birthday present but couldn't think what that could be. now i know: the best gift I can offer you is to spare you the agony that my worthless presence would cause you to suffer. hope you like it!

last night, i found a bit of clearing in a field maybe close by to your home. I fell asleep right away. maybe that clearing cleared my head because when i woke up this morning all i could do was keep asking myself these same questions over and over:

how can i be an evangelist if i've not yet heard the good news?
how can i preach love if i don't know what love is?

one more self-appointed evangelist of love finds out that he isn't the person he claims to be. not at all.
case closed, i feel washed-up. and stupid. such an idiot not

to see what I've been doing. trying to be more like dylan than dylan himself. even writing so that it could have been something that dylan wrote. dumb, arrogant, nothing-like-dylan me!

i've promised myself to stop all that. i'm gonna find my own voice now. my days of thieving are over.

i don't know what nature girl was up to when she gave me that tooth, and i guess i'll never know. it doesn't really matter. what counts is that i let her gift kid me into believing i was someone special. someone above it all. someone who could explain away why he didn't get the love he wanted because he was "chosen". a martyr whose job it was to make sure everybody else got the love they wanted. even if it cost me the chance to get the same.

love. love. love. nothing's more scary.

okay. looks like this trip's nowhere near finished. more like it's just beginning. so ... i leave woodstock today totally unsure of where i'm heading. i'm grubby and hungry and shattered and silent. i've also not met up with dylan and probably never will.

sad but true: i'm in one hell of a state. even the "i" who's writing this doesn't know who he is.

here's the road, then. and on the road, here's someone who has, for the moment, understood that he's understood nothing.

death and rebirth.

a shiver of shame.

and maybe of redemption, as well.

* * * * *

Next morning, Curly Joe's sitting in a strange car with New York City not too far in the distance calling out to him. He only woke up a couple of minutes ago, so it takes his not-quite conscious bewilderment a bit more time to re-establish recent history.

The car belongs to this wild-eyed Woodstock local who kept jabbering on about some sinister gunpowder plot to stop the planned music festival from happening. They had a flat tire part way along and then nearly ran out of gas so the driver took it as a message to give up on any thoughts of going anywhere else that night. Instead, he'd parked near a garbage dump and invited Curly Joe to snuggle up in the front while he stretched out across the back seat. The highway they were on looked deserted and Curly Joe wasn't in any hurry to get anywhere so he took up the offer. Now that he's awake, he can't recall what the driver's name is. But so what? All that he needs to know is that he's met up with one more person living for the adventure of it all.

Half an hour later, goodbyes exchanged, roads parted, Curly Joe is sitting on a snack bar counter stool drinking a glass of very cold milk. It's a humidly hot morning, but he's still got a bad case of the wobblies at the memory of how, while washing his face in the Men's washroom, he'd had to fend off an insistent customer waving his stiff prick at him. *Hello, New York ...* Curly Joe gazes up at the *Felix the Cat* shaped clock above the bar counter. No time like the present to pay a visit to *The Warden*.

Not long after that, back on *The Warden's* home turf, Curly Joe experiences that sudden time-jerk which reduces a year to mere minutes. Nothing — not the paint-work, not the stack of magazines piled up in the hallway, not even *The Warden* himself — seems to have altered one tiny bit. To add to his feeling of being unglued in time, the room he's being assigned to is the same one he'd stayed in the first time around. The sole, if vital, difference being that, instead of sharing it with Moe and Larry, now there's a Japanese student and some poor lost fuckhead from Wyoming who wants to Major in Agricultural Sciences at the University of Colorado and who (according to the garbled explanation of the Japanese guy) spends half his life on the phone 'carring his gurl fren rong dishance inna Carifonya'.

Rotsa ruck, fella, Curly Joe murmurs and then goes back to being amazed by how *The Warden* had recognized him right away. He'd even snarled that he thought Curly Joe had shed a few pounds. Lost for words, Curly Joe took this as a compliment and lied that *The Warden* was looking pretty fit himself. The response, of course, had been his trademark scowl. Seconds later, *The Warden* regurgitated his spiel about how no one was to touch the colour TV just to prove he was the same old barrel of laughs.

* * * * *

Combing the streets, straggling aimlessly westward and eastward along Broadway and Fifth Avenue and every other Avenue that lies between Eight and D, Curly Joe is blown away by how charged up he feels being in NYC. Its pulse beat maintains a constant signal reminding him to never stop being on the alert. The city is in full hyperdrive mode, showing off its uniqueness and beauty side by side with the obscenity and the bone-chilling psychic blasts coming from nowhere that make up its identity.

One day, not far from Columbus Circle, Curly Joe spies an old woman suddenly trip and sprawl face first onto the sidewalk. No one seems to care. Some people stop long enough to blink and then walk on, but nobody does anything to assist her. Even Curly Joe stands there, not moving a muscle. Seconds later, a *Yellow Cab* pulls to a stop. At first, the driver yells at her to get up. When she doesn't respond, he drives off. But then, minutes later, an ambulance appears and whisks her away. Shocked by his own inability — or is that unwillingness? — to act, Curly Joe tries to explain this away as one more example of how rapidly that *Big Apple* rottenness can spread. It's an excuse he'll return to more often than he wants to believe while he's here.

On another day, down one end of Times Square, Curly Joe passes by one of the many stores that advertise

BOOKS AND MAGS OF ALL TYPES
AND FOR ALL TASTES.

He has no doubt as to what kind of books and magazines he'll find inside, but he's fired up enough to step in anyway because in its shop-front window display, nestled between *Memoirs of a Coxcomb* and *S As In Sex* lies a book titled *The Love Songs of Kahlil Gibran*. Overcome by memories of Eve, set on owning a copy, he scrabbles into the store only to find that it's divided in two sections with a table running down the middle separating them. On the left side of the room are magazines and posters of muscle-flexing body-builders with pink-capped divining rods between their legs whose size causes Curly Joe to blush in disbelief and envy. The right side has similar photos and books composed entirely of nude women with their legs spread apart to the extreme.

Most of the men in the shop are on the right hand side of the room, hunched over, flipping through slick rags comparing glossy paper photos of models adopting squirt-all-over-me poses, while surreptitiously arousing themselves, their reddening faces darting right and left to catch anyone watching them at it. Some stand with hands in pockets, some laugh with friends and say things like 'Ain't this one swell?', some grit their teeth and try to recollect how much money they have on them. A few scutter to the cashier standing on the platform overlooking one and all, quickly hand him the correct change then study the room's ceiling while he stuffs the magazine they've selected into a brown paper bag. Grabbing hold of the treasure being shoved their way, hearts beating wildly, they race outside, swivel-eyed so as not to be noticed.

Curly Joe pictures them fancying themselves as magnificent lovers lying on their lonely bed, trousers unzipped and bunched at ankles, directing hard pricks into cupped hand or towel or open air or even straight onto the explicit magazine page photo itself while being transported into a makeshift ravishment that alters the two-dimensional dots on paper into something living which just might be offering them its love. Feeling distinctly ill-at-ease, Curly Joe does his best to come up with arguments insisting that there's nothing sordid about what he sees going on. If anything, he affirms, he's filled with sadness by what's being put on display. Still, it would be good to get out of this place as soon as he can. Deep breath taken, he drags himself over to the shop keeper and asks for a copy of Gibran's book.

The man offers a prolonged snigger. 'Not for sale, kid,' he rasps. 'That there book ain't even real. We just put this fake cover in the window so that you high and mighty college brats can give yourselves an excuse to come in here and buy what ya really want.'

Curly Joe smiles at this. What else is there for him to do?

That's New York for you ... *Howard Johnson's* continues to offer a BIG CHICKEN FRY every Monday and the high sign ten stories up on the side of an East Village building proclaiming that it sells CULTURE BY THE CARLOAD still hangs there fascinating Curly Joe with its irreconcilable message.

Washington Square hasn't changed either. Mediocre folksingers dreaming of being noticed by some hotshot record producer strum on guitars, banjos, mandolins. Even the occasional balalaika, auto harp or sitar. They attract tourists, pickpockets, dealers, street bums and, mostly, people strung out on alcohol or drugs ready to swoon over and applaud anything that sounds vaguely melodic. On an afternoon a couple of days after Memorial Day, while Curly Joe's sitting on a bench, taking in the sounds, a near-toothless, grey-haired Black drunk stumbles up to him and demands that he be given a dime. Needing every cent he has, Curly Joe shrugs an apology. Smiling back, the drunk pulls out an odd scythe-like curved knife and rests it so that it tickles Curly Joe's throat. Like some terrifying robot-machine, his face registers absolutely no emotion. Heart-stopping seconds later, he swiftly removes the knife, hides it away, and barks out one overlong, putrid laugh.

'I sure as shit put the fear in Whitey,' he gloats as much to himself as to Curly Joe. 'Yup. I surely did. Made Whitey go even whiter.' Then he hobbles off, still chortling at his own version of Tricky Dick's Presidential encouragement that all Americans offer up a Memorial Day Prayer for Peace this year.

Craziest of all, with no contender even close to it, however, is the daily festival ground that is East 4th Street with its stumblebums and prostitutes and addicts and sidewalk gambling

Puerto Ricans — all still as loud and dirty and noisy and stone pony broke as they've ever been. And yet, here too, in spite of all the muck and grime, instances of life-enhancing joy disport themselves for Curly Joe. On one particularly clothes-stickingly muggy day, the children of East 4th Street declare that they've had enough heat to last them a lifetime. Rebelling, they set about unscrewing the sides of all the fire hydrants on the street with a stolen wrench until, in minutes, the entire area becomes a miniature *Versailles,* fountains springing up all over the place, expelling freezing cold water for everyone to splash around in. One enterprising kid even solves a way to direct the hydrant spray so that it showers passing cars, while a fleet-footed partner-in-crime knocks on their windscreens haranguing drivers for the 25¢ instant car-wash they've just had imposed upon them. Caught up in the anarchic freedom of it all, Curly Joe finds no reason not to join in. Sneakers and socks removed, he splashes his merry way back to the hostel.

Given such moments, it's with little difficulty that Curly Joe's self-imposed burdens begin to evaporate. During that first week in the City, he renounces all further searches for meaning and identity. He is who he is and where he is without any need to fathom the wherefore and the why. If he's learned anything of importance it's that it's enough to just be aware that he's alive and experiencing what there is to experience. Anything more than that seems a waste of time and effort.

* * * * *

(from Curly Joe's Thought Book)

june 6
night-time already. another day in another week all gone. i wrote some poems but i tore them up afterwards because they said nothing. outside my window, a young puerto rican couple is caught up in a heated argument. he reaches over and takes hold of her hand, which is what she wants, but she's not giving in so easily. instead, she frees herself from his hold and crosses

her arms rejecting all further endearments. they're playing a game and they both know it. but they won't stop. or maybe they can't.

it makes me think of my own ritualized game that i've been playing for the past while. it's a game that doesn't have a winner and has to always end in tears. my tears. everybody else's tears. i'm sick of this game. i want to play a laughing one now. but i've got to work out its rules first.

from his bed, the italian who's playing the role of a cockroach smiles at me happy because he's at last found someone who'll listen with appreciative ears to the problems of a struggling would-be underground film director. it's better than listening to <u>the warden</u> who still spurts out garbage about viet cong and lurking communists. at one point, he was quite literally shouting about how great he feels because a "very very special" asian kid's coming to stay here tomorrow. some guy, kim from korea, who calls himself lee and chews lots of gum. kim's been hiding in st. mark's place trying to get high because marijuana's the cigarette of the poor over in the east and no one gets high on it. then, suddenly fascinated by some news item that appears on the perpetually "on" color tv which only <u>the warden</u> can adjust, he laughs hysterically at the report of some especially violent murder 'because it'll scare the right-wingers shitless and get them to finally do something sensible like bring down that socialist supreme court cabal!'

and, it hits me: who and what the hell is <u>the warden</u>, anyway? right now, I'd like to thump him in his fat belly just to shut him up for a minute.

i mailed a letter to moe that said nothing except that, like mark twain, the rumors of my death have no basis in fact. i sent him and emily some leaves from woodstock and told him about the festival they're going to be holding there in august that's causing all this fuss among the locals. still sounds nice to me.

i haven't written to larry. what i keep telling myself is that chances are he's with suzie q and i have no way of contacting him. that's my excuse, and i'm sticking to it.

morning next day

the warden's on a rampage. it began at 1.30am, when he took it upon himself to kick a guy out. this guy, incidentally, also goes to mcgill. why am i being repeatedly plagued by people who come from mcgill? the poor slob probably ended up spending the rest of the night on the streets. the warden claimed that the reason the guy had to leave was because he was only there while searching for an apartment — which, for some incomprehensible reason, is a no-no as far as the warden's concerned. but the real, honest to god, true reason — which only i and the warden and the now-homeless guy know — is because my fellow mcgillian was dumb enough to mention to the warden that, while at university, he'd become a member of the new left. that little incident occurred on tuesday night, and, since then, the warden hasn't let up on the schmuck, constantly ridiculing him, not listening to what he said, and, as planned all along, falsely accusing him. somehow or other, i got back to sleep after that but then, later this morning, more screams woke me up. turns out, some yank was getting kicked out because he hadn't made up his bed or washed the dishes.

i really don't get what the warden's up to and i can tell he's trying to bait me with all sorts of political questions coming out of the blue to which i respond: 'i don't know anything about politics', or, 'you're the one who holds all the facts, man.' what i really want to say though is: 'fuck you and your political purges, jerk-off! join the revolution!'

i recoil at my own weaknesses. i confess to levels of selfishness and self-protection that prevent me from engaging in heated dialogue because it's just too convenient and cheap to stay here. so I put up with it. it's either them or me. Today, i'm ashamed to say that "they" come in at a poor second place. a coward? probably. disillusioned? certainly. i tell myself that i'd fight for someone who meant something to me. right now though, i seem to be the only candidate. i'm revolted by my honesty. but at least i'm being honest for once.

here's another piece of honesty: i wish there was someone other than me around who meant enough to me to fight for ...

* * * * *

A couple of days later, Curly Joe's enjoying another lazy afternoon in Central Park getting ready to suck on a blueberry fruit-stick he's just bought from an ice cream wagon dealer who calls himself Happy Jack. Handing over the flavoured ice tube, Happy Jack lets him in on a secret: the fruit-stick is a magical one that will invoke the presence of a beautiful woman close to Curly Joe's heart.

'sadly, i can't think of anybody who fits the bill.'

'You just wait and see. The Magic Fruit-Stick is never wrong. But you watch that heart of yours. It should be warm, not ice cold like that delicious treat you're holding.' And with that, Happy Jack winks and turns around to push his cart further up the path.

It doesn't take long for Curly Joe to forget this exchange. He's more caught up in lying back on the dry green grass and allowing himself to fall into line with this slow-down-and-take-it-easy park life he's caught up in. Kids playing timeless games. Fat-bellied men sucking up air, wiped out from the exertions of jogging. Flawlessly outfitted secretaries chomping on their diet lunches and slurping 1-CAL soft drinks while they lap up as much sun worship as possible during their hour's break. Besotted couples gliding by. And, somewhere in the distance, someone playing a gentle blues riff on their guitar. Curly Joe shuts his eyes and feels at peace. How long has it been since he could say that about himself? Long may it last!

Too bad. Life has other plans for him.

Minutes later, feeling someone's shadow hover over his face, he looks up, his serenity all too rapidly dissolved. Before any logical explanations are able to take hold, he flashes to Happy Jack's prediction. He squints to make sure he saw things right the first time.

Yes, he did. Angel is beaming down at him. Angel! Of all people! Why hasn't he thought of her until now? Probably because there wasn't any point to doing so. First off, he wouldn't have had the faintest clue how or where to find her. Or even if she was still living here. And, more than that, short and sweet: what would lead him to suppose that she'd be remotely inclined to arranging a meet up?

Still, here she is, giving him this loopy look that makes all those sensible points and questions totally redundant. So what's he to do? How about summoning enough energy to leap up, ready to shake hands in greeting?

Paying no attention to his outstretched hand, Angel hugs him as though they're long-lost, lifetime friends. 'Oh, it's so mind-blowing to find you here! I was passing by and thought I recognised you but I wasn't really sure it was you, if you know what I mean. I nearly didn't stop. But then ... I don't know. My curiosity took over. I'm glad it did.'

'i'm glad it did, too. it's great to see you again.'

'Likewise. But whatever's brought you to this god-forsaken city?'

'you, of course,' Curly Joe jokes. w*here did that come from?* 'actually,' he blushes, rapidly backtracking, 'i've been trying to find out what i want out of life.'

'Aren't we all?'

'yeah, i guess so.'

'But this is way far out! Where are you staying?'

'oh ... same crummy place as last time. still ... it's cheap.'

'Nothing's cheap in this town. Except human life. Have you got any plans while you're over here?'

'nope,' Curly Joe's given in on an impulse and cancelled his vague decision to leave New York soon, maybe travel around some more. Or, more likely, head back to Montréal. 'i ... i'm half-trying to write a novel.' *what am i saying? what do i know about writing novels? and besides ... besides ... well ... uhm ... hey! why not?*

'Wow! That's so fantastic!' Angel gushes, jumping up and down. 'What's it about?'

'uhm ...' *what can it be about? think, man, think!*

'Oh ... Maybe that's a secret. You don't have to say.'

'no! no! nothing like that! it's just that it's hard to sum up, you know? it's a sort of fantasy-type allegory on what's going on in the world.'

'Do you mean politically?'

'uhm ... yeah. politically. socially. spiritually. whatever. i'm just starting to work it out, really.'

'How sensational, though! Good on you!'

'well ... i haven't gotten very far with it yet,' Curly Joe answers truthfully.

'I'm not surprised. How can you possibly write anything in *that* hovel?'

'with difficulty.'

'For sure. Say ... Listen, I've just had a thought: you have *got* to meet a friend of mine if you're trying to write a novel. He keeps saying he wants to do the same thing and I'm sure that he'd like someone to rap with and share ideas.'

While Curly Joe nods and thinks of what to say to show his expected appreciation, the gives Angel the necessary time to ask her next question. A self-conscious cough, and then she leaps in.

'Are you here by yourself?'

For a moment, Curly Joe feels Larry's ghost worming its way between them. *but larry's got suzie q now.* 'yeah, i'm all on my lonesome,' he answers.

As if reading his mind, but, more likely, laying her own anxieties on the line, Angel asks: 'What about Larry and Moe?'

'oh, they're doing fine. moe's in montréal, working. and he's got a girlfriend now.' He pauses to look for hints in Angel's face about what to say next. Still unsure, he does his best to sound devil-may-care. 'larry's got a girlfriend, too. well, she used to be my girlfriend, but that's a long story.' There. He's made it plain. And Angel doesn't seem to be too bothered by the news. 'she — suzie q, i mean — she's over in london for the summer, so i guess that larry's doing some traveling.'

'To England?'

'uhm?'

'Is Larry going to England?'

why would larry go to england? it's moe who's got the english girlfriend. hasn't she heard me ... oh! wait! 'no. suzie q's in ontario. london, ontario. sorry, i didn't make that clear.'

In spite of everything, Angel feels a flicker of jealousy. She castigates herself for being so possessive. Even about what she no longer wants. 'Oh ... Good for him. Is he happy?'

'yeah, i think so.'

'Great! And you? Are you okay with Larry being with your ex-girlfriend?'

'it's complicated.'

'i bet.'

'but it's all fine. really! the three of us are still great friends.'

'It sounds like the basis to a really hilarious novel,' Angel teases. A sudden thought switches her back to organising mode. 'Oh! I've just had an idea! This friend of mine I told you about, the would-be writer ...' She pauses to make sure that Curly Joe's paying attention. 'Well, the other reason you should try to catch up with him is because he's staying in a brownstone over in the East Village and he told me last time I saw him that there's a spare room going there. It's a weird place, but it's clean and it's cheap as well.'

It's not quite the offer that Curly Joe was hoping she'd make, but it has its possibilities. 'that sounds great. i could do with a change. and any weirdness that's different to the one i'm getting over at the hostel has got to be an improvement.'

'Sweet! Then I'll call up Victor and find out if the room's still free.'

Curly Joe is about to thank her again when he notices that all evidence of accomplishment reflected in her face has hastily morphed into a worried frown. 'what's wrong? did you remember something? maybe the room's already gone?'

'No. No! I'm pretty sure no one's moved in yet. No, it's ... Look, I better warn you about this place. The room used to be lived in by some guy who shot himself in there around five weeks ago.'

Curly Joe's eyes widen in amazement. *what would it be like to live in the same room where somebody'd offed himself?* Still, if he's going to write a novel — and, face it, the idea's beginning to sound more and more appealing — the gruesome setting could be a dynamite stimulus for his imagination. 'listen, if i have to put up with *the warden* for much longer, i might give that option a go myself!'

'I'd better not waste any time, then,' Angel snickers. 'There's a phone booth near the Park Entrance. Hopefully, it's working. You stay here and I'll go call Victor.'

'no, wait,' Curly Joe says. 'i'll follow you. you're doing more than enough for me already.'

Before he can add anything else, Angel runs off, leaving him to stand there reeling from the jumble of emotions that her appearance has set off. *my god*, Curly Joe whispers to himself as he ogles her moving body, *she's just so incredibly beautiful ...*

Next thing, he's standing outside the phone booth watching Angel in action. Another minute slides by and then she's out standing so close to him that he can smell her scented breath.

'There's someone in the room for the moment, but they're just passing through. They'll be out of there tomorrow or the next day at the latest. Victor says you can move in then.'

'hey! that's great! thank you so much!' Pleased as he is, Curly Joe has already come up with something else to trouble himself with. How to ask Angel out for a date without giving her the impression that he's on the make?

Just as he's about to muster up the courage to pitch his offer, Angel notices the time on her watch. 'Shit!' she complains. 'Listen,' she tells him, placing her left hand casually on his shoulder, 'I've got to run because I've got a rehearsal to go to. But why don't we meet up tonight and chew things over?' Misreading Curly Joe's reaction, she quickly adds: 'If you'd like to, of course.'

'i'd love it,' Curly Joe blurts out, hoping he sounds sufficiently nonchalant.

'Excellent! Come to my place around seven. I'll cook you a meal. Here, I'll write down my address for you.' She takes out a sheet of paper and scribbles quickly, then hands it over to him. 'When you get there, if anybody asks, say that you're meeting up with Jane.'

'who's jane?' Curly Joe asks, placing the slip into his shirt pocket.

'Just little ol' me. I had to change my name for the stage. Angel sounds way too whorish. So now, I'm just another Plain Jane.' She vamps melodramatically. 'Which brings me to a sore point.'

here it comes. now she's gonna tell me all about her live-in lover.

'I just can't call you Curly Joe,' Angel pleads guilty, then bursts out laughing.

'what?' Curly Joe's grinning more out of relief than amusement.

'I'm sorry. It's just such a silly name. I couldn't even say it to Victor when I phoned him. I kept talking about "this curly-haired friend of mine from Montréal". And there's no way on earth I'm going to tell any of my friends that someone named Curly Joe is coming over for supper. Sorry!'

Angel's insistence gets Curly Joe to thinking things over. Maybe he's outgrown the nick-name. Still ... 'all right then,' he offers, 'call me rick from now on.'

'Rick?'

'yeah ... it's another long story.' *kitimat. nora. vancouver. nature girl. it's flashback time again, folks!*

'I wanna hear all about it tonight,' Angel-who-must-now-be-known-as-Jane says. 'But, I really gotta go. Catch you later, *Rick*.'

'have a great rehearsal, *jane,*'

The both crack up at their newly-agreed aliases.

'See you tonight,' she repeats, then pats Curly Joe's shoulder before rushing off.

* * * * *

Two hours have gone by. Two hours devoted to chit-chat and gossip and a very spicy chili-con-carne. Their time together has sped by. No awkward pauses wondering what to say next. More like two old friends with tons of shared interests catching up after a long separation. Leonard Cohen's new album, *Songs*

From A Room, is playing. It's the third time that Jane's put it on. She keeps getting up to switch sides. Curly Joe can't help but produce a grin every time she does. Probably due to the joints Jane rolled so expertly and which have served as suitable after-dinner mints substitutes. They've succeeded brilliantly in getting them both stoned to point where everything thought of or spoken betrays its humorous side. It's taken this long for Curly Joe to get around to relating his recent search for Dylan.

Just as she's falling about laughing at the absurdity of his odyssey, Jane remembers. 'I saw your hero on Johnny Cash's TV show last night,' she crows, bouncing on the sofa they're sharing.

what? how could i have missed it? oh, wait ... the warden, of course. he who controls the color tv, controls the world. 'how was he?'

'he looked good. but also really nervous. he did a couple of songs on his own and then they duetted.'

'*girl from the north country,* i bet.'

'Yes! It was hokey, but still really beautiful. And Joni Mitchell was a guest as well.'

'no! are you kidding? joni mitchell! don't tell me: leonard cohen popped by, too.'

'I wish!' she laments, punching Curly Joe's shoulder. Shrugging off the fantasy, she starts to roll another one.

Curly Joe is kicking himself. But at the same time, being here, in Jane's company, even knowing that he's blown another chance to see Dylan doesn't feel like such a tragedy. So far, what news he's learned from Angel — no! *Jane* — is that, since Larry, and following a subsequent period of self-imposed isolation and self-assessment, she's become involved with Women's Lib. One result of this conversion is that she's begun to see that her issues with men and with herself, though personal to a degree, are also typical of the war between the sexes. Drawn in, she's joined a women-only weekly encounter group focused on freedom from male oppression. Not too subtly, she keeps trying out some consciousness-raising on him, which Curly Joe doesn't mind and, usually, his responses meet with her approval. What's mainly raising his consciousness though is that Jane must have burned her bra, since her pants-on-fire fidgeting makes it all too evident that she's not wearing one under her T-shirt. If this is part of Women's Lib, his libido is happy to agree with them all the way. Stoned as he is, Curly Joe thinks it's probably a good idea to keep this sexist pig conclusion to himself.

On top of that, everything's looking up for Jane. Modelling put aside once and for all, she's turned her attention back on an earlier dream of acting. Not long after enrolling at an independent acting studio, she hit it lucky and landed a decent role in an Off-Broadway play that's received good reviews and so seems set for a reasonable run.

When Curly Joe tells her he's eager to go see her in it one night, she absolutely forbids him from doing so. 'I'd get all nervous and flub my lines if I knew you were in the audience.'

'okay. i won't tell you in advance.'

'No!' Jane shrieks. 'Half the time I'm on stage, I'm practically naked. And I'm moaning away like I'm about to explode through a lot of it. I've banned all my friends from coming. So promise that you won't!'

Curly Joe promises. *how is this in keeping with jane's new found feminism?* Something else to keep his trap shut about.

Main thing: Jane's happier than she's felt in a long, long time. She's formed numerous friendships. She goes on demos against the war, against Nixon, against all sorts of restrictive laws set by The Straights. She's connected with a great dealer who sells his wares at a reasonable price. *And* does home deliveries.

Not so hearteningly for Curly Joe, there's also been a steady run of lovers to satisfy her more physical needs. Added to which, there's a somewhat unique curveball to this last revelation: Jane's subscribed to an unbreakable rule. All of her sexual partners can only last a total of three days — no more, no less — before being discarded, replaced and forgotten.

'No one-night stands and no dumb dreams about any lasting, long-term relationship,' she explains. 'If the guy can't accept my conditions, then I blow him off!' She giggles. 'I mean, I tell him to go look for someone else. Not give him head.'

'you could do both. as a going away present.'

Thanks to the grass, they both find this suggestion to be hilarious.

'It's my way of turning the table on all you men. I'm letting you have an inside look on how women are treated and used. I want men to feel that so maybe they stop doing it.'

Hearing this, Curly Joe can't prevent Larry from invading his thoughts again. Larry wasn't like these men she keeps going on about. He couldn't have been.

Now that he's there distracting him though, Curly Joe asks himself how Larry would feel if he could see the two of them right this second. Curly Joe can't deny it any longer: he's insanely attracted to Jane. He wants to see her naked. Be naked with her. Make love with her.

Is he betraying Larry by feeling this way? Another, even more disturbing, thought pops up: is he feeling this way because it's his revenge on Larry for having started a relationship with Suzie Q when she was still his girlfriend? Is Jane his means to get even?

He turns to catch Jane staring at him. *no. absolutely not!* he resolves, then quickly switches topics. 'so this guy who's got the spare room ... victor. is he one of your "three days and you're out" men?' He hopes that his voice sounds more detached than he feels it to be.

'Victor? No, I told you: he's a good friend. A great friend, for sure. He had the option, of course. I like him that way — sexually, I mean — too. So it could have happened. But it didn't. He decided that a lasting friendship mattered more to him. New York's a tough town for finding good friends. Finding three-day lovers is a hell of a lot easier. No, Victor's not in the running.' She smiles crookedly. 'Thing is, right now I'm in an in-between phase with regard to lovers. I'm just hanging loose and seeing what happens.'

As plain as Jane's challenge is, Curly Joe still misses it. She'll have to try harder. Thankfully, her Lord, Leonard, comes to the rescue. That song she loves so much. *You Know Who I Am.* Those lines about not following or being followed. The equality of it all.

'Well?' Jane prods.

Curly Joe coughs and passes the joint to her, thinking that maybe he's been caught bogarting it. Looking into her eyes again, he finally gets it. 'jane,' he says. 'you have no idea how turned on i am right now. maybe it's the grass, but —'

'Well! Thanks a bunch!'

'no, i didn't —'

She can't stop herself from dissolving into laughter. There goes her attempt to play at being offended.

Dramatically wiping his forehead, Curly Joe laughs too. 'i want to go to bed with you,' he says.

'Even if it means that after three days it's all over?'

'can we still meet? as friends, i mean?'

'Nope. If you stay over at Victor's we're bound to bump into each other. But you have to promise me that if you choose the three-day option all our interactions from then on will just be surface ones. No closeness. No jealousy. No friendship.'

'it's an awful choice.'

'Yeah, but you still have to make it.'

'i already did,' Curly Joe says.

* * * * *

It's mid-afternoon by the time Curly Joe makes it over to the hostel so that he can collect his belongings and then rush back to Jane's apartment.

Before leaving, he goes in search of *The Warden* to say goodbye.

best to get away on good terms just in case victor's room doesn't work out and i need to go back, Curly Joe tells himself.

'So where were *you* last night?' *The Warden* snarls.

'i stayed over at a friend's place. uhm ... she's invited me to crash there for a while, so it looks like you've got a spare bed for now.'

'*She*, huh? Well, guess who's getting his rocks off, then!'

Curly Joe can't think of anything to say to that without getting himself into trouble, so he shrugs instead.

'Ya missed some fireworks last night, lemme tell ya.'

'oh yeah?'

'Yeah. That Eye-Tie guy staying here, ya know who I mean, he just flipped out. Musta been on something or other. Hadda send him packing. He was gonna smash the TV to pieces because he couldn't take seeing more pictures of *The War.* Panty-waist.'

'sorry to hear it. he seemed like a nice guy.'

'Yeah, well. Ya never can tell.'

'guess not.'

'I've seen 'em all, lemme tell ya.'

'i believe you, man.'

'One more thing: before ya head off to this girlfriend of yours, I gotta tell ya that I don't do refunds. Ya got three days left on this week's bill, but —'

'no problem. i wasn't expecting a refund anyway.'

'Well, good. Because you wouldn't have got one from me.'

* * * * *

Their lovemaking is frequent and fierce. Jane is in total control, barking out orders.

'Put your hand there! No, there! Rub! Gentle now! Harder! Inside me, quick! Push it in all the way! Now out again! Faster! Slow down! Don't move! Slide your tongue lower! No, up a bit! That's it! Don't stop! Stop! Suckle my tit! The left one! I'm coming! Yes! Yes! Yes!'

The rawness of their coupling makes Kitimat's tawdry threesome seem like a rather sedate garden party. Curly Joe isn't sure what he thinks about it. Never mind. Plenty of time for that when his three days are up.

And when they're not having sex, they get on so well it's almost scary. Spending time with Jane is, for Curly Joe, as comfortable and revealing and rewarding as hanging around with Larry and Moe.

Maybe even more so. Because Jane's a woman. No question about that.

* * * * *

(from Curly Joe's Thought Book)

june 11

i see myself as a mirror
reflecting the shadow
of a shadow
from another mirror.

jane. i woke up this morning — our third and last morning — and she was still asleep next to me. one of her breasts peeked out from under the sheets and I wanted to fondle it, kiss it. i wanted the whole of her again. my desire seems insatiable.

jane. she tells me how fucked up she's been. how she learned to hate men. how our pricks repelled her because of their need. even larry's. yeah, her time with larry seemed to sum it all up for her. and afterwards, after that first time we came to new york, something broke loose in her.

jane. now, she says, she can live with men. or, at least, put up with them. she wishes that she could find other women sexually desirable. that would solve everything. but she doesn't feel that way. she's tried. even enjoyed the encounter. but it wasn't ... she doesn't know how to explain it, and i sure don't ... it just wasn't. instead, she jokes: 'i guess i like men's bodies too much. it's the creeps inside them i can't stand.' then she throws me a long hard look, daring me to nail down if her statement is all-inclusive.

jane. she said she'd give me three days. three days.
'and after that? what's gonna happen after that?'
'in three days time, you won't be asking such silly questions.'

later

- *goodbye, then. have a great rehearsal. have a great life, too.*
- *will you think of me?*
- *yeah, of course. will you think of me?*
- *no. you made your choice. now live with its consequences. I will. goodbye. enjoy your time with victor.*

* * * * *

Curly Joe writes that down as his last thought of his three days with Jane. Alone in her room, he clings to his memory of their parting. How much he'd enjoyed their time together. Even if there hadn't been any sex, he tells himself, it would still have been nirvana. Maybe he shouldn't have chosen the three days as her lover. If he'd stuck with friendship instead, he'd be able to go on seeing her, enjoy her company. The mention of friendship, annoyingly, gets him to thinking about Larry again.

Has he betrayed Larry?

Yes. No. Maybe.

But Larry's happy with Suzie Q now. Doesn't that make it something other than betrayal?

Yes. No. Maybe.

Curly Joe locks the door to Jane's apartment. He'll place the keys into the mailbox marked JANE and head off to have a look at his new room.

As to Larry, well, he can just fuck off and leave him alone for now.

Curly Joe smiles at his conceit; losers can afford to be magnanimous.

* * * * *

Having taken forever to find his way through the maze that is the East Village, Curly Joe knocks on his possible new home's front door.

Seconds later, it opens and ...

Did you Time Tripsters guess already? Yup. *It's fuckin' Vic from Vancouver!*

Vic smiles, totally calm. 'I figured it had to be you. When Jane mentioned Montréal and curly hair, I said to myself: it's gotta be Ol' Ricky-boy. Welcome. Come inside.'

As an added inducement, and instead of the customary hand-shake, Vic offers "Ricky-boy" a joint. Taking it without a moment's hesitation, Curly Joe follows Vic to the kitchen.

There's a very tall, long-haired kid who couldn't be much older than sixteen stands in front of the electric range mixing white sugar and water together in a pan. When it starts to turn brown bubble, he pours the hardening gruel onto a plate and turns to face Curly Joe.

'Caramel,' he explains matter-of-factly. Then, spurred by high hopes, he asks: 'Got any crystal, man?'

'He means speed,' Vic translates before Curly Joe's forced to admit to his ignorance of current hard drug slang. 'The place is full of speed freaks. Me excluded. Didn't Jane tell you that?'

'no, she didn't.'

'Probably didn't wanna scare you into not coming by,' Vic says.

'Wanna score some? I can get it real cheap,' the caramel-maker asks.

'nope. thanks for the offer, though,' Curly Joe answers, hoping he's not going to be dismissed as square and unworthy of sharing space with them.

'That's cool, man,' the speed freak reassures him. 'Do your own thing, right? I'm Jeff. What's your handle?'

'uhm ... rick.' Curly Joe says.

'Rick and Vic!' Jeff laughs. 'That's far out! Hey, Georgia!' he yells down the hall, 'Ya gotta tune into this!'

Then, half-eaten bowl of glop in hand, and laughing loudly at the humorous nature of rhyme, he goes in search of the mysterious Georgia.

'Aside from their eating habits,' Vic begins, 'they're pretty nice people. They won't bother you about crystal. As long as you're straight with them, they won't fuck up on you. A word in your ear, though: keep any cash you got on you close to hand. "When speed gets low, itchy fingers grow." Other than that, it can get hilarious to watch them when they're high.'

'but you don't ... ah ... shoot speed yourself?' Curly Joe asks, just to make sure he heard things right first time around.

'Naw,' Vic says. 'Dope and acid's still enough for me. I haven't given up on all that "peace and love" shit I was peddling last year.'

'glad to hear it.' *say! wait a minute! if vic's here then ...* 'hey, is nature girl around as well? i hope so. it'd be great to —'

'Nature Girl's dead,' Vic says, cutting him off.

'what? dead! how —'

'She O.D.'d. Smack. Happened round about last Christmas time. Some junkie she met made like Santa Claus and gave her a taste. Couldn't get enough of it after that. It's a long, sad story. But ... Come on,' Vic urges. 'I'll show you your room and then we've got to head over to Colin's so's he can meet you.'

'colin? who's colin?

Vic shakes his head. 'Something else Jane didn't tell you. Colin owns this place. He's got to approve whoever stays here. His place, his rules. I wouldn't worry about it, though. Colin's no fool. He knows what goes on here. So long as you've got the cash to pay upfront, he won't care.'

* * * * *

(from Curly Joe's Thought Book)

june 12 (2.00am)
can't sleep. too much buzzing going on round my brain.
vic turned out to be wrong about colin-what's-his-name. he took one look at me and just like that made up his mind that he didn't like what he saw. kept saying he didn't trust me. vic didn't argue with him. he just turned us both around and headed back to the brownstone. i thought he'd given up on me and was going to hand me my packsack, send me straight back to <u>the warden,</u>

tail between my legs. But, no. i was wrong. instead, he collected together the other residents, told them what had happened, and got them all to march back with him and me to colin-what's-his-name's and demand that he change his mind. or else. i don't know what they have on him, but, after telling everybody to go fuck ourselves, he gave in. so now i'm an official resident of "crystal waves house", east village, new york. lucky me!

what's keeping me awake is thoughts of nature girl. i keep reminding myself of all the curses i threw her way back in woodstock when i found out about the tooth. it's crazy shit, i know, but i can't get rid of the worry that, somehow or other, those curses had some role in her dying. which is out to lunch, because she died months ago. but still ... I latch onto memories of our time together even if so much of those days remains a total blur. Partly due to the drugs, of course, but more than that. we had all sorts of long, crazy all-night conversations. no idea now what we talked about. doesn't matter. forgetting the words doesn't mean i'm going to forget the person. never. I know she's gone. except, she isn't. hey, nature girl: for your being, thanks.

june 17

what happened to last week? i have a page of scribbled ideas for this novel i'm supposed to be writing. that's as far as i've gotten. not much to be proud of. but then, from what i can tell, i'm <u>way</u> ahead of vic, writing-wise. so far, neither of us is ready to admit that as much as we like the idea of writing a novel, the reality involved in doing so is not yet something we're ready to commit to. still, it's fun to play at it. vic and me are getting along just fine.

okay, introduction time. as i make it, there's eight of us sharing space here. we make an odd collective.

first of all, as well as me and vic, there's keith — tall, thin, and walrus-moustached, he's a friendly giant of a man who's staked his claim as undisputed "leader" of the household because he's been here the longest. keith's hung up on occultism, screwed-up by his mother, and shot-up with crystal.

he's taken kindly to my presence though because i told him about my candle meditation experience and that's proof enough for him that i'm a soul-brother who can relate to his mad blathering about "the arcane wisdom" in general and numerological palmistry (Keith's very own invention) in particular. as if he'd needed any more convincing, keith "palmed" me and confirmed, much to his disbelief, that every single digit corresponding to the letters in my name was odd-numbered. this, he explained, is a mega-freaky rarity on all counts, and it evidently signifies that the being in question is totally impractical. i had to agree with him on that one.

then there's a speed-freak dope-fiend named hal. like his hero, neal cassady (who hal tells me died back in february 1968 while driving some sort of hippie bus), he seems to be constantly coming in and out of the building, shaking like some bugged-out bum. he gives me the wobblies. he's also forever burbling on about crystal real rat-tat-tat style so that not even any of the other speeders can make out what he's saying. whenever he assumes that anyone cares to hear such things, he voices his conviction that he no longer requires drugs, merely uses them to further his psychic development. according to vic though, the sad truth is that the hospitals have certified hal to be too far gone to do anything with. veins bulging out of his skin, he's "the king of crystal", too high-minded to be bothered about the ferment brewing within.

the one female inhabitant is named georgia. hard to define, she's a pretty twenty-something with long straight black hair and an indelible smile that suggests awareness but is more likely the simple result of being off her rocker. georgia seems to sleep with everyone and no one in particular. her role in the commune is to be its main shoplifter. valued by her penniless compatriots, she rips off what she can. an expert in such matters, she rips off quite a lot. one night, for example, she returned with two loaves of bread, a pound of cheese, half a dozen packs of bologna, a quart of milk, and a chocolate bar. she'd paid for the chocolate bar. her philosophy is: "they fuck with you, you fuck 'em right back." more than anything else about georgia, though i'll always remember her as the first woman i've ever met who applies vaseline, not lipstick, to her lips. 'crystal makes 'em go dry,' she explains. 'same goes for down below,' she adds, hooting.

there's also, of course, jeff, the caramel-maker, who's clearly on the make for georgia who, in turn, doesn't seem to care one way or the other. when jeff's not to be seen hanging around with georgia, he passes a good part of his day playing with the house cat (named "dog", of course) which is also given regular injections of speed. some nights, poor dog literally claws at the ceiling. 'crystal,' jeff never tires of making known to me, ' is all that counts in the end. everything else, georgia included (but don't tell her i told you so), ain't worth shit and oughtta be cashed in on when a taste's on offer.' if jeff feels anything at all for me, which is doubtful, it's pity. 'if you'd only try it once, man,' he predicts, 'you'd see i was doing you the best favor in your life.'

after jeff, comes an even younger-looking guy called jody. he always dresses up "real spiffy" and, though probably only fifteen, appears to be the only one with any drive. he's involved with "the fillmore east" in some way or other and usually comes back every few nights with a bunch of new records that he's liberated for his private collection. have to say, he's got a really good taste in music.

lastly, there's a nameless entity who lives behind the locked door across from my room. he never comes out and is said to be hung-up on zen. he's rarely referred to, and it's only due to the cash for his weekly rent appearing outside his door every friday that anyone knows for sure that he's still there and alive. legend has it that he's really colin-what's-his-name's son on the run from the draft board.

All in all, an odd family. as a center for the drug trade, the place is visited regularly by edgy outsiders who come and go as quickly and easily as it takes for them to score. keith, the main man, greets all comers as they crawl out of the woodwork; the others, rarely engaged in anything too demanding to view their visitors as sources of distraction, hover like vultures waiting to fight over any remains.

    the acrid smell of decadence hangs over one and all.

    as to vic ... well, when i had a chance to get a word in, i asked why he'd left the west coast and ended up here, he just shrugged. 'the west coast turned into a dismally bad scene, man. too many tourists and weekend hippies tripping around in vancouver. and, from what i hear, it's even worse in san fran. i figured it was time to pick up sticks and head eastwards. the midwest was so dozy, it put me right off. next thing i knew, i'd come as far east as you can go without ending up in the atlantic. i hate the winter, but the thing is it hardens you in a positive kind of way. purifies you, is what it does.'

    all of which may be true enough, but i've got a suspicion that nature girl's death may have had a part to play in his decision. what vic studiously avoids mentioning is anything more about nature girl. i know for sure that she meant a lot to him. still does. as well as off-and-on lovers, they were also, and mainly, like a brother and sister to each other. turns out that as well as (not) writing his novel, vic is getting himself ready to go to university. says he wants to do psychology because he's interested in studying levels of consciousness.

    back to the present: it seems that, for some reason or other, i've been fated to spend time with these people. every morning, i wake up in a sagging bed under sweaty sheets that could do with a major clean. i look around myself: leather armchair. bureau. mirror. window. rickety wooden chair and desk. closet. half-drunk glass of water. i know that i can always choose to get up and leave any time i want. but here's where it gets really crazy: i don't want to. there's nowhere else i'd rather be.

* * * * *

Another week speeds by and the imminent arrival of July begins to nudge its way into New York consciousness. As ever, no one's holding their breath that there's any positive change in the offing. The news media keep cranking out the same sad stories from Washington to Vietnam. When death counts become bedtime lullabies, the nightmares are sure to intrude. In order to dull the brain, to supply it with moments of relief from tension, drugs have become the common option. The streets are full of them and demand grows by the day.

When he's not pretending to write the Great Canadian Novel, Curly Joe has gotten himself a job sticking propaganda leaflets for a New Left group into apartment building mail boxes. They pay him next to nothing but it's only a couple of hours in the morning, it's decent exercise and it goes some way toward easing his political conscience.

The dog days are approaching, and, with them, violence is always an option.

* * * * *

Curly Joe and Vic are arguing.

It's the 28th of June 1969 and the *Stonewall Uprising* has begun.

Very early this morning, the cops raided the *Stonewall Inn*, a gay and lesbian bar over on Christopher Street in Greenwich Village. Things turned explosive and by the evening there are protests everywhere with Village street people finding themselves becoming activists for gay rights and liberation. Curly Joe and Vic learn all about this from Jody who claims to have been walking by the scene on his way home.

'Oh, man!' Jody puffs. 'There's a full-on riot going on there! People outside shouting "Gay Power!" and singing "We Shall Fuckin' Overcome"! No kidding! I saw this dyke in handcuffs fighting off a bunch of pigs. And she was winning, too! Straight off, there were loads more people there surrounding the fuzz. So they started arresting and putting cuffs on anybody they could catch. Even this folkie who turned up there to see what all the fuss about got cuffed. Dave Van Ronk? Something like that. Anyway, next thing you know, they're all running for shelter inside the bar because the people started into throwing bottles, rocks, garbage cans, and what have you at the building, smashing all its windows. Then some got into lighting garbage on fire and lobbing it inside the busted windows. And, guess what? The fucking fire hose inside didn't work because there wasn't enough pressure or something to start it up. So not long later, more pigs arrive to save the ones trapped inside the bar. And boy! Talk about spitting blood! They were gonna Kill! Kill! Kill! Take no prisoners. They grabbed anybody they could. Even tried to catch me, so I just ran like hell.'

Vic shakes his head. 'You trying to tell me that a bunch of fags and fairies had it in them to beat off the cops? No way!'

'I'm giving it to you straight, man!' Jody insists. 'It was like they found something fierce inside themselves. They had it up to here with being pushed around and they wasn't gonna take it any more.'

'Yeah,' says Vic. 'I bet that now that they're so strong and brave, they're gonna go and chase off the Mafia and stop paying them their weekly "gayola", too. Because everybody knows that it's the Maf' who own the place.'

'yeah, but so what?' Curly Joe interrupts. 'cops or mafia or whatever doesn't really matter, right? i mean, calling them names lets you forget that these are people first of all. and what are they doing that's hurting anybody? nothing. they got rights.'

'Not yet they don't,' Vic reminds him. 'And, just so you know, I'm all for these people having the same rights as anybody else, but let's not turn them into knights in shining armor.'

'okay, so maybe their armor's a little rusty. but that's also maybe because it keeps getting kicked in and cracked, or whatever.'

'Right on, man!' Jody cheers.

'Yeah, fine. Okay. I give in,' Vic says, both hands open-palmed.

Curly Joe is looking back to the day he'd arrived in New York and how he'd been harassed by some gay guy. How angry and sullied he'd felt then. Possibly, Vic has had similar experiences. Well ... Maybe what they got isn't all that different from what Jane was going on to him about when it came to men thinking it their right to slobber all over her. *hey! i think i've just had my consciousness raised!*

'come on,' Curly Joe says to Vic. 'let's go over there and see things for ourselves.'

They're not the only ones minded to do just that. All Saturday, thousands of New Yorkers keep arriving to get a good look at the burn-blackened *Stonewall Inn*. There's so many of them that they've spilled over from Christopher Street onto adjoining blocks.

There's all sorts of Gay and Lesbian agitators shouting 'Hey! Hey! What do you say? Try it once the other way!'

Not far from them, a kick line of Drag Queens is singing

We are the Stonewall girls.
We wear our hair in curls.
We don't wear underwear.
We show our pubic hair.

It's a circus, but a good-hearted one.

Taking it all in, Vic and Curly Joe come across an older man, standing by himself and not bothering to brush away the plentiful tears running down his face.

'This was our special place,' he blubbers. 'Look at it now! It was the only Gay Bar with a dance floor where we could flaunt ourselves, put on a show. And, yeah, the toilets were a shit hole, and it had no fire exits or running water so that dirty glasses had to be scooped around in water tubs and then re-used. And also, it had no licence so it was like being in some speakeasy from the Roaring Twenties. But it was ours! Ours! And now ... Now almost everything inside is busted and it's already been turned into some sort of shrine that every visiting straight tourist is gonna want to have their picture taken in front of! It ain't fair! And you know what else? A couple of days ago, they legalized being gay up in Canada. And over here? Over here, we get a riot, instead! That can't be right! No Siree!'

That evening, the TV news reports that thirteen people have been arrested, four police officers injured and a number of onlookers and activists hospitalised. Maybe it's the broadcast that incites a second night of rioting. Once again, garbage can fires are lit and more street battles break out.

By then, Curly Joe and Vic have reconciled and are back at their place getting stoned and celebrating the birth of *Gay Power.*

* * * * *

(From Curly Joe's Thought Book)

30th of june
dog, the hopped-up cat is jumping around, growling and hissing at nothing. like everyone else, except for me and vic, he's on speed.

twenty minutes ago, i was telling myself i was in heaven. the communards got together to give me and vic an early independence day gift of a dime of primo hash. now that they've all shot up though, it feels more like i'm in hell.

georgia and jeff are just starting to get high on the speed they ripped. as a distraction, keith starts begging me to let a guy from florida sleep on my room's floor tonight. naturally, I say 'sure. be my guest'. the visitor says little and falls asleep in a few seconds.

dylan's on the record player, singing "desolation row" for all he's worth. I finish eating my french bread while keith grills some stolen hamburger meat rolled up to look like hot dogs.

'i feel like hot dogs tonight,' he grins, explaining all.

the speed catches up on georgia. she places jelly arms around jeff, a shaky hand runs thru his hair. he's not tuning in; too much left-over crystal to eye up.

i leave, heading back to my room. i'm feeling tired and its not through lack of sleep ...

july 1
morning.
knock knock. 'c'mon, man. gotta move,' keith's voice yells.
oh yeah. the guy from florida's leaving.

'thanks for the use of your floor.'

'any time. see ya.'

i wouldn't recognize him if I ever saw him again.

it's way past 11.00am and the freaks are still high.

weirdly, dylan's still singing "desolation row".

here's vic wanting to be let in for sanity's sake.

then jeff pushes his way into my room as well because the light here's good.

a couple that look like school kids follow him. they tighten belts around their arms, crook them.

one of them says: 'c'mon, man, we wanna rip.'

jeff yells out 'nurse georgia! nurse georgia! you're needed in ward nine!'

georgia enters, holding incense and a bunsen burner.

a needle's cleaned. 'which arm?' she asks.

male partner stabs a point on his left arm. 'there! stick it in right there!'

needle in. needle out.

'oh wow! oh wow!' he bawls while his girlfriend squirms.

'now me! now me!' she barks.

vic can't take any more so he gets up and leaves.

'i'm gonna flake out,' the guy says.

'more!' the girl screams after her turn. 'i want more. work all next week — a hundred and twenty bucks — put the whole shebang into me, man!'

all of them laugh, knowing just what she means.

and then i'm alone in my room again not wanting to know if I've just seen the future.

* * * * *

That afternoon, everything changes again.

Out of the blue, Jane shows up and says to Curly Joe: 'Happy Canada Day! Pick up your stuff and come live with me.'

Curly Joe doesn't ask any questions. Bag packed, he does the rounds and says his goodbye's to the various communards. Aside from Vic, he doubts they'll miss him much or even recall who he was a couple of weeks from now. Saying so long to Vic isn't quite so easy.

'You know, man, I really like you,' Vic says. 'We made a good team, there.' He pauses to let that sink in before adding the rest. 'But, seeing as you're about to take off with Jane and go live with her, it makes me think that she's finally given up on that nutty Three-Day Rule of hers. Which is a relief, let me tell you. But get this straight, here and now: because she has, you and me are rivals as of today. You got something cooking with Jane, and that's okay. Thing is though, I'm betting I've got a chance at it, too. And nothing's gonna stop me doing my best from making my dream come true. Not even whatever this friendship of ours might be. Get me?'

'i get you,' Curly Joe answers.

'Good. Let's you and me smoke on that,' Vic grins, bringing out the makings.

* * * * *

Inside Jane's apartment again, Curly Joe feels like he's being invited to live in unimaginable splendour. But what's the price?

'I want you to stop wasting your time with all that pamphleteering. There's a nighttime usher job going at the theater next to mine. It pays okay and we get to go home together. The rest of the time, I want you to concentrate entirely on your writing, okay? Except for when I'm home, of course. Agreed?'

What can he say? 'agreed.'

'Good.'

'so are we talking more than three days, or what?'

That sets her tears streaming non-stop. 'Maybe I deserve that. But don't be a bastard. Don't make me ask myself if I made a mistake.'

Stroking her face, apologising, he tries to explain that he can't get a hold on why she's changed her mind.

Jane pauses for one breath-gap second and whispers 'Because in spite of everything I tried to tell myself, I found myself missing you. I couldn't get my head around it. Don't take it the wrong way but it wasn't your looks or the quality of the sex and conversation. I'm not saying they weren't good — great, even — but, no. None of them was the reason. Still, there was something. I just couldn't put my finger on it ... When I looked into that some more, I realized that since our three days together, I'd changed. I didn't feel so angry and resentful about men. I don't know what did it. And I'm not suggesting that it had anything directly to do with you. But you definitely set something churning up inside me. I didn't want to accept it, at first. I waited. But the feeling wouldn't go away. What it comes down to is this: I have no idea why, but I feel like I can trust you. And that I can be honest with you. That *we* can be honest with each other. So here you are. Here *we* are. I'm glad I'm sitting down while saying this, but here goes: I want to love you. I want you to love me. No fucking idea why. Or why it should be you. But there it is.'

It's only when they express that love physically that Curly Joe fully gives in and believes her. Jane isn't as violent, self-centred and ferocious as before. No commands. Nor even words. There's a new-found softness emerging from her, an openness to give as well as take. Even the way she orgasms feels and sounds different; she's not fighting it any longer as if the insistent arousal she feels is too indebted to the man who's with her. No longer just bodies, their lovemaking is between two people now.

* * * * *

In the immediate weeks that follow, Curly Joe and Jane inhabit a fabulous tilt-a-whirl world designed for their private exploration. Thanks to Jane's fringe theatre contacts, on their free days and nights they gain unlimited entry to off-Broadway plays, experimental underground films, delirious studio loft parties that go on for days on end, even lunatic "happenings" where people strip off their clothes and run about screaming 'I'm not allowed to go to Albania!'

On less exotic excursions, they meander up and down the streets of New York, slide into art galleries and studios, soak up all the enticements that the city has on offer.

Even the kitsch setting of Coney Island supplies them with unanticipated delights. Pretending to be tourists, they are temporarily adopted by a middle-aged New York couple who lead them along the famous boardwalk pointing out, here and there, historical landmarks, places of interest, gossipy secrets that only Coney Island lovers would know. Then, just to ensure that their memory of this day stays permanent, they buy the young tourists hot dogs from *Nathan's.*

And in their quieter, private moments, they pass away the time in bed reading and eating crumbly bread sticks with peanut butter or cheese, smoking joints, sipping cherry brandy, and making love.

These times are cherished more than any other. Ever curious about what new unknown they might happen upon, they become tireless explorers.

A poem that Curly Joe writes about their "fieldwork" during these days easily encapsulates the time, as well as the joy they experience in sharing it.

> *some make love with their hands.*
> *many caress each other's feet.*
> *a few rely upon the use of their nose.*
> *even ears are employed at times.*
> *so are knees.*
> *then, there is always the armpit lover.*
> *and i've known several men and women*
> *who worked their elbows to a frenzy.*
> *while hair ...*
> *well, everyone knows what to do with* that.
> *but you,*
> *you taught me something new.*
> *you pointed out i had a prick*
> *and you a cunt.*
> *i'd always wondered what they were there for.*

* * * * *

Round about mid-July, there's a phone call from Vic.

'Janey gal, how's it going? Do you and Rickie-boy wanna meet up with me in Central Park? It's been a while, and it'd be good to touch base again.'

'Sure, why not?'

They don't know it yet, but Vic's about to become a regular visitor into their world. Way cool! They both look forward to spending time with him. And Central Park, in mid-summer, is utterly phantasmagorical.

Just to prove them right, their visit presents them with a parade of characters vying for unfading space in their long-term memories.

Near the archway leading to the park on 5th Avenue, a Bowery bum out of his skull, is holding two Aces from a pack of cards pretending that they're six-guns. Starring in his very own Hollywood Western, he keeps shooting from the hip at whoever passes by, then blows into their imaginary barrels and waits for his next victim to appear.

A little ways inside, a straw-hatted, lanky Black man with a falsetto to die for regales them with a medley of Jamaican songs just for the sheer joy of it then sashays away.

Four very drunken bachelor businessmen huddle on a nearby park bench and argue whether it's worth it to pay $20.00 each for tickets to an Erotic Magic Show. Everybody's imaginations run wild trying to work out what sleights-of-hand and prestidigitations would fit that bill.

Not too far from them, a couple — he blue collared, she in dirty mini-skirt and tank top — start up an argument. Moments later, she walks away in a huff. He allows her to head off for a few seconds and then shouts: 'Hey!' stopping her in her tracks. Then he stands, all up-tight and shaky, holding out his right arm crooked at the elbow as if walking arm in arm with her. She slips back to his side, looking like a sorrowful dog, and puts her arm in his. Happy once more, they skip off together paying no attention to the cheers and loud hand-claps from several bench-sitters applauding their play's ending.

Ambling along, Jane's arms linked to both of them on either side of her, she feels a joy that sets her off giggling. The couple of surreptitious joints they've smoked along the way help as well.

'what? what is it?' Curly Joe asks, he, too, now grinning.

'Yeah. What's the joke, gal?' Vic adds.

'It's you two. I feel so good and safe with you. You're Rick and Vic, my Heavenly Twins.'

Later, their park adventure at an end, they invite Vic back to the apartment, to smoke and rap some more, listen to music, chill.

While Jane's preparing her rice and tuna fish salad concoction, Vic gets round to informing Curly Joe that King Hal died three days earlier. Stupidly, just as stupidly as he'd lived out his life, he'd obsessed over some dried-up pigeon shit obscuring the view from his third-storey room window. Leaning backwards from its ledge to remove it, he'd pushed himself too far out so that he'd slipped, fallen, broken his neck and died comatose in an out-patients corridor, some four hours later.

All of the house-freaks had been upset, of course. But that was because they'd had to clear the place of all drugs before the cops called in. A total bummer. Still, someone else is just about to move into Hal's old room, grief being a passing thing.

Just from the way Vic tells the story, Curly Joe catches on that, close as they are, there's a self-serving cold-heartedness to Vic that he hopes isn't something else they share.

When Jane rejoins them, carrying plates and glasses, they both get up to help her.

Vic is full of praise over her culinary skills and can't stop thanking "his bestest pal". The cuddle he gives her seems spontaneous but to Curly Joe there's a reminder of Vic's desire for Jane in it.

twins we might well be, he reminds himself, *but, then, so were romulus and remus.*

* * * * *

On the 20th of July, the day that the first man sets foot on the moon and speaks the dumbest well-rehearsed words ever to be heard across the world, the three of them are together again. Invited over to watch the event on TV, Vic is riding high, thoroughly juiced by what's taking place. He sees the Moon Landings as the conclusive victory of scientific technology over Faith. Journeys to the Moon will eventually explain our origins, he insists. No Bible, no Fairy Tales. Just hard-gained facts. That's what appeals to him the most. What he wants to do with his life. Mysteries of every sort absorb him; but only because they're waiting to be solved.

Jane, who started off not feeling all that much one way or the other about the landings, finds herself agreeing with Vic. Sitting down on the sofa right next to him, she's cheering away, joining in on his euphoria.

Curly Joe is giving them dirty looks from the other end of the room. He's protesting and refuses to watch what he takes to be a horrible mistake, if not a crime. He can't bear to watch Goddess Moon being so defiled and keeps hissing and booing in counter-attack to the others' out of this world cheers and yowls of elation.

'That there guy you're living with is a hopeless romantic,' Vic tells Jane. 'He should get real, like you and me, kiddo.'

Curly Joe sees through the jokiness. When it comes time for Vic to bid them goodnight, Curly Joe knows that what could have been for them is over. In the end, they'll always be rivals.

Showing him that she's understood this as well, Jane presses herself tightly up against Curly Joe as soon as the door's shut. 'Let's fuck,' she says. 'I want you. Now.'

'you don't mind fucking a hopeless romantic?'

'When it comes to fucking, hopeless romantics are the best there is!'

'and what are realists like?'

'Oh, they always choose the best option available. Now shut up and take "one giant leap for womankind".'

* * * * *

If Curly Joe was starting to worry about what plans Vic might have up his non-existent sleeve to win over Jane, the 4th of August reduces those concerns into trivialities.

Yes, it's time to face yet another blindsiding change.

He can see from the moment that she walks into the apartment that something's the matter. It's the way that Jane's grinning and pretending to be all ears to what he's been up to today that raises alarms.

'what?' Curly Joe says. 'something's up. what is it?'

Jane sighs. She wanted to put him at ease first, before delivering the news.

'I've gotten a part for a new play,' she says. 'A really good one. Not quite a starring role, but as close as you can get.'

'hey! but that's great! at last! this is your chance!' Curly Joe prattles on, feeling calmer.

'Yeah. But the thing is, it's a touring role. We're going cross country. Maybe Europe if the reviews are good enough and we can get Union approval.'

'oh.'

'It could be a long tour.'

'how long?'

'Months. At least.'

'oh.'

'I really, really need to do it. You said it yourself: it's my big chance. I'd hate myself if I didn't give it all I had.'

'you're right. you gotta do it.'

'I'm sorry. I'm so, so sorry. I don't want to leave you.'

'when do you go?'

'We need to go through a whole bunch of intensive rehearsals. The Director wants us to bond while we get into character. So we're heading off to some place he's found for us all to stay. No distractions, he keeps insisting.'

'when do rehearsals begin?'

'On the 8th.'

'the 8th? wow. that —'

'Soon. Too soon, I know, but —'

'no. i was gonna say that gives us — me — three days with

you before you take off. kinda funny, really, when you think about it. back to three days.'

Jane wants to slap him for making the same connection she'd made an hour ago. Instead, she ruffles his hair and laughs as if she really means it.

* * * * *

(From Curly Joe's Thought Book)

august 6
i woke up at one point in the night recalling that, once, a long time ago, i was sure i had a purpose: i was to preach and bring glad tidings to one and all.

i thought that delusion had died in woodstock. but it wasn't a death at all. something grew instead. except, I'm not sure what.

it strikes me that by now the pieces should at last be fitting themselves together.

the summer's ending early and so my search should be, as well.

i should have seen the light. i should know.
'the killer is —. The cure is —. 'The answer is —.'
if only it could be so easy.

instead, it comes to me that we search and search and all we find out is that maybe we were searching for the wrong thing. so we start again and arrive at the same conclusion, each time getting more and more mixed-up.

some people will tell you that the trick is to stop searching. maybe that's just another con.

i was sitting alone today trying to write and jane just entered my thoughts. there was no getting rid of her.

it wasn't sexual. it wasn't possessive. it wasn't even emotional, somehow.

it was a touch of her soul. and it left me absolutely shaken.
this is the truth I've learned, then. this is it:
it all comes down to souls being brave enough to touch one another.

august 7

august 7.
it rained
and i noted that the daisies
i'd picked for you in july
lay still-dead and rotting.

august 7.
the person next door
played music
that didn't seem
to suit his character.

august 7.
i bought an ice-cream
though it was chilly
and, enjoying its taste,
was reminded of happy jack.

august 7.
my attempted novel
lies shredded and disdained
in a trash bin.
where it belongs.

august 7.
i've made up our bed
for the last time
and now
it is all yours again.

august 7.
i'm going back to montréal.
i have no plans.
we haven't spoken of the future.
what future?

* * * * *

Two days later, back in his parents' house, in a place he's no longer sure he can call home, a letter arrives for Curly Joe. From the handwriting, he knows it's from Jane. But how could it possibly have arrived so soon? Oddly, he finds that his hands begin to shake. Mustering his strength, he rips open the envelope, reads her words quickly, realises that she'd written and mailed it before they'd parted.

Me Darlin' Rick:

How can I tell you that I love you and yet tell you what I must?

The month we had together was our very own Summer of Love and it was beautiful.

Don't ever forget that. Promise.

There's no other way of saying this: I lied to you.

Yes, there is a not-quite starring role for me in this new play.

No, we're not touring.

I'm sorry. I am weak and confused.

And it is Victor's turn.

Victor will move in in a couple of days.

I couldn't say no.

Don't hate me, please.

Precious,

Very softly, I must go.

Very gently, I must go.

Your Sweet (and Plain)

Jane

A part of Curly Joe wants to understand. But most of him can only concentrate on continuing to stand.

Well, if he failed to live up to every other trademark associated with being an evangelist, he's managed to score a complete success in the one tagged "betrayal by one he trusted".

33. WOODSTOCK NATION

So here they are, together again, mud-splattered and smelling all too much like stale urine, laughing and rolling one more joint, and, most of all, praising the sun for having deigned to shine on them once again. They're whooping it up in yet another dream, sharing it with half-a-million other lunatics who've agreed to join in on the celebration.

As far as dreams go, this is a gentle and oddly moving one. People who aren't here during this long mid-August weekend will soon refer to it as historical. But for them, corralled and cornered into a patch of land besotted and strewn with tin cans, wasted food, lost clothes, wind-swept tents, and drugs of every variety and quality, it's enough to know that they're in the greatest disaster area they've ever experienced, and that, in the whole wide world, this is the *only* place to be.

Somewhere in the music that never ceases, somewhere in the bedraggled aura of the event, they have, all of them, broken down all resistance to truly touch each other. And, in so doing, they've heard the call and felt the presence of a force that doesn't lend itself to identification or appellation. It's because of this that many will come to see what occurs here as the birth of a nation, the true beginning of the much-proclaimed revolution.

But it is neither. It's simply a moment.

Oh, but what a moment.

Right now, it has just gone past 6.00am, Monday morning. The *Woodstock Festival* should have ended last night but insistent audiences and storms and you name it have meant that the show must go on. Hours ago, *The Band* played their set. And now, it's Paul Butterfield who's shown up to perform just because Moe kept hoping he would. Tons of people have already left Max Yasgur's farm land. Poor Ol' Jimi Hendrix will only get to strut his stratocaster in front of a minuscule gathering of 200,000 hangers-on.

Larry's scratching at the dirt-caked hair tickling his shoulders. Once Butterfield finishes, he makes it known, he's heading off to Filippini Pond and giving himself a good, long cold-water wash and scrub.

Moe is so blitzed out, he's convinced himself he's on stage playing back-up blues harp with his hero. He sounds real good, almost like a Pro. Must be all down to no longer being a virgin.

And Curly Joe is only half-listening to the music because this letter from Edna of all people that was waiting for him to open when he got home keeps butting into his thoughts. It doesn't say much other than apologise if her previous postcard had maybe been unduly rude. It's her last sentence, "Maybe we'll meet up one day and share our weird life experiences", that keeps bugging him for some reason. Last thing he wants or needs in his life at this point is some pushy woman, right? Right.

* * * * *

The rains that pour down on Woodstock Nation are nothing in comparison to the deluge that will come.

As if the message of the brutal, helter skelter murders carried out by the Manson Family just a few days earlier hasn't been warning enough, hand-in-hand with the fabled "3 Days of Peace and Music", there's another three-day communal riot going on, the Battle of The Bogside, that's taking The Troubles in Northern Ireland to a whole new level. Further afield, some mightily alarming disagreements over how to interpret the Communist Manifesto have led to violent border clashes between the USSR and the People's Republic of China that are giving a whole new meaning to "The East is Red".

And down the line for the rest of 1969? There's the Chicago 8 (or is that 7?) Trial starting up in September. And any remnants of the Prague Spring are being hosed down the gutter. And, as always, more death. Death in Vietnam. Death in "neutral" Laos and Cambodia. Death on the Gaza Strip. Death at Altamont. Death on Kent State campus. Death from police raids on the Black Panther Party. Death down the backstreets of Montréal thanks to the FLQ. Death everywhere. Even Jack

Kerouac can't get on the road to escape it.

On the other hand ... Sam Beckett is soon to be awarded the Nobel Prize for Literature. And *quark,* a word invented by Sam's old pal, James Joyce, is about to be turned into an elementary particle tinier than a proton. While, at just about the same time, something called the *arpanet is* sending out the first ever email. *Medium Cool, My Night at Maud's, Kes,* and of course *Butch Cassidy And The Sundance Kid* are lining up to hit the screens. And *Monty Python's Circus* is getting ready to take flight. Not least, in a time where diplomacy still has some value, the SALT I talks limiting the number of strategic weapons that the United States and the USSR can threaten each other with begin to take place in Helsinki, Finland.

Plus, there's still the music. *Abbey Road, Hot Rats, Volunteers* and *Let It Bleed* are just round the corner. And there's Festivals a-plenty from now on. *The Isle of Wight Concert* starring Bob Dylan is just a week away. Then there's *The Toronto Rock and Roll Revival* bringing on John and Yoko in mid-September. And the *Rolling Stones* do *Altamont* in December. Which circles us back to death again.

As for our Three Stooges ... They, too, will have to weather the multiple changes in their lives.

Up ahead for them lie more failed relationships, long periods of lives lived in solitude, marriages that last or don't. There's kids and not having kids. Rentals and mortgages. Hirings and firings. Spending sprees and pension pots. Holidays and trips to every part of the world except Antarctica. Tooth decay and dental implants. Freak flag hair turning grey and then white or worse disappearing altogether. Breakdowns and breakthroughs. Minor ailments and life-saving operations. Friendships dissolved and resolved. Drugs for fun taken over by drugs for depression, high blood pressure, cholesterol. Caring for ageing parents and burying their ashes. Clothes that no longer fit. Broken promises and dreams unfulfilled. Wonderments and epiphanies coming out of the blue. Years speeding up and walking slowing down. And Death, of course, sooner or later.

Whichever way you look at it, the message is clear: the long dream that is The Sixties will all too soon recede into an almost forgotten memory that can't quite be nailed down but which continues to haunt everyone's waking thoughts. A combo ready ripe for turning into Legend.

Still ... For now at least, the dream ain't over yet as as far as Larry, Moe and Curly Joe are concerned. Sure enough, September's about to descend upon them in a matter of weeks and with it will come McGill and countless unexpected journeys of body and soul. But who wants to look up ahead when there's so much to groove on right this moment?

* * * * *

As if it was the most natural thing in the world, here comes a bare-breasted hippie girl, all psychedelic smiles and mellowness personified. She's painted her front teeth purple and her jeans are torn at the knees.

Larry waves a joint and points for her to sit down next to him. It will be easy to talk her round into coming along later for a splash. And then, they're bound to want to fuck before they go their separate ways. Which is just how Larry wants all his relationships with women to be like from now on. He'll be too busy for anything romantically big-time, anyway. He's switching over to a BA degree at McGill. Going to Major in Art History. And, evenings, he'll enrol in drawing and painting classes. Put all he's got into becoming an artist himself.

Curly Joe's mesmerized by the scene he's taking in. There's something so liberating about it all. The revolution he believes is taking place goes beyond politics and social norms. It's a commitment to something far less easy to capture in words and ideas. It's a commitment to Life itself, in all its manifestations and possibilities. Maybe it's the hippie girl's laid-back presence, but for some reason, he gets to thinking about all the different women in their lives. How relations started and ended. And, mostly, how strong, in her own way, each of those women was. So much for "the weaker sex". He tries to imagine where they all are now. Then he shakes his head in honour and wishes every single one of them well. Somehow, this mélange of ruminations inspires Curly Joe to take another stab at novel writing. He's not kidding himself, either. He means it.

Moe? He's finishing his ten-minute harp solo and hoping to retrieve some of it when he gets back together with the *Les Blues Hounds de Montréal* and they're ready to do some top-notch recording. In-between that, Moe's going back to McGill as well. Those Westmount kids won't leave his thoughts. He knows he's got something to offer kids just like them so that maybe, just maybe, they won't go making a mess of their lives.

Right about then, Hippie Girl bends down to join Larry. Except she slips and Moe catches her right at the last minute only to get face-whipped by her generous breasts as a reward. Too bad she couldn't make it over, but thank heavens Emily's not here to witness this. Blushing, turned-on, his drug-addled mind improvises a musical response full speed ahead.

Monday, Monday, you fell on top of me.
Monday, Monday, your breasts felt so fine and free.
Oh Monday morning, how blessed can I be?
Hoping that by Monday evening you'll still be falling for me.

And the three of them laugh like loonies.

* * * * *

Hey, Tripsters! Your last chance:
Can you see them?
Yes, there they are.
It's their time.
Always and forever.
And even more.

A GOODBYE FROM YOUR TRIP GUIDE

Ah, The Sixties!

Well, Tripsters: as your Trip Guide, I hope that you've found some worth in visiting way back when.

Different times, right? Or maybe not quite so different from today as you'd imagined?

Are you left wondering what makes The Sixties so exotic that we keep wanting to re-visit them?

Me, too. I've got my possible answers but, more importantly, it's what answers come up for *you* that matter. And what are you going to do about them?

In case you're interested, I first began to write a version of this novel in 1972. Completed in 1974, I passed it round to various friends for comment but they knew, as I knew, that it was a young man's attempt to glorify his recent past. Basically, it was rubbish.

Not all that long ago, a good friend of mine, while clearing out her home for a move into a new life, came across a copy of that early draught and passed it back to me. I approached it with suspicion. Reading it again, it was still rubbish. But ... It drew me back to pinning down what I'd wanted, and tried and failed, to write. So I began again.

In 1795, William Blake completed the painting of a masterpiece which he titled *Newton*. It depicts a man, compass in hand, ensnared and enthralled by the single-mindedness of discovery. In his eyes, there exists not the slightest hint of a social conscience or concern with moral implication. Deep into the vortex created by his curiosity, certain that nothing truly matters other than the continuation of his act, he follows its dictates, regardless of where they may lead him.

Then, in 1965, at the height of his visionary fever, Bob Dylan recorded *Highway 61 Revisited.* It was like nothing anybody had ever heard before and that just about everybody's tried to copy since. Dylan included. It's a reckless, bravura performance with a back-beat so tight that no one could lose it. On it, there's a song titled *Tombstone Blues*. One of its lines says something about geometrising innocence. When I heard that, I couldn't help but frame a link to Blake's painting.

The last song on *Simon and Garfunkel's* 1968 LP, *Bookends,* is titled (unsurprisingly) *Bookend.* Its melody and lyrics evoke an innocent time, when the confidences between friends matter more than anything.

Discovery. Creative ferment. Innocence and confidences. Connecting together these separate strands provided me with an entry into The Sixties. My task, as I saw it, was to gradually expose and begin to clarify the internal structures of how that time was lived by my characters — to "geometrise", if you will. The source of reference was my chaotically ordered/orderly chaotic mind.

And because it is that, I make no claim to provide the definitive *Truth* about The Sixties. But I did try my damnedest to stay *truthful* to their spark and exposition.

And maybe, after all that, what I've accomplished is still rubbish.

Only this time, it's old man's rubbish.

Oh well!

As to The Sixties ...

If the German philosopher, Friedrich Nietzsche, is correct, we're all condemned to repeat our lives eternally, endlessly recycling the same exact thoughts and deeds, with every instance of angst and nausea, epiphany and serenity, intact and unalterable. Every incident and encounter that has come and gone will come and go again and again, forever, like some perpetual *Groundhog Day* without the Hollywood Happy Ending.

'Just think,' I tell myself, 'Lifetime after lifetime of having to live through The Sixties ...'

'Tee, hee,' laughs my eager soul. 'Tee, hee.'

ACKNOWLEDGEMENTS AND NOTES

A whole bunch of people read early draughts of parts of this novel and, thanks to their advice and comments, significant re-writes were undertaken. My gratitude and love to them all: Pauline Buchanan-Black, Betty Cannon, Maggi Cook, Todd DuBose, Kate Du Toit, Mark Ellerby, Fiona English, Jon Fitzmaurice, Nicole Gehl, Peter Hannon, Michael Harvey, David Higham, Caroline Horner, Penny Jones, Greg Madison, Frances Middleton, Dida Mitchell, Michael Montgomery, Marion Phillips, Paola Pomponi, Neil Rodgers, Helen Runciman, Colin Ryall, Sally Ryall-Fletcher, Lucy Solymar, Paul Swift, Gary Willis and Michael Worrell.

As ever, I am deeply indebted to David Higham for his splendiferous cover artwork. If only it were true that a book could be judged by its cover.

Many real people who I got to know during The Sixties were the inspiration for their highly-fictionalised novel counterparts. Without wanting to impose on their lives after so many years, I've thought it best not to name them. Nonetheless, as the saying goes: "I am who I am because of you." Peace and Love to you all.

And, in case you're left wondering, most of the events you've been reading about really did happen. Especially the ones that couldn't possibly be true. But *who* they happened to shall forever remain a secret.

The Daniel Cohn-Bendit quote that opens Part Three is from a dialogue between Daniel Cohn-Bendit and Claus Leggewie published in the May 10, 2018 edition of the *New York Review of Books* and titled *1968: Power to the Imagination.*

The Bob Dylan quote at the start of Part Four appears on page 315 in James Miller's book *Democracy is in the Streets: From Port Huron to the Siege of Chicago,* published in 1988 by HarperCollins.

Milton Keynes UK
Ingram Content Group UK Ltd.
UKHW020816300924
R3695700001B/R36957PG448786UKX00002B/1